Mitzi

Mitzi

By
Robert W. Greenwood

For Carolyn —

Robert W. Greenwood

E-BookTime, LLC
Montgomery, Alabama

Mitzi

ISBN: 1-59824-391-8

First Edition
Published November 2006
E-BookTime, LLC
6598 Pumpkin Road
Montgomery, AL 36108
www.e-booktime.com

1

Jesse and I were sitting on the ground under a huge, stately, patriarchal oak, a silent, battered witness to the lives of over a half score of generations of the hill folk whose labors from the time this country had been given a name had cleared the forest with axes and oxen, hewn and assembled the logs into homes, divided and fenced these fields, plowed them, manured them, planted and harvested them, pastured their stock on them, tended them painstakingly, passing their lives wresting sustenance from them for themselves and their broods and passing them on, unchanged, as their fathers and their father's fathers had done. The manners, the customs, the language, the hopes persisted without measurable change. Strong in religious faith and uncomplaining in adversity, they doggedly preserved tradition and aspired to little more than what had been given them as their patrimony.

It was late summer now, the air still and warm, the foliage dusty dull, the fields shorn and stubbled, a thin blue haze nearly obscured the outlines of the mountains. My mule stood patiently, switching at the flies, waggling his great ears. Jesse sat idly with his head lowered, scratching lines in the hard, yellow dirt with a piece of stick. He was a strong, broad, quiet boy, soft spoken, reserved, a tireless worker, a loyal friend. His heavily callused bare feet protruded from patched, sunbleached overalls. Like his father and his grandfather, he had a coarse thatch of reddish hair and the bright blue eyes that centuries had bequeathed them, together with the skin that never tanned.

"Get all your 'bakky in?"

"Finished last night just before dark. Looks like a pretty good year." There was a long pause as Jesse prepared to gradually enter into what was on his mind.

"When are you fixin' to leave?" He perfectly well knew that answer to this. I had told him a dozen times, but it still bothered him and he wanted to go over it again, I suppose.

"Wednesday. First thing in the morning. We're going to stay for a couple days with a cousin of Mom's who has a place there. They won't let me into my room at the school until Friday so we're just going to look around and see the sights."

"Think you're goin' to like livin' in a big city?"

"I don't know. It's not really in the city, you know. It's out sort of on the edges. I guess it'll be all right. Not much I can do about it if I don't like it."

"You can come on home and just forget it is what you can do. Nice girl like Carrie Jane waiting for you. I just don't see why you want to run off. You know your Pa would give you the old Brandon place. You and him could fix it up just as pretty as could be. There ain't any better land around here than what's there. And you know your Pa would at least go shares with you. More likely give it to you. You and Carrie Jane could settle in there and have everything a man could want. Good big spring, that old orchard you could clean out. Put a little more tin on the barn and she'll be dry. Cut through that little boundary of timber and run a juice wire up from the road. I just don't see why you want to go off to learn more than you need to know anyway. OK, so you get an education and all, what good is that going to do you around here? Won't do you no good at all. I can read some. Not as good as you, but I do all right. And I can cipher some. My Pa nor none of 'em can read nor write and they're doin' all right. We ain't got noth-ing' to complain about. You think those Rafferty boys or Rory or Buck is any better off than me because they stayed in school? Not so's you'd notice. Just a waste of time and a waste of money the way I look at it. You get to be a scientist or somethin', you're go-ing to have to live in a big city somewhere, ain't you? That ain't no place to live. You talk to anybody who's lived in one. What's your Pa goin' to do without you to help him with his fixin' places up and all? You two are makin' good money and there's more to be made just like you're goin'. You got all that comin' to you and you're going to walk right away from it. Don't make sense to me. The way I see it, you're cutting' loose from this place forever if you go on the way you're goin'. Why can't you settle down like other folks and have kids and a nice place and not go makin' a lot of trouble for your folks, spendin' all that money for school. Way I see it, you got everything here a man could want. And you just walkin' away from it." We sat for a time in silence. "What does Carrie Jane say about it?"

"Not much. She's still pretty upset about it, but she knows there's nothing she can do."

"She goin' to wait for you?"

"Can't say, Jesse. That's up to her. I hope not. I never gave her the idea that I was going to ask her to marry me and she knows I can't think about marrying anybody for four years. Carrie Jane wants to get out of that house and away from her old man awful bad, and I don't blame her, but I don't want to mess with it. That old man of hers is nothing but trouble."

"Best thing would be if somebody would just shoot her old man."

"I wouldn't be surprised if somebody did, there's plenty that would like to. Maybe the sheriff will plug him someday."

Jesse snorted. "Not as long as he's getting paid to lay off the old man's still, he won't. When you going to get a chance to come home again?"

"The catalogue says they let out for four or five days at Thanksgiving, but that's a lot of money for the train just to be here for a couple days. I expect I won't get back until Christmas. That's for two weeks."

"You're goin' to miss the early deer season"

"There'll be plenty left when I get home at Christmas. I expect we can go over to that place we went last year. That was pretty good."

"Yeah. I guess we could do that." We sat again for a time as Jesse brooded and scratched with his stick.

"You goin' to the dance tonight?"

"Uh huh. You coming?"

"You need a ride? I've got the Ford."

"No. Dad's letting me take his car. We'll get there about six, I expect." He stood, dusted off the seat of his overalls, ducked through the barbed wire fence and vaulted up onto his horse. He sat, twisting the fuzzy rope reins as though he had something more to say, then raised a few fingers to signal his departure, and set off down the hill.

Not many miles from where we were sitting, two narrow, rutted gravel roads intersected. At some time long gone by, this meeting of paths generated the impetus to create a community of sorts. The only remaining evidence of this little social center was a small clapboard church with a tiny steeple, a mercantile building unused now except for a small portion of it where a limited selection of general merchandise was sold, a swaybacked, roofless barn, a stock pond covered with a thick layer of bright green scum, the remains of a small shed, a limestone chimney that had once served a home, long since burned down and identified only by some foundation stones and a tangle of rubbish filled brush. Across the road from the church was a lovingly tended cemetery with row after row of expensive looking granite headstones proclaiming the Celtic and Teutonic origin of the inhabitants, and behind them in a sudden transition from this polished granite, tilted, thin tablets of a softer white stone, the dates going back to Revolutionary times, so many of them commemorating the passing of infants and children, dates and names blurred and indistinct.

A little farther down one road was the school where my mother had first taught. It was a rather large frame building divided down the middle inside by an aisle, a large open classroom and a tiny, one hole toilet for boys on one side, the same for the girls on the other side with a dining room between them. At one end of this refectory was a large black cast iron stove and a lead sink with a pitcher pump. Not long after my mother retired from teaching, a new school had been built some distance away where the population had shifted, leaving this sturdy memorial to the old community to be adopted as a social center for those who remained. Whether those who built the new school appropriated the bell from the bell tower on the roof, I have never heard, but the bell which my mother used to ring with a rope that came through the ceiling of the dining room was gone, leaving the heavy oak beam and chain from which it had hung undisturbed. The huge oaks that had grown up around the building at one time had had ropes and swings tied to their great limbs. They now represented a threat to the building and there was always talk of cutting them down, but nothing ever came of it.

From this extensive area, farmsteads widely spaced and scarcely seen, there magically and improbably materialized each Saturday other than in winter a number of souls far out of proportion to the visible population. They converged on the school on foot, in wagons, on horseback, in rusted trucks and automobiles with the intention of playing music and dancing. Stringy, weather beaten tillers of the earth and their plump, plain wives were now scrubbed and pink, wearing freshly ironed overalls, cleaned shoes, white shirts, long skirts and colorful blouses, for the women their only chance to dress gaily. Almost every family had musicians so there was a constant rotation among the fiddle and mandolin and banjo and bass players. There were mouth harp players, gut bucket players, washboard players and even a ukulele. It wasn't called 'bluegrass". It was just music, our music, loud, cheerful, played at breakneck speed, the physical release at the end of a hard week's work. There was socializing and gossiping and joking that would be unacceptable the following morning in church. Some men danced but most stood around in groups and talked about tractors and livestock and crops. The women converged in corners and in the kitchen and discussed births and marriages and quilts. Those women that danced for the most part danced with another woman. Many of the girls belonged to school groups being taught clogging and practiced their routines. Some of the men, too, were expert cloggers and danced dazzling solos which drew a respectful circle of admirers and enthusiastic applause. As for the kids, they just ran wild, the way kids will when they know their parents are distracted. They would be shooed outdoors where they yelped and chased and threw things at each other.

There was food and most people took their supper here instead of eating at home. A group of women, always the same ones, it seemed to me, cooked up great messes of soup beans and cornbread on the big stove. These were served in chipped, thick crockery bowls with big thin spoons. There was jello and cake for dessert. The charge for the meal was ten cents, children free. For a nickel more, there was unrefrigerated Nehi soda and Dr. Pepper to drink. Mostly the kids took the pop and their parents plain water. Out in back when it got dark enough, there was moonshine.

I drove over to Carrie Jane's about five-thirty. She was sitting out on the porch in the wooden glider, just as pretty as a picture in utter contradiction to the squalid house, the jumble of junk scattered everywhere on the ground. How that huge, coarse bully could have fathered such a sweet girl is hard to imagine. Of course, maybe he didn't father her, and I much preferred to think this the case. Far and away the best looking girl for miles around, she was intelligent, she was proper and she yearned for a chance to be somebody. When we talked, she told me of all her daydreams, not impossible dreams but unlikely dreams. Nevertheless, I supported them, I encouraged her to believe in herself and a better life but all the time recognizing that in these dreams that I was expected to be the medium through which they were to be realized.

We went to the dance, a melancholy affair it was for Carrie Jane who was obsessed with the knowledge that it might be the last time we would be there. She tried hard, dear girl but it was just not working, and by an unspoken mutual consent, I drifted away to be with the guys while she tried to take comfort with a few girl friends. And that was the way the night went. We left early, not a word spoken on the way to her house. In the dying light, we sat on the glider as we always did when I came over. I had never once been inside the house. Neither of us had much to say but just sat and slowly rocked, my arm around her, her head on my shoulder. She wasn't making a sound, but I knew she was crying, tears just silently sliding down her cheeks. I reached over and touched her face and found the wetness. Her misery revealed, she began to quietly shake, muffled sobs and pathetic stifled little cries fairly breaking my heart. Nothing had ever been said between us of 'love'. That word was not in the vocabulary of our people. A fellow might be 'sweet on' a girl but he was never 'in love' with her. These things were unspoken but understood at different levels by the two parties. When a fellow wanted to marry a girl, he didn't tell her of his love, of his adoration, rather he might suggest the 'maybe we should get hitched' or possibly ask if the girl 'would like to settle down' with him. I think we felt all the emotions that more demonstrative people felt. They were just never articulated. They were left to conjecture by both parties. And so I had nothing to un-say. It was simply a matter of telepathically projecting to Carrie Jane a sense of my withdrawing from competition for her hand without saying anything to that effect. Conditioned to this style of courtship, she knew and she was miserable. We sat thus until the muttering and heavy tread inside the house foretold the abrupt appearance of her old man bellying through the tattered screen door. "Time for you to git on home, Hawkins"

"Yes, sir." We got up and picked our way down to the car in the dim lantern light coming from the door. Now in the darkness and away from her father's hearing, she could talk and we could hold each other warmly and lovingly and kiss and caress as we dared not on the porch. "Will I see you again before you go?"

"I'll try. But I can't promise. I've got so much stuff to do to get ready." I felt like a heel but I was beginning to be anxious to put down this burden which had suddenly become so very much heavier.

"Will you write to me, Peter?"

"Of course. Just as soon as I get there."

"You won't forget me?"

"I couldn't ever forget you, Carrie Jane."

"You'll come home at Christmas?"

"Yes. For a couple weeks, at least." The dim light all but disappeared as the bulky figure filled the front door. "You git in here, girl, before I come out there to you, you hear?" It was an ominous bellow and Carrie Jane gave me a fierce hug and a hard, smeared kiss as she broke away and ran to the porch. That was the last I ever saw of her. We wrote a few times, then her letters stopped. When I came home at Christmas, I learned that she had run off to Knoxville and married an automobile salesman.

2

My mother was a Yankee, the product of a long line of old Puritan stock that had prospered since their arrival here, deep roots in their area, the women often artistically talented, the men largely in law, academic pursuits, a couple respected scientists, several authors of some reputation, a number of State level political figures including a governorship in the preceding century. My mother had inherited not only a good intellect but also the artistic ability of her mother, a successful painter in an era when lady portraitists were uncommon. My mother's talent lay not in painting but in music. She studied under good private teachers from an early age and when she entered a fashionable ladies college, majored in musical theory and composition and was headed for what appeared to be a career as a pianist. Her family had long been identified with all manner of charitable causes, so it must have come as no great surprise when my mother, in some sort of spasm of social consciousness, announced that she was going to Appalachia and teach children to read and write. Apparently undeterred by not having any teaching credentials but with a most permissive family's consent, she took a train to Knoxville, Tennessee. The story is a little fuzzy here, but somehow she was assigned to the little school I have just described and having arranged boarding at a private home, undertook to teach the girl's side, a real, shore 'nuff school marm.

My father had come back from service in the army in Europe during the war with a wholly new ambition and outlook. He had always been good with anything mechanical as so many farm boys are, and as a consequence had been assigned to the motor pool. By the time he was discharged, he had been promoted as far as he could go as an enlisted men, oversaw a big operation of considerable complexity and foresaw an entirely different role for himself when he returned to East Tennessee. Once home, he bought up surplus equipment with borrowed money, hired a few good men and set about picking up abandoned farms and completely rehabilitating them, putting in electricity, plumbing, repairing the house and barn, rebuilding fences and generally transforming nearly derelict properties into comfortable quarters. There was money in pockets such as there had not been in years. Returning servicemen were getting married and looking for properties, business was booming, and my father found himself in prosperous circumstances. He was all over the countryside with his business activities, working right along with his crew, and in this way came in contact with my mother.

Uncharacteristic of this prudent, proper lady, she fell head over heels in love at the first sight of him. He was tall, strongly built, handsome in the Gary Cooper mold, polite, gentle with the ladies, a hard driver of his help. He was fair and he was honest. He didn't smoke and didn't chew and never swore which truly set him apart and must have deeply impressed my mother. She was certain that this was the man for her and settled in to wait to be asked. That doesn't seem to have taken very long and by the time the first year of her teaching was completed, they were married. My mother quit her teaching and the two of them moved into one of the houses my father had just finished. It was here a couple years later that I was born, then after an interval, my two sisters, nearly age mates. From that time on, we lived in a succession of houses, each something better than the previous one as business grew. We finally got the house my father had wanted for years, old Henry Sensabaugh dying, leaving what local folks called his 'mansion', a big, handsome old brick house that must have been the wonder of the area when it was build a little less than a century before. My parents felt that they had at last fulfilled their dream.

I was allowed to grow to a certain point like any of the other farm kids, a marvelous childhood full of freedom and adventure, but after my second year in the local grammar school, my mother insisted that I withdraw and from that time on, my education was in her hands in one way of another. There was a downside to being treated in this special way and not socializing each day in school, but the summers and weekends made up for that and while I was vaulting past my peers in academic pursuits, I managed maintain my status as one of the gang, learning and living one culture at home, learning and living quite another one with my pals. When the requirements my education got to a point beyond my mother's liberal arts background, she had me enrolled in a quirky local boarding school, Jefferson Academy, an eccentric institution that accepted a child of almost any age who had the wherewithal, and tutored them as well as taught them up to a level that was equivalent to at least the first year of college. This institution had somehow endured over a great period of time, through some thick and some pretty thin times. The faculties seemed to have been largely recruited from among those talented but troubled college level teachers whose taste for alcohol or whose other weaknesses had caused their fall from grace. Jefferson was willing to give them a second chance, and in many cases reaped rich rewards of gratitude from these fallen angels. My mother, so clever and so prescient, understood all this and had the credentials and charm to seek out and befriend the best of these men and see to it that I got into good hands. It was here that I was first introduced to general science and biology in particular. After a good bit of inquiring and reflection, my mother had selected Dr. Casper Ord to undertake to be my mentor in general science. Admittedly, our laboratory facilities were spotty and the budget for the department rather lean, but this man had a gift for making the living world become brilliantly alive for me in a way that completely absorbed me and determined me to pursue a career in entomology. How I came to love bugs! Whole new worlds opened to me with his inspired teaching. I managed after a little over two years of attendance to have earned the equivalent of a high school diploma.

After considerable consultation among the active faculty members of my mother's family and friends, it was decided that for college, Corinthian University would be a sound choice. It did not come as a complete surprise on applying to this famous institution that my Academy's credentials were suspect and that I would be obliged to take an entrance examination. I had no way of measuring my academic progress other than by the grades I got at the Academy. Even these were not traditional but tended to be written opinions along pass/fail lines rather than letter grades. So it came as quite a pleasant surprise to find that not only had I passed the entrance examination but that I had gotten a rather gaudy grade. Dr. Ord was particularly pleased, of course, and took the initiative to contact the head of the biology department at Corinthian, a Dr. Charles Baxter. Whatever transpired there I was never told, but the result was that I was urged to apply for a scholarship, did so and was bowled over by being accepted for very generous support. What an exciting end to what had seemed to me to be only a delightful few years of study!

My mother's family was thrilled, letters went back and forth with congratulations and suggestions and offers of more support should it be needed, a certain note of surprise that I could have done so well, living in such a benighted backwater. It was a great triumph for my mother, a final vindication of her precipitously defecting from her ancestral halls. My father was terribly proud, I knew, but took it all very calmly as though he expected nothing less.

I had the entire summer to bask in this glory and the prospects of attending a prestigious university, but otherwise nothing changed. I worked with my father at his building business and on our farm, getting a crop of tobacco raised and harvested, putting up a couple cuttings of hay, feeding the stock just as any farm boy might, vague images of 'college life' appearing in some of my daydreams, but the whole vision of leaving the only life I had known nebulous and unreal. I simply continued to do what I had always done, waiting for summer to end.

3

On the day of our departure, my father drove the two of us to the nearest railroad station where we got aboard in late afternoon. Arriving in Bristol we got on our Pullman car and settled in, the train not yet made up. My mother had brought some chicken and biscuits on which we nibbled until we got under way. I had never imagined anything as luxurious as the dining car in which we took our supper, the heavy linen, the heavy silver, the attentive service all while rattling through the countryside in regal splendor. It was afternoon the next day before we arrived. I felt like a boy again instead of a young man as my mother expertly handled the tipping, the calling of a cab which whisked us madly through a portion of this great metropolis that was to be my home and out to a suburban section where my great aunt lived. She was a very dignified elderly lady, gracious and cordial but with what I misinterpreted as a lack of warmth. We were pampered and settled by a maid into two bedrooms, dined elegantly and at length went to bed. I recall distinctly not sleeping well because of the touch-me-not perfection of the room.

The following morning, my mother was given the keys to the Oldsmobile sedan and we set off along a parkway that led to the university. I must have been distracted by a large park on my side, a small, pretty lake with older men tending small sail and power boat models which fascinated me. I was still craning behind me to see when the car stopped and my mother announced that we were there. We were parked under some large trees, and it was not until I had gotten completely out of the car and walked around to my mother's side that I saw the campus. Even now it is hard to describe what happened. I was utterly dumbfounded. Spread before me was a Gothic fairyland, what seemed to be castle after castle, majestic, towering, timeless constructions of ivy-covered carved stone, great blue slate roofs, yawning entrances, all surrounded by great expanses of manicured lawn and paved walks. I felt suspended in time and space, completely overawed at the thought that this was mine, that this was to be where I was to live and learn, that I should have the privilege to simply be allowed there. In the same instant of humility at the grandeur of the sight came the flash of insight that here lay not just my further education, but my destiny. I stood transfixed as this epiphany washed over me, an ecstatic and exhilarating feeling that left me giddy with delight. My mother, of course, was no stranger to such sights, but she seemed to have caught my mood and stood quietly while I recomposed myself.

"I had no idea,' I mumbled. "I had absolutely no idea."

"Impressed?"

"Impressed. Yes. Overwhelmed, yes. I simply had no idea. None at all."

"You're going to love it, Peter. I'm so glad the way things have gone. I just know you're going to be happy here. And I know you're going to do well. You're going to be astonished at all the wonderful things there are to learn. Don't try to do it all at once."

We followed the sign that indicated the way to the Administration building, announced ourselves to a very pleasant lady who gave me a whole sheaf of handouts about all manner of things. There was a fixed curriculum for the first year for all liberal arts students, so dormitory selection and roommate selection were almost the only loose ends. I entered myself as having no roommate of choice and was given a room number with the understanding that any incompatibility of roommates would be adjusted later. In a short time we were free to leave and walk about. It was a perfect day of weather and the campus could not have been seen to better advantage. I continued to be staggered at the number and size and beauty of the buildings. We toured all morning and then went back home with the car to have lunch. The rest of that day and the next were a blur or tramping around downtown, having parked the car near a subway station and using public transportation. We 'saw the sights', shopped for my mother, lunched in crowded restaurants, trying to adjust to this violent dislocation of my senses that suddenly being in the Big City for the first time had caused. Saturday morning found me making my goodbyes to my mother on the campus where she had deposited me, intending to take the train home that afternoon.

For all of her valuable experience and advice, I was secretly happy to be on my own. My trunk and my suitcase were recovered from storage and with the help of a college porter, I got them to the dormitory and into my room. The room was comparatively spacious, sparsely furnished with a double bunk, a pair of large desks, a couple desk chairs, a double closet, a pair of bureaus. There was a large bathroom and shower room down the hall. Well, not overwhelming, but adequate. Beautiful view of the golf course out of this second floor window. I got unpacked and made up the lower bunk with the pile of bedding that lay on the mattress and sat down to reflect. There were comings and goings in the hall outside, voices calling out, laughter, a radio turned on, signs of life appearing. At one point a guy poked his head in and asked if I were so-an-so and abruptly left when I denied it. I was on the point of going out to explore further when the door opened and a body started backing in, struggling with a cart on which were heaped a trunk and several suitcases. There was nothing much I could do except wait until he got in. He was muttering and cursing in truly expert fashion when he finally completed his entrance and with a huge exhalation turned to survey the room. He was tall and skinny, physically graceful I thought, with a somewhat delicate, handsome, beardless face, an air of slightly baffled distraction. He wore an open collar shirt under an expensive looking lightweight sleeveless sweater, neatly pressed trousers of a fashionable cut and tassel loafers with no socks. In short, my idea of a youthful dandy. I was grinning at his performance. He seemed a little surprised to see me sitting there.

"Oh. Hi. Kind of small room, huh? Damn! Too much stuff. Oh, man. This is going to be tight. That the only closet? Oh, man. This is really tight. You Ed?"

"No. I'm Peter Hawkins."

"What happened to Ed? You're not Ed?"

"No. I'm Peter. I don't know what happened to Ed. Was he supposed to be your roommate?"

"I guess so. That was the name they told me. Ed something. You're sure this is the room they gave you?"

"Yup. That's what it says on the paper," and I waved my assignment at him. He wasn't interested in looking at it after all, and just shrugged. "Maybe Ed won't come. Well, I guess we're roommates, huh? What did you say your name was?"

"Peter. Peter Hawkins."

"Well, that's easy to remember. OK, Hawkins. Welcome to four years of living hell, I suppose."

"If we're going to room together, I'd better know what to call you."

"Oh. Right. My name in R. G. L. M. Oldfield, but my friends call me Barney because I like to drive fast. And also because I can't stand my real name which I won't tell you just now. All the ones in the middle aren't too bad, but the first one is disastrous. Call me Barney." We shook hands formally. Barney was still unsettled and edgy, looking around him disconsolately and muttering to himself and he unloaded his bags and pushed the cart out into the hall where he abandoned it.

"Man. This is a really small room. I guess I'll just have to get some of this stuff sent home. My God, do they expect us to dress decently out of that little closet?" He poked around in the closet. "Is that all the stuff you have in there?"

"That's it."

"Would you be willing to let me use a little of your side? I guess I just brought too much, but man, I just don't see how half my stuff is going to fit. Could you spare a little on your side there?"

"Sure. Help yourself and welcome to it."

"You won't mind?"

"Not a bit. Help yourself."

"Well, thanks. I really appreciate it. That's all you brought?" gesturing to my half dozen hangers.

"That's all I've got," I said. He looked at me closely now for the first time. There was something about his look that said 'What have I gotten into, here?'

"Where do you come from, Hawkins?"

"East Tennessee."

"East Tennessee? Where is that?" I really had to smile.

"It's underneath Virginia and on top of Georgia."

"Right. Underneath Virginia. And you say you're from the east part of it? I've never been anywhere down there. How'd you end up here?" I told him briefly.

"Scholarship! My God, a brain! How as I going to live with a brain? Hawkins, don't go brainy on me. Brains intimidate me. I hope to God your not going to sit there and study all the time. Too depressing. Are you a drudge, Hawkins? Are you going to sit there and grind away at the old books all night? I don't know if I can handle that, Hawkins. I'm much more of a free spirit, you see. I have to go through this college crap because my parents insist on it and all, but that is not the real Barney. Whatever I am destined for has nothing to do with grinding away at books. Gentleman's C and that sort of thing. You won't hold it against me if things get to the point where I think we should split up, will you? I don't want to offend you, you know, but it might just turn out that we weren't meant to be roommates. You see? Well. We can just go along and see how it works. No harm in trying. Have you ever had a roommate before? No? Neither have I. I guess we'll just have to make the best of it and see how it goes. That suit you? I hate to get off on the wrong foot, but I think it's better that these things are out in the open right away so there won't be any hard feelings. Where about do you live in East Tennessee? Not that I'd know the place, but I suppose I ought to know if we're going to live together."

"I live on a farm. There isn't any town there anymore. There used to be a little village where I live, but it more or less disappeared." He stared at me without any visible emotion, that thousand yard stare that I came to know so well when there was a major disconnect.

"A farm? You live on a farm?"

"Yes. On a farm."

"What do you do on the farm? I mean, do you grow things and all? I guess you must. Or maybe you don't. Just what do you do on the farm?" I told him briefly about the crops and the livestock. He listened quietly. He was so totally non-plussed that I found it amusing and I was almost tempted to lay it on a little for the fun of it, but decided to play it straight until I knew him better.

"I have never met a farmer, you see. I know there must be lots of them, but I didn't expect to meet one. At least for awhile, you know. There are farms out where we live, I think, but we just drive past them. I mean, I've never gone in to see one.

"Well, not much more I can do here. What do you say to a beer, Hawkins? Pulling that cart around gave me an outrageous thirst. Do you drink beer? I suppose you must. Everybody does in my crowd. What do you say, a beer to start things off on the right foot?" I was fascinated by this oddity of a roommate and anxious to hear more, so with my assent, we shut the door and walked off to one of the several taverns that ringed the school at a nearly respectful distance.

4

arney turned out to be a good guy after all. You just had to cut through the haughty, aristocratic crap he was attempting to invent for himself at that period in his life to find the real Barney of whom I became very fond. He came from a wealthy family, an older child of parents who married late, the father an investment banker, his mother a self effacing, motherly lady of impeccable pedigree but no other attainments. After we had gotten to be much better acquainted, he invited me to his home in an exclusive suburban area where I spent a number of weekends very pleasantly. Barney (whose entire name was Rupert Grant Lawson Marshall Oldfield, commemorating a number of distinguished ancestors) was an entirely different creature at home, almost normal, nothing of the bored sophisticate which would never have been permitted by his father, just a bright, engaging, amusing and lively companion, much better read and smarter than he was willing to let on. He made good marks and studied seriously, but almost always in the library so that he would not be found studying by his classmates, to whom he wished to be seen as succeeding without effort.

His father and I got on very well, Mr. Oldfield a warm and considerate gentleman, sincere in his interest in my welfare and a first rate conversationalist. Our reading tastes were similar and he was pleased to find that we had both enjoyed so many of his favorite books, an interest which Barney had only marginally absorbed from his father. During our second year, certain that my influence on Barney was beneficial (he had told me as much), Mr. Oldfield unobtrusively staked us to a much grander suite of rooms, our own bathroom, two bedrooms with a central study room, a couch and couple easy chairs. He would hear nothing of my offer to contribute and so we passed from relative austerity to near palatial quarters.

As planned, I had become involved as heavily as my scheduling would permit in the biology department. I had come in contact with Dr. Charles Baxter in a preliminary course in our first year, back in that dim past when professors actually taught classes. I developed a great affection for this odd little duck who was constantly mimicked and joked about for his odd mannerisms and what seemed to many students his absurd enthusiasm for all things biological. For the student taking this elementary course as part of his obligatory freshman sampling of the arts and sciences, it was understandable, but for me, his intensity was exciting, an appreciation that must have been apparent to him. Whatever the reason, I found that he was looking directly and nearly exclusively at me during his lectures as though at least in this one student he had found a reception. The result was that in my junior year when I came in regular contact with him, he made it a point of taking a personal interest in my progress. This flattering attitude on his part led me to prodigious efforts, rather dazzling grades, and a closer relationship with him. I took every course to be had as well as non-credit Saturday seminars that Dr. Baxter moderated himself, attended by only a few of us hardy souls. I idolized him and he clearly liked me. He had taken me under his wing, almost literally and had decided that my thinking about a career in medicine was not challenging enough to fully engage me. All this was very flattering, and as time went by under his influence, I abandoned my plans to become a physician and decided to hitch my hopes to Dr. Baxter's star.

5

The fourth year had just begun. Whenever there was a gap in my scheduling of science classes, I tried to fill it with a course in some aspect of history or literature. On this last occasion when it would have been possible, the opportunity arose to attend a class I had long planned to take, Elizabethan Drama. The principal attraction of the course that made it so hard to get into was that it was given by Dr. Alvin March, who in addition to his credentials as a teacher, was a successful Shakespearian actor of considerable reputation. On the second day of class, of all things unimaginable, there appeared in class a lovely female student, something unknown previously in this hidebound men's institution. She was introduced to the disbelieving class as Miss Grafton, a senior attending Willoughby College, the prestigious women's college nearby, who would be auditing the course.

No one could possibly have objected to such a treat, in spite of the all male atmosphere. We looked at each other with the looks and gestures that young men my age exchanged in such situations. Her beauty was along classical lines, the sort that one sees on the covers of fashionable women's magazines, but with a modesty and a reserve alien to those models. She appeared poised and proper with an unmistakable aura of wealth and good breeding. She simply reeked of money and social position. Beyond that, there was an intimidating, cool self possession about her that invited no liberties.

Above average height, she had long straight, naturally blond hair held back with a dignified silver and tortoise shell clasp, blue eyes under real, unplucked eyebrows, a delicate nose and an interestingly curved but not sensuous mouth. She was dressed simply in a longish skirt of muted fall colors, a simple moss colored cashmere sweater that revealed (I think to her dismay) a lovely figure, burnished loafers, no jewelry other than a simple gold chain with a green stone pendant and a delicate, expensive look-ing gold wristwatch. Her carriage and her posture were impecca-ble, regal without a sign of haughtiness. She had nodded politely and smiled imperceptibly as she was introduced, but then took her seat, erect and poised as she had no doubt been coached to sit at her fancy school. I found myself unconsciously sitting up straighter myself, just in case. I was impressed. I knew there were girls like this somewhere, but wherever they hung out, I had never met them. She was elegant, refined, composed and clearly beyond the reach of mere mortals. Whether her indifference to the rest of us was aloofness or simply the defensiveness that the only girl in a classroom packed with guys was entitled to, I had no idea.

I was not above fantasizing about her, however, and although she didn't seem any more accessible as the next couple weeks passed, I became more determined to create a chance to talk with her. An opportunity finally arose a couple weeks later. In the course of reading and discussing "Romeo and Juliet", our profes-sor assigned several of us to roles involved in a few of the scenes that he felt encapsulated the essence of the play, a great favorite of his, he said. It was to be done as a play reading. We had read and discussed the play and he now wanted us to have the experi-ence of actually uttering the lines in these particular scenes. You have never seen so many heads ducked quickly to check notes or shoe tops as Dr. March looked about for candidates. When he an-nounced that first he needed a Romeo, one of my pals with whom I had shared a few confidences pointed to me and said, "There's your Romeo."

This got a laugh as well as landing me the part, to my cha-grin I might add, not anxious to make a fool of myself. Their could be no doubt as to who was assigned the role of Juliet. Miss Grafton was understandably surprised, as her role was one only of observer and auditor. She seemed about to protest in embarrass-ment when with an effort she rallied and accepted the assignment, although visibly uncomfortable. Charitably, our professor picked up on this and spent some time on further analysis of the scenes we were to read, and then when Miss Grafton's flush had subsided, set us to our task. We were seated loosely in a circle, Juliet across from me. I had never even made eye contact with her, nor had anyone else that I was aware of. She had resolutely remained distant from us, silent during class, going to the professor's desk for a brief conference at the end of each class by which time we had all left. We had never exchanged a word, never heard the sound of her voice. Now it became nearly inescapable, and during the lines spoken by the professor that led to my own opening lines, she glanced up from the text and our eyes met and my gaze held hers for just a moment, and in that moment the flush reappeared. I felt very sympathetic toward this lovely creature, thrust so unexpectedly from her preferred privacy into such exposure. We read portions of a couple scenes, chosen to illustrate this most famous of all examples of 'love at first sight'. In an effort to put an end to her discomfort, I was reading as quickly as I dared, and she in turn read so softly as to be nearly inaudible.

The professor stopped us, shaking his head as though in despair. "Wait, wait, wait, gentlemen and Miss Grafton. These are some of the most famous lines in all literature. Try to make them live for the rest of the class. Come now, let's put some life, some feeling into this. Think! Think about what you are saying…imagine yourself living these moments. You, Romeo," looking at me and gesticulating, "you have just seen this lovely young girl for the first time in your life, you are deeply in love with another girl, but at the sight, the simple sight of Juliet, you are helplessly, hopelessly in love with her, your heart is pounding, your legs are trembling, you can think of nothing else but meeting and speaking to this girl, you are burning with passion and love and God knows what else! Make us feel it! Don't mumble! Look at this beautiful creature," gesturing to Juliet, "get yourself into Romeo's mind and let us hear you sound like you are dumbstruck with her beauty! Now, let's start again and see if you can make us believe you!"

I looked over at Juliet who declined to look up, visibly flushed again. I felt so sorry for her and for myself as well, convicted probably of being a party to this unwelcome experience. I took a deep breath and tried again. It helped that Juliet resolutely studied her script while I tried to emote effectively and failed, I thought. When we got to the balcony scene and Juliet's turn came to speak, the professor encouraged her and treated her very gently, and she managed to read her lines, but just audibly, head down, uncomfortable and conspicuous. The reading went on to another couple scenes equally unsuccessful, and finally came to a merciful end. We broke off to listen to a dissertation on how to read Shakespeare, Dr. March now acting all the parts as he had wished us to, an exciting performance, actually. I tried several times to catch Juliet's eye, but she resolutely looked down or ahead until class was over, then went up to the professor's desk as usual while the rest of us filed out. It was partly because I wanted to apologize for her having been put in such a difficult spot and also because there was something about her modesty and distress before that attracted me. I waited for her in the hall. She came out of the room arranging her books in her carrying bag and almost walked into me, startled as she looked up and identified me.

"I wanted to tell you that I'm sorry for whatever I contributed to your ordeal in there. It must have seemed natural for him to pick you to read that part, but if it makes you feel any better, I think I was just as uncomfortable as you were. I don't think he'll do that to you again. Did he have anything to say about it just now?" She shook her head. "Well, anyway, I'm sorry you had such a time of it. I hope that won't sour you on the class. Are you going to keep on coming over?" Yes, she would. It had been something of a shock, but she realized she had allowed herself to make too much of it. "Do you mind having an escort to your car or wherever you're going?" She didn't mind, but I didn't feel any encouragement and I honestly thought she might regret the whole business of coming over to this men's campus and toss it up.

"My name is Peter Hawkins. I know you are Miss Grafton but I don't know what comes between the Miss and the Grafton." She smiled pleasantly enough.

"I'm Susan Grafton. How do you do?" and with this held out her hand. We had to stop walking briefly to perform the shaking of hands, a convention that seemed odd coming from a girl.

"How do you like Dr. March's histrionics? This may be a bad time to ask, but I think he's really impressive when he reads from the play. He still does summer stock, you know. It shows, don't you think?"

"Yes, I do, he's really quite good. Actually, I knew that he was active in the theater. I was told that at Willoughby before I came over. Someone on our faculty had seen him perform before and knew he did some acting in front of his classes. Actually, that's largely why I decided to audit the course. It's just that I didn't think I'd be drawn into anything personally like this. I don't usually get upset by being asked to recite but this was so different and I just wasn't prepared."

"You weren't prepared? Believe me, I wasn't prepared either. I'm not the volunteer type and when he picked me for Romeo, the first thing I thought about was escape. Here I've hardly seen you in my whole life and I'm supposed to be passionate and jelly-legged and smitten and burning and...have I missed anything?" By this time, she was laughing and I thought maybe this was going to come off all right after all. "It's bad enough for me. I know these guys, but you being a total stranger...well, I thought you were brave not to run. Were you able to enjoy it at all?"

"In a way, I suppose. I mean, yes, after I got started a little I began to get a grip on myself, but the words seemed so artificial and strange when I spoke them out loud compared with just reading them.. I've always enjoyed reading Shakespeare, and I've seen several of his plays, but somehow speaking that way myself and saying things I would never say in real life was difficult. How hard it must be to be an actress and have to play a part that she doesn't feel. I suppose they get used to it, but I found it very unnatural to pretend to be Juliet. She certainly didn't show much restraint, did she? I suppose Shakespeare felt he had to keep things moving along, but the whole business of Romeo being in love with some other girl and then in one glance, head over heels with another...that's not very credible, do you think?"

"Well, actually, I don't have any problem with that. I don't think Shakespeare was just trying to pick up the pace. I think he understood the crushes that kids have. Here's Romeo, sixteen or so, and Juliet, fourteen maybe, both of them rich, maybe bored, time on their hands, so they dream about what their genes insist they dream about, namely romance. Romeo was probably cruising around Venice romancing everything in skirts, a seething mass of hormones doing what every male organism on the planet is programmed to do, looking for a mate. I mean, love at first sight is just standard animal behavior and we come by it honestly. That's why we're still around."

"Oh, Peter! What a thing to say! I'm sure you're right as far as animals are concerned, but don't you think that human beings have the intellect and the discrimination and the...cultural background to do better than just blindly seize on a potential mate like that? That seemed awfully unrealistic to me. It seems to me that after millions of years we can do better than just allow our emotions to rule our lives. Think of how much pain and waste must result from matches like that where no one takes the time to think things through, but just...pounces! I think that people who have so little emotional control must be responsible for much of the world's unhappiness. I can't imagine much good coming out of such irrational behavior. Am I wrong?"

"Well, I don't think it's a matter of right or wrong and I'm *really* sure it's not a matter of reason. It's just the way we are and always have been. If reason were the rule, I don't think there'd be a single human being on earth. It's that lack of control and pouncing that keep things going...no pounce, no people. Like it or not, a lot of what we do has nothing to do with reason. No question reason has kept us out of a lot of scrapes and has been terrifically important to our being as successful as we have been, but we're not all that far removed from dragging some lady into a cave by the hair. You aren't by any chance religious, are you?"

"No, I wouldn't say that I am. I believe in evolution, if that's what you're getting at."

"More or less. I didn't want to offend you, talking about something that might be objectionable. The point I was trying to make, is that almost everything we've got was handed down to us by all those bugs and fish and furry cousins of ours, so we shouldn't be surprised if something pretty animalistic surfaces now and then. It's our honest inheritance, and I personally think we should recognize that and accept it as part of the package. As far as being rational is concerned, I'm all for it most of the time, but I think emotions are really important, so I don't feel guilty when I occasionally do something a little nutty if it makes emotional sense to me. I think that having fun is important and if that takes a little irrationality you know, then OK, why not? I don't think you should let your emotions run away with you, but that's different from just doing something totally spontaneously, without dissecting it and scrutinizing it and agonizing over it, but doing it just because it feels right and you feel like doing it. I think being able to do things like that at least once in awhile is good for a person. It kind of clears the air. I think it's a good idea to just give things a shake now and then and see what happens." She laughed and I saw nothing that suggested I was going to get my head handed to me.

"I can't do that. Sometimes I wish I could. I know what you mean about getting into a rut, but some people feel most comfortable that way. I have a friend at school who is a little wild…I don't mean she does bad things, but just silly things, and I must say she seems to enjoy life more than a lot of other people. Sometimes I think I envy her, but I just don't feel right trying to join in and if I do try, it just doesn't work. She laughs at me and pokes fun at me, but I just don't have any inclination that way." I shrugged. "I didn't mean all that to sound critical. Everybody should do what they feel comfortable with, I think. Go with what you've got." There was a pause, then Susan asked what year I was in. We were both seniors. She asked me what I was majoring in. I told her biology and she asked what I intended to do after graduation.

"My professor thinks I have a good chance to get in with a pharmaceutical house he has some clout with. He's sort of grooming me for a research project that he thinks he can get a grant for and help me with, something that might turn out to be fairly big stuff for the company if they can be persuaded to let me try it. I thought at first I was going to go to med school and I started out in pre-med, but then I got involved in biology with this professor and gave up the idea of being a doctor. My family was a little disappointed, but everything considered, I think this is the right thing for me."

She looked at me with something like respect and said, "That's wonderful, Peter! That sounds very exciting. You must be very pleased to have something like that to look forward to. I see now why you felt the way you did about Romeo. I suppose I should take back some negative thoughts I had when you talked about animal instincts. You must know a great deal more about it that I. Somehow Darwin has always seemed to me to be so brutal about things. I really hate to think that I'm descended from an ape."

"Shame on you. When was the last time you saw an ape?"

"What? When was the last time I saw an ape?"

"Yes, when was the last time you saw an ape?

"Well. I suppose when I was little. Actually, I can't remember ever seeing an ape, if that's what you mean."

"You're overdue." Now she was puzzled and uncertain whether this was humor, where it was headed or what was expected of her. "I'm sorry but I don't understand what you're getting at."

"Do you have plans tomorrow from about ten to maybe three?"

"I'm not sure I want to answer that question. Why do you ask?"

"I want to show you an ape, is why. Several apes. Lots of apes. I don't know what they are teaching you at Willoughby, but the fact that you have never seen an ape is totally unacceptable. If you will permit me, tomorrow I will show you some apes." Now she was really laughing, frustrated."

"Are you perfectly sane?" She was just about to get into the spirit of the matter.

"Quite."

"How do we go about this if I should agree?"

"How we go about it is that you pick me up here tomorrow morning and we go to the Zoo. Beyond that I will be playing it by ear, but it will definitely include apes."

"Is this your idea of giving things a shake?"

"It is." I think if it weren't ladylike, she would have stamped her foot. She was laughing, frustrated, perhaps annoyed, but enjoying it.

"You're really serious about this?"

"Dead." More hesitation and uncertainty.

"No one would ever believe this…oh, dear. When and where would I pick you up?"

"Ten A.M. and right here." We stood and stared at each other, smiling, mine confident, hers tentative. "Susan. You're doing the right thing. I'm a good person." I think that helped. At least, before she got in her car, she held out her hand again and I shook it briefly. Odd, this hand shaking, but it felt good, sincere, dignified, so adult and I wondered if this was the way the smart set did things.

6

The day at the zoo was a success, I thought. I was aware that she was dressed very prettily when I got in the car, but when we got to the zoo and she got out, I was absolutely blown away and made no effort to conceal it. Entirely spontaneously, I made an expressive male sound and immediately regretted it. She was a picture. Beautiful, billowy, flowered print dress, light and delicate, her blonde hair slightly blown by the breeze but her face suddenly immobilized with a self conscious lowering of the eyes. Anguished, I quickly took her hand and tried to make amends. "Susan! I'm so sorry! You deserve so much more than that. I don't know if I have ever seen a lovelier sight and I got carried away. Where I come from girls just don't look like this, and I was simply bowled over. Forgive me? You look so pretty!" My sincere contrition was received with some of her own embarrassment and with a tiny smile. She dropped me a little curtsey. I bowed slightly and we both laughed and this little bumble of mine was forgiven.

"You must forgive me, too, Peter. It's so silly, but for some reason I find it hard to accept compliments. I don't know why, I just do. I hope you aren't offended. I should be more appreciative of nice things like that. I'll try hard to do better if you will promise not to..." "Say no more. I won't. What ever it is. For instance, I'm going to tell you once more that you are the prettiest girl I have ever, ever seen and I can hardly believe that I have a date with such a vision." She smiled, such a lovely smile, still not at ease with my praise, but pleased, I thought.

Now she reached inside the car and fished out a hat, a big floppy hat with a blue ribbon hanging down in back. The breeze ruffled the hat and the hair and the ribbon and the skirt and I couldn't take my eyes off her. "You have no mercy. That did it. The hat is just too much. Why don't girls wear hats anymore? It makes you look so special." Flattered but a little disbelieving, she put on a pair of sunglasses and now the movie star image was complete, and I told her so. She was that striking. And all this for the zoo!

"I promised you apes today. Ready?" She was, and I took her hand and we headed straight for the primate area, Susan relaxed, a graceful, long gait, admiring this and that which I resolutely passed by, assuring her that we would return.

There is a god somewhere whose particular pleasure it is to confound the innocent and upset the most sanguine of schemes. I had spent endless periods of time watching these fascinating creatures whose behavior I had read about, studied onto, come to understand to some extent and toward whom I felt a tender kinship. To admire them, I had brought this ethereal creature whose society I hoped to cultivate, this refined and modest maiden, and before my eyes, to my utter mortification, the whole thing backfired miserably. The gibbons refused to swing, well, no matter. To my dismay, it was a down day for the chimps who were just sitting around, one of them, wouldn't you know, right in front of us, sitting and dreamily picking excrement out of her butt and smelling it. Inwardly furious with the perversity of these creatures on this of all days, I hastily moved on, Susan silent but determined to see the apes as she had pledged. We passed on to the gorilla enclosure, one great handsome silverback sitting with his back against the thick glass panel, a wedge of lettuce held loosely in the enormous fingers, the head with it's tiny brown eyes turning occasionally to look at us, an exciting moment for anyone, Susan no exception. The two of us stood gazing in admiration and I was offering some observations that I thought illuminating when I sensed Susan tensing. Better attuned now to her signals, I quickly glanced around and there, not twenty yards in front of us, the other male gorilla lay idly on his back, masturbating. I drew a deep breath and led my lady away, away, as far away as I could before I stopped and faced her.

"Well!" I said with deliberately artificial brightness, "so much for our ancestors, the apes. No doubt I have made my point, yes?" and then screwed up my face and hung my head. I think that Susan commiserated with me. She surely understood my embarrassment and disappointment. "Ah, well", I continued, "perhaps we should press on to less...ah...functional sights."

From here on, although anything would have been can improvement, things went immeasurably better. The zoo was one of my favorite spots on weekends and I had gotten to know a number of people on the staff. As they got to know me better, I was extended little favors. These kids for the most part were my age and understood that I was a regular and studying biology so things were pretty relaxed. Whenever I ran across a staff member I knew, I introduced them to Susan and told them it was her first time there and naturally that opened doors. One of the girls that worked training the birds took us back into a large arena behind the display area where they train the raptors to fetch. We watched one of the girls training a hawk and now Susan was excited and appreciative. When she put the bird away, at my request she got out an owl and a peregrine and a macaw and let Susan see them close up and touch them. Susan was delighted and very grateful for the privilege and I began to feel like things might come around. We went through the insect house and watched the ant and the termite and the bee colonies behind their glass walls. I never tire of watching those creatures, but I wasn't at all sure that Susan felt the same way, but she seemed to want to linger, so I began to tell her about their social life and how many of the things they did, we did also. I wasn't sure that she was willing to accept the notion that they had passed on these things to us, but I think she was enjoying herself, and that, beyond anything else now, was my goal.

The African lions were sound asleep and hardly visible, but a keeper friend led us around to where the three cubs were dozing and rattled her keys and these tough little creatures came to the fence and pawed and rubbed and put on a little show for us. Susan was thrilled, of course, and I was very pleased that things were going so well. The girl at the snake house let us in back and got out a corn snake that was sort of their demonstrator and while I held it, Susan was persuaded to stroke it's skin, probably not the high point of the visit for her, but she carried it off nicely.

The elephants had always been a big favorite of mine, so after the sea mammals and the giraffes and the bears and feeding the wolves, we went to the elephant house. I banged loudly on the employees door until a girl opened it and confirmed that Don was there. Don was an interesting guy whom I had gotten to know fairly well. He was one of these trim, short, heavily muscled guys who looked to be straight out a carnival but had a good head and knew elephants. He was obviously impressed at Susan and after the introductions, while she was distracted, gave me the huge thumbs up gesture and look, which didn't surprise me.

We wandered into this gloomy, cavernous room, walking a safe distance from the thick steel columns that served as bars, trying to accommodate from the sunshine, when suddenly Susan became aware of the enormous bulk and presence of Tantor, the big bull African elephant, towering what seemed several stories over us, the huge trunk swinging slowly back and forth. She audibly gasped and recoiled and clutched my arm and only slowly relaxed as she made out his form and realized she was safe. Don was pleased at such a spontaneous tribute to the intimidation this colossus inspired, such a magnificent and dangerous beast, and he put on a little show, giving this brute a series of voice commands, to pick up each foot successively, kneel down, lie on his side, get up, take and return a baton Don held out to him and so on. I had seen this many times and every time was awed by the power of a tiny human to command this great beast to perform such ponderous and at once delicate tasks. At the conclusion of this performance, just as we were coming down from the thrill of watching him, Tantor gave a tremendous, ear splitting bellow, the likes of which I had never heard from him. Susan uttered a muffled scream and Don loved it. He turned to Susan and said, "He likes girls." We gave him our thanks and tottered out into the bright sun, Susan still wide-eyed and clinging to me, which made it worthwhile.

"I just can't believe it! Have you ever heard such a sound in your life? Imagine what it would be like to hear that out in the jungle! That was so exciting! I can hardly believe what I've just seen and heard. Oh, Peter, that was such a wonderful experience. I'm so grateful to you for going to so much trouble. For everything. I had no idea! Thank you so much! This is a very special day for me."

I was perfectly content to take credit for this dramatic and unplanned climax and felt that the apes excepted, the tour had been just about everything I could make it. I suggested a bite and we got a couple dull hamburgers and some ice cream and sat at a table under some trees. It's times like these that I wish someone had taken our picture. I asked her about her school. She enjoyed it but thought it was too snooty, standards very high, faculty brilliant. She was majoring in Fine Arts, had a studio of her own at home, did oils and watercolors mostly, had talent but felt it was only modest. She was very easy to talk to, it turned out, poised, articulate, confident, mature, just about all the things I had never met in a girl my age, and I was thoroughly enjoying myself.

We drove back to the campus and sat and talked in the car for a long time. I had the feeling that she was as reluctant to break the contact as I. It wasn't love, there was nothing I would call lust, but I was excited and fascinated by meeting such a good mind, the first girl I had ever met who was truly bright and engaging and beautiful and what else? Who knew? I wanted to talk and talk some more and as we were eventually obliged to part, told her that I hadn't begun to finish all the things I wanted to talk about, and could we continue the dialogue sometime soon? She would love to and would I like her to take me to the art museum sometime? I said that that would please me enormously, especially if it were very soon. As though it were her turn to be cute, she allowed that the earliest that she could make it would be tomorrow. How did I feel about that? I felt very good about that and told her that I would sit and wait on the curb until then.

I was walking on air. I had met a lovely girl, she seemed to like me and we were going to get to know each other. Something I had projected had been right, something had appealed to her, there was something that had encouraged her to allow my attentions at least for the time being. I had no idea where we were headed. I only knew that she was the most interesting girl I had ever met, that the immediate future looked pretty exciting. She seemed to acknowledge without prejudice my limited resources; she was willing to take my lead and beyond that, offer her own. She was bolder and warmer than I had imagined.

My band had a gig that night at a fraternity house bash. I played piano in a band that I had put together with a few other guys a couple of years before. We played mostly rock and roll, and some rhythm and blues. That wasn't my kind of music but it was what people wanted. I preferred jazz to just about anything else, but there wasn't much interest in jazz in my age group, so we played what paid, and although it didn't pay all that well, it kept me afloat and got us out and around, meeting people and having a little fun. We had a really good vocalist, Peggy, a girl I had met about a year ago, just an office chick with no musical background, but when we started dating I found out she liked to sing and after she came to a few rehearsals, we figured she was pretty good and she had been with us ever since. Peggy and I had times when we didn't get on all that well, usually a result of her being hell bent on marrying someone and trying to interest me in the job. She was a lot of fun, cute as a button but pretty wild and irresponsible which is great to a point but Peggy had a way of getting past that point too often. At this particular time, we were getting along pretty well and I stayed at her place after the gig.

We were having coffee and doughnuts the next morning and just relaxing and taking it easy when she suggested we go over to one of her friend's apartment. The friend had just gotten some really great pot and was having some people over and so on. I told her I had to study and she told me she knew I didn't and after we'd gone round and round for a time, I got annoyed and told her I wasn't interested in sitting around stoned all day and left. I hated to do that because I didn't really want to get Peggy mad in case the Susan thing wasn't what I hoped, but it seemed like the thing to do at the time, so I took off walking, Peggy in no mood to give me a lift. I got back to school in plenty of time to meet Susan. She was right on the dot, as I sort of expected.

The museum trip was nearly as much fun in its own way as the zoo had been. I had very little artistic talent but had long been an admirer of what then was still called Modern Art, which in my limited art education, personally arrived at, consisted largely of only a dozen or so famous names, van Gogh way out in front for honors. I had been to the museum many times as it was free, an undeniable attraction, but my interest had been confined almost exclusively to those rooms featuring my favorite modern artists. Susan was very respectful of my tastes as we visited my favorites, but then patiently led me through areas that I had scarcely visited, pointing out all sorts of things that I would never have dreamed of. It went on like this for a couple hours, Susan animated as I had not seen her, a little color in her pale and perfect cheeks, introducing me to her world, this world of art that must have been a large part of her life. I listened attentively, nodding, asking questions, serious now, impressed at her knowledge. A couple times she caught herself and asked if I had had enough. No, no, by all means, please go on, I was enjoying it immensely. Even with this assurance, she looked closely at me from time to time as though to give me another chance to demur.

Eventually we came to a pause point. "Susan", I whimpered, "I am eternally in your debt for your patience and your sharing of all this delicious material. This has been an outstanding adventure for me, but if I don't get something to eat pretty soon, I'm going to have to be carried out."

She laughed and apologized. "I am totally unreliable when I get wrapped up in something like this or when I'm painting. I almost always come here alone, and when I'm with others, they are most likely to be art students. This is the first time I have come in here in ages with someone either not involved in the art department or the museum. I'm having fun. I hadn't thought about a lot of the things I was telling you for such a long time. I do hope you really did enjoy it and are not just being kind. And I am hungry, actually. Where shall we go?"

"I promise you that some day before too long I'll take you to a real restaurant, but rather than walk a mile to some hash house, how about the coffee shop here, no stars but they have lost very few people." So we ducked into that chaste room and took a table, almost the only people there. We wolfed down a couple drab sandwiches and then rather than linger there, I suggested we go out on the grounds where there was a pretty little lake, a pond, really, with thick beds of fall flowers around it, winding walks, benches and so on. We sat and talked, in the course of which I mentioned that I had tried my hand at a little painting. She turned to me on the edge of the seat and seemed surprised.

"Did you really? How wonderful! What have you done?" I had not expected to generate quite so much interest.

"You won't believe this. I'm not sure I should even tell you about it. It's going to sound awfully dumb. I tend to plunge into things and try to figure them out after I get there which isn't the soundest way to do business. This will not reflect well on me."

"Don't feel that way. Do tell me. Everybody has created things they're not proud of, but the fact that you were willing to try is what's important." She remained poised in this expectant way so I felt obliged to go on.

"Well, OK. But this is so dumb. Anyway, I decided one day that I'd like to have some original art in my room. It just came to me that that was the thing to do, no other reason that I know of. Obviously, I couldn't buy anything, but I had the notion that I could copy something I liked. You know, if they can do it, I can do it sort of thing. Several times when I had come over here to the museum, there was this guy sitting in front of one of the really great paintings like you were just showing me, copying it. He had an easel and a stool and a big box of all kinds of paint and brushes, you know, the whole works, and there he sat, painting away, and doing an absolutely beautiful job. I never saw him finish anything, but you could tell that they were going to be really good copies, so I decided, why not me?"

Susan broke in. "Was he a small man? Thick bushy hair? Big bristly mustache that sticks way out on the sides?"

"Must be the guy. Sure sounds right."

"That's Mort Nadleman. Isn't he simply marvelous? He does the most beautiful work. I've seen him over here a dozen times and I always stop and watch. Jim Nance, one of our instructors knows him. He lives in a dreadfully run down place not too far from here. Mr. Nance says the walls inside his apartment are just covered with reproductions he has done. When he had covered the walls, he just started stacking them in piles. He says it is just like a museum basement. Everybody knows he could sell them for really good prices, but he's not interested. He just seems to want to live in the midst of all that beauty. They say he doesn't do anything original, which seems like a pity. But go on. I'm sorry. I just thought you should know something about him."

"Interesting. I figured he was sort of a character. He acted like he owned the place. Anyway, it was old Mort that gave me the nudge to try something, so I scrounged together some dough and went to a little art supply store right around from school and bought one of those canvases that are all ready to go, and about three brushes, totally guess work, plus one tube each of red, blue, yellow, black and white. Pretty smart, huh? I figured I could make any color I wanted if I took my time. Then I went to the library and looked at a few books of modern paintings, picked out one by George Braque that looked easy, took the book home and started painting.

"Oh, man, what a time I had. I mean, you could tell it was a supposed to be a copy of the painting in the book, but something was really, really missing. Like talent. But I was determined to get it to the point where I wouldn't cringe every time I saw it, and gradually, by fooling around here and there and painting over and over until I got something like the right colors, it improved a little. Talk about reinventing the wheel? I was so excited one day to realize that the effect I wanted in a part of the painting could only be had by painting one color on, letting it dry and then painting another over it lightly so that the bottom color showed through. I felt like Columbus. Can you imagine? I just didn't know anything. Anyway, I finally got to a point where I didn't think I could make it any better so I propped it up on my desk and after awhile, it began to look a little better, so I went out and got another canvas and picked another Braque and did that one, a little larger and a little better. Boy, I was easily satisfied, but you know, I wanted something on the wall and I had gotten them. So eventually I sprang for a couple cheap unfinished frames, put a pickle on them and hung those two masterpieces in my room at home. And there they will stay, safely out of sight, just like Mort's. Well, maybe not quite like Mort's."

"That's wonderful! Good for you! I'm so pleased you told me. If only more people would let themselves do something like that. There must be so much talent in the world that we'll never know about. It seems such a shame that people think that something must be professional to be enjoyed. I know from what you said that you must have enjoyed doing them. And you needn't apologize for the way you went about it. Your instincts were right. You wanted something and you did it rather than just sit around and wish. Have you done anything else?"

"Ah, dear lady, you are lifting the curtain on my secret life. You see, I had been bitten. I have had a long running love affair with Van Gogh that verges on the pathological. My mother and several of her sisters had some modest artistic talent—and she had bought a coffee table book on Van Gogh. This was right after my Braque Period. I had never seen anything like these paintings. I went through that book time and time again. Something about them was intensely personal for me. I admired them to the exclusion of almost everything else, but there wasn't a single one of his works in this museum, so I had to settle for what I could get out of the book. You probably remember the touring exhibit of a whole bunch of his paintings that came through here a couple years ago? Well, I was here at the crack of dawn the first day of the exhibit. OK, not the crack of dawn, but the first day. It's hard to tell you what it was like. I'm not even sure I should try, it was so weird. I had this nervous feeling that something very special was going to happen to me, that this was a big day in my life. I know that's silly, but as I stood in line waiting to get in, I was as excited as I can remember being.

"The minute I found myself face to face with the first of those crude, thick masses of paint and realized that the hand of the man I so admired had actually put them there, I could scarcely believe it. I actually had a rush of adrenaline. Isn't that crazy? I was staring more at the individual brush strokes and blobs than I was at the painting as a whole. I had this feeling that in some mystical way, I was in the presence of this tragic man. I realized that in my mind I was actually putting myself in the position of putting that paint down and feeling the emotion, the overwhelming emotion that he must have been experiencing with every stroke. I actually felt that I knew how he felt as he painted. Am I making any sense? I've never talked about this before. Anyway, I could see that pathetic figure tortured by the genius that drove him, actually putting that stroke and that stroke and that stroke on that very canvas. Does this found too absolutely dumb? It's so hard to explain. You remember just a couple days ago we were talking about Romeo and his sudden passion for Juliet and how I more or less agreed with you about the problem of emotions running away with someone and all that? I knew there was something I wasn't saying about how I felt about strong emotions and I just now realize why 'passion', I guess you could call it, is important. When I look at one of van Gogh's paintings, I don't see anything remotely resembling reason—they are just pure passion, and I think van Gogh must have been passionately in love with the whole world and everything in it, and I think we would be much poorer if he hadn't listened to that passion. You just know people like Michelangelo were pure passion, and loads of other artists, probably most of them, even the ones that seem so controlled and serene, must have been in a passionate state when they painted, so let me go back a bit and add something to what I said before. I think passion is very important. I think it makes an ordinary life exciting. So it was the passion of Van Gogh that I guess I had picked up on and which completely transformed my appreciation of his paintings. I seemed to have been able to vicariously share that passion of his. It resonated with something in me that I had never been aware of." Susan sat perfectly still not taking her eyes off of me.

"I spent the whole day there, no lunch or anything and the mood never changed. I was literally awestricken. I felt kind of numb or detached or something. Now, I know there are a lot of other artists more famous and more respected, but I have never been able to feel this way about any of them. In some way, I guess, van Gogh and I are on the same wave length, or whatever you want to call it. His paintings affect me in a certain intense way that others just don't." I paused and sat and thought some more, trying to think of a better way of explaining. I was beginning to feel terribly self conscious. "Well, I kind of got wrapped up there. I may not have expressed it very well, but this seemed like the time to tell someone about it. I hope I don't sound too much like a nut of some sort." There was a long pause.

"No. You don't sound like a nut at all." She looked distant and pensive, thinking about something personal, I thought. "Actually, I think you're very lucky. I've never had a feeling like that. It must be very special. I love so many of the paintings here and I love to paint and draw, but I've never felt anything like you have. I don't know if it would even be possible for me to feel like that. I can't honestly say that I have ever felt very strongly about things. That doesn't seem to be my nature. I see many of my friends getting deeply absorbed in things and very emotional and upset and all, but I don't seem to be that way. My mother is very calm and completely in control, and guess I get it from her. I admire that in her so much. She is the Rock of Gibraltar. I don't know if I could ever feel the way you just described. Perhaps it's just not in me. But I envy you. I envy you your 'passion', as you called it. I would give a great deal to have had such a thing happen to me." There was another long pause. This whole line of thinking seemed to be somewhat painful for her and she sat absorbed in thought. After a bit, she continued. "What you were saying just now sounds like those people that have a sudden experience of deep enlightenment about something that changes their lives. Like Joan of Arc, or Buddha or someone like that. A girl I know at school has been studying Zen for a couple years and she talks about trying to reach a point where she experiences a sudden transformation that she calls 'satori'. So far, she hasn't had much luck, which makes me wonder if it isn't rather uncommon."

"Well, I can't make anything as dramatic as all that out of it. You'll have to take my word for it, but I'm really a very down to earth, nothing spiritual or mysterious kind of guy. It just happened, right out of the blue, no warning, nothing like it ever before or since. It just happened."

We sat for a time, each with personal thoughts, and then I felt the wave of all this confessional carrying me forward again. "There's more. We've come this far. I guess I might as well do the whole thing. Want to hear the rest of the story?"

"Oh, of course. I was just thinking."

"Well, after that, I just had to have some Van Gogh paintings, so I dragged out my paint kit again and decided to give it a try. I know what you're thinking and you're absolutely right. But

I not only wanted the paintings to look at but I wanted to go through the experience of putting something on canvas that resembled the real thing at least, just have that thrill I was just talking about, of making those big, thick, bold splotches of color myself. Actually, I had gotten a little smarter by then, and I got some better brushes that looked like the kind he might have used, and I got a few tubes of colors I simply figured I'd never get right otherwise and sat down to go to work. It was so strange. I found I could work only so long at a stretch, because after awhile, I would get into some sort of peculiar mental numb, more or less what I would imagine being hypnotized would be like, and I would have to stop and walk around some and get my focus back. It was a pleasant feeling, it wasn't scary or anything like that, but if I didn't get up and wander around some, I'd just sit there in sort of dreamy state. I more or less came to the conclusion that this feeling was what I had come for, that this was the experience I was looking for, and just let it go on the way it wanted to go.

"The first thing I copied was of an old guy in a blue smock or cloak, big yellow hat, gnarly old hands. Great painting. I don't mean mine, I mean the original. But actually mine wasn't all that bad. It was at least good enough that while no one would take it for an original, they wouldn't guess that I had done it. I was so tickled. I loved it. I framed it and put it up in my room. And of course, I couldn't stop there. I made another, and a third, always a portrait, and then finally one day in a magazine ad, of all places, I came across a photograph of the ultimate, at least for me, a little self portrait that had only recently been discovered, all greens and oranges with a little line drawing of a Japanese head that I guess he had done for some reason and didn't want to paint over. So he left the head there, and I guess just put the portrait away unfinished and maybe unloved, considering that it was not found for so long. I tore the page out and painted my copy of it. Not only was it better than the others, but something about the thought that he had not valued this treasure, that he could afford to discard something as exciting as this, made me feel as though I had done enough. This wasn't his last painting, but I decided it was the last of mine. Maybe it was just because I had finally turned out one that pleased me. Anyway, that was a couple years ago, and I haven't had any desire to do any more and I doubt I ever will. Odd. It just came to an end."

We sat silently. I had been talking to the space in front of me, and now, unburdened of this sensitive material, I glanced at her and her gaze dropped and she continued to sit quietly for some time. "You're so lucky. You're so very lucky. I don't know what to say. As I said a little bit ago, art has been my major interest for years now, and yet I have never felt anything like what you're talking about. I paint and draw because I have a certain amount of talent for it, I guess, and it gives me great pleasure, but somehow, I've never felt anything that I would call a passion for art, whether it's mine or someone else's. What a strange experience! I mean where you get the feeling that you said was like being dazed. I don't know what to say about that but I have the feeling you were sort of possessed or something. Is that the right word or am I getting it all wrong?"

"Possessed? I don't know. I guess you could say something like that. I don't want to try to make a lot out of it. I've never mentioned it to anyone before, so I haven't thought much about what to call it. It was just a peculiar feeling that I had only when I was doing those paintings."

"And you don't have any interest in doing anything more?"

"No. I think that was it. I seem to have satisfied something that I don't understand but that I value. I have my paintings to look at and to look back at me, and that's the end of it, as far as I can tell." Susan continued to sit quietly some more, and I was satisfied to do the same, the story having been emotionally tinged enough to dull my interest for more conversation. Telling something this personal for the first time takes the wind out of ones sails, I suppose. She turned back toward me now. "Would it be proper to ask if you would show me one of your paintings?"

. It seemed almost inevitable that something like this should come up as a natural way to put an end to the story. I had no serious objection, although I felt a little reserve at the prospect. "There's the risk you know, that seeing them will spoil the story. It might be better off to just let your imagination fill in the blanks."

"Peter, please. I'm not trying to embarrass you. I really would like to see one, any one you'd like. I don't care at all about how good or bad they are, I just want to have a picture in my mind to go with the story. Please understand."

. I did, of course, understand, and I told her that maybe I could somehow arrange to show her at least the last one, but I really had no interest in the idea. More than anything else I was feeling self conscious about having paraded something so private before someone I scarcely knew. The spell was over, both of us a little relieved, I think, as we walked to the car and drove back to school. It was an odd parting. I told her that I had so much enjoyed her company and her tutelage and as she was in the process of expressing similar thanks, she held out her hand to me, this unusual gesture that seemed not only natural to her but very flattering to me. I remember that her hand was warm. I held it just a little bit longer than necessary, feeling very pleased with my new friend and thinking that I could do without Peggy if I had to.

As I might have expected, Barney weighed in on the new girl friend the minute I walked into the room. "Hawkins, you drifter, with my very own eyes I saw you climb into a late model yellow Buick coupe yesterday in the company of a debutante of surpassing beauty. Nothing was said to me about this though our paths crossed frequently before bedtime. Further, it is reported by an unimpeachable witness that you repeated this performance only today, same vehicle, same bimbo. This is not the way we play the game here, Hawkins. We share. We respect the need of our roommates to know about such things. You have let me down, Hawkins. What can you do to make amends?" I was not entirely surprised that my new companion had been spotted.

"You mean that hooker that picked me up the other day?"

"Mind what you say, Hawkins. This was a creature of breed and quality. You mistake my seriousness. Unload, you degenerate."

"You've got me. OK. I will admit to a brief dalliance with the lady you mention. To clear the air, we went to the zoo on Saturday, checked out the wildlife, scored a bit to eat and parted friends. Next question. I know there will be a few."

"You took a ravishing creature like that to the zoo?"

"To the zoo. Yes."

Mitzi

"The last of the Big Spenders. You pathetic oaf, you. You took that goddess to the zoo? And you are unrepentant? Hawkins, you really depress me. You are wearing shoes now. You have stopped dragging your knuckles almost entirely. You are beginning to appreciate the refinements that civilization has to offer, and what do you do? How do you reward my attempts to make you presentable in decent company? You march right off and take the tastiest morsel to set foot on this campus since the founding, to the ZOO! How can you justify such an affront to the homage due such divine creatures?"

"Ah, Barney, old shipmate. There is a kernel of truth in what you say. I will try to keep you better informed but as you have been told, we just happened to have two dates in quick succession, today's starting before you had opened an eye. I suppose you want to hear details?" Yes, by all means he did, so I told him of the Romeo episode, about the day at the zoo, about the museum and a little about Susan but not much. He loved the story about the gorilla ("Splendid! Show 'em what's what, what? Stout fellow!") wasn't very interested in the museum story and was highly critical of the Van Gogh business.

"Don't for God's sake tell me that you even alluded to those ghastly daubs of yours on the wall. You will surely frighten her off, you boob. Be cool. Now tell me the important stuff. What does her old man do? Sounds like lots of loot in the background there somewhere, right?" I told him I had no idea. "No idea! Dear fellow. You simply must find out something about the ancestor. We simply can't have you squiring around a shop girl! Aim high, man! Go for the gold! You have nothing to lose but your poverty! Now seriously. My impression and that of my informant is that she has definite class. Does she have class, Hawkins?" I allowed that she did have class. "Son. You need me. There are things you must know about that I am thoroughly familiar with and that are no doubt foreign concepts to you. If you have found a dame as classy as this one who is willing to be seen in your company, you really need advice. We will discuss this further when we have leisure. With guidance, you may be on the threshold of the most momentous event in your undistinguished life. I will help you." On this note, we went out for a couple beers.

7

We saw each other after classes on Monday and Wednesday, frustratingly brief encounters after having been spoiled by our weekend. She had obligations after school, I had obligations, and while we were so much more at ease with one another and the limited time we had was better spent, we scarcely got beyond classroom comments before she was off. On Wednesday, I asked if she would like to do something Saturday, and for some reason was surprised when she said she would let me know Friday. I shouldn't have been, of course. I realized that unconsciously I had begun to think of us as a twosome and had no thought other than that she would say yes, and now found myself vaguely uncertain and a little deflated. Maybe I hadn't hit a home run. Besides, I knew she must date other guys, she had a family, she had girl friends, she goes shopping, God knows what all. Don't be possessive, Hawkins. Friday came, and I wasn't nearly as interested in class as in after class. We walked to the car and I asked if she would be able to break away tomorrow for maybe a picnic or something. I didn't know how I would go about arranging a picnic, but I thought it sounded like something that would be hard to turn down.

"Oh, Peter, I'm sorry. It's just impossible for me to make any plans for this weekend. We have house guests and I'll have to be there. I'm so anxious to see your painting and all. I really do want to. But it will just have to wait." She inquired about what I was going to do over the weekend and I told her something, I forget what. We talked a little more, and I said I hoped she'd have a nice weekend, and said I'd see her Monday. I didn't act like I was disappointed, but I was. I affected a casual attitude that I didn't feel.

Mitzi

It may not have been entirely convincing as I thought she looked a little concerned, but if she was, nothing was said and we parted.

The band was playing at a club that night, and Peggy was plenty hostile at first, but after a couple numbers and a couple drinks she loosened up and by the time we folded up, we had patched it up and I went home with her and the next day we went to the friend's place and smoked dope all day and sat around and grinned at each other. I shouldn't talk that way. We had a good time. There was no question about my enjoying these freaks. They were a lot of fun, a lot of laughs and it was the right antidote for classes and study. I took Peggy out to a joint that featured a jazz group I knew and they let me sit in some and it felt great, but whenever I was playing, the regular piano player was making time with Peggy. I got the distinct feeling that she was giving me a piece of what she thought I had given her last Sunday, so I couldn't object much. The fact was, that for all her faults, Peggy had things to recommend her that I couldn't expect in Susan, one of which was her own apartment.

We got a little tight and I decided to do the driving back to her place. We slept in until nearly noon and really got everything sorted out and by the time I got back to school, I figured that all things considered, I was probably just as well off to not try and include Susan in my plans. If I tried to juggle both these girls, there was going to be trouble. I just couldn't face offending a girl like Susan, and I surely didn't want to get into a big fight with Peggy. Susan seemed to me to be the type of girl you would have to be serious about if you went with her steadily. Girls like Susan didn't date around, I decided. I was just getting things arranged to start a career and I had no intention of getting serious with anybody yet. All I wanted was a cute chick with a good disposition who would settle for some weekend frolic and not try to nail me down. For the time being, even though Peggy didn't fill that bill too closely, it was close enough. If Peggy defected, there were lots more chicks where she came from.

The problem was, that in the back of my mind was the thought that I might never meet a girl like Susan again. What if she was the 'the mate that fate had me created for'? Maybe this was fate telling me to wake up and claim my prize. Well, just now there wasn't anything I could do about it. But even if we did get to be close, how could I make any commitment that wouldn't mess up my career plans. I had a lot going on at that point. I was dead serious about my studies, I was taking extra courses, I had the two piddley little campus jobs that my scholarship required, I had interviews coming up soon with several big companies that I was interested in working for, I had a term paper that I thought was going to be important to me, just a lot of stuff going that was more important than trying to hang on to a girl who might not think of me as someone she wanted to hang onto herself. Besides, she was rich, I had concluded, she came from a different world, and she would return to that world without me. We had had a very nice weekend, I had had an attentive and interested listener, but we came from very different backgrounds. True, she seemed interested in me and we got on really well, but then she was so polite and cultured, that what I took for interest might have been just good manners.

I was in a low mood for the next couple days. It wasn't depressing, it was just disappointing. I had fantasized every imaginable situation. We would fall in love and marry, we would meet later and marry, we would have a big romance now and part forever, she would wait for me, she would marry someone else and leave him for me. I didn't dwell much on the most realistic scenario in which I just put an end to the relationship. Everything considered, it appeared to me better not to start chasing her, which I realized I was about do. I tend to plunge into things, as I had told her, and sometimes I have to stop and slow down some, and this seemed like the time to do it. So I decided I would be friendly, walk her to her car, talk the way we did, take it easy and give her a chance to back off without it being awkward. If she didn't seem to miss any special attention, I'd just keep the whole thing at arm's length. If she showed some interest again, well...I didn't know.

Monday after class we walked out to her car. I had rehearsed this neutral attitude until it had almost gotten to be negative. Susan seemed unusually quiet and serious and it occurred to me that maybe it was over and I could stop agonizing. Talk on both sides seemed awkward and came to a halt. I was mad at myself for being so ambivalent, for not acting like a man about all this. I was doing badly and it seemed like the time to excuse myself and face this some other time, but just as I was about to sign off, Susan asked me to stay and talk a minute. It was chilly, so we got in the car. I figured she was going to say some things I didn't want to hear, so before she could start, I decided to make my presentation after all.

"Susan, first of all, I'm sorry I'm being such a jerk. I'm embarrassed to admit that I've been sulking because I had gotten the idea that I'd be seeing you over the weekend...." She started to speak but I waved it off and continued. "Look, you don't have to explain anything. I keep forgetting that you've got a whole life I don't know anything about, and here I am, expecting you to be ready to go when I say go. I just wasn't thinking, so I let myself be disappointed that I wasn't going to see you. Then I got to thinking about the whole idea of how different we are. I mean as far as where we come from and where we're going. I've never dated a girl as pretty as you, as bright as you, as talented as you and if we stop seeing each other, I'm going to really miss you, but I don't want to waste your time. I'm out of my depth here, Susan. You're serious stuff and I'm just ...." I sat for a moment, trying to get it right and still looking anywhere but at Susan. When I finally did look over at her, not knowing what to expect, I was stunned to see her on the verge of tears. As our eyes briefly met, she lowered her head and tears began to slide down her cheeks and drop into her lap. There was not a sound, just the tears running down her cheeks. I felt stricken, certain that I had deeply offended her, and I seized her hand.

"Susan! Don't cry, babe. What's going on? Hey, sugar, take it easy, don't cry, please don't cry. I didn't mean it the way it sounded...Susan?...Come on, babe...I wouldn't hurt your feelings for the world...Please don't cry." Even at such an emotional moment it was not instinct to hold her or even put my arm around her, so I just sat, with her hand in both of mine and patted and rubbed and waited, disgusted with myself for having provoked this. I couldn't imagine Susan in tears, she was so self possessed, so controlled. The tears slowed, then stopped, and she abruptly reached across me and fished a tissue out of the glove box and held it to her eyes. There wasn't anything I could do except wait, and it didn't appear she expected anything more. At length she looked at me, red eyed and still miserable. "It's not your fault. It's not anything you said." There were more tissues and presently she seemed calmer and continued.

"I've had a perfectly dreadful weekend. May I tell you about it?" I nodded. "I'm so upset," she said. "Please forgive me. I never carry on like this and I'm so ashamed to have you see me this way, but all of a sudden it just overtook me again and I couldn't help crying. I don't want to be a burden, but I need to talk to someone and get it out of my system and I don't know of anyone else who would understand. Would you please hand me another tissue." I did, and she continued. "Thank you. I'm sorry. Just give me a minute," and she gradually began to recover her composure and after a bit, she drew a deep breath and began to talk, almost calm then.

"This was a very unpleasant weekend for me. The people I mentioned who were staying with us are old friends of my parents, a very dear couple that we have known for a very long time, all my life as matter of fact. They used to live just a few blocks from where we live still, and I grew up with their son, Brad, almost as closely as if we lived in the same house. He was an only child and I was an only child. Our parents were the best of friends, so inseparable and so much alike that they might have been related, and Brad and I were just like brother and sister. If they weren't at our house for dinner, we were at theirs. They had a house on the lake, we had a house on the lake. They had a place at the shore and we had a place at the shore. If they went skiing, we went skiing. My father and Brad's father were both doctors and at that time in the same hospital, so they had a great deal in common between themselves, aside from the family contacts. Brad is a very nice person, he's loyal, he's gentle, he's honest, he has a good sense of humor...he's good looking, athletic. Sounds like a maiden's prayer, doesn't he? I think if you met him, you'd like him. But for all his charm, he is really a very shallow person. He's fun to be with and to have around, but he is just...meaningless. I don't mean to sound cruel, but that's just the way I feel about him.

"We had good times and were so comfortable with each other that it seemed natural when we got older and started going to parties and dances and what not, that Brad was my date. He must have been attractive to other girls, and I suppose I flirted some with other boys, but we almost always gravitated to one another. Our friends began to assume that it would be like that forever, I think. Nothing was ever said by either of our parents, as far as I know, and Brad never so much as hinted at our ever being anything more than best friends, but I realize now that there was a general idea that someday we would get married. Certainly it never occurred to me, but it seems that it had occurred to Brad." She sat quietly for a few moments, collecting her thoughts, I guessed, and I waited for her to continue.

"Last spring, actually it was June, everything changed. School was over, we had the whole summer ahead of us. This was the time of year when we saw the most of each other, and I had no reason to believe things would be different than they always had been between us. It's hard to tell you just how it came to me; it wasn't anything specific that I can recall, but I began to be aware that Brad was sending some puzzling signals that I couldn't define. From the easy going, sort of careless person I was so used to, he began to tease in a way that he never had. He had always teased me in a totally inoffensive way, which we both got a kick out, but now the teasing was sort of …challenging. As though he were somehow testing me about something that wasn't part of our friendship. I found myself asking him from time to time what had gotten into him. I can't put a name to it, but it was something that made me feel I wanted just a little bit more room than I was getting. Then there were more or less suggestive remarks. I don't mean the kind of thing that everybody does for laughs, but sort of personal, as though he expected some sort of response from me. We just never behaved this way toward each other. He had always had my complete confidence that he would treat me with respect and courtesy, no matter what. It was just the way we had been brought up."

There was another long pause before she resumed. "Do you have a sister?" she asked.

"Two," I said.

"All right...oh, dear. How can I say this? I feel so uncomfortable. I said that Brad was like a brother. I mean, that is just the way I thought of him, even though of course he wasn't. Can you imagine having any...improper thoughts toward your sister?"

"Certainly not." I had screwed up face in distaste and Susan caught my anticipation of what was to come.

"Of course not! So you can imagine how I felt when he began to act as though he was no longer my brother but a boyfriend. Here we knew each other as well as two people can, and from a loyal and trusted friend, I began to feel I was dealing with a predator. We had always kissed when we met and kissed when we said goodbye. But it never meant anything, it was like kissing your father, and now suddenly, the kisses came with an embrace, and the kisses were not what they should have been between friends, and I found myself trying to avoid even the occasions that might call for a kiss. Of course, this didn't work. We were so often with family and it would have looked odd, and I didn't want to get into any explanations if I could handle the thing myself. I had the feeling that he was saying 'Look, we're not children any more' and it was most uncomfortable. I told him so. He laughed and told me I was acting like a kid. I became angry, genuinely angry and told him that if he couldn't behave properly, I wanted nothing further to do with him. I actually cried, I was so upset, and this seemed to have an effect and he left me alone the rest of that day.

"How is came about, I don't know, but to my enormous relief, Brad and his family decided to move over to the shore for the summer, which they had never done, and my parents decided we would spend some time at the lake. It was the first time I can remember our being at the lake without Brad and his family, and I felt very self conscious and a little guilty because this rift between Brad and me might have been the cause of such a big change. I had just about decided that this was going to be a disastrous summer, when one day, not a week after we had arrived at the lake, in came Brad's parents and no Brad. It turned out that they had sent Brad packing off to Italy to join some archeology group that his Dad had an interest in or something. Anyway, it seems that it was possible to arrange for him to go over there in some capacity. I never knew Brad to be interested in anything for over a week or so, but anyway, he went off and I was saved.

"So we had a pretty good summer. There were other kids I've known all my life and we had a really good time. Nobody pairs up much out there, we all just enjoy each other as a big group and swim and sail and play bridge and things like that, so I didn't really miss having a regular partner. It's actually only been a few weeks that we've been back in town. Anyway, last week, we got word that Brad was back from Italy and the whole family was coming to spend this past weekend with us.

"At first, everything seemed fine, Brad had a lot if interesting stories and he seemed like his old self and I had no reason to feel that my message had not gotten through to him. Saturday everything was just as it should have been, all of us together and enjoying catching up. Sunday, yesterday, Brad and I found ourselves alone in the house, the others out in the garden with their coffee. I was uneasy about being separated from them and suggested we go out too, but Brad wanted to apologize, he said, and I thought I should hear what he had to say. There was an apology of sorts to start with, but then it gradually came to a point where I was the one being accused of spoiling our relationship. It may have been overreacting, but I had the sense of being slightly threatened, and I was determined not to have a lifelong friend make a fool of himself and alienate us again. There was so much at stake. Our families would be very embarrassed and I'd be embarrassed and I wanted no part of anything like that. So I told him that in case he hadn't gotten the message, I thought of him as a brother and always would, but under no circumstances could I ever regard him as anything else. Instead of having the moral high ground, I found myself on the defensive, Brad insisting that I was all wrong, that we were meant for each other, that he would never stop loving me, that I was all he had ever wanted for a wife, such nonsense, on and on in spite of my telling him it was utterly impossible, out of the question, wrong, and anything else I could think of.

"Oh, what a scene! He just wouldn't listen, and I had this sinking feeling that something had gotten terribly out of control. I knew that I had to put a complete end to any ideas he had right then and hope to salvage something of our friendship. At some point in all this unbelievable scene, while I was really scolding him, he got this…stupid grin on his face and tried to pull me toward him… to hug me, I guess, and without even thinking, I slapped him. I mean, I slapped him with all my might and I got him right across the whole side of his face. Oh, it was dreadful, dreadful, dreadful!" She put her hands up and covered her mouth, and I thought surely she would begin to cry, but she didn't. She stayed like that for some while and then the hands came down, her face flushed and unhappy.

"He was stunned. I have never done such a thing in my life. It was a terribly sad sight. He looked completely defeated. All the life was out of him. He just stood there, staring at me, not saying a word. I wanted so to break right down and cry, but I forced myself to just stare back and not say a word, and then he just turned and walked away and when he had gone, I cried and cried and cried." She looked at that moment as though she might do just that, and I sat very still. There was a tiny sniffle, a furtive wipe, and she took a big breath and went on.

"I went to my room and stayed there until I could send word for my mother to come to me and I told her the whole story. I just had to tell someone, and although I knew the pain it would cause her, there was no one else I could count on to understand. And I thought she and my father ought to know what had happened. My mother was horrified when I told her I had slapped Brad, and slapped him hard and in real anger. I could hardly believe it when my mother told me that the two families had 'always' assumed that the two of us would marry! Marry! That I would 'marry' my 'brother'! "I told her that I would never, ever consider marrying Brad, that I felt toward him in a totally different way than I expected to feel for my mate, and that nothing could change that. I have rarely been upset with my mother, we are so close and she is so understanding. There were more tears and apologies and promises and, you know…both of us upset and unhappy at having a scene.

"We eventually talked it out. I could scarcely believe it when she told me that everyone was so certain of this union, that Brad's parents had hinted that he ought to get a move on before I got tired of waiting and went off with someone else. Can you imagine this? I felt so betrayed! Everyone seemed to think that I waiting for Brad to propose. Well, my mother and I got through it, and my mother told my father, and he came to my room. My father is such a wonderful man. Just the sweetest and most thoughtful person you could imagine. He told me that he completely respected my wishes, that he and mother had been wrong in making any assumptions about Brad and my marrying and that I should not be concerned about the parent's friendship, that this episode would pass and that they would all see to it that there would be no further awkward situations for me to deal with. I didn't know just how my father was going to work it out, but I knew he would. I stayed in my room until my mother told me that the two couples had had a talk, that everyone understood my position now, so that I could come out of hiding. The things parents have to go through for their children. I swear. I know this has been awfully long, but I'm almost done. At least, we're over the bad part." She took a big breath and smiled for the first time in the whole story.

"It couldn't have gone better. A simple apology from Brad, one from me, dinner, conversation and a dignified goodbye just about twenty-four hours ago. That was my weekend." I sat wide eyed and stunned.

"Oh, man. You've really had a weekend. Poor Susan! I'm so sorry you have had such a rotten time. You must have been feeling awful. The first thing I thought when you started to cry was that I had said something and I was really feeling pretty bad."

"No, no, it had nothing to do with you except that you said some nice things about me and that ruined my control. I hate to show emotion like that, it's so unfair to you. I'm sorry," and for a minute I thought she might cry again. I slid over and put my arm around her and drew her to me and stroked her hair and she melted and we sat like that for the longest time.

Without lifting her head, she began to talk very quietly. "You sounded as though you didn't want to go out with me any longer. I think I know what you were going to say, and I think I understand why you might feel that way, if that's really the way you feel, but I wish you didn't feel that way. I think you're a very nice person and I wish you didn't feel that I belong to a certain group that somehow excludes you."

"Susan...I didn't realize a lot of things a few minutes ago. I just felt I ought to make it easy for you to break something off that you knew couldn't go on. I think you're the kind of person that would bend over backward to avoid hurting someone. I couldn't believe you didn't have a boyfriend, or someone in your own crowd waiting for the chance to be your boyfriend, and I just couldn't see a place for me. I don't want to lose you, but I don't want to be some sort of marginal acquaintance that you dated a couple times and hate to refuse after that out of politeness. To tell the truth, when you said you'd go to the zoo, I was surprised. I mean, what in the world does she see in me? Don't get me wrong, I've got as much ego as the next guy. But it did seem like a major social mismatch, and I think that could still be a problem. Maybe I'm being too sensitive about something that isn't a factor at all, but somehow I feel like I'm here under false colors." She sat up and turned to look at me with that absolute candor and honesty that completely disarms me.

"Oh, Peter, please try to understand. I don't know what I have done to make you so defensive. You're making this much more complicated than it should be. I'm not one of the rich girls you seem to think so little of. I know the type you mean, but I'm just me, and I want you to treat me just for what you find me to be and not what you imagine me to be. Don't let's give up on each other just yet." Nothing could be plainer than that. I dragged her over to my chest again.

"Thank you so much for saying just what I wanted to hear. I think you're right. I do believe there's a little life left in this relationship. Think you can handle it?" She nodded.

"If you want to end it, will you promise to speak up?" She nodded.

"You too?" she asked.

"Me too."

It was dark now and the windows of the car were all steamed up. Susan seemed perfectly content to stay quietly. "I guess we've done enough damage for one day, huh? Ready?" She nodded and sat up. I took her head in my hands and kissed her, then got out, blew her one more and closed the door.

Was I in love? Not as far as I could tell. Sympathy, empathy, by all means, but nothing I could detect beyond that. There were no bells, no thunderbolt, no walking on air. She wasn't the type of girl that would provoke bells and thunderbolts as far as I could tell, but she was certainly a very appealing, very sweet girl. It was more in a mood of reflection and analysis that I returned to my room. Barney took one look at me and groaned. "She dumped you! Oh, you bumpkin! I knew it! I told you, don't play around, don't give her line, set the hook! Reel her in! Oh, Hawkins, the look on your face tells all. Simply pathetic." I told him we were thicker than ever and he didn't believe me. At least in a way this friendship had gotten simpler—at least we had cleared the air, but where that led, I had no notion. I certainly hadn't felt any compelling sense of direction with the two ladies currently in my life. I was right back to start with the Peggy problem but I didn't have to worry about that until the weekend.

When I walked Susan to her car Wednesday, she was as pretty as I had ever seen her, cheerful, smiling, animated and I could only believe that I had done the right thing. She told me some anecdotes about her school and her friends, no allusion to any part of the Monday affair, but it certainly seemed to me that we were on a much more personal footing and it felt good, in spite of some of the tentative feelings that lingered in me. Before we said goodbye, I asked her if she thought a picnic sounded good for Saturday, and she said she'd love it, how about going to the lake and that she would like to bring the food, OK?

8

Saturday turned out to be one of those perfect fall days, bright, cool morning with warm sunshine, the leaves only about a week from being at their best, a calendar picture day. A totally transformed Susan met me at our spot. My goddess had on jeans, a men's lumberjack type shirt, scruffy old sneaks and a sweater tied around her waist, all of this topped off by a broad brimmed, low crown cream colored western hat, it you can imagine that.

"You said you liked hats on girls. I hope I won't disappoint you to tell that this one is borrowed."

"Howdy, partner. Well, if you ain't the purtiest li'l filly on the ranch. After that Cosmo girl outfit at the zoo, I appreciate your dressing down a little. I looked pretty shabby there at one point. The hat looks great, by the way. You can wear that any old time." She was obviously pleased in spite of her outfit being so clearly out of character. I had been out to the lake several times before. The only narrow sandy beaches were private, made with sand that was trucked in, so it wasn't the greatest place to swim, but it was pretty and a couple of the guys and I would come out occasionally. Susan must have known it like the back of her hand. At least, she drove right to a nice spot with thick grass and lots of sunshine and I hoisted that hamper out. Susan had thought to bring a thick old automobile robe with fringe on it that looked like it had lived in an attic for a very long time. We spread it out and sat down in the warm sunshine, Susan looking very pretty but still incongruous in her country clothes. She had a camera and she took a picture of me and I took one of her and then we got a man who was walking his dog along the shore to take one of us sitting together on the robe.

We took the long walk around the lake, stopping to admire the occasional view and the reflections where the tree line was open. I took her hand for the most part as we walked, not trying to make a statement but just because it seemed like the thing to do. I picked a bunch of asters and gave her this bouquet and when we got back, she took a wine glass out of our picnic basket and made a centerpiece for our lunch. Hungry now, Susan unpacked the hamper. I could hardly believe what was inside. There was a table cloth, real napkins, silverware, cold chicken and potato salad and deviled eggs and Italian deli meats and French bread and French cheeses and pears and apples and carrots and celery and two different kinds of French pastry and a bottle of French white wine and a corkscrew.

"I never saw a picnic lunch like this in my life. If you tell me you put this together, you are going to seriously damage my impression of the idle rich."

She laughed. "Have you forgotten that I am a child of privilege? I told our cook that I would like her to pack a picnic lunch, and here it is. I deliberately overdid it. I was having such a good time looking forward to how you'd look when you saw it. Isn't it scrumptious? Are you shocked?" She was enjoying this. I looked at her and rolled my eyes and nodded. "I love picnic lunches. This is the sort of thing we do so much of in the summer when we're here. Now when I tell you some story that involves a picnic lunch at the lake, you'll know just how glorious it is."

The lunch was as delicious as it looked. We didn't quite finish the bottle of wine. I could have, but I thought it might look bad and since Susan didn't want any more, I stopped, too. We tidied up more or less and took off our shoes and walked along the edge of the water. "Do you see that little building over there just to the right of that big tree?" I did. "That's a boat house where they rent canoes. We used to have a beautiful old canoe, but someone stole it from under the cottage one winter, and we never replaced it. The ones they rent are awful looking, but they don't have to be babied like the one we used to have. The whole gang of us would rent canoes and paddle all over the lake and swim and picnic, you know. There are all sorts of neat places to explore. Did you ever do any canoeing?" I had never been in one and I told her. "We could to do that sometime if you'd like to. It's lots of fun. All summer long on Saturday nights they have concerts in a little cove around that point over there. Do you ever come over to the lake? Have you ever seen the bandstand? It's right on the edge of the water and you can paddle up and tie onto poles they have stuck in the bottom and listen to the music. It's such a great thing to do."

We walked some more, throwing pieces of left-over bread to a bunch of ducks that spotted us and came over. You could tell they were used to picnickers tossing bread. At least, they seemed to me to be pretty good at it. Susan stopped, thinking. "Would you mind if we just drove over to the bandstand. You could at least see it. I think the concerts are over but I remember going to one once when the weather was pretty cool. Wouldn't that be something if they were still going on?"

We packed up all our stuff and drove along the winding road under a canopy of stately trees with their festive foliage, such a pretty drive. We came on an old fashioned bandstand, all wood, heavy with gingerbread trim, crisply painted white, not as large as I had expected, a few rows of plain wooden benches for the musicians and a cleared area all around the base of it. There were stacks of folding chairs padlocked underneath the bandstand floor behind lattice work. It looked to me as though the season were over, but Susan spotted a middle aged woman whom she seemed to recognize, and approached her. They had a pretty cordial conversation, and she came back radiating good news. The regular concerts were over but a smaller group of some sort was going to give a performance this very evening, she thought about eight.

"Let's get a canoe! We can paddle around the lake some and then come over here for the music. There's plenty of food left over. I'll have to call home and tell them what's going on. What do you think? Let's!" Back in the car, we found a public phone and while I stayed in the car, Susan called her mother. They had a rather long conversation, and I began to think that there was some concern on the other end of the wire. That would certainly be natural enough. Their daughter out at night with some bozo they had never met. Susan returned very much at ease and reported that she had told her mother where she was and that she would be home about ten-thirty or so.

She got behind the wheel again and we drove around to the canoe place, a ramshackle affair with an ominous lean. A caricature in soiled sweats, old, grizzled and grumpy, acknowledged our presence by allowing his chair to come upright. Susan smiled at him and called him whatever his name was, but either this didn't register or was of no interest to him. Susan told him we wanted a canoe for the rest of the afternoon and until after the concert. He named his fee, I paid it and he slid a badly dented aluminum canoe into the water. As he wouldn't be here at that hour of the night, we were to slide it back up onto the float and turn it over before we left. Susan dredged up a couple cushions and a pair of badly chewed paddles. The hamper and robe went in the middle. I was regarding that treacherous cockle shell mistrustfully when thoughtful Susan got in and steadied the thing while I gingerly got seated in the stern.

My introduction to canoeing was inauspicious. Susan told me to just paddle on the same side until we agreed to switch, and this went generally fairly well, but in spite of her best efforts, we were zigzagging badly and I knew it was my fault, but nothing I did made any difference. When we had gotten well clear of the boathouse, Susan stopped and gave me a quick lesson and things went much better. There were only a couple other canoes that we could see, and they were nowhere near us. We glided along the shore, in and out of little coves, no place to go and all afternoon to get there.

About five-thirty, we pulled into a short stretch of rough beach. Out came the hamper. We were a bit short of wine, but there was still plenty of chicken and deviled eggs and fruit. If this was what came of going out with a child of privilege, I was all for it. We talked about all kinds of things. Susan was a good reader it turned out, and we talked about favorite books and movies we had both seen. We talked about what we were going to do after graduation in June. She told me she had a chance to go to Europe and study painting but thought she would rather stay here. What a bright girl. What an easy pleasure to be with her, just talking. As the sun got behind the trees, it began to get cool and we packed up and got into the canoe.

The paddle to the bandstand was in near silence. I let Susan set the pace, and we just poked along. She would occasionally point to something of interest, but mostly we were alone with our own thoughts. The utter stillness, the reflections on the smooth, black, viscous surface were mesmerizing, and I was content to simply be surrounded by the scene. When we arrived at the bandstand, there was only one other canoe there, an older couple bundled up in jackets and hats. We glided into one of the slots between the poles and got tied up. Susan pulled the hamper toward her and somehow backed over it and got seated in the middle of the canoe. She was sitting so far to one side that it appeared I was expected to sit beside her, although nothing had been indicated. I was actually amused at feeling so diffident about assuming this position of closeness. There was something about Susan that didn't invite quite this degree of intimacy, but I managed to crawl forward and get seated beside her. We fussed and wiggled and adjusted and finally got settled with one cushion under us and one behind us. That didn't work. Each of us had half a butt and half a back on the cushions, so we got both cushions in the bottom and just leaned back against the thwart. I was almost dark now, still but cool. We got the robe around our backs and shoulders and pulled it across so that we were snug. Canoeing had just taken on an entirely new attraction. We were sitting as close as two people can sit, my arm around her, robe-wrapped, warm. Could have been a lot worse.

There was activity around the bandstand. From out of cars and station wagons that were pulling up came an odd assortment of older men, a few women, most with instrument cases, sheet music. The door under the bandstand was unlocked, chairs and music stands were being dragged out. We heard laughter and voices and snatches of conversation, a group beginning to collect as the performers and a small audience chatted and milled about. The musicians were dressed as they pleased, a few in jackets, some sweaters, one particular extrovert in a sort of pinstripe gangster suit. They took their time getting organized, and finally after a number of hails from friends in the audience below, more laughter and clowning, a pink faced, cherubic, white thatched old gentleman introduced the group, thanked us all for coming, made a few jokes about certain band members and at last turned to his musicians, a-one and a-two and a-three and off they went into some high energy, really tight Dixieland jazz! I couldn't believe it! I was so tickled. It was such a surprise! These old dudes were good! They played Dixieland the whole first set, Cherub on trumpet and the Muggsy look-alike on the clarinet, Pinstripe on drums. On the piano, and really taking it apart was a delicate, middle aged woman with a lot of gray in her hair. The other lady was on the standup bass, not inspired, but competent. I could hardly believe what I was seeing. They must have played for nearly an hour. When they finally took a break to very thin but very enthusiastic applause, I asked Susan if she had any idea who they were and whether she had ever heard them before. No, she hadn't. I told her they must be retired professionals.

When they came back after the break they may have been sort of tuckered out because the whole second set was all slow blues and a few popular tunes. The trombone player had a pretty good voice and he growled out a few blues numbers including an old Jack Teagarden standard which I suppose he did because he was a trombone player. Anyway, the whole show was just great. At the end of the second set, which was fairly short, they all stood and clapped and we clapped back and they thanked us for coming. It was a great show, such a complete surprise.

We sat there while the musicians broke down and packed up. Susan explained that she had expected something else in the way of music. "They usually play light classical music, operettas and that sort of thing, which seems so much more in keeping with lake and the quiet. I have never heard this group before. Did you like it?"

"Like it? I loved it! I grew up on jazz. Well, not just jazz, but when I was a kid, I used to listen to the radio a lot, almost just for the music. I liked almost everything and I knew the words to all the popular songs, but it was jazz that really got to me. I couldn't get enough of it. It just had some quality that felt right to me and after I got to where I could play the piano, all I wanted to play was boogie-woogie. We could get one station on Saturday night that was all jazz, live and really great stuff. I used to take my radio under the covers and listen to it until I fell asleep. My mother had absolutely no interest in jazz, but at least she didn't get after me for trying to play it. I wasn't doing especially well until I got into the old prep school I went to for a few years. One of the teachers heard me banging away in the lounge one day, told me to get up and then sat down and started playing, jazz every bit as good as what I had on records, as far as I was concerned. He was one heck of a jazz pianist. He had a terrible drinking problem, but that didn't hurt his playing as far as I could tell. He volunteered to teach me, took me on as a personal project, I guess you could call it, and taught me just about everything I know today. A great guy and a great teacher, but such a mess otherwise. I got a few guys together at school and we call ourselves a band. Play at fraternity parties and a few clubs in town. No jazz, though. I have to sit in at one of the places in town that features jazz to get in any licks at all, but the guys there are pretty good about letting me sit in, so I get some time with the pros." Susan was respectfully quiet during this explanation. "You know, I have a hunch you aren't much interested in jazz, right?"

"I'm afraid I don't know anything about it, Peter, that's all. I've heard it, of course, but I don't know anything about it so I really can't say anything. I grew up with classical music and that's the only music I'm familiar with. Well, popular music too, but I guess I just haven't been attracted to jazz. But don't give up. Maybe you can help me appreciate it and I'll love it."

I laughed. "You remind me that Louis Armstrong once said that jazz is something that if you have to explain to someone, they're never going to get it. Don't be discouraged, Susan. It's just one of those things that grabs some people and won't let 'em go, and if it doesn't grab you, don't worry about it. It's like the Van Gogh business. Both those things just hit me a certain way and there was no choice to be made. I'll play a little for you some day and maybe I can come up with something that you'll like, who knows?"

We were both nearly paralyzed when we tried to get up, but with lots of giggling and grunting, we got sorted out and into our old seats, a pretty big letdown after the cuddling in the canoe. I didn't have the foggiest notion of where to go, but Susan kept directing my efforts and after a fairly long paddle we came up on the boathouse and got unloaded and out to the car. She stopped and turned to me and told me how much fun she had had and thanked me for a wonderful day. She stopped talking and stood there, and I had to interpret this as some sort of acquiescence so I put my arms around her and kissed her. It was dark and I couldn't see her face really well, but she was still looking very quietly at me, so I kissed her again, just lightly, and now her eyes fell for the first time. After a moment, she looked up and held the car keys up to me.

I don't think either of us said a word all the way to school. When we got there, I turned off the motor and took her hand and just held it for a time and then got out and she scooted over. "Kiss," I said, and she turned her face up toward me and we did. I rapped my knuckles a couple raps on the door and took off. I was nearly at the quadrangle before I heard her start up and drive away. It was fairly late, but I didn't feel like going in just yet, so I walked to John's Cozy Bar which was such a crummy place that nobody I knew went there. I got a beer and thought about the day. It was difficult to decide what was going on. I was strongly attracted to this girl, but I was having trouble just relaxing with her and being natural. In no way did she invite romance, nor did I feel inclined to offer it for some reason. Something lacking in the chemistry department. I figured that she must surely have spent her share of evenings parked at the lake or somewhere, but then again, maybe not. If she was so hung up on Brad for so long, maybe she was really new to dating people she didn't already know. When I kissed her at the boathouse that there wasn't much response, I didn't think, but on the other hand, she seemed to have waited for another one. Then again I thought of the kiss through the car window, and that was kind of nice. She had seemed willing and it seemed natural, so maybe I was imagining things. It was a nuisance to have to analyze what should have been just a spontaneous affair. Was I projecting some sort of restraint of my own or was it all on her? I decided it was all on her. I mean, we had sat in that canoe and were warm and tangled up for a couple hours and it seemed right cozy. I thought that by the time we got to the boathouse we should have been on the other side of some threshold, but I couldn't make a case for it having happened, in spite of the isolated smooch. I finally figured that I'd better keep going very slowly. I didn't have a clear idea yet of where I hoped to go with this, but there was an aura of importance about this girl that I couldn't ignore. I wished that she would thaw out a little. I hate to push a relationship. All I wanted was a little encouragement to guide me and I wasn't getting much. Some, but not much. She had such self control, such a sense of propriety that I had no way of knowing where I stood for the longest time. I decided the best approach was to concentrate on keeping things on an even keel and wait for intuition to give some guidance.

We continued to date on weekends, which was the best I could do with my studies and the jobs. The weather was colder now, and most outdoor things weren't practical. We went to movies fairly often. They were cheap and it took some of the pressure off of me. The best part was talking over the movie afterward with a pizza between us. It had never occurred to me how much one could learn about someone by discussing something like a movie. I found how she thought about so many things that we might never have gotten to. We discussed complex motivation and character that took us into each others most deeply held convictions and attitudes. I had had no idea how deeply she thought about things, what good insight she had and how sensitive she was to subtle things that I might not even have picked up on until she pointed them out. For a girl who I thought had led a sheltered life, she seemed awfully well prepared to face life. She was completely grown up. I like movies and I was getting a lot of mileage out of them, but I'm not addicted to them. I was looking for some sort of novelty to get away from the same pattern of movies and pizza when a break came from an unexpected quarter, Susan's parents. She told me one Friday afternoon that she had a surprise for us for our date the next afternoon. I had figured on going to an indoor polo match which was free. Now, it seems, her father had given her a pair of tickets to a popular musical that had opened not more than a month before. I had been to exactly two plays in three years.

Mitzi

It was absolutely marvelous. We had incredible seats, the songs were witty and memorable, the dancing, the costumes, staging, everything a great treat. I had never seen anything like it. I had no idea what a thrill a hit musical with a professional cast could be. I couldn't shut up. I talked and exclaimed and hummed the tunes and reexamined the playbill, on and on, Susan laughing, obviously enjoying my enthusiasm. I told her that this was what happened when a privileged kid took a hick to a show. It wasn't until years later that I learned that her father had gotten these tickets for the matinee to save me the expense of dinner, as though I would have had the sense to know that that might be expected. He was that kind of man.

Technically, this was a violation of my stiff-necked principles about paying my own way, but I was waking up to the reality that Susan wanted to share, was able to share and this was her contribution to our having fun together. My instinct was to mention it but better sense prevailed and I settled for asking her to express my gratitude to her father. She had dismissed my implied misgivings by telling me that her father 'got these from time to time' as though to diminish the value of the gift. I didn't believe this, but I told myself I did. Just as well because before much longer, her father seemed now to be getting tickets to other things as well. I began to be aware that Susan was trying to introduce me to her world, to the things that were important to her that she hoped I would enjoy also and thus give us more common ground. I had to admit that my tastes in so many things were poles apart from hers. One afternoon after class she asked me if I would like to join her to hear some friends of hers play chamber music. I thought that sounded interesting and said so. "My father knows this couple, Irene and David Bernstein, who are both very talented musicians. He is the head of a big real estate firm--maybe you've heard of him. His name is on signs all over the city. Anyway, he and his wife have invited two other fine professionals to join them for an evening of music and asked me if I'd like to come over. There will just be the two of us, nothing fancy. No dressing up. I think you'll like it. Shall I tell her we'll be there?" I told her I thought it sounded great, something of an exaggeration really, but I was anxious to please Susan.

She picked me up at school. I had put on the old all purpose dark suit, which in subdued light was passable. Susan drove us to a quiet, formal residential cul-de-sac of elegant looking town-houses, the street cobbled, the sidewalks of patterned red brick overhung with dark leafless trees. Wrought iron fences with gilt finials defined the tiny front yards of these stately old three story dwellings. We parked on the street and passed through the low iron gate and up three steps onto a tiny porch, a large ornate glistening brass light illuminating an elegant old paneled mahogany door flanked by leaded glass sidelights. Susan pushed a lighted bell button and after a time, there were muffled steps and the door was opened by a petite, older lady in an evening gown of rather somber dark gray material with an elaborately embroidered jacket. Her gray hair was pulled back from her broad face, serious and foreign looking, and gathered into a tiny knot in back of her head. She greeted Susan politely but I thought rather coolly and when introduced to me, simply bowed without expression and preceded us down a long, thickly carpeted hallway, the walls covered with photographs and drawings, to a room at the back of the house. We entered into what was not only a well used and serious library but a music room, a grand piano cluttered with musical scores at one end, a little row of handsome occasional chairs in the center of the room and a pair of arm chairs facing these. Instrument cases lay on the floor beside the chairs and there were four delicate music stands in front of them, a cello semi-reclining to one side. The room was so hushed and the lighting so muted that it took me a moment to identify the three men in evening clothes, quietly conversing with each other near the heavily draped and curtained windows.

Mrs. Bernstein took us to the group and introduced us, first to her husband, David, who smiled and shook each of our hands without comment. Turning to the second man, she introduced him as Avrim something of other, I never did properly hear the last name, and then presented us to Paul Wolf, who she identified as the conductor of our famous symphony orchestra, this identification for my benefit I thought. Of the three, he was the only one to express his pleasure at having our company, a gracious, urbane gentleman whose very presence commanded respect. Irene indicated that we should be seated. Now for the first time the uniqueness of the situation fully dawned on me. We were the sole guests privileged to be invited to a private evening musicale starring a world famous violinist and conductor. They had been waiting for our arrival before beginning. As unfamiliar as I was with classical music and as totally ignorant as I was concerning chamber music, here I was in this rarefied atmosphere feeling unbelievably humble and out of place. Avrim, I learned was also a member of the symphony orchestra, the Bernsteins' role apparently that of affluent amateurs whose patronage and talents could command such a performance in their home.

We sat in respectful silence while our musicians talked in low tones, chuckling over some remark, getting out their instruments and plucking at them until they seemed to agree with each other. Musical scores were selected from the piano and placed on the stands, tiny lights turned on and the quartet took their seats. Mr. Bernstein was the second violin, Avrim the cellist, Mrs. Bernstein playing the viola. There was more quiet banter, adjusting of seats and scores, more string plucking, a few little practice phrases of music, adjusting of handkerchiefs then a brief silence. I wasn't aware of any cue. It must have been something too subtle for me to note, but in perfect unison this ethereal music began. I could hardly credit my senses. It was utterly hypnotic, indescribable, the rich resonances, especially the deep and lyric voice of the cello filling my mind and seducing me completely. What a glorious introduction to chamber music! The first piece went flawlessly, a few little appreciative smiles and remarks among the musicians, nothing that reached my ears, no eye contact with us, and then after a bit of retuning and that mysterious cue, they were off again. I scarcely dared look at Susan for fear of seeming to have broken my appreciative attention when suddenly with a little laughter, they all stopped, chuckled over what must have been someone's mistake, and took off again from the beginning, this time apparently all going well. It dawned on me after this happened again, that the amateurs felt obliged to repeat a piece if they made some error. In addition to being a concert for us, it took on the air of a highly refined music lesson for them, honing their skills under the tutelage of this master.

We were all conscious of the wind blowing hard outdoors on this mild but blustery night. As though she had had the same thought, Irene passed behind us and drew aside the drapes and curtains and the sound of the wind and the sight of the shrubbery careening, the intermittent illumination of the entire garden as clouds occasionally parted for the moon, created an unworldly effect. I was concerned that the musicians might find it a distraction, but it seemed by tacit agreement that on the contrary, it enhanced their pleasure as well, and the music resumed and mesmerized me as before.

I could have sat there indefinitely, but again, after an hour or more as though on cue, the musicians finished, turned to each other smiling and softly applauded themselves. Susan and I clapped equally softly ourselves, uncertain if this were proper, but determined to show our gratitude. Without any acknowledgment of our tribute, they began to pack up their instruments, talking reservedly among themselves. It was almost as though the quartet had been unaware of our presence. They were deep inside their own world where we were not invited, nor could enter. It was not awkward, it didn't seem rude. We were simply superfluous to their pleasure. Susan knew her cue and we both arose as Irene came over to us. We thanked her profusely, made the rounds of the other players and were escorted to the door. I was probably too effusive, trying to express my gratitude for such a gift, Susan more restrained and appropriate in her thanks, Irene smiling dutifully, politely but with no suggestion of friendliness and scarcely a word other than to extend her greetings to Susan's father.

We got into the car and Susan drove me to the dorm. I asked her how all this had come about and how she fitted into such an incredible opportunity. She shrugged. "It's a strange arrangement. My father has been a supporter of the symphony orchestra for years and years and it surely has to do with that. He has never had the slightest interest in any acknowledgement of this support, but for some reason, the Bernsteins at some point felt obliged to give something in return, so each year about this time, they invite my father to this performance. To be perfectly honest, my father has no ear for music so he declines and sends me. This is the third time I have been here and I'm always the only one, so it must be for my father's sake alone. I'm sure they get together like this more than once a year, but just once a year they invite my father. I asked if it would be all right for me to bring you. I don't think Mrs. Bernstein was especially happy with the idea, but I was sure you would enjoy it and I wanted you to see it and hear the music. Did you enjoy it? Wasn't it beautiful, that lovely music and the sound of the weather outside and all?" I told her it was the most magical musical experience I had ever had and how much I was taken by the sound of a string quartet. She seemed very pleased that she had been able to introduce me to something I thought so highly of. I thought for the longest time that night before going to sleep, what a marvelous world of music there is, how much joy it brings and how happy I was to find that something so rarefied had enormous appeal for me. I promised myself to buy a couple re-cords of chamber music and learn more about it. Well, you know how those things can go. Yes, it was a thrilling experience and I meant all I had said to Susan, but for some reason I couldn't build on the initial enthusiasm. I never did buy the records. So far, I was doing great at learning to enjoy the things she liked. I wasn't nearly as optimistic about her making the leap to mine.

The band had a number of gigs at fraternity houses, and that meant that I couldn't see Susan on Sundays, because Peggy and I were doing all right, and I would spend the night there and then Sunday we would go to somebody's place and drink beer and smoke dope and hang out. I didn't want to get started ducking out Sunday morning and having the arguments with Peggy that that involved. It was tough enough to beg off on Saturdays. Susan had wanted to hear me play and since I couldn't have her go to the dives where I occasionally sat it, the fraternity parties on Satur-days nights were the logical place for her to hear our band, but this would mean a big stink with Peggy, so I kept making excuses to both these girls and was feeling rotten about it, but selfishly I didn't want to lose either one of them. Each one had her special attraction, and those attractions didn't overlap at all. So I just kept hedging, waiting for a sign. It's embarrassing to admit to all this, but that was the way I was playing it. If Peggy had found out and dumped me, I would have regretted the loss, but it wouldn't have hurt much. If Susan had found out and dumped me, I would have been humiliated and miserable, she was so decent and trusting. But I continued to take the chance.

We broke for Christmas and I took the train home. This long break was uncomfortable and I found myself wanting to get back to school after a week had gone by. I had Susan's telephone number, but never used it. Instead, I wrote, every day but never more than once. I even wrote to Peggy a couple times, but she never answered. Susan did, very nice letters, no perfume, but long and upbeat, lovely penmanship, fancy paper. I saved them all, just in case. I went back a day early and as I had suggested in a letter, met her the next morning at the usual spot. It was pretty nice. Kisses and blushes to start, then out to get breakfast in a family restaurant around the corner. Susan had eaten but kept me entertained while I wolfed down a stack of pancakes and sausage. It was warm and cozy at the front table by the window in the sunshine, and we sat and sat, drinking coffee and telling about what we had done on vacation. Our semester together was coming to an end in a few weeks, and there were things to arrange about that. Susan had her own phone number at home, it turned out, so I need not go through her parents. We took in a movie and a pizza and she took me back to school. It was the season for enjoying all sorts of entertainment that would have been beyond my means. The tickets continued to appear and each Saturday we attended a play or some musical event. The band had a gig somewhere every Saturday night this time of year, so Susan and I were restricted to matinees on Saturday and an hour or two after class three afternoons a week. Peggy pretty much owned Sunday. I was getting a big dose of culture and having a good time getting it.

During the last week of the semester, just before we said goodbye in her car after class one day, Susan turned to me with the bright, pleased look that usually announced something I was going to like. "Do you have plans for Sunday afternoon?" I didn't. "Would you like to go to a horse show?" I thought that sounded great. "Really? Oh, that's perfect. I really want very much to go. The girl who puts it on is my close friend and I told her I'd come. Now…when I told my parents that I was going to go and that I was pretty sure you would like to go with me, they asked me to invite you to join us for breakfast that morning. Would you like that?" She was beaming. "Really? Breakfast? Sure! This Sunday?" She nodded, still beaming. "I'm about to be vetted." She laughed. "Of course you're going to be vetted. Don't you think it's about time? I guess my parents do, anyway. Plus I think my father wants to see who he is squandering all these tickets on."

"I knew it. Are they nice?"

"Of course they're nice. Nice girls have nice parents."

This posed an immediate problem with the band and Peggy. Between the two, the guys were a lot more forgiving than our chanteuse, so I called Eddie and told him that I had the world's heaviest date with Susan that I just couldn't ignore and would he try to get another piano player or do without me and for God's sake tell Peggy I'm sick or whatever, anything but the truth. He gave me a really bad time and I took him seriously and was backing and filling when he owned up and told me to go for it and they'd figure out something.

Sunday morning Susan picked me up. I had two jackets to my name, so it wasn't a difficult decision to pick the tweed one. The problem was with the tie, that is, whether to wear one. I decided I'd better, and knotted on a black knit one that didn't go with anything but didn't clash with anything. My fashion plate didn't disappoint me, long dark plaid wool skirt, black sweater, black beret, black polo coat. That girl sure could wear clothes. She was all smiles, chipper, a little excited I thought. In a way, I was, too. I knew it was a big event for all of us.

"Hungry?"

"Ravenous."

"If you liked the picnic, you'll like the breakfast. Sunday breakfasts are always special. Just wait." We drove for what seemed like quite a long way, all strange territory to me, finally turning onto a handsome boulevard with a nicely landscaped median, old trees on the curb side, lovely homes. I was looking along my side of the road when Susan made a U turn at a break in the median and drove through a pair of huge, ornate iron gates between massive stone pillars, following a curved drive that led to the entrance of what I had to imagine was her home, a home that seemed to extend almost out of sight. We stopped and I stared. Only two stories, but raised substantially above the level of the drive so that it appeared higher, all white brick, huge wings extending from either side of the main building, massive porch supported by great columns, the roof of thick slates. I looked at the house in awe, gaping, then looked at Susan. She was grinning from ear to ear.

"Impressed?"

"Impressed."

"Isn't it enormous?"

I nodded. "Think they'll let us in?

"Let's chance it."

Susan led the way up the long flight of stairs to the porch and simply walked in, holding the door for me and closing it. We were standing in a foyer with black and white marble squares, wide, curved heavily carpeted central stairway veering off to either side at the top of this lofty first floor. A man's voice came through the archway to the left, "I'm in here. Come in and enjoy the fire." Susan tossed her coat on a chair and led me through a parlor at the far end of which was another archway. We walked into this further room, a warm, masculine looking place. A pleasant, distinguished man in an open shirt and cardigan looked up from some material on a long table and came quickly toward me, hand extended. "Peter! Welcome. I'm Walter Grafton, Susan's father. I'm so pleased to meet you. Won't you come over here and get warm? No matter what the thermostat tells me, I enjoy an open fire. Would you care for some coffee? There's a carafe and cups over here. Coffee, Susan? Those little pastries by the coffee are rugelachs. They're awfully good. Hungarian or something like that, I think. Martha, our cook, makes them for us every weekend. Please do try them, they're quite special. Breakfast is always a late affair on Sunday, and I like to have a little something before we sit down to serious eating."

I had agreed to the idea of the coffee and Susan was pouring two cups. I was still in a daze at the magnificence of everything there was to be seen. The floors were wide, pegged boards of what I thought must be cherry, the carpets old, oriental, of intricate design, faintly patterned silk fabric covering the walls, the fireplace of green marble surrounded by a tall, wide carved mantel, the furniture largely red leather, deep, wide. Paintings, prints, marble and bronze sculptures, vases...I tried to take it all in.

Dr. Grafton watched my inspection. "It's too big to be a den, but it's comfortable and this is where I like to come to read. The library doesn't have those big French doors, and I like to read by natural light when I can. Do you like my hideaway, Peter?"

"To tell the truth, Dr. Grafton, I'm trying to think of some way of expressing my total awe as I look around. I had no idea of what to expect and when Susan turned in here and I saw this incredible house, I was just overwhelmed, no other word for it. I'm trying to absorb some of this and I hardly know where to start. It's just unbelievable. Unbelievable." He laughed.

"It may sound strange, but I have the same feeling from time to time, even though I've lived here all my life. My grandfather built this house nearly a hundred years ago. He had a famous architect, he had good taste, good advice, adequate funds and he did it right. I've personally added comparatively little. It's much too big for our little family, but we're very attached to it and it's nothing I want to give up just yet. I suppose someday we'll have to find something smaller, but for the time being, it still serves us well. If you'd be interested, after breakfast, I'll show you around."

I sampled the pastry and had a second cup of coffee while Susan and her father talked about her school and some friends who had just called on the phone. Mrs. Grafton had been tied up with the call but now came briskly into the room, a handsome, dignified lady who came directly up to me with her hand extended.

"How do you do, Peter, I'm Emily Grafton. I'm so glad you were able to come. Are you being taken care of? I'm so sorry I wasn't here to greet you. I heard you drive up but I was on the phone until just now. Susan! Hello, dear. You're looking very well. Does the cold weather agree with you?" There was an exchange of more mother-daughter talk and then Mrs. Grafton addressed all of us. "Please do excuse me for just a few moments more. I do want to get some flowers. Giuseppe is cutting them and I thought it would be nice to have them at the table. I'll be back shortly," and she left briskly.

"We're very fortunate to have a splendid Italian fellow for a gardener. He raises things in the greenhouse all winter long that are simply amazing. Are you interested in plants, Peter?"

"As a matter of fact I am. We've always have a big garden at home. Ever since I was little, I've helped my Dad with it. And then he raises the most beautiful roses you've ever seen. Well, anyway that I've ever seen. He wins prizes with them every year at the county fair. I've never gotten into flowers much, just the vegetables." At his point, Mrs. Grafton returned with a large vase filled with freshly cut flowers, a beautiful mixed bouquet.

"Aren't they exquisite! What a privilege to be able to have such treasures in spite of winter." Turning to her husband, "I think I'll put them on the sideboard, dear. There just isn't room on the table. I had no idea Giuseppe was going to cut so many. I think I'll just put them in here for the time being so we can enjoy them." She put the vase on a table and took a seat near Susan. Dr. Grafton addressed her.

"Em, Peter was just telling us that he's a gardener himself." Then to me, "Too bad it isn't summer. I'd take you around our own vegetable garden. I doubt we have as large a garden as you're used to, but Giuseppe does such a marvelous job. I know you'd enjoy it. He's terribly shy and even though his English is quite good, he absolutely will not speak to anyone I show his work to. Now if you don't mind, tell me where you do all this gardening. Where is home?"

"East Tennessee. That little corner way up in the northeast part of the state. Right up against the mountains. People in East Tennessee are very particular about not being confused with people from anywhere else in the state. It's very different from the rest of the state in just about all respects, I think." He was clearly more interested than I thought this simple information would have justified. "East Tennessee," he repeated, "I don't know a thing about that part of the world. What's it like? Have you lived there all your life? As a matter of fact, I don't think I know a soul from any part of Tennessee, east, west or in between."

"That doesn't surprise me. Aside from the mountains, it's rolling farm land, pretty little family farms for the most part, hay farming and corn and dairy cattle and of course tobacco. We don't have much industry to speak of, just a nice, quiet, friendly backwater about fifty years behind the rest of the country that nobody seems to go to unless they live there, and if they live there, they don't seem to want to leave. We're just a bunch of farmers and hillbillies. The mountains are kind of wild, but the rest of it is just plain old pretty farmland." Dr. Grafton seemed to like the sound of it.

"Now it would seem to me that you should have an accent of some sort, and yet I don't detect any. How do you account for that?" he asked. "Oh, I've got an accent, all right, if I'm home. My Mom was a teacher and a Yankee and all my life she insisted on my speaking the way she did without any accent, which was OK at home, but when I was in school, or working with my Dad or out playing with my buddies, I talked as they did, accent and bad grammar and all the rest, so I was more or less forced to be bilingual, if that's not too fancy a word for it."

"Fascinating! What an odd arrangement, although from your mother's point I can certainly see it. I imagine your father has a regional accent. How did he take to the idea? I would think he might be a little offended."

"No, Dad isn't like that. He had to quit high school to help at home and has always felt that he missed out, so he's a big supporter of my learning anything that will make my chances better. He and Mom always agreed about grooming us kids for something more that farming. Mom has high hopes for me and figured I'd have a better start if other people could understand me." He smiled. "Is the accent that thick? Can you give us a sample?" I overdid it just a little to make the point, but for the next few minutes I talked the home dialect, much to the amusement my audience, for whom it was more as though I were putting on an act. They had never heard anything like it, expecting something of a southern accent. Dr. Grafton was particularly impressed for some reason, and taking up a magazine from the table, asked me to read a few paragraphs. I did and got a big kick out of it, not having had any occasion before to perform in this way. Susan especially seemed stunned.

"Now do I gather that you live on a farm?"

"Yes, sir. Where we live now used to be a regular farm, but my Dad sold off most of it because he was too busy with other stuff to farm it. We just have the old house and about twenty acres for the orchard and the gardens and so on." "Twenty acres? That's what we have here. That's a big piece of property to keep up with. Sounds like a marvelous place to call home. Have you've lived there most of your life?"

"Well, no, we've only been in this house for a few years. I really hope it's the last one and that my Dad will settle down for a change."

"So you've moved around a good deal, I gather?" By now we were well into the vetting that I had expected. I couldn't blame him and it didn't bother me. Actually, Susan had almost never inquired about my home or family or background. For all I knew she was afraid of what she might find out. I figured this way I'd just have to go through it once, and if it wasn't what they hoped for, well, no problem. I didn't have any apologies to make. I told them about how my father and mother had met, about fixing up farms and selling them and moving to the next and so on. "I can't even tell you how many places I have lived in. This last place is a big old brick house made out of handmade brick that were actually made and fired right there on the property in a portable kiln, just digging up local clay. Big rough bricks, so pretty. The walls...well, I notice, like this house—solid brick about a foot or more thick." I glanced to a window where I could judge the thickness of the wall. "Yours must be closer to two feet thick. Anyway, it was a pretty fancy house for that part of the country, the woodwork and trim special, and great wide old planks for flooring. I've been admiring your wonderful floors. Ours aren't nearly as nicely done, but they look a lot alike. I imagine they're about the same age, actually."

"Well, well, I'm impressed. What a fine success story. You must be very proud of your father's resourcefulness. Living where we do and how we do, such ingenuity is very refreshing to hear about. I'd love to see a picture of your home sometime. Are there any other children in the family?"

"Two younger sisters. They're still at home, but the older one will be going to college somewhere next fall. She's my Mom's star pupil."

"Then your mother teaches?" he asked.

"No, sir. She used to teach in public schools, but when Dad began to prosper, she quit and taught all of us at home."

"Really! How did that suit you?"

"Oh, it was great. A lot harder, of course, as my mother was a really tough teacher, but we sailed through the regular curriculum in no time each day, and I had time to help my Dad, which taught me a lot of things I'd never have learned in school, like driving the tractor and the trucks, building things, installing plumbing, simple electrical wiring. I know that sounds weird, but kids there do a lot of adult things. It's surprising how much practical stuff you can learn if you have someone to teach it and some reason to learn it. Mom had a good library and when we got through that, she bought books as fast as I read them so I soaked up a lot of stuff that most kids don't get to until much later."

"How very interesting! Quite a different approach to learning than I'm accustomed to. When I think of my own school years, bored to death because of the kids that weren't interested in learning and just holding the rest of us back. I did have a tutor finally, but for the longest time, my father was obsessed with the democratic notion that I should go to a public school. Now, the schools here were probably a cut above what you report, but they were still geared to the group average, no wiggle room for the bright students. It was terribly frustrating, and it wasn't until I got to college that I began to appreciate learning. So your mother taught you until you came here?"

"No, sir, not quite. When I was thirteen, my Mom felt I needed to be somewhere where there were laboratory facilities available, and science and math teaching beyond what she was capable of giving me, so I was enrolled in a local boys boarding school that was more or less half high school and half college and that was where I went until I came here." Susan and her mother sat quietly, so much alike, while Dr. Grafton sat forward in his chair, attentive and curious.

"I don't know if I understand this last school you mentioned. You said half high school and half college? How did that work?" I smiled at the memories.

"This is a very strange school. Maybe unique for all I know. It is old as the hills, is constantly short of money or about to shut down. They seem to go broke from time to time, but then somehow they get financing again and things resume, and everybody locally seems to understand. The only time it happened while I was there, I just studied at home and after a time, they called and said to come back. The tuition was reasonable, it was near enough for my Mom to drive me, and they had pretty good equipment in their labs. What made the school so different was the weird faculty. You wouldn't believe some of the teachers. I think they were men who had lost their positions in various colleges because of drinking or something like that. You could tell they were too smart to be in such a dinky little school, but there they were for some reason. They were the nicest bunch of teachers I have ever met. The policy of the school was like nothing you ever heard of. There was no pressure, there weren't all that many exams, and even if you flunked, they just kept on working on you until you got it or gave up. If you didn't show up for class, that was your problem. The kids that enjoyed learning could write their own ticket out of a bunch of electives in addition to a core of studies much like college, so the smart ones who were interested could go at their own pace and really cover a lot of ground. The classes were small and the teachers really seemed to care about our learning if we were willing to be taught. The year I graduated the entire enrollment was just fifty kids. Everybody was friends with everybody else. I used to love to go to school. Some of the kids just never did anything when they found out they didn't have to and after awhile their parents took them out and probably thought they had been soaked, but for most of us, it was great."

"Such an odd story. I've never heard of anything quite like it. I wonder that the faculty was able to get anything at all done. It's hard for me to visualize effective teaching without discipline.

Don't you think that that much latitude is going to be abused by the students?"

"Yes sir, no question. It was abused plenty, but the main thing seemed to be not to let discipline or pressure or a rigid schedule turn off the kids that had soured on school someplace else. And that part seemed to work with most of them. The idea was to get them to enjoy learning just about anything no matter how dumb, then slide in the solid stuff and hope their attitude held up. I'd say that it worked with more than half of them."

"But did you get the impression that when these boys were graduated that they were ready for college? It would seem to me that someplace along the line they would have to toe a line of some sort."

"As far as I could tell, it seemed to work on two levels, meaning that the kids that weren't college material got a decent high school education while the interested kids got a much better education than in a public school, or for all I know, a lot of boarding schools. There was no question they were preparing us for the college entrance exams, but they didn't point things that way. It was a very broad approach, and when I sat down to take the entrance exam for Corinthian, I felt pretty well prepared."

"And I gather that you weren't disappointed?"

"No, sir. They were a breeze. I had chosen Corinthian because of their biology department and they not only accepted me but offered me a four year scholarship and here I am."

A harassed looking little woman in an apron appeared silently at the door and caught Mrs. Grafton's eye. Mrs. Grafton interrupted signaled to me for my attention.

"Peter, I hate to interrupt, but breakfast is ready. Let's go in. I'd love to hear more, but I know you all must be starved." I was happy to have the reprieve, and we went in to the sun drenched porch, as they called it. The table was a revelation to me, heavy cloth, heavy napkins, heavy silver, gorgeous china. I had no thought of being blasé about anything I encountered in that house and exclaimed over this scene, the room, the table, the sunshine, the buffet with its ornate silver chafing dishes. I was certainly not going to pretend that I wasn't impressed even if wasn't the thing to do. I was enjoying it immensely and I wanted them to know it.

Following Susan's lead, I took my plate and shamelessly heaped it with bacon, eggs, sausage, biscuit, pastry. It must have looked as though I had no prospects of ever eating again, but at that age and in my circumstances, I felt an obligation to treat myself. Whether out of politeness or amusement, Dr. Grafton endorsed my approach, by wishing he could return to the days when he could eat like that.

We took our places and enjoyed a memorable breakfast. The food was piping hot and excellent, the atmosphere one of refinement beyond my dreams, the company cultured, interesting, the conversation lively and intelligent, none of it showcasing my history further for which I was thankful, none of it concerning things in which I could have had no interest. It was my first exposure to this world of theirs, and I was impressed at the thoughtfulness which characterized it. We sat for a long time over more coffee, everyone at ease and seeming to enjoy the leisure and each other's company. At length we arose and as though by custom, although possibly by design, Susan and her mother set off to some interest of their own while Dr. Grafton invited me to a tour of the house. It was more a museum than a home, walls covered with watercolors, landscapes, lots of portraits, big portraits, brooding portraits of stern looking men, imperial looking women. We stopped in front of one particularly fierce looking gentleman, whose resemblance I had noted in a couple other paintings, and Dr. Grafton introduced me.

"This is my grandfather, the man who built this house. I never knew him. He married quite late in life and had been long dead when I was born. My father told me a great deal about him. He had come from a modest background, it seems, the youngest of a rather large family, no other one of whom seems to have amounted to anything special. He left the family, apparently with their blessings and a little money, and set off into the coal country in Pennsylvania where his relatively good education and his toughness recommended him to a mine owner who took him on in some sort of office capacity, but also as what was called a supervisor. My father was always cautious about details as to what constituted 'supervision', but I had the impression that it included some rather rough tactics with the miners, whom I imagine were a tough lot. Grandfather had a group of assistants, and although they did most of the 'supervising' Grandfather apparently was right in the thick of things. My father was a strong person and fearless, but he was always vague when he talked about Grandfather's role in the brutality that was part of that life. He mentioned that there had been shootings and serious beatings and I have no doubt, some deaths, although this was never stated. It was considered, at least by the owners, as just part of the business, and I never heard of any legal action against the company.

"In any case, eventually the owner took Grandfather as a partner, died, left the mine to Grandfather who went on to buy more mines and enlarge those he had and what with one thing and another, accumulated a fortune and had this house built in anticipation of a family. At that point, he went out and found a mate, brought her here, got her pregnant, left her with a staff of servants and I suppose a checkbook, and went back to Pennsylvania and the mines. He no more than got there that he turned around and came back, turned over the operation of the mine to his manager, and never had anything more to do with the day to day business of mining after that. He didn't manage to father any other children, not surprising considering his years, but he seemed to have lost his ambition to make money when he discovered the joys of making love. My father remembered him as anything but the tyrant he was reputed to be. I suppose that shows what the power of a good woman can do for a man."

"Knowing my father, it is remarkable to me that he was in the least interested in any business, let alone such a tough business, but he nevertheless studied business and mining in college, joined the company and became a very successful and respected manager, much like his father but without the rough stuff. I never did understand the fascination of the business for a man of so many other, opposed interests. It was he who put together the library I'll take you to in a minute. I hope I'm not boring you. You were so forthcoming about your own background I thought you were entitled to know a little about the history of this house. As you can gather, I've had little or nothing at all to do with it, nor did my father. In fact, I have always been somewhat self conscious about the family fortune. I don't dwell on it, because it is ancient history and I don't subscribe to the notion of the 'sins of the father' and that sort of thing, but I do have moments of remorse for the suffering that others endured to provide us with such plenty. I take refuge in giving gobs of it away. Years ago, I created a foundation and that provides me with an outlet for my guilt. Susan is very much interested in the foundation and I expect she will be a help to me there some day. Let me show you the library. You sound like you're a reader, am I right?"

"Yes, sir. I sure am a reader. I can't say it's been much but science in the last couple years, but that's going to change one of these days. I've got a huge list of stuff I want to get into when I have some time again."

"Well, you're going to enjoy this. Come on in here," and he led me into the type of library that I had only seen in movies, all wood paneled, thousands of books in handsome leather bindings, great matched sets of books that I suspected no one had ever cracked, but which sure lent atmosphere. There were a couple of those ladders on tracks to reach the upper shelves, reading tables, Tiffany lamps, writing desk, more Oriental carpets. The entire room was interior with no windows, quiet as a consequence with a large fireplace that looked rarely used. I started looking and found nothing that I recognized except leather and gilt which was everywhere. Dr. Grafton interrupted to direct my attention to a farther wall.

"I think you'll find this section more to your taste. This is where I keep my own collection. Some of those books you were just looking at are volumes that you're probably are familiar with, but I found it almost a sacrilege to read them in those intimidating bindings, so those I wanted to read I have bought in less elegant editions. I think the majority of them have never been opened and heaven knows when or if they ever will be, but they are so pretty and they smell so good that I wouldn't part with them. My wife thinks it strange of me, but it's part of my pleasure in this room." He waited politely while I looked enviously along the shelves until I reluctantly indicated my willingness to move on.

We passed through a huge parlor that Dr. Grafton explained was used for entertaining only a few times each year when they had large groups, the room very formal, opulent, almost out of human scale. Now we passed across the foyer into the first room I had seen but had passed through with scarcely a glance. He led me around, pointing out some of the details of the woodwork elaborately carved, flawlessly finished. In the far corner, somewhat hidden by the light pouring into the center of the room from the porch where we had dined was a grand piano, an enormous concert grand that seemed to extend to infinity. I walked over to admire it and Dr. Grafton lighted a large floor lamp near the bench. I had never seen anything like this instrument, the wood strange to me, the name unknown to me, the whole effect that of great importance. Dr. Grafton anticipated my questions, it seemed.

"It's a Beckstein as you can see. They tell me it's about as fine a piano as there is. Beyond Steinway, I know nothing about pianos myself, but I have never seen the equal of this one. It's all rosewood and I expect very valuable. I keep forgetting to have it appraised and insured separately. Neither Susan nor my wife plays, but I have been advised to engage an expert to go over it a couple times a year. There is a German fellow downtown who keeps it in tune for us. He seems to know his business. My wife tells me that after he tunes it, he sits and plays for a half hour or more. She says that he has told her it has the best tone and the best action of any piano he knows, and I suspect we can trust his opinion." Almost reverently, I played a few chords, then a little run, just to get a feel of it.

"Peter! Do you play? Well, obviously you do. I should have asked you. Please do sit down if you like and play something. Don't be put off by all my bragging. It needs playing, I'm sure, and we never hear it unless we have a guest who plays, and that isn't very often. Do play something." I didn't need any urging. Dr. Grafton opened the top and propped it, and I got a rush of some sort, never having sat at the business end of such an instrument. I sat down and just noodled a bit, the feel of the keyboard so very different. It took some time before I felt comfortable, and then I did a long introduction to a Cole Porter favorite of mine to get loose, scarcely believing the richness of the tone, then got into the chorus with more confidence and began to just play. Most musicians would know what I mean when I say that I felt myself getting into a groove. I was barely aware that my host had seated himself somewhere nearby out of my vision, and with this exception, I felt alone with an inspirational instrument. There is a kind of sublime joy that can come to a person at times like this. I've had it happen now and then when for some reason I just got completely into the music. This was one of those times. I became completely unconscious of my surroundings and my listener, and just played what came unbidden into my mind, a play list just as real as if written down, leading me from tune to tune, the lovely ballads that meant so many things to me, singing the words in my mind, living the lyrics, melody after melody, just letting it all hang out. I had no consciousness of the passage of time until I felt the mood coming to an end. In keeping with the time of year, I played a rather slow, thoughtful version of "My Funny Valentine" and finished it with a long, tinkly treble run up to last key on the keyboard. I sat for a few moments, just readjusting to my return to earth. It takes awhile to come down from a trip like that. I turned on the bench to say something to Dr. Grafton and found the ladies standing behind him, with a quietness and expressions that suggested awe. Very embarrassing.

"Oh, my. I didn't know you were there. I'm afraid I got carried away there for a minute. Somebody should have yelled or something. When the fit comes on me like that I have to be dragged away. I just can't get over this piano, it's like nothing I have ever played before, just absolutely too much." That seemed to break whatever spell I had cast and now came all the exclamations of surprise and praise and utter disbelief and all that stuff, you know. I'm aware that I play pretty well and I understand how much people like to hear someone play, but it still embarrasses me to be praised for something that's as easy as that for me, and they really layed it on..

"Where in the world did you learn to play so divinely? Mrs. Grafton asked. "I don't think I have ever enjoyed anyone playing that piano as much as I have just now. How wonderful that you should have such talent! Do tell us about your training."

"My Mom taught me at home. Just as simple as that, I'm afraid. She's a really good pianist, one of those people who can hear a song and sit down and play it right off. She had real talent, so her family saw to it that she had good instruction all her life. She majored in music in college and went to graduate school and was going to make it her life when she decided to come to Tennessee and teach school. She says she can see the music in her head when she hears it. I don't have nearly that gift, but she did pass on some of it, and I can usually pick out a tune after I worry over it for awhile." Well, this set the theme for the rest of the visit and we just sat around the piano, everyone talking about their favorite songs, and asking me to play this and that. I abbreviated things a little by just making up a couple medleys of the things they liked, and we passed the time like this until about two o'clock or so. They served a neat little snack of fresh baked bread and French cheeses and a bottle of wine and fresh fruit and we sat and talked some more, just as pleasant an afternoon as you could imagine, the parents at ease for the first time, I thought.

"Are you two going to try to get out to your horse show this afternoon?" Mrs. Grafton asked when there was a little lull in the conversation. Nothing had been said about it until now but Susan answered, "Yes, and we really must leave pretty soon. When we talked yesterday I promised Nancy that we'd come by. It's just the kids showing, but I'm anxious to see how she's doing. I haven't seen her in ages, it seems like."

"What ever became of that unfortunate Roger? Did you ever manage to come to his senses?"

"Not from what little I hear. I really don't know any more than that he went into some institution and after a time they released him and I think he didn't drink for a time. One of the girls at school saw him a month ago or so at a party and said he was drinking again. I really don't have much hope for him ever straightening out. He is such a nice boy when he's sober. I feel terrible about what it's been like for Nancy. I don't know if she'll ever come back and finish school now."

"Poor dear. Do bring her around sometime soon, Susan. She is such a lively thing. I got a short note from Blanche not long ago. They're still down in Florida. Bill is not doing too well, it seems. She didn't mention anything about coming home soon. I think they might be just as well off to stay down there. It must be rather lonely out there for Nancy in that big place. Is she seeing anyone, do you think?"

"I don't know but I doubt it. I get the impression she just wants to be alone and get over all the divorce business. The riding school is probably a good thing for her right now. I do wish she'd finish college, though. I think she could have a career with her acting if she'd get serious about it, but she doesn't even want to talk about it, so I just don't bring it up."

As the nibbling wound down, Susan looked at her watch, announced that we had to leave and there was the bustle of getting wraps and the good-byes and thank yous. I had had a very good morning, and it appeared that they had as well. Mrs. Grafton particularly seemed to have thawed, and I felt she genuinely meant it when she thanked me for coming. Dr. Grafton had the air of someone who had made a new friend and mentioned he hoped we could finish the tour sometime. We got in the car and drove out into the country. Susan was almost giddy. I knew that she was very proud of me and the impression I had made on her family, and actually, I was pretty well satisfied myself.

9

The horse show was indoors, thank God, and a lot different than I thought it would be. Horse shows in my neighborhood consist of halter classes and Western pleasure and some barrel racing, that sort of thing, but this one was all about high jumping and a hunt course. The arena was just about as big as a barn can get, room enough to have eight or ten low jumps spotted around for the riders to sail over in a certain pattern. I had never seen anybody jump a horse deliberately. I've seen and been involved in a certain number of unplanned jumps, but these kids looked like they knew what they were doing. The high jumping was amazing as far as I was concerned. I had no idea horses could jump that high, especially with someone on their back.

We had stood and watched for a time before Nancy could break away from her job coaching the kids. She came over excitedly and threw her arms around Susan and exclaimed how good it was of her to come and how wonderful to see her again. They turned to me and Susan introduced Nancy, another one of these smartly turned out, classy looking girls, definitely from Susan's society. She was voluble and outgoing with a bold, self assurance that caught me off guard. She insisted on getting us settled in bleacher seats along the middle of the arena, then quickly excused herself as she was to perform for the parent's benefit, taking her big, dark bay thoroughbred over some very big jumps with not the least suggestion of effort, that brute just sailing like a gazelle without missing a stride. Very impressive. I had to presume that this daredevil horsemanship was what these parents were paying her to teach their children to be able to do. She suggested we come with her while she walked her horse back to the stable where a groom took him. There was a small office at one end of this barn, just a desk, a few chairs and a coffee table. Nancy told us the next few classes were just halter classes and suggested we sit and talk over a cup of coffee.

She and Susan brought each other up to date, the conversation nothing I could join, so I just listened and watched. Susan asked her if she had seen anything of Roger at which Nancy gave a little look of annoyed exasperation. "The Fergusons gave a party several weeks ago and I decided at the last minute to go, which turned out to be a mistake. Roger was there, not quite drunk but trying hard to get there. I couldn't avoid him and he came over and wanted to go over the entire divorce again, so tedious, so pathetic. I wish to God he'd find someone and go away." She turned to me. "As you probably gather", she turned to me, "I was married to Roger at one time, one of those charmers that everyone loves, life of the party, spoiled rotten and unknown to me, a problem drinker. Well, I shouldn't say unknown. I knew he drank a lot but I didn't know he couldn't leave it alone until it was too late."

"That's so sad. Doesn't anyone have any influence with him? He's such a nice person and such fun to have around. It seems such a pity that he is just wasting himself like this. Are you going to come back to Willoughby sometime?" Susan asked.

"I doubt it. This is fun and it gives me the excuse to buy horses and ride and that's enough for me right now. I'm not sure that the theater would have suited me all that well, and I doubt that one can be really good unless one works at it full time and I'm not sure I wanted to work at it full time." Susan turned to me. "Nancy is a very good actress. You would have been impressed," then turning to Nancy, "Speaking of acting, you would have gotten a huge kick out my own acting debut. I told you that I was going over to Corinthian to audit a course in Elizabethan Drama, didn't I? Well, that's where I met Peter. The professor had an impromptu play reading, Peter was assigned the part of Romeo and --can you believe it--I was Juliet and that's how we met. Can you imagine me being involved in something like that? I thought I'd die!"

"Don't tell me--I can guess the rest. By the time you were done, you realized you were destined for each other. I can't think of a nicer ending." And she turned from one of us to the other with a smile of false innocence.

"Nancy! Don't tease! It was nothing like that. It was the most uncomfortable experience I've ever had in a classroom. I was just mortified! The professor tried to smooth it over and Peter was very understanding, but I was just about in tears, I was so miserable!" Susan's protest came with a flush to her pale skin. "Forgive me, Susan. There's actually something touching about visualizing you in such a situation. I know how upsetting it must have been. I don't think I would have done a bit better. You can imagine I've seen a lot of stage fright, even in people trying to do it for a living. It's not anything to tease about. I didn't mean to make light to it"

She turned to me. "What are you up to beyond your acting career, Peter?" I told her I was graduating in June, hoping that my professor would get me placed in a local pharmaceutical firm. She listened politely. "If that means you'll be around town for awhile, maybe Susan can be persuaded to bring you out here again when we aren't so busy. She was looking at me very directly and I murmured something about being happy to. There is a certain length of time to look at someone after a given remark that is appropriate and we anticipate to a split second when that should occur, and when the look is prolonged, there is the sense that something more than the remark is intended, some subtle challenge has been offered, something in addition is implied, and I got this momentary but unmistakable impression. Nancy turned to Susan.

"What have you two been doing for fun?" I explained that Susan was trying to turn a hillbilly into a cultured escort.

"Hillbilly?" She laughed provocatively. "Are you a hillbilly, Peter? I don't think I've ever met a hillbilly. At least, not a self confessed one. Good for you, Susan! How are you working this transformation?" I looked at Susan and saw that she wanted me to handle this.

"Hillbillies have limited budgets, as you can imagine, so after I had completely worn out Susan's patience with an endless diet of movies and pizzas, a mysterious benefactor began to give her tickets to all sorts of cultural events that she was to share with me." Nancy immediately smiled knowingly and turned to Susan with raised eyebrows to silently inquire if her supposition that Dr. Grafton was responsible was correct, so we were all in on the secret. "As a result of the generosity of this anonymous benefactor, we have been to the theater and recitals and gallery openings and ballet and opera....well. You are looking a cultural glutton. In the short space of a few months I have been transformed from sharecropper to sophisticate. Two more cultural events and I get my badge and will then be allowed to come indoors when it rains." Nancy gave an appreciative hoot and squeezed my arm impulsively "Love it!" she giggled. More of that direct look. Susan appeared to be a little embarrassed but pleased that Nancy found me amusing. Having brought up the subject of theater again, the two of them got into spirited girl-talk, comparing notes about the shows they had recently seen. I watched the interaction of these two opposite personalities and wondered at their having been roommates for a year and close friends thereafter. Nancy must surely be the girl Susan had mentioned as being a little wild but seeming to have the fun that Susan was unable to join in. Each surely had something to offer the other in spite of the obvious mismatch. Nancy turned back to me. "Has Susan shown you any of her paintings?" No, she hadn't, I had only just this morning been to her house for the first time and the subject had come up, but we hadn't had time.

"Oh, Nancy! You should have been there! Peter played the piano for us, a regular concert, just beautiful! You've never heard such wonderful music! We just stood there and listened for the longest time. I knew he had a band, but I had no idea...somehow, Daddy got him to play. You must hear him sometime!" And now Nancy turned suddenly to me with a squeal and a look of triumph. "Now I know how I know you! You play the piano at the Jazz Village! I saw you there just a few weeks ago!" Turning to Susan, "I knew the minute you two walked in here that I had seen Peter before, and I just couldn't place him. Jim and Rudy and Irene came cruising by one evening, looking for a drink, and after awhile we decided to go down to the Village. I haven't been there in ages, and there was Peter! So!" waiting for my explanation.

"Unmasked," I groaned.

"How do you fit that kind of life into a B.S. degree?"

"Well, I'm not in that band, really. I just sit in with them for fun mostly. Once in awhile if their piano player doesn't show up or something, I play the whole gig which is great, because I get paid, but that doesn't happen very often. I've got my own band that plays on weekends, pretty much only Saturday nights and not every Saturday, actually, so it doesn't take up too much time." Nancy was beaming. "I'm so tickled! A real, live jazz musician! Susan! How are you going to handle that?" Susan just smiled and shrugged. "When we roomed together, I would play jazz and Susan would play her classical music and I don't think either of us ever converted the other. Susan, you simply must break down and let Peter take you to the Village some night and hear him play with a group." I took a deep breath and looked at Susan who clearly didn't think much of this proposal. Nancy of course picked up on this immediately and added, "Maybe you should take up the violin, Peter." This was kind of a cut and I didn't think it particularly fair, but I tried to turn it into a joke by playing air violin briefly, both girls smiled and I guess Susan wasn't offended.

Nancy suggested we go out and check the progress of the show, temporarily being directed by an advanced student. We all sat together and watched a couple hunter classes, very exciting for me to see these kids sailing fearlessly over the fences. I had a great many questions to ask Nancy about their training which meant talking behind Susan who sat between us. It was subtle, but as this exchange of remarks went on, I was certain I was being sent those indescribable telepathic signals that one occasionally gets from another person and I began to think that my interest, my personal interest was being cautiously solicited. A couple times she reached behind Susan and touched me to get my attention and pass on some observation that might interest me. While I was flattered at this familiarity, I was equally aware of how inappropriate it was unless I was misreading it. It was reasonable to assume that she might have sensed that whatever bond there was between me and Susan was tentative and therefore exploitable, considering our different temperaments and interests, but the idea of a close friend cutting in on what at least passed for a twosome trying to happen was unsettling. I had seen this happen with guys, but somehow I didn't think girls were like that, and I wondered if it was the money these girls had that made them different from the girls I had known. Or had I just missed something? Knowing that she had been married and only recently divorced, aroused some ignoble thoughts of my own. The ignobility got as far a couple flashes of fantasy before I told myself I should cool it. It came time to go, and we got up before the kids had finished and went out to the car.

"I'm so glad you came out. I wish we had had more time to talk. I've scarcely said two words to Peter. I meant that about you two coming out sometime when we can all take a ride and have a little peace and quiet. I know you'd enjoy it." Susan turned to me for my approval and of course I said sure. "They've extended the trail along the river since you saw it last. It makes a long and very pretty loop now, through the woods. They put a thick layer of wood chips the whole length of it. You'll love it. Do plan to come out sometime soon. Do you ride, Peter?"

"Do you have a mule back there somewhere?" She smiled, a broad, warm smile. Her gaze was disconcertingly personal and lingering. "Don't worry. I'll see that you're well mounted."

Well mounted! Well mounted? Was I imagining things? Was I seeing innuendo where none was intended? 'Well mounted'? Oh, man, what was going on here? Or was it all just my imagination? Undeniably Nancy was an exciting girl, very pretty in a less delicate way than Susan, her dark hair and eyes, stronger features, her confidence and quick wit making her seem so bold. Maybe it was the horse business that brought these things out. "I don't know what the rules are, but this is all I have to ride in," gesturing to my blue jeans and loafers. "Don't worry about that. You look great. I'm going to hold you to it. I'll give you a call, Susan. I look forward to it." She gave Susan a hug and extended her hand to me, this last with another look which as far as I was concerned was definitely intended to mean something unless I had completely lost my touch. Unsettling business. I mean, here are two close friends as far as I know. I get introduced and bingo, the friend is messing with my mind. Was this just a straightforward invitation to a fling? We got into the Buick and started back to school.

I was annoyed that all I was thinking about on the way back was Nancy and how to handle whatever was going on. There was no question that some sort of attraction existed that might very easily develop into something unless she was just one of those girls that flirts with everybody and anybody, just to see how she stacks up. I accepted that such disloyal thinking on my part didn't do me much credit, but for all the respect and affection I had for Susan, and all the nice things she had done to please me, and all the loyalty I owed her, Nancy was projecting something undeniably tempting, and at that age, temptation is not easily resisted nor it's consequences clearly foreseen. To put it more accurately, consequences are usually not even considered.

It had been quite a day for both of us. Susan was on a high for her, just glowing and happy because things had gone so well that morning. She talked at length about the piano 'recital' and how surprised she had been to learn about my childhood, what I had told of it, how pleased she was at how well I had been received by her mother and especially at how her father had seemed to take to me. We sat in her car and necked some, poor Susan always glancing around to make sure no one saw us. It teased her about it, but she said she was just shy of any display of affection in public, and even though the interior of her coupe was a long way from being public, the windows steamed up and all, I decided not to mention it any more.

The semester ended that week. It was a letdown to think that we wouldn't be seeing each other regularly during the week. I looked forward to these hours of sitting in her car and talking, Susan having gotten over some of her reserve and more animated and relaxed. I asked her if she'd like to go with me to a jazz concert the next day. I was doing pretty well with my classical music education under Susan's tutelage, but since the subject had come up at Nancy's, I thought I'd do what I could to improve her opinion of jazz. I don't think this was high on her list but she was a good sport and I think really wanted to be able to take part in the things that meant so much to me. She was not enthusiastic I knew, but she agreed so we went to hear a group I had followed for years. They were playing an afternoon program at one of the high school gyms as part of the school's cultural enrichment program or something. I thought what they put on was great, even though the guys seemed a little bit subdued, possibly because of the school atmosphere, the fact that it was only the afternoon, no booze and all. They weren't at their best but even off stride they were live and playing tunes I played too, way better than anything on records. I felt a little sorry for Susan. She was totally out of her element, but she took it with good grace.

I knew the alto player fairly well and I'd talked with him a number of times before, so when the thing ended, I grabbed Susan by the hand and we shoved our way through the kids and got to the edge of the stage and I hailed Jimmy. He remembered me and put his horn down and came over to the edge of the stage and gave me the big "Hey, Bro! How you is..." and all that jive. He was a wild looking cat, always mugging and clowning around but a really good musician. Not all that long ago he had been for some time in a rehab program to get him off the hard stuff. His career had just about tanked, but now he was clean and sounded as good or better than I had ever heard him. I decided not to mention this to Susan. We cut up a few touches about the recent past. He finally looked at Susan as though aware of her for the first time and then with extravagant gestures, paid her his idea of the ultimate compliment to her beauty.

"YEOWWWEEE! Oh...MAN! I is BLINDED! I been struck BLIND! Great God aawmighty! Peee-TAH! Man! What is you doin' to me, Bro? Wheah you get this mama? Wheah she come from, man? OooooWEE! Take me now, Lawd! I done seen it all!" Of course I was getting a huge kick out it, Jimmy such a crazy dude but what surprised me was that Susan was laughing. Blushing, yes, but laughing in spite of herself. Jimmy abruptly abandoned the clowning and holding out his hand, said, "Happy to meet you, little lady. Not meanin' any hahm, but you is some treat for the eyes, ain't she Petah? How come you hangin' out with class like this, man? You hit the numbahs or sumpin'?

I explained that I was trying to introduce Susan to the finer things in life and that I couldn't think of anything finer that coming out to hear Jimmy. Jive like that. He laughed and we shot the breeze a little more and then he said, "You had anything to eat since yestidy, man?" What did he have in mind? "Couple of the brothahs and me goin' over to the club and get some ribs and blow a little. Why don't you and this little lady come on over there and live a little while you got the chance?"

I didn't defer to Susan this time. I wasn't going to miss this, so I asked how to get there and he asked if we had wheels and I said yes and he volunteered to show us the way personally if we had room for him and his horn. We put the horn in the trunk and the three of us got in the front. I didn't know how Susan felt about this, but whatever she felt, I thought it was time she busted out of the cocoon, so off we went, into a pretty bad part of town where I had never gone. It had long been dark and the street was empty and very unfriendly looking.

We pulled up across from a neon sign that said 'Brown Derby', sticking out from the front of an unhappy three story row of store fronts. A faded banner spelling out 'Live Music!' hung across the top of the big front window which was shielded with chain link fencing. I could sense Susan's anxiety, and I must say I wasn't feeling all that good about the neighborhood, but sometimes you just have to have faith and I was sure Jimmy wouldn't let us down. We got out and Susan locked the doors, looking a little miserable.

"What about the wheels, Jimmy?" I asked. He made me the 'gotcha' sign and motioned to a black kid who was sitting on the steps of an apartment on our side of the street. "You wanna make you some money, boy?" Nod. "We going ovah to the club, you heah?' Nod. "When we come outta theah, I don't wanna find nothin"..NOTHIN'—you unnahstan'—Nothin' wrong with this car. You unnastan? Nothin'!" Nod. "Now you have any trouble, you jes come in the club and git me, unnastan"? Nod. "Now when I come outta that club and I find that car OK, I gonna treat you right, unnastan'? And if they's anything wrong with that car, I gonna wipe the street with you, you unnastan'?" Nod. "OK—you a good boy, now you jes take care a things and I'll treat you right. Now git to wuk." He winked at us and the threatening face split into a huge grin. As we approached the club door, he turned to Susan and said, "Now don't you worry, little lady. That car is gonna get took CARE of." Susan still looked quietly unhappy, but if he noticed it, Jimmy passed it off and we went in. It took a few moments for our eyes to see anything, the room narrow, poorly lit.

There was a bar along the right wall, booths along the left and beyond these a half dozen tables and beyond that a small bandstand. The music was going to be loud. To the right of the bandstand was a door propped open beyond which we could hear the laughter and banging pots that identified the kitchen. Jimmy was hailed from several parts of this cave, loud, indecipherable cries of recognition and welcome. He waved at the bartender, a huge black figure with a lot of gold in his mouth who shouted something at him. One inebriated giant lurched out of the darkness and threw his arms about Jimmy, and they fell to smacking each other and laughing and yelling things that I couldn't understand. It was as though we didn't exist. I never saw anyone so much as glance at us, and Jimmy made no effort to introduce us.

The entrance ceremony over, Jimmy motioned to us and we sat down at a wooden table with a threadbare oilcloth cover. Jimmy shouted a question at the bartender in this second language he had, the language in which one could only pick out occasional words. The bartender yelled to the kitchen, the kitchen yelled back, the bartender looked for further instructions from Jimmy who yelled them back to the bartender who in turn yelled them to the kitchen once more. There was the sound of assent in the kitchen, and presently a tall girl with a black bandanna around her head came from the kitchen, snuffing out a cigarette as she passed the bandstand. She came over to the table and raised her eyebrows at Jimmy, haughty, disinterested, annoyed. It seemed that Jimmy expected something better and looked over at the bartender who was taking in the whole scene. He yelled at the girl.

"That Jimmy Mooney! What's th' mattah with you, girl?" Jimmy sat waiting, looking up at her. The light seemed to dawn on the girl and the face slowly recomposed itself to one of respect and apology, suddenly shy. "You Jimmy Mooney?" she asked. Jimmy said nothing, but the bartender answered for him. "What's the mattah with you, girl. I tol' you that's Jimmy Mooney. Now ask the man what he want!" She seemed to have lost the power of speech in her embarrassment. Jimmy had no intention of consulting us. He told her we wanted three rib dinners and three beers and she smiled and simpered off, looking back once, smiling coyly, reassuring her unbelieving eyes that he was who he was.

"Looks to me like you might have played here once or twice, Jimmy. I never see anything in the papers."

"I ain't been in this place for years. I used to play here a lot back in the bad ol' days, back when I was doin' all the bad sh--- stuff. I got some good memories heah, I got some bad memories." He was uncharacteristically somber as he mentioned this, then suddenly beamed and said, "But that's all behin' me now, baby, all behin' me and nevah coming back. No indeed. I has paid my dues." A new patron had come in and looked around quickly until he spotted Jimmy and came yelling and laughing over to the table. Jimmy got up with a mock angry face and then burst out yelling himself and they pounded one another, yelled more sounds at each other, almost upsetting the table. Poor Susan. I didn't dare look at her.

"I heah you heah, Jimmy! Man, I jes hoof it ovah heah as fas' as I can! Damn! It good to see you Jimmy. You famous now, man! You famous! I surprised you come back to this ol' place anymoah, Jimmy. Man, you shoah lookin' great, Jimmy! You gonna play? You gonna play some, Jimmy?" Jimmy told him that a couple of the boys were coming by and they might play some for old times sake. He left, beaming and took a stool at the bar facing Jimmy, got a beer and sat grinning.

Our dinners and beers came, an empty heavy plate for each of us and an enormous platter of steaming ribs drenched in dark sauce. Jimmy told her to bring us some napkins and she came back with a metal container bulging with paper napkins. Jimmy was making sounds of anticipation and picked out a rack of several ribs and rolling his eyes at us, started in. I realized silverware wasn't part of the dinner and we pitched in ourselves. They were delicious, and I'm not just saying that because I wanted them to be. Those ribs were downright good but there was no possible way we could get through all of them. I noticed that Susan had a pretty good pile of bones on her plate when we got done, and was pleased that she had gotten through two beers.

About the time we finished, two more guys from Jimmy's band came in, carrying their horn cases. The yelling started all over again, the smoke now thick and the place getting so crowded that we had to pull our table toward the wall to let people past. We remained completely invisible. As far as this crowd was concerned, we weren't there. Jimmy had gotten up and left without a word, and we sat, non existent to our fellow patrons, in the heat and the smoke and the noise. I got through a couple more beers, Susan declining and quiet. Susan and the waitress appeared to be the only two women in the place. Finally there was an increase in the yelling and we could see the neck of a bass moving slowly through the mob, propelled by a diminutive guy whom no one seemed to know. He got up on the bandstand somehow, there were some snatches of playing on the piano, more greeting sounds and gradually the bandstand cleared except for the band. Jimmy came up to Susan and asked her for the keys to the car. Poor Susan. She complied and sat very quietly until Jimmy came back in with his horn and put the keys down on the table. He grinned at her. "Now don't you worry about that cah, little lady. That boy doin' a good job. I done take care of that boy, so don't you be givin' him moah. I remind him and he not goin' NOwheah!" Susan smiled wanly and put the keys away. Poor baby.

The music just blew me away. There is a natural tendency to imagine something better than it really is when you hear it in a joint like this, about as authentic a spot as you could imagine. I had never heard really funky jazz played in a really funky place. Maybe it was the atmosphere, but whatever it was, it sure was the real thing. At one point, Jimmy dedicated the next song to "that little white lady over there at the table". A few faces turned to look at Susan and she tried to smile and didn't even come close. They finally broke and I turned to Susan and before I could even ask, she nodded and I knew she wanted badly to go, so when Jimmy came to the table, I told him we had to go and how much we had enjoyed hearing him in a place like this. We shook hands and we yelled, then he shook Susan's hand and yelled in her ear over the dim that she should take good care of me. Susan smiled and nodded and we made our way out into the night. The street was completely deserted except for the boy who still sat on the steps, now wrapped up in a blanket. I gave him another buck which he took without a sound. Susan handed me the keys and we got in and drove to school. We sat in the car for a time.

"Too much?" is asked.

"Oh, Peter. I was scared to death. I know it's silly, but I was just petrified the whole time."

"Sorry, Suze. There was no telling how things were going to go. I knew Jimmy wouldn't let us take any chances. He's a good guy. He's worked so hard to get straightened out. I must admit I was little worried. That's not the greatest part of town, you know. I was mostly worried about your car, but maybe you noticed too, Jimmy was just as concerned as we were. I think he took good care of us. So here we are, safe and sound, and you've got a story to tell now, haven't you?" She laughed, and took a deep breath.

"I guess so. I don't know who I'd tell it to, though."

"How about those ribs?"

"They were very good."

"What did you think of the music?"

"Oh Peter. That's just not my kind of music. I'm sure it was very good, but I don't understand it and it seems so frantic. Maybe that's not fair. I'm sure they are very talented, but I just…I don't know what else to say."

"Susan, you are very possibly the first white girl to ever spend an evening in that place. I think you did awfully well. It's all over now, and we have some great memories and someday when it all sinks in, in about thirty years, you'll tell your grand-children about this evening and they'll think Grandma was quite a number." She snuggled closer, probably reliving all the insecurity, the noise, the smoke, the sea of black bodies, our helplessness. "You done good, kid. I'm proud of you." She only sighed. Well, so much for Susan and jazz. I had struck out. There was no faulting the music. With the exception of a little hard bop that they played, it was mostly funk and I would have thought that funk would appeal to almost anybody. If that was the most inspirational evening of jazz I had ever heard, then or since, I just had to accept that we weren't ever going to get together in that department. Well? Well, what? That was just the way Susan was. So, we move on.

10

For the next few months until graduation, Susan and I were to see each other only on weekends and not very often even then. My new schedule which Dr. Baxter had designed for me, put the two of us together all day on Saturdays, no credits involved, just his personally coaching and walking me through a very esoteric theory based on some hypothetical areas in molecular biology that he felt would earn me a master's degree nearly simultaneously with my bachelor's. What his theory eventually led to is now well known, but at the time it was at the cutting edge of what is proving to be an incalculably important scientific frontier.

There was a tremendous amount of reading for me to do simply to get grounded in the basics of this new vision. What literature there was on the subject was scanty, a good bit of it foreign and difficult to come by, and much of what I needed was stored in Dr. Baxter's mind. There were new courses in fields either new to me or in which I had had only entry level exposure. I read endlessly, then we met and talked on Saturdays or after his class hours and occasionally even in the evenings.

I had told Susan that this was going to be a real charge to the finish line, and she took it all in good grace, as I expected. I called her the morning after the Mooney jam and we talked a little. I got to feeling a little lonely and asked if she could come over for awhile and she said yes, so we met and drove over to a little park near her campus and took a walk and then sat in the car and talked. I told her the next Saturday was out, and she said she understood and asked me if I could come to breakfast again. This posed a problem because I felt obliged to play that night and if Peggy showed up it was going to be hard to turn down staying over. I might break away gracefully about noon without a fight, but not for breakfast. Mind you, I didn't feel entirely good about this line of thought, and I knew that sometime soon I was going to have to break with that chick, but I didn't want to rush it. I wrestled with the options a few seconds and finally decided that Peggy was just going to have to go home alone. I told Susan that breakfast sounded great.

The next Sunday she picked me up and we drove to her home, and had one of those memorable breakfasts. Susan and her Mom paired off and Dr. Grafton took me out to the greenhouse and introduce me to Giuseppe who bowed and smiled and made some soft sounds. Beautiful flowers, dozens of orchids many in exquisite bloom, vegetable seedlings rack after rack, everything spotless, humid, warm, green. Outdoors the fruit trees had all been pruned neatly, the garden freshly turned, a great heap of compost, forsythia bulging yellow. In spite of most of the trees being leafless, I couldn't see the wall at the back of the property. As we walked back to the house, Dr. Grafton asked me if I ever played pool, and I told him I did. That seemed to please him. We bore off to the right and entered the house through a door in the back of the wing on that end and came to an interior door.

"I can't vouch for the conditions in here. I haven't been in this room for months." We entered and he turned on the lights, revealing a long, pool table under wraps, heavy, ornate legs protruding under the cover, two great green lamps overhanging it. He looked around in some satisfaction. "Not the worst looking table in the world, I guess". It was a little chilly, and he fussed briefly with the thermostat and a soft whir could be heard and warm air felt. "Haven't had that on since last winter. I added this room on years ago. I love the game and put all this together and would you believe it, not one in ten of the people we have over here are the least interested, so I play some by myself but that gets boring after awhile."

He walked over to a handsome mahogany cabinet on the wall and opened it. "I think I have about twenty cues in here and use only one. Isn't that a pity, all those lovely sticks just standing there going to waste. He turned and took the cover off the table, spotless felt, rich looking laced leather pockets. "I actually built the room around the table. I can't guess what it weighs, but I put it in first and then we finished the exterior wall. I don't intend to move it and I like the idea of no one else moving it either. Would you like to try a game?"

Dr. Grafton took out his cue and after sorting through a half dozen, I found one that seemed right and he racked up the balls. "Straight pool OK with you?" I said it was fine with me and he told me to break. I didn't run the table, but I wasn't that far from it and when I finally missed, he grimaced. "I think this might be long morning for the doctor." We played a couple more games, Dr. Grafton getting steadily better and almost taking the third game "OK, I give up, but just wait. And all this time I thought you were studying biology. Where do you get your pool time, young man?" I smiled and told him that we had a couple tables at school. "If you'll lay off practice for a week or two, I'll have you back here again and take my revenge. We put our cues away and covered the table and walked down a wide hallway to the library.

"Susan mentioned a long time ago that you were interested in biology, but somehow I just lost track of that information until recently when it came up again. I imagine you must know Charlie Baxter pretty well, by now." I was surprised at this casual reference and asked if he knew Dr. Baxter. "Charlie and I have been good friends for many years. Not long after I started in the pathology department at City Hospital, Charlie was hired to run the bacteriology part of the laboratory. He was older than I and had kicked around at a couple different hospitals in the Midwest, just not able to settle for some reason. Well, it wasn't just some reason. Charlie was too eccentric for most people, and I believe he lost a couple positions because people couldn't figure out how to deal with him. I'm sure you know by know that he is smart as a whip, a very bright man, but you also know that Charlie is a most opinionated and uncompromising man. Plus, he is certainly not attractive. I'm not being disloyal. Charlie knows it and it's sort of a standing joke. That round pink cherubic face, the tiny watery blue eyes and the thick lenses, the tic he has, all that nervous fidgeting used to put people off. He was completely bald even at that relatively young age when we first met"

Mitzi

"I had never had anything to do with him until one day, he came to me in considerable agitation to give me a verbal report on a specimen that had come down from our department. The upshot of his compulsive oversight of everything in his lab was that he had noted something in this specimen that completely altered the cause of death in a patient we had signed off on, saving the hospital from a very expensive legal action. I was impressed and I made it a point to make his acquaintance. I soon came to realize that Charlie had an extraordinary mind. That mind cut two ways: it made Charlie a brilliant laboratory man, but it drove everyone around him nuts. He was a perfectionist, not just with himself, but for the people around him who for all their willingness and hard work could never satisfy him. He wasn't abusive, he didn't rant, but he checked every thing that anyone did, check, check, check until people were leaving. True enough, some of these people should have gone. The lab got better and better, but the administration got tired of the complaints and I learned that there was move afoot to dump him, so I went to the Administrator and pleaded his case and then went to Charlie and tried to talk him out of his compulsive behavior. That didn't work, as you would expect, but at least it bought some time."

"Em and I had been married only a short time, and we were giving a lot of parties as young people will, and I decided to invite Charlie. He had absolutely no social life that I knew of and I thought it might do him good, so he came, dressed in an outfit that you would have had to see to believe. Poor Charlie. And I'm sure he knew it, but he just came anyway. Well, what with my friends and Em's friends and friends of friends, I usually didn't know many of the guests, but I introduced him to several in the course of getting over to the bar and getting him a drink and then turned him loose. Sometime later, I saw him talking to a tiny creature, rather attractive and lively, and I felt good about having asked him. When some while later I noted the two of them still in conversation and Charlie nodding and smiling and laughing, I asked Em if she knew who the lady was. It turned out that her name was Ellie something and that she was a close friend of a classmate of Em's from college who was staying with the classmate for a time until she found a job."

"You never saw a more unlikely looking duo, as though they were from different planets, the nearest thing to Beauty and the Beast you're likely to meet. And yet, he wooed her, he won her and to everyone's astonishment except Charlie's it seemed, they got married. Well. This was the making of Charlie. You probably have never seen a diabetic in insulin shock swallow a glass of orange juice and before he puts down the glass is recovered. I'm exaggerating some for effect, but it was nearly like that for Charlie. Whatever Ellie told him or did for him is not important. The result was that he became a changed man. The mind, to be sure, was just the same, but somehow Ellie flipped a switch and Charlie came down to earth calm, patient, understanding, forgiving, all the things you must see in him now yourself. Let me tell you, it hasn't always been that way. Well, to finish the story, the administration backed off, they shook loose the funds for him to considerably enlarge the lab, new equipment, more staff, better pay. In the end, they made him head of the lab. At about the same time, I had been given the Pathology department when my chief retired. So there we were, each of us at the top of his heap. We weren't social pals. Charlie and Ellie were rather private and while Charlie and I saw each other every day, I had very little occasion to be in Ellie's company."

"About this time, the medical college was given an unbelievable gift by a local real estate tycoon who wanted the school named after him. Somehow, the school talked him out of that part of the deal and ended up with the money and embarked on a major building program, included in which was a brand new Pathology section, the old one just deplorable. They had given the old professor the sack and had lined up a new man who had a fine reputation, only to find out at the last minute that he was abusing drugs of some sort and was in trouble over it and that was the end of that. Sorry to say, but this sort of thing does happen. Anyway, in desperation, as I modestly like to think of it, they came to me and made me a very fair offer. I'm not referring so much to money as to authority. I wasn't ready to retire, but I must say I had gotten to the point at the hospital where the prospect of something less demanding sounded good. They let me put together my own staff and I've gotten good men under me to do the real work.

I have only a couple lectures a year to give and otherwise I just supervise and troubleshoot, and with a staff like mine, there's not much of either."

"I didn't lose track of Charlie by any means, but we saw much less of each other. I asked him to lunch one day, and we had a good visit. Everything at City was thriving, and he was excited about a number of things that he felt would occupy him for a long time. We parted and I felt very good about how well everything had turned out for him. It was not more that a week after that that a mutual friend called to report that Ellie had just been killed in an auto accident when a patron of a local bar had pulled out in the highway, knocking Ellie's little car into the path of an eighteen wheeler." Now he turned to me, "Did you ever hear anything about this?" No, I hadn't. I had no idea what Dr. Baxter's private life might be.

"I was terrible for Charlie. He is a very sensitive man and I was deeply concerned about what it might do to him. We all gathered around, of course, and did what we could, but poor Charlie was just destroyed. He took some time off and even talked about retiring, and then things settled down a bit and I thought perhaps all would be well again, as well as it could be, but the wind was just out of Charlie's sails. He came to me one day, in this very room as a matter of fact, and we had a long talk about his situation. My foundation had not long before given a sizable unrestricted grant to Corinthian. I knew the situation in the biology department where the professor had become an appendage, simply because of his age. As Charlie seemed completely burned out at the hospital, I asked him if he would consider teaching, thinking that I might be able to wield the power of the purse in getting Charlie a berth. I told him my thoughts, he reflected at some length, and allowed that it was worth an attempt, so I got in touch with Corinthian and after some hand wringing and feather smoothing, the incumbent was tactfully promoted into a meaningless position and Charlie was appointed interim professor, or something like that. In any event, the old gentleman promptly retired, possibly with a little urging, and Charlie was given the chair and that's where we stand today. Incidentally, I would suggest you not pass any of this on. There is still some feeling in the department on the part of one of the associates, and the less said, the better, I think. So now you know more about your professor whom I gather from Susan's remarks, has taken a shine to you. Tell me something about your relationship, if you don't mind."

I told him how Dr. Baxter had plans for me getting installed in Phillips Pharmaceuticals with his help, that he had connections there.

"Industry? Somehow I don't think of you as the type to be a cog in a big machine. Have you ever thought about going into medicine, for instance?"

"Yes, sir. I thought about it a good deal at one point and I guess if I hadn't met Dr. Baxter, I'd be headed for medical school next fall."

"Really. What did Charlie say that changed your mind?"

"He didn't talk me out of going into medicine, but he made biology so interesting to me that I just decided that might be a good career, and when it looked like I had made that decision, we had a long talk about structuring my last year to get the most out of the time I had left, and one thing led to another, and before long he had gotten me interested in a research project that he wants me to take with me to the research department at Phillips if he can get me in. He has some connections there and he feels pretty sure he can arrange it. I can't go into any detail, but he has an idea about a breakthrough in cellular chemistry that he thinks has great potential." Dr. Grafton asked me if I had gotten any inkling that this referred back to something he had been working on years ago, and I told him I was pretty sure it must be, because of things he had told me.

"Charlie has had that dream for some time, and you know, I can't discount it's having something in it. He is an awfully bright man, as I said, and I think you're very fortunate that he has taken such an interest in your career. Very interesting. So you're going to carry the mail, you think?"

"If I can do it. I sometimes have my doubts, it sounds like such a wild idea, but he seems to think he can whip me into some kind of shape and pass me on to these people. Right now, as you suggest, I don't think I can go wrong whatever happens. He's teaching me a lot of valuable stuff and it's got to fit in somewhere, so I'm going to give it my best shot and hope it works." There was a long pause as Dr. Grafton seemed to be considering something. "Peter, do you mind if I stick my oar in some, get in touch with Charlie and go over this with him? I'm sure you realize I won't interfere. There is just a possibility that I can help in some way. I haven't gone over this ground with Charlie in a long time, and I'd like to know what's gone on in his head the last few years. Would that interfere with your plans, do you think? Does he know you have been seeing Susan? He's always been very fond of her."

"Boy. Small world. No, that would be great if you'd like to talk to him. This whole thing is getting pretty intense. I gather from what you say that you have some idea of what he's up to?"

"I think so. I'm sure his thinking has evolved a good bit, but it must be basically the same grail he's been stalking all this time. You realize, of course, that if he can pick the lock, there is no telling the magnitude of its significance?"

"More or less. So much of it is really beyond any concept I can have other than what Dr. Baxter hints at, but so far, he's just scratched the surface, and there's a lot I don't know yet. You and he can probably see a lot of things that just don't register with me yet. I'll get it sometime, but right now all I can do is just study and keep my mind open and do the best I can to follow his lead." Dr. Grafton sat for awhile more, just thinking.

"Peter, I think you are going to have a very exciting life. I could be wrong, of course, but if I judge you accurately, and knowing the regard Charlie has for you, I think you are going to have a very rewarding career. I'm so glad to be close to this story. Well, well….. come on. We'd better get out of here. I have a feeling we've been missed by now. Are you and Susan going out this afternoon?" I said that nothing definite was planned, but I thought we might. "I'm so sorry, Peter. I'm being very selfish. I realize you probably would like to see something of Susan. Forgive me. Thoughtless. Well, let's go and apologize."

We found them sitting in the solarium sipping cocoa. "Well, gentlemen! How nice of you to join us!" Mrs. Grafton offered. "Yes, yes. Sorry, ladies. My fault entirely. This young man plays pool, a little too well I might add, but when I tell you that it has provided me with a half hour of pleasure, beyond the humiliation of losing every game, I hope you'll forgive the inattention. Not only have I found a pool opponent, but young Dr. Pasteur and I have advanced his career by light years, and that is something not to be taken lightly."

"Dr. Pasteur, is it?"

"In the wings. Not yet, but in the wings. Em, this will surprise you some. Guess who has taken Peter on as a protégé?"

"Charlie?"

"Isn't that wonderful? They're thick as thieves, and Charlie is sponsoring him over at Phillips after graduation and the two of them are going to rock the scientific world. Can you just picture it?" Mrs. Grafton seemed appropriately surprised and very pleased.

"Well, Peter! How marvelous! It never even occurred to me that you knew Charlie. Of course, I should have guessed because Susan did tell me that you were majoring in biology, but somehow I just didn't make the connection. How wonderful! He's such a dear. We have seen so little of him since he started over at Corinthian. Well! Charlie Baxter. We should have him over some time, Walter, sometime when Peter could come."

Dr. Grafton laughed. "We'd better ask Peter about that. It seems that the plan is that they are spending all Peter's Saturdays, some of his afternoons, and an occasional evening together for the rest of the year, and I suspect that might be enough contact with Charlie for Peter."

"Oh, dear! That sounds awfully formidable, doesn't it? What in the world would possess you to take on such a burden, Peter? Is this the Dr. Pasteur business Walter mentioned? Is Charlie going off on one of his tangents, Walter? He can be so impulsive, you know," she added, addressing me.

"Not a bit, Em. Charlie has been involved with this idea for years, and he wants Peter to help him get it funded and checked out at Phillips. Or so I believe. I'm going to get in touch with him and see what's going on. If you two are going somewhere, I'll let you know what I find out, Peter. Are you coming over next Sunday?" I told him that sounded just fine. I knew I had to accept with Dr. Grafton going to much trouble on my behalf. I also realized that this was definitely the end of Peggy and no hedging. There was a great deal more at stake now than I could risk for the sake of a few rolls in the hay.

Susan and I drove to the lake and parked where we had picnicked and talked in the fall. She wanted to know all about what Dr. Baxter and I were up to and I did my best to explain the basic notion. She asked me more about growing up in Tennessee, so I asked her about her own childhood and she told me a lot, so very different from mine. I gathered that Dr. Grafton had never been very seriously tied down with his professional work and there were lots of vacations, skiing, dude ranches, cruises, Europe, the shore, the lake, parties, so much different from anything I had ever known. I told her how much I enjoyed her father's company and how good he was about taking an interest in my studies. Susan volunteered that she felt her father missed not having a son, then realizing that she might have said too much, added that I mustn't feel I was expected to fill that role. She blushed and I pretended to be indignant, "And all this time I thought you wanted me for yourself!" and at this, she opened her mouth in distress and having nothing to say, dropped her head in embarrassment. I took her face in my hands and raised it. She opened her eyes, still upset. I kissed her, unresisting. "Put your arms around me." She did. "Hold me tight." She pulled me to her. "Tighter." She did. "Now kiss me." And she did, and it appeared to me that there was room for hope.

Dr. Baxter and I spent the next Saturday morning together at his home. I was still struggling with absorbing a number of difficult concepts integral of understanding certain features in molecular metabolic processes that were the basis of Dr. Baxter's hypothesis. We had spent several hours going over chemical bonds and protein synthesis and I was getting restless and feeling ungrateful about it. It must have shown.

"Peter, let's call this enough for today day. We've covered a lot of ground and you need a break. Besides, there is something I want to discuss with you that is personal, I realize, but touches me in several ways. Walter Grafton came to visit me Tuesday and we had a long and very pleasant talk. I had no idea that you knew him at all, nor that you had been seeing Susan. Needless to add, I was very pleased to hear about it and told Walter just that. Quite a coincidence that you two should get together. Walter and I have been very close for years, and he has done a great deal to help me, a truly fine gentleman and the best friend I have in this world. After we caught up on the news since our last contact, a much longer time than I ever should have permitted, the subject turned to you, the newest interest in both our lives. Are you impressed?" I smiled.

"I don't think I am violating any confidence to tell you about the substance of his remarks. First of all, he is very impressed with you, as I have been, and I value his judgment which confirms my own. He is anxious to help you and I assure you, he has resources that I can't begin to command. He is a very valuable ally for you and I have no doubt will continue to help you in every way he can, regardless of any other involvement with his family. By that I mean whatever your relationship with Susan might develop into. He mentioned that you two had been seeing a good bit of each other, and even though you may know it, I'll tell you that both he and his wife approve of you as a companion for his daughter. I doubt you have any idea how flattering that is. Now, if you don't mind, there are some things I need to hear from you personally. First, can you characterize your relationship with Susan for me?"

I told him about our meeting in class and going out pretty regularly and how highly I regarded her, everything in general terms as I had no clear idea of where this was going. "Is there any other young lady competing for your attentions?" I had to squirm at this. Whether he had hit on this sensitive spot by accident, or was more intuitive than I would have guessed I couldn't tell. I thought candor was called for, reluctant as I was to admit my double life to a close friend of Dr. Grafton's. I asked that he assure me this was all confidential and when he did, I cleared the air as best I could, telling him in the broadest terms about Peggy, leaving much to his imagination.

"Are you serious about this Peggy?"

"No, sir. I won't be going with her anymore. I decided this week that it's bothering me and I'm going to call it off tonight after we finish playing. She might quit the band, but we can get somebody else. So far, Susan doesn't know anything about Peggy and I've never had to lie to her, but I'm beginning to feel guilty about the whole thing and I think it would be better to just break it off." He digested this without comment.

"Are you serious about Susan?" he asked.

"Well, in a way. But I'm not sure I should be serious about anyone right now."

"If circumstances permitted it, are you fond enough of her to ask her to marry you?" I squirmed again determined to be direct with him, but embarrassed that I couldn't come up with an answer. Before I could respond, my hesitancy having answered partly for me, he asked, "What are Susan's attractions for you?" I was on solid ground now, and I explained that I admired her composure, her maturity, her self confidence, her honesty, her intelligence, her beauty, her intuitiveness, her manners, her talents. I explained that we seemed to be perfectly compatible in temperament and that I found her an excellent companion.

"That's an impressive list. I think I would agree with you in every particular, but unless I am very much mistaken, something is missing, am I right?" I sat somewhat dejectedly, reluctant to get into these waters, worried that in spite of his pledge, something might make itself known to Dr. Grafton and prejudice my friendship there.

"Well, maybe nothing is exactly missing, but I just don't know…I just get the impression that she wants a pal and maybe nothing more. I honestly haven't been able to figure it out. I get the feeling that if I were to try to express myself by getting romantic, you know, that she'd object, that she wouldn't like it, and maybe be offended so we go along with a kiss here and there and I don't get a feeling of much warmth. I mean, as far as marrying Susan, what if she turned out to be kind of cold as a wife? I don't think I could handle that, and so far I don't see Susan as very emotional in the way a guy wants his wife to be. I realize that I may be entirely wrong and I hate to say anything that isn't exactly flattering to Susan, because she is such a great person, but so far, romance just isn't in it and I don't know if it ever will be." I felt really badly about going into this with such an old friend of

Susan's, but I knew Dr. Baxter and I were going to be close for a long time, and I didn't want to mislead him in any way, so I just sat and waited.

"I see. I'm not entirely surprised to hear what you have to say. Let me give you what comfort I can. Nothing I have to offer should be misconstrued as disloyalty to the Grafton family, and I tell you these things in the strictest confidence, of course. Susan's mother is a fine woman, strong, intelligent, protective, proper, totally dedicated to her husband and daughter. As fond as I am of her for many reasons, I cannot describe her as a particularly lovable person nor a particularly loving person. Very protective, very loyal but rather stern in her social values, something almost Puritanical about her. For whatever reason, she has seen to it that all through Susan's adolescence her circle of friends was restricted to the point where she had as a male friend, for all practical purposes, only one boy whom Emily felt she could trust. Mind, you, I did not and do not approve of this sort of arrangement, and I think Walter was mistaken to permit it. It was definitely not his idea, but on this one point at least he has always deferred to Emily. I believe that Emily intended that Susan marry this boy and join two close families. Well, the whole thing blew up recently, according to what Walter has just told me, and a good thing it did. From what I have just told you, you will not be surprised that Walter was actually relieved although Emily took it rather badly. In my opinion as the result of this exclusion from wider contacts, Susan never had an adolescence. She went from childhood to adulthood, and this to me is the reason for her advanced maturity. Susan is a very obedient girl and I doubt very much she would ever violate her mother's trust. Whatever else, I suspect this trust includes that she remain celibate until she is married, something that is not negotiable with Emily, nor, I presume, with Susan. I am not in a position to know what goes on in her heart, and I'm not sure that she knows either, if it comes to that." He paused to fuss with his pipe again, while I reflected on the story Susan had told me about Brad and how our present closeness had begun after this confession.

"I gather that perhaps the most important deterrent to your courting Susan seriously is your concern about her ability to respond to you emotionally, whether she is capable of romantic love, is that fair? Whether she is capable of taking Peggy's place?" This stung a little, but he had identified the problem and I was obliged to agree.

"Peter, let me make an observation or two. There are in this city probably ten thousand young ladies with whom, in the right circumstances, you could feel yourself in love. Of those, not more than a dozen would make you happy as a wife. Looking at me you can tell that I wasn't the sort of person girls would readily fall in love with. As it turned out, not a single girl of my acquaintance ever had such a thought. But I had such thoughts about them. At your age I went through all the agonies of love for any number of girls that never gave me the time of day. It was very lonely and very humiliating, but as Walter indicated he had told you, I waited them all out, they got married, often divorced, and eventually I forgot them and then my turn came, and the result of my waiting was that a lovely, lovely lady who had grown up and gotten over her adolescent fantasies came to me as a mature, stable, sensible and bright companion, and turned my life around during the years we were given together. I could not have wished for a more perfect mate. I submit to you that the communion of two like minds, the companionship of two people who think and feel alike, will last indefinitely, long after the excitement of the lust that so often passes for 'love' has vanished.

"I promise you that I won't speak to this subject again, Peter, but this once I want you to think over what I have just said very carefully. I don't know how you feel about money, but leaving the Grafton fortune aside, having a father-in-law like Walter and a wife like Susan—I'm assuming now that she thinks highly enough of you to marry you if you proposed it to her—is something that you may never meet with again. I assume that you want to have children, and I think you should consider very carefully the breeding of those children and their rearing. Does this sound too clinical? It may seem so because I mean it to be. You're going to live the rest of your life with your children, and you should begin to accept responsibility for their breeding before you select a mate. If I were you, I would want the best genes I could find for producing the finest children I could and I would want for their mother a woman who would give them the intelligent dedication they deserve. I recall reading something in Montaigne to the effect that regardless of what we think, we marry less for ourselves than for our posterity. Personally, I don't believe that to be true in most cases, but I dearly wish it were. It is something to aspire to, in any case. I know something of the background of both Walter's and Emily's families. They were capable, decent, people, strong, resourceful, industrious people, what we used to call 'quality folks'. I've known Walter and Emily very well for many years, and the way you have been treated tells me that if you decide you want to marry Susan some day, that you will be accepted." He emptied his pipe and went through the ritual of loading and firing and then resumed.

"The hormones that run rampant in young men your age are deceptively dangerous. Those powerful urges that torture us so intend that our genes be passed on. The instincts that they command have absolutely no other interest. They don't care in the least for you beyond bullying you into fertilizing as many ova as possible. We are powerless to ignore them, but recognizing their tyranny, we should be smart enough to understand their recklessness and guard against letting them distract us from making wise choices of a life partner. I do not intend to act as a marriage broker for Susan but I have her interests very much at heart. I have known her all her life, I have watched her grow up and I am admittedly very fond of her and anxious for her happiness. I have had little personal experience with girls of her age, but I am a good observer, and I have no difficulty recognizing when a girl is exciting. Susan is not an exciting girl by what I imagine your standards to be and I would have to agree with you, but I submit that what she represents beyond this shortcoming is compelling and strongly recommends her as a mate. It may be that the time for recouping what has been denied her is past, but we can't speculate about that, can we? Nevertheless, I have some reason to believe that if you are the man for her in every other way, that you might be surprised at what a gentle and determined courtship could turn up in terms of emotional development. At the very least, I would ask you to think on this. Give Susan a chance. You might be pleasantly surprised. And even if you are not.....Now, I've said enough. Possibly too much. I hope you'll forgive me for intruding in your personal affairs, Peter, but knowing and having a high regard for both principals in this matter, I feel gives me some license. Now why don't we put all this aside for a couple days and you call Susan and take her to a movie or something."

I was impressed and humbled at how perceptive he was about our relationship. This uncertainty and frustration I felt at Susan's reserve and propriety nagged at me, dissuading me from being more overtly affectionate, fearing a rebuff. This was the first I had ever mentioned my misgivings to anyone. It was disappointing to find that unburdening myself gave me no comfort, but I was impressed at the wisdom of his advice and the importance he assigned to rational choice in such a long term commitment as marriage. In my most serious moments, I would agree that Susan was a highly desirable mate, and I found myself experimenting with the idea that an affectionate nature and wit and spirit were not really important in the long run. But the short run continued to bother me. I had often considered what it would be like to be married to Susan. Maybe her lack of warmth was due simply to inexperience. After all, she had scarcely had a boyfriend before I came along. I did a lot of thinking about our conversation and then took Dr. Baxter's advice and called Susan. She was surprised and happy that we would have some of this day together. We took in a movie and the traditional pizza and she dropped me at school.

One of the guys in the band picked me up. I had rehearsed my farewell address to Peggy and thought it sounded pretty noble and decent. Actually, about the only thing that concerned me about dumping her was that she might quit the band, not an irreplaceable loss, but nevertheless, putting the band in a bind for a time. As we drove to the gig, I told my buddy that I figured I had to give Peggy the boot and that I was afraid she might get sore and quit. "What gives you that idea?" he asked.

"Well, you know...it might be kind of awkward working together. We've been pretty tight, and for all I know she may think something is going to come of this, even though I've never given her any reason to. I just don't want to make any waves, you know?"

"Are you serious?" He was looking over now and then and grinning from ear to ear. "Do you seriously think you've got the inside track with that chick?"

"What are you getting at?"

"Look. Casanova. Haven't you ever noticed The Suit?"

"What do you mean, what suit?"

"Not what suit, man, The Suit. The guy at every gig for the past…what? Couple months? Three piece suit, no date? Smooth looking operator?" I thought a moment and remembered that I had seen such a guy, strictly out of place, always alone.

"Yeah. I think I know who you mean. What about him?"

"That's your competition, man, and you're running second, know what I mean?"

"Where did you get this stuff, man? You're telling me this cat is beating my time? Who says?"

"Irene told me a long time ago. It's a going thing. He wants to set her up in her own apartment, the whole works. Of course, he's married, but that doesn't seem to bother Peggy. She's adaptable."

"Are you serious? Is this on the level, no kidding?" I was pretty annoyed. Here I was feeling sorry for her and worried about doing the right thing and not hurting her feelings and she'd been messing around with some other dude.

"Look, man, you haven't got any beef. You've had a free ride for a long time. Did it ever occur to you to take the girl out once in awhile? Girls like that, you know? You just shack up over there when you have the time and then walk off. Now, mind you, if you can get by with a deal like that, more power to you, but don't feel sorry for yourself. And don't worry about Peggy being sore. You're doing her the favor of not having to dump you, right?" Can you beat that? I was really deflated.

"You know, somebody could have said something. There's no law against letting a guy know about something like this."

"What's your beef, man? You were happy, she was happy, the Suit may not have been but that's Peggy's problem. So who wants to stick his oar in? I think you should just leave the whole thing alone and let it die a natural death. What's to be unhappy about? You haven't got any complaints the way I figure it." It was the ego that was suffering. After a bit, I realized that the best thing to do was just that, let it die, not say anything, just be friends.

"What do you suppose she's been telling the dude when he sees her drive off with me after a gig? How does he take that? I'd sure like to know how she's been getting around that. Maybe being married he doesn't want to rock the boat. Oh, brother. She's going to have a mess on her hands some day. Apartment? Crazy business, huh?"

"Peggy can sing but she is not known for being over bright. You've been playing to the cheap seats, man. Time to move onward and upward." Not that there was much choice. Sure, I was relieved not to have a scene to go through, but for a few minutes there, I was actually a little disappointed. I had planned the thing and seen myself playing the role and carrying it off with some sort of credit and now I was going to have to swallow the fact that I had lost out to a guy in a three piece suit. Peggy was just the same as ever, and when we finished, I just packed up and when we got outside everybody said goodnight to each other and I got in with Ronnie and off we went and that was that.

11

Susan picked me up the next morning, and it was odd how relieved I felt to have just one girlfriend. I was actually kind of euphoric, probably showing that it had worried me more than I realized. I got in the car and grabbed Susan and gave her a big kiss and she laughed, pleased but taken back and asked what had gotten into me. I told her that I suddenly realized how much I had missed her during the week and she said she thought that was flattering, so I kissed her again and I think she actually blushed a little, which really tickled me. I was thinking some about what Dr. Baxter had told me, and there was no doubt about, it, the welcome I got at the Grafton's was beyond what an ordinary date would get, I felt. Even Mrs. Grafton who seemed so self contained, was cordial to the point of being warm.

In this short period of time I realized that our Sunday mornings had taken on a very informal and comfortable air. Susan's parents had come down to normal size, the house was no longer as intimidating, the conversation had become relaxed and easy between us as the early stiffness disappeared. By degrees, I found I was being integrated into the family in a way that was flattering. This urbane couple had accepted me on such even terms. They respected me, they trusted me and I came to agree with Dr. Baxter's appraisal that if I chose to become their son-in-law, that they would approve. There was also no doubt now that this was Susan's choice as well. I had been tested and had passed. The responsibility for what came of this courtship now rested with me, a daunting thought that I regularly shuffled to a corner of my mind, waiting for a sign to give me the nudge I needed.

Barney was no help at all, but nevertheless I got a kick out of using him as a sounding board. When you have lived with a guy night and day for over three years, you can hardly avoid leveling with him about your love life. I had kept Barney up to speed in just about all particulars since I had met Susan. He knew all about Peggy, of course, and highly disapproved of my double life, not so much on moral terms as for the danger of it causing me to lose my 'heiress", as he persisted in calling Susan. He had researched the Grafton family through his father and came away with enormously exaggerated estimates of their wealth and power. "Hawkins, you hopeless dullard, can you not get it through your hayseed head that you have stumbled upon the Golden Fleece? This is IT! It's show time, champ! Get in there and show me your stuff! You've got her on the ropes, boy. Give her the old one-two, bring home a scalp for God's sake! Get up off the mat--do something!" Then a change of tone, and abject pleading: "Roomie. Roomie. My good pal. My sole comfort in this scholastic sinkhole. Make me proud of you. I say such good things about you behind your back. I encourage people to look up to you as a gink that can make things HAPPEN. And what do I get? You dither. You vacillate. When you first got here, you had backbone. You had determination. There was a raw energy about you that you brought from Appalachia that was masterful, intimidating. And where has that fled? You, Hawkins, are becoming a major disappointment."

Barney was also put out that I had never introduced him to Susan. The nature of our dating, the fact that our dorms were strictly off limits to female visitors made it awkward. When I told him that Susan's money was a matter of indifference to me, he tore at his hair. When I told him about Dr. Grafton's offer to assist me with his connections, he fairly howled in frustration. "Rube! Do you realize you could own that Phillips outfit? Can't you see that the old man is absolutely handing you a major slice of the American Dream? Handing it to you! And you sit here like Hamlet. Please excuse me. I think I am going to be sick." And so on. I confess I enjoyed setting him up and all, but the truth was he was right. I was just plain unable to persuade myself that Susan would ever be an emotional fit. In spite of everything else she offered that was so special, I just couldn't see myself marrying with the idea that breeding quality stock would justify such a union.

If I had any other complaint, it was with the stability of this life I was slowly drifting into. It was not only my age that craved some fun, it was my nature as well. Up until very recently, my life had been pretty carefree and casual, lots of laughs, lots of beer, late nights, permissive liaisons, parties, horseplay. The experiment of stepping into a previously unimagined world of wealth and sobriety and responsibility and restraint had been very pleasant and I was pleased to see that my behavior and manners and conversation were acceptable to a stratum of society that I had never encountered. It was heady stuff and I was even growing comfortable with it, but I missed 'the life that late I led'. Susan was just not a girl to take out with my old gang, I felt. It was not entirely a matter of her meeting old girl friends I was anxious she not meet as much as that I thought she would be uncomfortable with my gang. I wasn't even sure if my buddies would especially like her and after all, that does count for something. Chances are I would continue to choose for friends the sort of people I chose now and how would that work out, if Susan didn't particularly like people of that sort. I could see her being distant and polite and proper and coming across as dull and I didn't want her image tarnished by putting her in situations where she wouldn't show to advantage.

Annoyed with myself for being so protective of her, and telling myself that maybe there was more flexibility in Susan than I credited her with, I decided to take her on a pub crawl, a mindless diversion I was fond of and that might shake her loose a little, give her a chance to unbend or whatever. With the same unconscious motivation that prompted the Jimmy Moody night, I was trying to change Susan, trying to make her into what I wanted her to be, an unacknowledged measure of my vague unease regarding our compatibility.

We started off one Saturday afternoon, just one beer and one pickled egg in each bar, Susan not drinking much at all, but seemingly enjoying the experience. She had never sat at a bar before, had never played a jukebox, never played a slot machine. She appeared to be having a good time, and I felt encouraged. We took our time, drifting down this same avenue, looking in store windows, stopping in a couple more of my favorite quiet, dark bars, watching baseball on the TV. We ended up at Delaney's. There, wouldn't you know, sitting around a pair of tables pulled together with a half dozen glasses and couple pitchers of beer, was the Gang, Barney among them. Totally unplanned, the big meeting was about to take place. My first thought was to back out, but we had been seen and there was nothing to do but put a good face on it. There were loud, beery hales and a lot of chair scraping and fumbling as another table and a couple chairs were arranged to make room for us. They all knew that I had been hiding something special and that this was it. I introduced her all around, Susan polite and smiling her lovely smile, the guys suddenly more respectful than usual, sensing a different dimension in this lady, I think. That didn't last long though, and the table was soon the laughing, noisy, verbal free for all it always became. I had a strong feeling that this was a mistake, but there was nothing to be done about it, and well, so what? These were my guys. She might as well meet them and I'll just hope for the best. I had never been more aware of the gulf that existed between us.

At one point I went to take a leak and when I came back the jukebox was playing some polka or something and one of the guys was dancing with Susan who looked rather baffled but game. Then another guy cut in and pretty soon it was obvious that every one of them was going to have a dance and they did. She took it very well, I must say, breathless and laughing and very, very pretty. I did a lot of loud complaining and threatening which they enjoyed, and then as soon as I decently could, begged off and amid lots of pleas to Susan to get rid of me and come back herself, we made a retreat. I decided that that was enough pub crawl for the day. We got back to her car and drove to the campus. I apologized to her for getting her into a situation that I had never intended and that I knew wasn't much fun for her.

"Please don't apologize, Peter. It's just that…I'm not very good at things like that. I didn't know what was expected of me. I hope I didn't spoil your fun. I'm glad to have met some of your friends. They're nice boys and they certainly are fond of you. I hope they didn't think I was unfriendly. I don't know much about dancing and when they asked me, I tried to get out of it, but they insisted. I didn't know what to do, so I danced with them as best I could. I had no idea what I was doing. I felt terribly foolish."

"My fault, Suze. Those clowns. I just thought you'd enjoy seeing a few old timey, Irish pubs without the chrome and glitz, the way a bar ought to be." She assured me that she had very much enjoyed the tour, but I knew she was never going to be comfortable or amused by certain parts of my world. I had found her world generally to my taste and knew I could accept and enjoy the things it had to offer. My attempts to show her my world hadn't gone at all well. Was it so awfully important that she should like those things? Wouldn't it be enough to me to enjoy my jazz and my male friends in such a way that it didn't interfere with a shared life in her world? I just didn't know, and I didn't seem to be getting any closer to a resolution of the problem.

Things went along about like this into spring. The Graftons had one of those nice green tennis courts out back and as the weather got better, Susan undertook to teach me to play the game. I had struggled from time to time when somebody asked me to play at school and had decided it was a dumb game. When she first came out in a tennis outfit, I realized that I was wrong about tennis. Like Nancy and her riding habit, tennis clothes were meant for Susan. I had never seen her in anything quite so abbreviated. Unconsciously without realizing it for a moment, I was giving this newly revealed figure the very appreciative review a that guys go through when a girl appears looking like this. Even though I had quickly readjusted my look, Susan had picked up on it, was embarrassed and threatened to go put on jeans. I doubt she would have, but it was that kind of touch and go with the modesty.

The lessons actually worked to some extent. She coached and she demonstrated and I did what I could, but I must say, most of the time my mind was on my coach and how she looked and moved. We had never done anything remotely athletic, and I was impressed at how graceful she was as well as how her modesty suffered at having me see her in such skimpy outfits. She was visibly embarrassed every time she came onto the court, knowing her appearance was the focus of my attention and it always took awhile for her to settle down and play normally, even though I made it a point not to appear distracted. That was just Susan, actually glamorous in a shy way with a graceful, enviable figure she was never at ease with. And that was just Peter, longing for her not to be so shy.

Sometime in May, the Graftons opened up their cottage at the lake and Susan and I went out for lunch and rented bikes and rode around. The park surrounding the lake was beautiful this time of year and we rode a long way and finally stopped and flopped on the grass in a sunny spot. Susan lay on her back, I beside her on my elbows, looking at her as she watched the clouds moving. It was one of those moments when all sorts of good things blend, the day, the ride, the grass, the fragrant breeze, and the girl. I looked at Susan and thought and thought, and I was seriously thinking about the future when she looked over and caught my eye. I was not conscious of being different, but she caught something instantly and turned her head. "What is it?" I looked puzzled by the question I suppose. "What are you thinking?" What I was thinking was that I was a fool not to ask this girl to be my wife forever and forever and forever. "Just how pretty you look." She looked at me very seriously and long enough that I began to feel it. I realized I wasn't ready to reveal any more than I seemed already to have revealed, so I inspected the grass. Susan was quiet for a time and then she suggested we go, and we walked hand in hand to the bikes, not saying a word. No telling what she was thinking.

It was not more than a week after this that Susan told me that Willoughby was having their 'Spring Fling' and would I like to go. We had never had an opportunity to dance except at Delaney's and I had resolutely declined to dance there. I said that would be great and was it formal? It was and I had to rent a tuxedo and get a haircut and buy a corsage, not a very usual experience for me. Of all things, Dr. Grafton arranged to pick me up and take me to their home where he gave me the keys to their big black Packard sedan and told me to enjoy the evening. Susan was absolutely stunning in a most becoming gown, the corsage in place, a light cape fastened at the neck. She was so elegant! I could scarcely imagine being the escort of a vision like this. Susan flushed with the awareness of the image she projected. Her parents exclaimed at how nice we both looked and what a handsome couple we made and I got that feeling again of fate taking me by the hand, a certain inevitability impending.

Willoughby was impressive. The campus was gorgeous from what I could tell with all the outside lamps lighting the walkways, the majestic buildings, everything so manicured and imposing. The ballroom was huge with great tall windows framed in heavy dark green and gold velvet drapes, upholstered couches and chairs all around the room, serving tables with enormous silver punch bowls dispensing streams of some beverage, high pitched laughter and low pitched laughter, a crush of people just inside, reluctant perhaps to commit themselves to the vastness of the ballroom.

We passed in, slowly squirming through knots of squealing beauties and their beaux, strangers to me except a couple guys I knew from school, who gave me a hail, but no one seemed to be hailing Susan, and I became aware the she seemed as much a stranger here as I. We stood and talked about the decorations, the bandstand decked out very festively with huge potted plants and flowers, the Spring theme. Suddenly, a large girl came loping over to us, shrieking at Susan as she came up behind her, "Susan! What in the world! I had no idea I'd see you here! What a surprise! Oh, your gown is just beautiful! It's about time you did something like this! Did this handsome gentleman persuade you to come? Well, whatever, I'm so glad to see you here, and looking so marvelous!" We were introduced and she continued on this not very gracious theme, "I never thought I'd see the day! Look, I'll talk to you later. Got to go. Have a wonderful time!" and she loped off, leaving me a little provoked at what seemed rudeness to me, and annoyed that Susan, even if this was a rare occasion, should have it thrown up to her like this.

"Who'd the Valkyrie?"

"She means well, Peter. It's just that I never come to any of the dances or any other social function for that matter. I don't enjoy mixing with the girls the way almost everyone else does. Nancy told me that they think I'm conceited, that I think I'm too good for them. Most of them have just given up on me, I'm afraid. We just don't seem to have that much in common. I guess you could say that I'm not very popular." I felt that this admission had cost her something and I felt very defensive for her. "I doubt you've missed all that much, Suze. That popularity business is kid stuff, as far as I'm concerned. They'll grow up one of these days." I had never heard of dance cards before Susan told me about them. It seems that guys were going around getting signed up for dances with whomever they wanted to dance with, so there was no cutting in and everyone knew just who to dance with every time. I didn't like that idea too much and I asked Susan how she felt about the card business and she laughed and said she scarcely knew one boy there besides me and her card was a perfect blank. I told her that was the way I wanted it and if it were OK with her, we'd just dance the night away, the two of us.

About this time, a dignified looking woman came out on the stage, greeted everyone, hoped that we would have a good time and made her exit. This was the cue for the band and they launched into an up tempo tune that I liked, a really good big band sound, big horn section, two percussionists, one for the Latin tunes that were just getting popular. I approached Susan as though to jitterbug, not knowing at what to expect, and was met with a little frown and a shake of the head that said, no, no jitter-bugging, and we fell into a clinch and slow danced. It didn't take very long to realize that Susan didn't enjoy dancing. She was so graceful at tennis, at diving, but here, she was defeated, not clumsy, just wooden, and there is nothing like dancing a whole evening with a partner who doesn't enjoy dancing. We got through a couple slow tunes and when the tempo came up again, I asked her if she'd like some punch and we got a couple dips of it.

"I know I'm not much of a dancer, Peter. Brad wasn't either, and he's about the only one I ever danced with and I'm afraid I'm not very good at it." She was not at all happy. "Hey, you're doing just fine. Slow dancing is just fine with me." Well, something had to be said. What is going on in that fine mind that has possessed you to do this to yourself, I wondered? Why had she had wanted to come here at all, and before I had finished asking the question I realized what the answer had to be. Susan had come to show me off. To show that she had a boyfriend, that someone cared for her.

It had to be. There would be a prom, and that would be the end of her college career. Poor Susan. I determined to be as gallant and attentive as possible. I had no more than formed this resolution, that a couple came hurrying up to us, a cute little thing dragging with her a tall, serious looking guy who seemed a most unlikely looking escort for this lively number.

"Susan Grafton! Marcia told me you were here and I couldn't believe it! I've been looking all over for you! Wow! Look at you! Great gown! Love your hair that way! OK, who is he?" and she looked up at me with a very winning, mischievous cocking of her head. Introductions were made, she was Bianca, he was Stanley. "Peter. Ask me for this dance. If you don't ask me, I'll ask you. Stanley, you dance with Susan. Come on, Peter," and she simply took my hand and dragged me off onto the dance floor.

Well, well. Could that girl dance. She was an utter joy to dance with. Jitterbugging, she made me look like a pro. She was clever and nimble and she danced with abandon, grinning from ear to ear with sheer high spirits, doing dazzling spins and steps I had never even seen before, goading me with gestures to imitate some of her stuff, just a wild chick. All she needed was someone to twirl her around and be there to catch her, and she was gone. I realized we had cleared a pretty good piece of the dance floor for her performance, and I felt both self conscious and tickled at the same time. The piece ended and the dancers around us laughed and clapped and said "way to go" and stuff like that. Slow dancing, she was like a cloud, somehow letting me lead but making me do things I had not even thought of and we must have really looked pretty good. She was grinning, I was grinning. "Hey, you're a good dancer," she whispered at one point. "Me? Are you kidding? You're the one who's the dancer. I'm just along for the amazement. Man! You are something else!" and she giggled. She knew she was good. I was all for having a break, partly because things had gone so well and I didn't want to mess up, and partly because I belonged with Susan, but the music started, a Latin beat, and I froze. She asked me if I could meringue, I said no and she said sure you can, just watch, and right there on the spot she showed me a simple little step and told me to just keep doing that and let her do the rest. What a sketch!

By the time this dance ended, I was getting edgy about Susan and must have gotten caught casting an eye around. Bianca said, "Time to get back?" with an innocent little grin. I told her I thought I had better. "Look. Peter. You're a really neat guy. You're just what Susan needs. Underneath all that is a really neat girl. Good luck. And it if it doesn't work out, call me up." She gave me a very cute smile, and before I could answer, took me by the hand and snaked through the dancers to Susan who was standing there with Stanley. She grabbed him and pulled him out onto the floor.

"Bianca is such an outgoing person," Susan said. "You two looked very professional out there just now."

"I didn't mean to put on such a show. That little minx is wild! And I didn't intend to strand you with Stanley. Would you like to dance some more?" Yes, she would and she smiled very nicely and I was relieved to feel that I hadn't messed up. I would have been very happy if there had been no more swapping. This was Susan's invitation to me and I was naïve enough about protocol to feel that we should spend the evening together, but that wasn't the way things were done, and a guy would come up to Susan and off she'd go, and a girl would come up to me and off we'd go. Bianca made it a point to come back a couple times and I had to admit, these were the highlights of the night, guilty as I felt about this disloyalty to my lovely lady. I never did ask any girl myself because I didn't know them, but that didn't seem to make any difference to the girls that came to me.

The evening wound up with 'Auld Lang Syne' and 'Stardust' and hugs everywhere and calling and gesturing and waving and the same crush going out except everyone looking a little wilted now. The night was warm as we walked to the Packard and I got Susan in and her gown and cape settled. "I need a kiss", I said, and she obliged before the words were out of my mouth. It was a nice moment, and instead of starting the car, we just sat and necked and cuddled and said nothing. I had no idea what her thoughts were. I'd have given a great deal to know, her mind so closed to me. Eventually the reverie was broken by headlights that suddenly flooded the front seat, followed by a couple whistles that I thought were meant for us, so I fired up that big machine and very carefully drove Susan home. I might have known. The doctor was waiting up and drove me home. What a family. Nice people.

Nothing had been said about even a late breakfast at the Grafton's, not surprising after the late evening, so I trudged over to a little hole-in-the-wall restaurant and sat over several coffees, thinking about the night before and Susan in general. I had never seen her with her peers, her friends of four years standing, and I was puzzled by the cool reception she got almost everywhere. No question, she was a genuine loner. I wasn't the rah-rah type, but I enjoyed a wide range of people and had no plans to tuck in somewhere and peek out. As it was already, I had gotten so closely involved with the whole family that if I decided that things with Susan were at a dead end, I didn't know how I was going to gracefully bail out. I didn't want to bail out as things stood now, but I was having so many misgivings that it was sapping some of the pleasure I took from the relationship. And the relationship was not just boy-girl. It was boy, girl, the girl's father, the boy's professor, the boy's career with a lot of obligation thrown in. The Graftons had treated me like the anointed and Dr. Baxter seemed to be actually counting on me to make the big move. I had gotten into a position with very little wiggle room.

Then I would say to myself where will you ever find such a girl again and about the time I had gotten comfortable with the obvious answer to this, I'd recall the emotional vacuum, the humor and fun problem, the antisocial tendency. The wealth business was not much of a factor. It was an undeniable comfort to know that money would never be a problem, but I didn't think it would be anyway, once I got started. This morning had something of a non-alcoholic hangover quality to it, so I sat and pondered and ended about where I had begun. I went back to school and played the piano for a couple hours, and then after lunch called Susan to thank her for the dance and to express my appreciation for her father staying up and driving me home. Susan asked if there was any chance we could take a drive that afternoon, as the whole family would be in Boston the following weekend to attend a cousin's wedding. We drove out to the falls, the spring foliage nearly full and everything so lush, the river high and the falls raging. We found a big warm rock to sit on and go over the evening again.

As we sat and drifted, I got the feeling that Susan felt the previous evening needed some explaining. We were holding hands and just watching the water when she brought it up. "I've never been to a dance at school before, but I knew it was going to be the last chance I had to see what it was like, and I thought you would like to see the school and the kids I have known there. Only I don't really know them, to be honest. I recognize so many of them and I know their names, but I have really had only one person I could call a friend there in all the four years, and that is Nancy. We didn't pick each other as roommates, we were just somehow assigned together and we became best friends in spite of being so different. Living together for a year forced me to be more outgoing, and Nancy simply insisted upon it and with her help, we got to be very close and I have enjoyed her so much these years. She tried to get me over my shyness around other people and do the things the other girls were up to, but even though I tried, I don't think I did awfully well. I'm just naturally more serious and I suppose… duller..than my classmates. It all seemed so frivolous and careless. They all drank, far more than they should have, and they did drugs and some of them were openly promiscuous and I just didn't want to be part of that, so I came home after the first year and became a day student, and of course, that separated me almost completely from the girls I had known. I disapproved of a lot of things they did and they knew it and they resented my being so goody-goody, as they called it, and it drove a wedge between us that you must have been aware of last night. I'm all but a stranger in my own school, and you must have wondered what was going on. Bianca always seemed to like me, but she is so different from me and we never got to be real friends. There were a couple other girls that I thought well of, but they weren't there last night." She turned to me for emphasis, I thought, and continued, "But I don't think of myself as being lonely. And I'm not a hermit in spite of what it may look like. I so enjoy talking with my father. And with you." And so my heart melted. I was that important to her, the closest she had ever come to saying anything that suggested as much.

12

I spent the greater part of the next Saturday with Dr. Baxter. At some point when we were taking a breather, he asked me how Susan and I were doing. I told him about the dance and what fun we had had, even though Susan felt self conscious about her dancing because her friend Brad had no interest in it and she didn't care for it much. Dr. Baxter, I realized, had known Brad and must have met him on many occasions.

"I feel I am quite tolerant of other people's failings and foibles, having so many myself, but that young man, Brad Morrison, was a fellow that I simply could never take a liking to. Good family, nice looking boy, outgoing and polite, amusing, if you like his type of humor, and for some reason, possibly the friendship between the two families, highly regarded by Walter and Emily. I could never see the fascination, myself, and I always wondered what they saw in him. I suppose Susan thought him a fine fellow, but Susan is so hard to fathom, I may have been wrong. Anyway, to my satisfaction, although I shouldn't admit it, after the break I mentioned to you before, the boy was packed off to Italy to study art or something. I never heard of him being interested in art or anything else for that matter. He seemed purposeless to me, yet Emily approved of him. Personally, I thought she pushed the two youngsters together unnecessarily and I'm very happy to have him gone. Walter denied they had any thoughts about the two marrying, but Walter doesn't know everything Emily has in mind, I can tell you. Walter is man of the utmost integrity where matters of principle are involved, but when Emily puts her foot down where Susan is concerned, Walter steps back.

"I personally felt a little sorry for Susan, always with the same boy, but you know how stoic Susan is. If she was deprived in any way, she certainly never gave any sign of it. Wonderful girl, Peter. I don't mean to be harping on that subject and I told you I wouldn't, but I mean it all the same. Be kind to her, Peter. I think you can do her a world of good, and I don't know of anyone I think would be better for her than you. Well, let's get out of here and go home. I'm busy Monday--let's meet here Tuesday about four, OK?" So now there were two votes for my being someone who would be 'good for' Susan, not what I would call a ringing endorsement of the match-up.

The band played for a private party that night. There was a certain amount of drinking to be done, and I slept in and felt not too swift the next morning, but got some coffee made and was about to go to breakfast, when a guy came to the door to tell me I had a call. It was Nancy, and I got an unexpected rush when she identified herself.

"Good morning, Peter. I hope I didn't disturb you. You remember the bargain we made? It's such a perfectly gorgeous day, I thought you could call Susan and come out and go riding. You'll never see the trail as pretty as it is now. Not only that, but I'm all alone and really need some good company. How does that sound to you?" I told her that it sounded fine, but that Susan and her family were out of town.

"Oh, Peter. What unfortunate timing. Well of course, we can always do it another time. It's just that this is such a lovely day." There was a pause that I was about to fill with my thank yous when she resumed, "Listen…This is just too good a day for you to waste with all your studies. If it wouldn't seem improper to you, why don't you let me come in and pick you up and we can at least ride some around the property. I hate to ride alone. What do you think?" I won't pretend to say that I didn't know what was going on. I had to assume that one way or another, she knew that Susan was not in town, and that this created an opportunity. I am reluctant to admit it, but my conscience was unequal to the task of saying no and I gave her the directions, heart pounding, quick clean up and change of clothes, in time to get downstairs.

Nancy pulled up to the dorm in a red MG roadster, top down, Nancy in her riding habit, black hair pulled back in a long braid, bare headed. Quite a sight. It was only a twenty minute drive and we pulled up to the barn. With the engine off, the silence was complete and I sat for a few moments enjoying it, Nancy pleased that I appreciated the tranquility of the place when I commented on it. She had already tacked up a couple horses and we led them outside. "I would ordinarily ride my jumper, but he's such a handful sometimes, I thought we'd be happier with this pair. I think you'll like your mare. She has a very nice gait. Let's take them down to the ring and make sure you feel comfortable. You said that you had ridden some. Have you ever ridden an English saddle?" I admitted that I hadn't, looking at it and finding nothing to hold onto, just in case. We went in the ring and Nancy pulled the stirrups down on my saddle and suggested I mount and let her check them for length. It started right there, or at least it started right there for me. She would take my ankle and put my foot in the stirrup, look at the bend in my knee, take the foot out and re-adjust. It was the same thing with the hands as she showed me how to hold the reins for this kind of bridle and to plow rein as I called it. "You're probably used to a curb bit. This is just a snaffle, very easy on her mouth, but that's all she will need. Just keep the tiniest feel of pressure with your reins. She's very sensitive. Do you know how to post?" No. "Let me show you. It's very simple, and really easier than sitting a trot, although your mare's gait is so smooth, if you feel more comfortable, you can sit."

Nancy mounted and came up beside me, showing me once more how to hold my hands and what she meant by light contact, and then set off around the ring the picture of grace, a nice square trot, rising barely out of the saddle in rhythm to the trot. She had urged me to watch how little she rose each time, thereby directing my attention where it didn't need any directing, very unsettling, those perfectly filled britches rising and falling. It's going to be a long day, I thought. She had me trot around, stopped me and made some suggestions, started me off again, now calling out encouragement and having me stop and start a couple times until she thought I had the fundamentals. "How do you feel about cantering? Nothing very fast, just a nice rocking chair speed." And she told me how to urge this horse from a trot into a canter. The mare was so responsive, so willing, so smooth gaited and well mannered, so anxious to please, I could have gone on like that all

138

day. She asked if I felt comfortable going out on the trail and off we went.

Nancy set the pace for the most part, at least at first, the path wide enough for us to be side by side. I was getting the hang of the posting, fighting it a little less, looking over at Nancy's can, sometimes for guidance, sometimes for inspiration, thrilled with this mare, the solitude of the trail, the beauty of the river, the new foliage. As I suspected from our first meeting, she was great fun to talk to and kid with, quick to catch any little bit of humor and turn it back with interest, an easily provoked laugh, articulate. A couple times we got to laughing and giggling so hard over something that we had to stop and settle down.

"You clown! How in the world are you ever going to make it as a scientist? You and Roger are a pair! Now damn it, let's straighten up and ride right. Someone might see us." We stopped just before we turned off from the river, dismounted and tied the horses and sat on the bank to enjoy the scenery. In addition to the light heartedness and her easy familiarity, Nancy had a serious side as she told me a little about her family and her childhood. Another child of privilege, to be sure, but with more ups and downs than Susan's life, Nancy's father a speculator, a first fortune lost, some very plain times before he recovered and became successful and retired at an early age to improve his golf game and travel. She told me about meeting with Susan at college their first year, rooming with this painfully shy and private girl, with whom at first she was exasperated and then came to understand, a close relationship developing. Nancy became sort of the liaison between Susan and her fellow students, Nancy's popularity attracting interesting girls into her orbit, Nancy insisting on Susan being part of this clique, teasing her out of her isolation.

"We'd finish studying, Susan such a brain, everything so easy for her, and I'd say, let's get out of here, let's go over to the Slipper--you know, the Silver Slipper, that place on 12th avenue?--and she'd start to make excuses and I had to almost drag her, but usually she went. There was always a gang over there and we'd sit with people I knew, and boys were coming and going and sitting down and even buying a drink for us once in awhile. She didn't really want to drink, but generally she'd get a Tom Collins or something like that and nurse it along forever. Two drinks, maybe, never beer. Can you see her drinking a beer?"

"Actually, I have."

"OK. Maybe I had an effect after all. Anyway, she is so pretty, boys would sit down and talk to her and ask her to dance and she'd just smile and be polite and answer only what she had to and they'd try awhile and give it up. That seemed to suit her. I'd tell her for heaven's sake, loosen up, have some fun, talk to these boys, they don't bite, and you might like one or two of them, but she didn't seem interested. Then there would be that talk that maybe she liked girls better than boys, and I'd have to really unload and put an end to it. But it didn't bother Susan. I know she was aware of it. She used to say that she'd know the right boy some day when he came along, and I'd say fine but you're going to have an awfully narrow field to pick from at this rate.

"She had a straight 4.0 grade average all the way through last year, did you know that?" No, I didn't. "Anyway, at the end of the first year, she said she was sorry but living in the dorm just didn't suit her, and she thought she'd be happier at home. I spent a lot of time over there on weekends until I got married. She was maid of honor at my wedding, the type you'd see in that job and say there's the next bride out of this gang, but not Susan. She is such a peach of a person but she won't let people get near her. I could hardly believe it when she called and said she had a friend she wanted me to meet. Unheard of! I asked her about you and she told me only that you were at Corinthian, that she had met you there, that you were very nice and she had been seeing you for months! She was very nervous and excited. I could tell that she wanted my opinion. Of you. An opinion from an expert, you know. I tried but I couldn't get any more out of her, so naturally I told her to come out anytime, and how about Sunday to the kids show, and there you are." I was smiling at the story, so like Susan, but not taking it any further.

"Do you want to know what I told her?" She was looking at me with an odd look, now, smiling but not meaning to, some tension in her voice, getting onto shaky ground here now, I thought. I was interested to know but having mixed feelings, suspecting the

Mitzi

unexpected, not certain I wanted to get into her feelings about me, the sense of a trust being violated disturbing me again.

"Maybe not just yet. I don't think I'm ready for any bad news right now. Hate to spoil a nice afternoon." Now the smile had become genuine as some decision had been made that defused a situation that I thought was getting tricky.

"Good choice. I think I'll let you brood some about it. I'll be interested to hear what you think." She was smirking a little now, being a tease and maybe hoping I'd take the bait. I thought I wouldn't.

"Gettin' on, girl. Boots and saddles, what?' I thought she was reluctant to leave, but nothing was said, just a feeling I had. We got aboard, riding along what must have been the old path, not as wide, and Nancy riding ahead of me and leaving me to my thoughts. Now that we were headed back to the barn, I began to come down to earth, reluctantly accepting that I was not here in innocence, feeling the impropriety that somewhat diminished the pleasure of the ride, rehearsing how I would present this to Susan, determined to dwell on the riding lesson aspect and very anxious to return here someday with Susan which I thought would wipe the slate clean. At least the laughter and the kidding helped make it seem less inappropriate.

We dismounted, led the horses into their stalls, took off the tack and put it away. I closed the stall door and the mare put her head out. I had a feeling of great warmth for this graceful, intelligent animal. I stroked her warm neck, tidied up her forelock and smoothed it down, rubbed the velvet nose and lips with my hand, the great nostrils flared and sniffing at me. She had a long white blaze set starkly down the length of her coal black face. I ran my hand repeatedly down this mark to her soft black nose, looking affectionately at the large dark eyes, reluctant to part company. Lost in formless thought, I finally became aware of Nancy's presence. She was standing just outside the shaft of mote-filled late sunshine coming through the doorway, watching me. In contrast to the light mood on the ride, the atmosphere had become charged. There was an unnatural silence, a suggestion of tension that was palpable. I wondered whether Nancy might be sharing some of my guilt about this questionable tryst we were having.

"Would you like a coke?" she asked, quietly. We walked down to the end of the barn but instead of turning into the office, Nancy walked through the door across the aisle. I followed her into a small apartment, presumably intended for a live-in groom. There was nothing suggesting occupancy. Nancy was fetching a couple cokes out of the refrigerator in the kitchenette. She put them on the counter without opening them, went over to the door and closed it. The moment the latch clicked, I had a momentary suffocating sensation, an indescribable psychic alert, a giddy sense of something immense and uncontrollable about to happen. She turned slightly, took the pin out of her stock and removed it from around her neck and unbuttoned her jacket, to all intents simply cooling off, but these simple acts were performed so slowly, so charged with sensuality that I found my thoughts suspended in a vague anticipation of I knew not what. She turned to me and took the few steps that put her all but against me, and all I could see was a long strip of bare white skin from neck to navel, so white and stark, framed by her black jacket.

She stood there, arms at her side, looking up at me. Not a sign of emotion other than a suggestion of tears, slightly trembling on the lashes, not falling. It was a devastating, irresistible invitation, and I had no thought of declining. To hesitate was not an option. There was nothing to do but succumb and let instinct take what course it would.

I have no wish to particularize the next couple hours. This is not one of the scenes that nowadays I rerun in memory to reconfirm that I have had a good life. It was an afternoon of mindless, reckless abandon with which I have difficulty identifying myself. It was silent, it was intense, it was messy and it was emotionally wasting. There was no question of tenderness, no breathless interludes of reflection, of whispered confidences as one might expect of lovers. It went on and on, each of us insatiable yet without any sense of excess although excessive it was.

After a time, an unspoken truce was reached and we reassembled ourselves into presentable condition, opened the cokes and sat together on the couch, each with private thoughts, mine disturbed, self condemnatory, apprehensive. I was determined not to allow my negativism to offend Nancy and equally determined that there must be no repetition of this encounter. Neither of us wanted to be the first to speak, it seemed, and so we sat and drank the cokes, holding hands, sorting things out. The light was beginning to fail and neither of us chose to turn on a light. Nancy broke the silence.

"What are you thinking about?" "Today." I said. "What about today?" How much I wished that she would not ask. I groped for words that wouldn't hurt, ambiguous words, words, meaningless words, not at all what I felt at the moment, without a clue as to where her mind was, what the intent of this whole encounter had been, anxious to escape and get this day behind me without further pain. "Nancy…you are such an incredible creature, such a…", and here came the tears, slowly, relentlessly, falling this time, Nancy anticipating…was it my tone?…or her guilt possibly…whatever it was, she seemed to anticipate the negative to come, the deadly 'but' that I was approaching, knowing that this was not a beginning but an end and that I was about to tell her so. And finally I did in as gentle and oblique a way as I could, the whole garnished with every tender sentiment except the one she sought, it appeared. There was no note I could strike that softened her disappointment, her despair. She had risked a great deal this afternoon, and she now was dealing with the humiliation of having thrown herself at me to no purpose.

She told me she felt sick, that she felt like a traitor, that she could never face Susan again. She sobbed and I clung to her and tried to console her. I didn't even have to offer an explanation. She knew my apologies and articulated them for me, taking all the blame herself, and there was nothing much to add by the time she finally began to regain her composure. I felt rotten, disgusted, unnecessary. I was equally responsible for the mess we had made and I told her so but she wouldn't hear of it. Well. She was going to flagellate herself no matter what I pleaded, so I let her get through it and eventually, nearly dark now, mercifully, there was a period of quiet, and we got up. I embraced her again for a long time and told her that this day had never happened. It didn't seem to register for a time and her face lay quietly on my chest. Then she seemed to understand, and looked up at me. I repeated what I had said. "I think that's best. I see no reason for this day ever to be known other than to us."

"All right...." Then, "Are you going to marry Susan?" Damn, damn, here we go.

"I've thought about it.... that's all. I'm very fond of her...I just don't know. Maybe. I just don't know. Nothing has been said, if that's what you mean."

"Peter! You mustn't! You mustn't, Peter. Don't you see? You would be making a terrible mistake. You are so different from Susan. I know Susan so much better than you and I love her as friend, and I respect her for all the good things that she is and that she represents, but she is not the mate for you, Peter, trust me. She will never respond to you in a way that will satisfy you, you must believe I know what I'm talking about, especially now. I'm not pleading my own case, Peter. In spite of this unbelievable... collision we've just had. I was right about you. I knew it when you first came to visit and I thought to myself what is he doing with Susan, of all people. Oh, God, what a mess I am. But I knew it and I'm right." She was looking up at me with an expression that would melt the firmest determination. Don't do this to me, Nancy.

"Peter, please listen to me. I love Susan. She is like a sister to me, in spite of how different we are in many regards. She will make someone a wonderful wife, Peter, but not you. Susan is bright, she is stable and dependable and pretty and incredibly loyal, but Peter, Peter, where is the spark? Where is the life, the laughs, the fun, the excitement? I can't accept that you are unaware of who you are and what makes you tick. When you think of carefree, does this suggest Susan? She is deliberate, traditional, inflexible, and these are traits I admire in her and sometimes envy but they are not you, Peter, don't you understand?" I sat silent. The doubts all this raised were unwelcome but they were no strangers to me. I had become integrated into the Grafton and Baxter complex as the prospective husband of the heiress, the protégé of both those men who were now my friends as well as mentors, who were depending on me to represent their interests in my generation, a huge responsibility that I had assumed I would discharge somehow, in some role, almost certainly as Susan's husband. I had gradually persuaded myself that in spite of all my misgivings, so frequently revisited as to be ritualized, that on balance, this was the best arrangement I would ever encounter, and that my best course was to just do it. Now, with all my procrastination, what should probably have become an engagement to marry was facing a serious challenge. Nancy, scarcely more than a brief erotic daydream a few weeks ago, had become a persuasive contender, too authentic to be dismissed.

"I know you don't want to hear this, Peter, but I'm going to tell you anyway because I have been there, Peter, and I know what you're thinking. When I was going with Roger, people who were close to me kept telling me not to get serious, that he was wrong for me on any number of accounts, but I wasn't in the least bit interested in advice because I had decided that living with Roger would be such fun. Everybody loved him. He was the most amusing person I have ever known, always cheerful, never a cross word, loyal to his friends, ready for anything. He was the first one to be invited to anything we did, and the last one to go. He turned the most ordinary party into a howl. It was true that he drank a lot, but he never seemed drunk. He just got funnier and more lovable and the next morning he was right there for whatever else was going on. I adored him. I was flattered that he seemed to have chosen me as the girl her preferred, even though he never really courted me. I courted him. I simply decided I wanted him, the way I might have wanted a toy when I was little. I thought how marvelous it would be to go through life with such a lighthearted, lovable dear. So I more or less seduced him and told him we should get married and because Roger hated to disappoint anyone, he agreed after some very comic scenes. I was so angry at those friends of mine that tried to take me aside and tell me I was crazy. I had some doubts, sure, but the more I heard that I shouldn't, the more I wanted to get married. And we did.

It was great fun for a time, a very short time, and then reality set in and I knew I had made a terrible mistake. Roger was like a wildflower, charming and perfect in its natural environment but almost impossible to transplant. Roger's natural environment was our whole crowd. He was never intended to be private property, and I had snatched him out of this environment and thought I could have the enjoyment of him all to myself. He wilted and the pain I felt at having spoiled him still bothers me. He did the only thing he knew how to do to protest his captivity. He took out his frustration by drinking to the point where he was no longer fun even with our friends and I knew I was being blamed for it. Of course, he was no longer fun for me either, and I was furious with myself for having been so selfish. I did the only decent thing left to do and that was to divorce him, put him back in the wild, but it didn't take. He went from a wonderful guy who drank too much, to a drunk who was a no longer fun to be with, and it all but broke my heart." There was no doubting the pained sincerity of this confession. There were depths here, depths I had only suspected, a sensitivity she was reluctant to show, the humor a cover for her as with so many amusing people, people awash in delicate emotions.

"You're going to say that falling for you is a rebound thing. I promise you, Peter, it's not. I had gotten over everything about Roger except the guilt when I met you. And it had nothing to do with either trying to save Susan from a mismatch or gratifying my ego by showing that I could steal her boyfriend. When you first came out here, I had absolutely no intention of getting involved with anyone for a long time. The school was taking my mind off things and giving me a purpose, Roger was long behind me except for my worry about his safety, I had learned a lesson and I was taking time out to grow up and do it right. And then out of the blue, you. And of all people to introduce us, Susan.

"There was something magical, some totally spontaneous attraction that I felt between the two of us, and I know for a fact, no matter what you say, that you felt something too. I sincerely believe that when things are just right for two people, that they know it right away. With Roger it was a matter of gradually imagining myself winning him to me. With you, I had nothing to say about it. It just happened as though it were supposed to happen. I hope that doesn't sound as though I'm trying to be dramatic or making something up that I want to believe. A feeling like that just happens and can't be ignored, and you know it must mean something special because it's never happened to you before. I just know you must have felt some of that! It wasn't just some wild idea I dreamed up. I'm not lonely. I have plenty of interesting things to keep me busy, but I couldn't ignore this. It kept nagging at me and nagging at me until I knew I had to do something about it. OK. I deceived you. Or tried to. I knew Susan was out of town this weekend. I had plenty of time to think about it before I called you. I knew it was being unfair to Susan and yet I did it." I interrupted her, uncomfortable that she was taking all this on herself.

"I made a big mistake by coming out here today, Nancy. It's not your fault. I'm not naïve. I came out here with an idea that there might be some fireworks. You're right about my feeling that there was something between us that first day. I thought about it all the way home and decided that it was something that I shouldn't permit, that I should put it out of my mind, that it was disruptive and finally, that it was unworthy of me. If that sounds like I'm posturing, I'm not. I really think about things like honor and daydreaming about you when I was that close to Susan seemed dishonorable, and I didn't like the feeling. You're very exciting, Nancy, you have a tremendous appeal for me and I probably shouldn't say so, but you don't give away much to Susan. There is no doubt you could get to be habit, and I can't let that happen. I'm not even sure it would be a good idea for us even to be friends. I'm not sure I could be around you without getting in over my head. I can't risk anything like that now, Nancy.

"Oh, Peter, what are you so afraid of? Think, Peter, think! You're the kind of person who would marry forever, no matter what. Have things gone farther than I think? Do you really want to marry Susan or are you just too decent to disappoint her? She very much wants you to be hers, you know. Or do you know? It's true. I know Susan. I have never seen her like she was that day. She wants you, Peter, she wants you very much. Do you know that?" She was willing to wait to hear my answer, and I was in no hurry to agree.

"Well...not really. I think she is very fond of me, but as you know, Susan is hard to read. As far as marrying is concerned, I admit that there are differences between us and I've given them a lot of thought. If we do get together, you're right about it not being a perfect match, but what match is? All the good things you

said about Susan are just the reasons I'm attracted to her. I've
known a lot of girls and I've never met anyone who so nearly had
everything I think is important. I guess I should be flattered that
you think I might marry Susan just not to disappoint her, if you're
right about her wanting me. I don't think I'm particularly noble. I
mean I wouldn't marry Susan because I feel sorry for her. On the
other hand, I just haven't felt a strong urge to go beyond where
we are right now. I don't want to go into it, but I have the feeling
of a lot of pressure from a couple sources. Not that I'm being
pushed into anything. I mean, I think I'm still calling the shots
and I'm not going to be bullied into marrying Susan, but everything seems to point to it as being the best for all parties. I do
have a gut feeling that she would be good for me and probably
that I could be good for her. I know that sounds pretty lame, but
that's about where things stand right now." I felt I had set out a
shamefully weak case to explain my ambivalence, feeling very
uncomfortable to have these tentative feelings exposed to such a
partisan audience.

"Peter. Do you love Susan? Are you in love with her?" Did I
have to answer?

"Come on, Nancy. That's not something that can be answered just like that. Give me a break."

"Do you love her, Peter? I don't think that's an unreasonable
question. Do you love her or not?" I squirmed. "You realize that
you should be able to answer that without a doubt, don't you?"

"Not necessarily. I mean, come on. There are so many kinds
of love."

"Oh no, you don't. You know what kind of love I mean. You
knew it an hour ago, without any coaxing." She had me there. Of
course I knew exactly what she meant.

"Look. I said some things to you this afternoon. Things I
shouldn't have said. Don't misunderstand. I meant them. I really
did, and I wouldn't take them back if I could. But I shouldn't
have said them. OK. Of course I should have said them. Oh,
Nancy, damn it! I'm making a mess of this. Yes, I meant all those
things, and now we both know it and we have to live with it.
Look, I don't expect anything like this afternoon to happen to me
again the rest of my life. I mean that. Even more important to un-

derstand is that I wouldn't look forward to such a repetition. I couldn't live like that. That sort of experience is way beyond my idea of plain sanity. Knowing that without intending it I could get to where we were is scary. I don't want that kind of responsibility. I have no desire to find out where that might lead. Do you understand what I'm saying?" Her head was down and it was only after a time that I saw the tiny nod. I held her closely for a long time, the aisle dark, secret, silent except for the felt presence and soft sounds of the horses.

"I don't know where we're going to end up, Peter, so I want to tell you something that I'll probably never have the nerve to tell you again. I absolutely adore you, Peter, you're the one I've dreamed of and finally decided that I would never meet. But we have met, and I know now that you exist, the one I've been waiting for, and what can I do now but plead my case and hope you will realize that this is terribly important to both of us? Peter, I ask you to please take time and think about me and what we can be together. I know you feel what we share. I'm yours if you want me, Peter. You may think I'm a nut and that I'll forget all about this by morning, but I won't. This isn't a whim, Peter. I'm deadly serious. I'll keep our secret, but don't forget me, Peter." She drove me home in silence.

13

I could think of very little else that next week. I gave a great deal of thought to what that afternoon implied for the future, what the message was, if there was a message, and how to interpret it. Nancy had touched a number of nerves that I realized I was sensitive about. If this had just been a roll in the hay for the fun of it, it would have bothered me some, but it wouldn't have possessed me as the memory of that afternoon did. I could see her face and hear her voice and I found myself fantasizing about her and what life would be like with her and I had to admit there wasn't much lacking. On the other hand, I felt I had been carried to the very limits of my emotional response to physical love, and had found it almost intimidating. Just how important to me was it that my wife be that passionate? How much less than that would be acceptable? She was smart, attractive, and so easy and so much plain fun to be with. I realized again how much I missed laughter. In the end, the defining argument against further consideration of Nancy was the utter impossibility of letting the Graftons and Dr. Baxter down. It would have been such an indictment of my constancy and I simply couldn't face the prospect of being thought fickle and unreliable. Besides, living with and dealing with Nancy's volcanic love making while great in daydreams, in practical fact seemed unrealistic. And so I left it until Susan came home.

I called her and she drove over after class that day and we drove to the park and just sat and talked. My, did she look good to me, and I made sure that she knew it and believed it. It was like a breath of fresh air to be with her again, almost as though there were a healing element to her presence for the contagion I had been exposed to. Silly, isn't it? But it was as real as Susan, and I felt that my decision had been made for me and that Susan was my destiny. We talked until it got dark and then went to a restaurant in the neighborhood where she called home and told them we were eating there and she'd be home later. She told me all about her trip and the wedding and the parties and so on. I figured that if I kept the conversation focused on her trip, my own weekend would not come up, and it didn't. I have no idea what we ate and couldn't have told you an hour later, it was so nice to have Susan home.

We slipped back into the same pattern that my obligations required, Saturday afternoons with Susan, usually at the lake, Sunday mornings at the Grafton's. Dr. Grafton had bought a new canoe, I suspect at Susan's request, this one chained to a foundation pillar under the cottage, a handsome vessel compared with the beaters at the boathouse. There was always a lovely lunch, wine, conversation, a paddle on the lake, home to play the gig, then Sunday for breakfast. Dr. Grafton and I usually walked together after breakfast or played some pool, but at some point sat somewhere and talked. I enjoyed his opinions and he seemed interested in mine. He had grown enormously in my estimation and of course it was flattering to have a man of his age and position treat me as an equal. Susan continued to try to turn me into a tennis player, nearly a thankless task although inescapably, I slowly improved by dint of sheer effort, not talent. With warmer weather, the cover came off the pool and now after our tennis, we changed and swam and lay in the sun and talked. There was no question that I had been selected by this family for their daughter, and that it was now up to me to make a move. I had come to a position where there simply was no other course of action that was open and yet I continued to procrastinate. It gnawed at me, mercilessly, that knowledge that in fact I did not feel 'in love'. Nancy had known perfectly well that I wasn't in love with Susan and had forced me to admit it to myself. I was constantly aware that I was on the verge of asking a girl to marry me with whom I was not in love.

Perhaps a week or two after this, sometime early in May, I was at the Grafton's on Sunday and Susan and I had had a couple sets of tennis and I had changed into swim trunks and was sitting on a beach towel on the grass, waiting for Susan. There were a couple of changing rooms in the building where all the pool and tennis supplies were kept. Susan's modesty was legendary and her taste in swim suits tended toward the Mother Hubbard variety, voluminous and frilly enough to effectively defeat any attempt at a critical appraisal of what was underneath. I had almost despaired of her coming out at all when the door opened. I looked up and here came toward me an unbelievable sight, a statuesque, voluptuous, curvaceous Susan clad in a light blue, skin tight one piece suit of elastic material that left no question unanswered. Completely nonplused I gaped, and she suddenly flushed and stopped.

"Peter! What are you staring at?" Something in my face must have answered for me, and she said in embarrassment, "Oh...You're awful!" and ran and dived into the pool. I dived in myself and in a few strokes caught her standing in shoulder high water. I was so excited at seeing this transformation and so anxious to complement her that I came up with the sort of remark that a guy would say even to a girl he had never met, just as humorous flattery.

"I think I'm in love. Will you marry me?" I said it in a tone I thought would be received as comedy, but it was very evident that Susan was not taking it as humor. She stared at me with a look I had never seen before. I was crushed as I realized my stupid gaffe. There was only one decent thing to do, and I took the plunge and did it. I repeated my proposal, entirely seriously. The silence that ensued as we stared at one another lasted an eternity, and then Susan's now trembling face, on the brink of dissolving, gave me a tiny smile and she fell into my arms. As I held her, so many things came to me. This painfully modest girl must have had to go to a shop, pick through suit after suit, agonizing over her decision to deliberately appear before me, half nude by her standards. She must have decided that her lack of any overt sexuality was the cause of my hesitancy and deliberately set out to force the issue. It had to be. Having declared it once, I was moved to declare it again. "I love you, Susan." I leaned over and kissed her cheek and her nose and the corner of her mouth as a tiny sob sounded and the tears rolled. "I love you, Susan," I whispered again, and the sobbing resumed briefly. When it stopped, she laughed uncertainly, wiped her eyes and smiled at me.

"I'm sure I look perfectly awful..."

"You look beautiful." She laughed and gradually regained something like composure.

"Susan...what I said about marriage. Would you like to get married some time? I mean, to me?" She visibly held her breath but never changed her contented half smile as she slowly nodded. I simply held her tight while the enormity of what had just happened consumed us. "I'm so happy, babe. I have no idea why in the world it took me so long to get around to this." Surely that was nowhere near the truth, but having at last crossed the bridge I felt I had to do a little apologizing. We stood there in the pool just holding each other until Susan seemed to have relaxed some. Her head came up and we looked at each other. I was uncertain how to proceed from this unplanned event. "Suze. Look, that's about as far as I can go today. I just haven't got anything left. Would it be OK with you if we take a breather and keep this to ourselves until we can figure out when to tell people?"

"Yes, Peter."

"I'm awfully, awfully glad you said yes." She just smiled, closed her eyes and had nothing more to say than I. Quite an afternoon.

We got dressed, I made my good-byes and Susan drove me back to the campus. What a tender goodbye!

I got something to eat and took a long walk alone. So much had happened and so quickly that I wanted badly to get it all sorted out before I went to bed. I went over and over my stupidly clumsy proposal. God, what a jerk! It had taken this painful scene to make me finally recognize that for all the composure she radiated, Susan was much more fragile than I had ever guessed, and my sudden awareness of this fragility was what had melted me. How many times must I have said or done things that were painful for her? The jazz joint. The afternoon at Delaney's. Painful to reflect on now. What forbearance she had shown, and no other explanation for the forbearance than a desire to please me. I had a lot to make up for. I simply mustn't let this girl down, she was too precious.

We saw each other every afternoon that week, Susan driving over after her last class and the two of us generally walking on the campus now, over by the athletic fields where we could have some privacy. Susan had come to terms with the swimsuit business to where I could tell her that she had genuinely looked particularly attractive and that I hoped very much that the dumb response she had gotten the first time wouldn't keep her from wearing it in the future. She smiled and made evasive replies, but she never wore it again. We agreed to tell her parents on Sunday, even if we were together with them on Saturday at the lake.

After breakfast as agreed, a visibly nervous Susan lured her mother away on some pretext and Dr. Grafton and I were left alone. We sat at the breakfast table for a time over coffee, talking about baseball. Having no very graceful entry into the subject in mind, I asked if I could talk to him for a few minutes in the library. As casual as I thought the suggestion it was very apparent that Dr. Grafton knew perfectly well that this was the moment. With uncharacteristic formality, having possibly rehearsed his response to the prospect that every father knows must come some day, we went into the library and took our usual seats. By now, he must have come to terms with the idea he was certain I was about to broach, and he smiled and said, "Does this by any chance have something to do with Susan?" I suppose it was written all over my face.

"Yes, sir, it does. You see…well, last weekend it came to me that Susan and I were so well suited to each other and …we got to talking and I asked her if she'd like to get married and she said she would. It had all happened so sort of unexpectedly that we thought we ought not to say anything until now. Of course everything would depend upon your and Mrs. Grafton's approval and that's what I wanted to talk to you about."

"Peter, I am very happy to give you my personal good wishes and approval, and I feel sure I speak for my wife as well. This doesn't come as a great surprise, you must realize. We have gotten to know you, and have watched the two of you together, and I think you are very well suited, not only to each other, but to Emily and me. I am confident that it will be a very successful match and one that gives me a great deal of pleasure. I think we ought to tell my wife very shortly but before we do, let me mention a few things that I think we should share." I sat back down.

"Susan is the apple of my eye, as you probably have noticed. She is very dear to me and I am very concerned for her happiness. Susan is a very complex girl, perhaps much more so than you realize, although that may not give you enough credit. I have a good bit of respect for what appears to me to be your appreciation of what I find best in Susan. As far as character is concerned, I don't have to point out to you that she is exemplary." He paused and reflected for a bit before resuming. "Susan's mother has been a very devoted mother. Possibly too devoted, although I would not want that repeated. She has some deeply imbedded ideas about certain things that she has gone to pains to inculcate in Susan, ideas that I have been responsible for creating, unfortunately. And in which effort she has been successful, as far as I can tell. Let me draw a curtain of confidence over what comes next, if you will accept that?" I nodded.

"As a young man, I had freedom, and I had money. College and medical school were easy for me, and I seemed always to have time for romance. I led a very carefree bachelor's life. I think you understand my meaning. There came a time when it was appropriate for me to marry and settle down, so shortly after I had begun my residency training in pathology, I set about selecting a mate who would be more acceptable to my mother than the young ladies I had previously enjoyed. Emily and I had met on many occasions, our two families had a number of interests in common and it came to be recognized that this would be a good match. Emily and I had never been sweethearts, but that didn't deter either of us. I had had my fling, as it was thought of in those days, and now it was time to settle down to respectability.

"Emily came from a rather strict family and had been brought up is an atmosphere of the utmost propriety. She was nevertheless a charming girl, pretty, intelligent, cultured if somewhat severe with herself. It was a match that occurred so naturally that it was almost as though it been prearranged. In a sense, it had been prearranged though we both would have denied it. The wealth that we both had permitted us to play far more than is good for people, in my opinion. For Emily, this took the form of clubs and attending cultural events and entertaining. There were always people for dinner, it seemed, parties every weekend, opera, theater, concerts. My training involved regular hours, so I was able to participate in all this socializing and was expected to. The problem was that much of it bored me to distraction. I enjoy cocktails and I enjoy dining but I have no interest in cocktail parties or dinner parties. Regardless of these preferences, it was my duty to my wife and our friends to be the host at these events.

"In our hospital, the pathology department and the laboratory were right next to each other so that I was often in or through the laboratory and knew its people as well as our own. There was a young lady employed there who came to attract me. She was lively, amusing, unconventional and not the least intimidated by my name or my position. I began to make it a point to have something to check in the lab and she was always willing to stop and flirt. She was the type of girl that I had left behind and now realized that I missed very much. From a simple sense of my position and the danger of censure from my chief, I kept the attraction at arm's length until a chance--I choose to think of it as chance--encounter outside the hospital made it possible to arrange to see each other privately. After a time, this liaison was brought to my wife's attention and a very grave crisis in our marriage followed. Divorce was out of the question in our circle and in those times, the disgrace simply unacceptable, so we patched it up over time. Susan was born a year later. We were both very happy to have this new interest and responsibility in our lives but Emily decided that we would have no more children. What with my transgression and Susan's arrival, our style of living changed dramatically and we stopped almost all the socializing and kept only a small circle of close friends, among them the Morrisons, whom you have heard about in connection with their son, Brad.

"Emily had very determined ideas about how Susan should be raised. I did too, and we were poles apart as you might guess, but I had lost much of my credit, you see, and felt I must yield to the superior moral force. Susan attended private schools all her life. All girls, of course. The few friends that we remained close to had several boys among them, so that Susan grew up knowing more than one boy and playing with them on occasion, but Brad

Morrison was the only boy permitted any regular association. When Susan last summer proposed taking a course at Corinthian, you would have thought the earth was coming to an end. Emily was firmly opposed and I believe would have preferred that Susan meet no other boy until she and Brad had married. I have to give most of the credit to Charlie Baxter here. He had gotten after me pretty hard about Susan when he found out what a short leash she was on and he insisted that I make a stand. To be sure, I should have long before, but I have never gotten completely over my guilt. I was in a way sacrificing Susan's proper development to my own absolution. So I insisted that Susan be permitted to go to Corinthian, and to my surprise, Emily yielded and the rest you know, including Susan's long overdue break with Brad. I think in retrospect that you can take some credit there."

We sat for a time. I could imagine what was being replayed in Dr. Grafton's mind. How different this family now appeared to me, what undercurrents I hadn't picked up on but that were now to be part of my life and responsibility. While I had guessed at much of the sheltering in Susan's background, I had had no idea of the depth of the deliberately orchestrated constraints that she had grown up with. What image of men in general had her mother instilled in her daughter? I had to consider once again the prospect that her ability or willingness to respond to love might have been so damaged as to be irrecoverable. The slinky swimsuit argued against this, but on the other hand, she had been unable to carry it off. I was dismayed to find how little influence her father had had in her life, and I wondered if she had been told about his fall from grace. And was I to be the next Walter Grafton caught in an infidelity brought about by her frigidity, a strict wife dominating the emotional life of our children? What I figured should have been a warm and happy conversation had now taken on some worrisome overtones. Was this uncertainty ever going to end? I was beginning to have my doubts.

"I wish I could tell you more about Susan. So much of her is hidden to me...likely hidden to you and her mother as well. She finds it very difficult...impossible is closer...to reveal intimate feelings. To me, to her mother, to anyone. I know she feels them, I have seen too much evidence of that to doubt it, but she can't seem to let those feelings out. Whether she will ever overcome that, I can't say, but you should know, if you presently have doubts, that she is a very feeling, very emotional girl in my opinion. She just can't bring herself to show it. She has protected her own privacy all her life and I'm not sure if anyone will breach it. I hope you will make allowances for that. She is very sensitive, as you must know, very perceptive, very intuitive. If you were unfortunate enough to make the mistake I made and have it discovered, I don't think Susan would ever say a word, but she would be devastated. I believe her loyalty to you will be absolute and eternal, she has that way about her. And that loyalty with her sensitivity makes her terribly vulnerable. Beyond any other wish I have for her, Peter, is that you not let her down. She will forgive you anything, but you would never forgive yourself."

I was shocked to hear his voice slightly break over these last remarks. His eyes had reddened and the sight almost broke my own composure. Susan was her father's daughter...her father's daughter. What a pity he had not more to do with her rearing. I tried to imagine the burden he has been carrying, the knowledge of what his philandering had cost him and cost Susan. There was nothing for me to say until the mood changed, and I sat and reflected on all this. When it seemed appropriate, I attempted an answer.

"I want to thank you for telling me all this. I don't imagine that was easy and I appreciate your thoughtfulness. There's not much I can say that will compare with just doing the right things, so if you don't mind, I'm not going to promise a lot of meaningless things. I've thought a great deal about Susan and what makes her tick. A lot of what you just told me I've figured out, I think. There have been a number of times when I wondered what was behind such and such a response and gradually I have come to the same conclusions you have. I've made a couple dumb mistakes with Susan but I learned something from them. She's an extra special girl and I'm going to do everything I can to make her happy. And I think I can. I don't think Susan is capable of complaining, so I'm going to have to keep my wits about me and learn to read whatever signals I can. If you ever see any signs that concern you, please tell me. I wouldn't consider that interference. I want to succeed with Susan, whatever it takes." He expressed his gratitude and suggested that we go out and find his wife and tell her the news.

As it turned out, that wasn't necessary. When we came back into the family room, Susan was sitting bolt upright, wreathed in smiles, flushed. Mrs. Grafton immediately got up and came quickly to me, arms outstretched for our first ever hug, tears in her eyes. Well, that was something of a surprise and a great relief, both to be so well received and also not to have to break the news. We were roundly congratulated and happiness was expressed liberally and then Dr. Grafton fished out a bottle of champagne from the bar and we had an official toast. It was all very exciting, all of us rather stunned. Eventually Mrs. Grafton got down to practical matters, but both Susan and I agreed that we would be grateful if nothing could be said or done until we had a chance to think about when the wedding would be. Susan, bless her, had the courage and the foresight to speak up and ask her mother if she would consider the notion of a very small, very quiet ceremony. Mrs. Grafton said they had best talk this over later and the rest of the afternoon we were encouraged to tell little anecdotes about our courtship. I left this all to Susan who made it all sound very conventional. We had another bottle of champagne and then a light dinner and Susan drove me home. We sat for the longest time in her car and talked. She was so very happy and I felt much, much better about the botched proposal which now seemed unimportant.

The remainder of this month is something of a jumble in my memory. Scholastically, beyond just getting through the courses on my schedule, there was frantic work on my master's dissertation and studying for finals. Somehow I saw Susan every day with few exceptions, mostly for the contact but also to try to make the decisions that seemed to be necessary. For my part, I would just as soon have put the whole wedding business to one side for a time until my school affairs were behind me, but there were families to consider and they wanted action. Unable to take any time off for a visit home, I was obliged to break the news of our engagement over the phone. My mother was in something of a dither for her, anxious to meet Susan and full of questions even though I had told them enough about Susan to persuade them that it was a serious relationship. It was impractical for them to break away until they came to my graduation so meeting Susan and her family would have to wait until then.

My next Saturday morning with Dr. Baxter was memorable. I told him what had happened, and he wrung my hand and clapped me on the back and acted as though I were his own son getting married. He insisted on all the details of my conversation with Dr. Grafton and nodded sagely at the latter's admission of having not been forceful enough in directing Susan's childhood. I said nothing about the reason for this, of course. I told him that his concern about the choice of genes for my children had been an important consideration in my decision, not just to flatter him but because it was true. To be sure, this was skimming over a lot of material, but I didn't want to air the rest.

He had been in regular contact with Phillips and that they wanted a meeting with me which he recommended we put off until after graduation. I had thought at some length about who would be my best man. I knew Barney seemed like the logical choice. He had come around to being supportive for all his kidding, but I thought the solemnity of the occasion required a more serious choice. It came to me that if he were willing that Dr. Baxter would be a perfect one, so I asked him if he would take the job. I might have offered him the moon. That was the only time I had ever seen him astonished. He seemed to take this as an extraordinary privilege, and in great seriousness told me he would be honored. The rest of that morning he was uncharacteristically subdued and I had to conclude that he was deeply touched by my invitation.

Saturday afternoons with Susan were out now and the Sundays at the Graftons almost our only personal contact. There was constant talk between Susan and her mother about the engagement announcements, where and when the wedding was to take place, the guest list, the parties, bridesmaids, the gowns, the reception…it went on and on, and all Susan and I wanted was to graduate and get married and get an apartment and be alone. Susan represented our wishes as best she could, but things like this are pretty much in the hands of everyone but the bride and groom, it seems, and about all we could do was make our wishes known and then take part in whatever production emerged from the doting mind of the bride's mother. While those too huddled over a notebook and papers and whatnot at a desk, Dr. Grafton and I discreetly withdrew either to the pool table or the library or the grounds and talked. I told him about my having asked Dr. Baxter to stand up for me. He praised it as a wise and generous choice and knew that Charlie had been pleased by the honor. It came out that Dr. Baxter had referred to me in their conversations as being like the son he wished he had had, and certainly there is nothing more flattering that could be said, as far as I was concerned. What with Susan having reported something similar having come from her father, I began to feel something of a prodigy. There were no two other men besides my father whose esteem I more valued and to have this returned was heady stuff.

Susan and I graduated on different days so that I was able to attend her ceremony with the Graftons. In a cap and gown, she looked positively professorial. If that sounds ungenerous, one would have had to see her to appreciate its aptness. With her regal carriage and outward calm, she radiated a dignity that was striking. Had I not known her, I would have been nudging the person next to me and asking who she was. She graduated summa cum laude, no surprise to me. We had a celebratory dinner in a private room at a very fancy restaurant afterwards, a festive evening. I had thought about having my parents come to town a day or so early and show them the town, but my Dad was temporarily minding a farm for a neighbor who had just had a stroke and didn't feel he could stay over more than a night. I explained the situation to the Graftons and it was decided that my parents would pick me up at school and the three of us would drive to the Graftons for a visit, then the graduation, dinner at the Graftons and home the next morning for my folks.

They arrived at my dorm about noon, my mother looking very pretty and trim in something new and summery, Dad looking strange and vaguely uncomfortable in a dress shirt and tie pulled open and the trousers of a new, sober suit the jacket of which hung in the back of the front seat. The truck was spotless and the two of them would have turned eyes at home. We squeezed into the front seat and drove to the Graftons. I had told them in detail about Susan's home, but nothing could have prepared them for the real thing, especially at this time of year with everything leafed out, flowered out, manicured to perfection. We got out and got into our jackets and rang the bell. Susan opened it and we entered as Mrs. Grafton could be seen approaching from deep in the family room, Dr. Grafton behind her. I advanced with my mother and presented her to the Graftons, looking back to locate my father who had stopped and was standing with Susan, towering over her as she extended her hand. He reached out with his own great, sun blasted hand and hers disappeared in it and stayed there as he looked down at her and talked to her softly and earnestly. My father is an impressive man. Craggy, manly good looks, the deeply furrowed, strong neck, the heavy shoulders, the long, thick arms. Susan listened quietly as my father spoke to her in what was clearly more than an introduction. Whatever he said, I never did learn, but the handclasp broke and Susan threw her arms around him and put her face on his chest. We don't kiss cheeks in Tennessee. My father held her closely for a few moments, and then she looked quickly up at him and then us, asked to be excused for a moment and disappeared.

My father, unruffled, now came forward and very gravely held out his hand to Dr. Grafton as I introduced him, then shook Mrs. Grafton's hand with a 'howdy' to each of them. It was even more of a shock to see my father in this room and with these people than I had thought it would be. My father is truly rustic, something I don't think of at home which is the only place I ever see him. Now, trying to put myself in his place, I realized what a strange experience this must be for him. He was not ill at ease, but he was waiting to see what was expected of him, I imagine. There was the usual exchange of questions about the trip, how glad the Graftons were to meet and have them at their home, all the things that well bred people extend to their guests, my mother carrying it off quite naturally and unaffectedly, my father quiet, immobile. Good old Dr. Grafton to the rescue! He started a conversation with my father while I stood by with the now returned Susan and monitored the three women getting acquainted. My mother was very flattering and loving to Susan, made some appropriate remarks about the house and soon the three were laughing and off to more comfortable quarters which ended in a tour of the house while I sought out the two fathers.

I spotted them out on the grounds in back, Dr. Grafton gesturing and no doubt explaining the layout and before long they set off to the garden area. I thought this a good time to let the two of them thrash it out and went with the ladies. My mother was thrilled with the furniture and the art and of course the piano. Knowing that she had taught me, Mrs. Grafton told her how much they enjoyed the playing that I did when visiting and how impressed I had been at the piano. I could see that my mother was inwardly calculating just what such an instrument sounded like and I urged her to sit down and just feel the action and hear the tone. She balked at first but with urging from all three of us, sat down and gingerly played a few chords, then a few phrases, now quietly exclaiming and after a little, playing 'Moonlight Sonata". This never fails. Her training was all classical and it showed. Susan and her mother were in raptures, and however my father was getting on with his host, the Hawkinses had made at least a little splash.

This round of applause and praise was my cue to see how my father was getting on. I found Dr. Grafton standing at the edge of the vegetable garden, my father crumbling a handful of dirt he had picked up, walking along and commenting on the vigorous plants and the neatness of everything. We then proceeded to walk the entire back area, my father asking about certain trees he was unfamiliar with, admiring the stonework in the walls and the greenhouse. We went in and looked over the orchids and the perennials and the dozens of trays of seedlings, my father in his element now, talking with Dr. Grafton about the automatic watering and ventilating systems which seemed to intrigue him and about which Dr. Grafton seemed to have the answers. Pretty soon a clipboard came off the wall and a pencil was handed back and forth between the two men while I wandered about, content to let them puzzle over whatever had so caught their interest. All I wanted was for these two men to appreciate each other's so different qualities, and as this seemed to be getting on well, I wandered out again and returned to the house. My mother was admiring the table setting, the flower arrangement, the silver, the china and Mrs. Grafton was giving her the history of the various pieces. I saw Susan in the next room and made a lunge for her before she could rejoin the ladies, anxious to find out what had so upset her at her meeting my father.

"Oh, Peter. He is the dearest man! What a wonderful, wonderful father you have! He just took my hand as though he had known me all his life and he just talked to me in a way...he said...oh, Peter. Forgive me. I can't repeat what he said or I'll cry again," and she was suddenly somewhat distressed again. "Please don't ask me again. It's just too...I'm very fond of him and that's all I can tell you. Now let's see how everyone is getting on."

The fathers returned, talking a blue streak, and we had a surprisingly gregarious lunch, my father overcoming his reserve and acting completely himself, amusing all of us with anecdotes about Tennessee, and thank God not having offered to say grace. The food was elegant, my mother asking about a particular recipe and somewhat abashed when Mrs. Grafton said she would have to ask the cook, but in general, I thought the folks carried off their introduction to high society particularly well, especially compared with some of my apprehensions. Lunch over, we prepared to leave for my school. My father insisted that we three would go as we came. If Dr. Grafton was stunned by the sight in his front drive of a Chevrolet pickup truck, he carried it off well, and left us to bring the Packard around and follow us.

As cool as I fancied myself, I was charged up with the realization that I was poised to begin my career as an adult. I was actually a little nervous as I strode across the stage for my diploma and inwardly excited at the congratulations, the general atmosphere of latent energy and promise, corny as those things can be made to sound. For my father, who had never even finished high school, it must have been a particular thrill and he looked like a very proud parent. We drove back to the Graftons where we had a grand dinner, so much more congenial an atmosphere than a restaurant. Did I detect that the courses were designed to be recognizable and pose no uncertainty as to how to consume them for the guests? It would have been in character for Mrs. Grafton to do this, not out of snobbishness, but out of consideration for guests whose background had never included an elaborate dinner. Now the talk was all about the wedding, the first time this had been so openly broached, and my mother particularly was involved, the three men helpless to contribute and eventually withdrawing. My father wanted to see that Packard, so we went out to the garage. When a man from Tennessee says he wants to look at a car, he is referring to what's under the hood, and sure enough, after a cursory glance at the elegant interior, my father raised the hood and studied the engine with great care and admiration. There was also an elderly Lincoln touring car about a mile long that was never used but immaculately kept that got the next critical inspection. My father had come into his own.

After some port in the family room with everyone together, my mother, judging my father's restlessness, announced that they had better get some sleep as they had a long drive in the morning. The farewell was very warm on all sides, especially between Susan and my father, I thought, and we piled into the truck and drove off. My parents had only three things to discuss on the way back to school, the opulence of the Grafton estate which they could hardly believe, and the warmth and genuineness of the Graftons themselves, and Susan's beauty and poise. For my part, I was greatly relieved that all had gone so well, in part due to my parent's innate good sense and part due to the Grafton's tact and thoughtfulness. The contrast between the two cultures represented that day was dramatic. One could hardly imagine people more conspicuously different than these two couples, but each had an inherent dignity and decency that bridged the gulf between their lives and backgrounds and fortunes. I was not so fatuous as to visualize a communion between them in the future (there never was), but I was anxious that there be respect and tolerant affection on both sides. As it turned out, there was.

14

While Susan and her mother went about the exhausting work of planning the wedding, Dr. Baxter and I set about getting me employed. My first interview with the head of research at Phillips, Tony DeMarco, was an eye opener for me. Dr. Baxter knew the man well and there was a good bit discussion about people I didn't know before the subject turned to me. Tony was a slick, brusque sort of article, fashionably and expensively suited and tied, carefully manicured, polished nails which gave me gave me a start, never having seen such a thing in a man. Was this guy a swish? He looked more like a prize fighter, and in any event, it was none of my business. Dr. Baxter treated the whole interview as though he were pleading his own case, which in fact he was. He went over my background, my academic record, gave a synopsis of the intense coaching he had given me and what he considered to be the fruit of these hours, explaining the potential of the work for the health and wealth of Phillips and so on. I was convinced that Tony knew most of what was being presented, but out of courtesy let Dr. Baxter go through it largely uninterrupted. He turned to me.

"What do you think about all this, Peter? Do you think your professor has something too hot for us not to turn down?"

"I really can't answer that, Mr. DeMarco…", "Tony," he corrected. "…Yes, sir,…Tony, but it seems to me that if the premise is correct that the potential is just about unlimited. As for the validity of the premise, I have to go along with Dr. Baxter, because he is the only person I know of that has approached it from this angle." Tony turned to Dr. Baxter.

"You think Mr. Hawkins here can deliver the goods? Are you going to keep and eye on him? Am I going to have to hire the two of you? We're talking about a real bundle of dough, here, Charlie. If this baby doesn't fly I'm going to have a lot of fast talking to do. I've grown accustomed to the good life, and I want to keep it that way. I'll tell you very honestly, you aren't the first guy to come in here with something very much like this, and nothing, never, nohow, has ever come of it and as far as most people are concerned, this is pie in the sky." Dr. Baxter started to interrupt, but Tony waved him off. "I know, I know. But I'm telling you, it's not going to be cheap just doing the background to establish the barest possibility that we can go on to just the beginning of the real work. Now, Charlie, let me put it to you this way: If I thought there was a one in a hundred chance of it working, I'd give you the go, but even those are awfully long odds and it's my neck if you fall on your face."

"And if I'm right, you'll be rich beyond your wildest dreams."

"Hey, come on. I don't sell this stuff, Charlie. I just try to get it manufactured. Surely you don't think I have a pecuniary interest in something like this?" They both smiled.

"I tell you what I'll do, hotshot," turning to me, "out of consideration for this old geezer here, I'll take you on and we'll see if we can work something out. I'd better make it plain, you're not going to start right out saving humanity. There's a lot of learning of just how to work for an outfit like this that you're going to have to get through. I'll introduce you to a couple geniuses--at least that's what they think--that you can try to seduce with your magic, but everything that happens or doesn't happen goes through me. If one of these geniuses tells me that you need some dough and convinces me that we might get a return on it someday, you'll get some dough to work with. If that pans out, we can go on to the next step, but you're going to have to go a step at a time. There's no great rush about this that I'm aware of. I'm not worried about anybody scooping us. Have you any reason to believe anyone else is working along these lines, Charlie?"

"Very likely. Almost certainly. There's no way of being absolutely sure, of course. There's a group in Russia that have something similar in mind, but from what I've heard, they are going at it just differently enough to fail. Also, they don't have anywhere near the funding I think is going to be required."

"Don't talk about funding in those terms, Charlie. Makes me nervous."

"Tony. Please. I know more that you think about the funding your division can command. And admit it or not, you know this is worth attempting. Now can this young man assume that he has a position here?"

"You twisted my arm. Welcome to Phillips, Peter, I have no doubt it's going to be a profitable association. I'm going to introduce you to a few people and then we can work out the rest of the details when we come back here." It was their choice that I come in for orientation on a schedule to be determined by them, compensation to be allowed on an hourly basis, but that I would not be salaried until after our honeymoon. Dr. Baxter had engineered this deal to allow us more time together and to keep me solvent. And that's the way it all started.

Corinthian had been persuaded to let me stay in my room a few extra days until I could locate an apartment in town. That wasn't as easy as I had thought. Whatever quarters I decided on would be the home to which I took Susan. I was at the Graftons the day after graduation and I brought it up to Susan, feeling that we should both do the picking. Dr. Grafton got wind of it and after lunch he asked me to sit with him in the library for a chat. This chat marked the beginning of my formal association with the Grafton wealth, as it turned out. I had made it very plain to Susan that I wanted us to be as independent as we could of her family's support, and in my naiveté, I genuinely felt that with my salary at Phillips, that we could make it. Dr. Grafton disabused me of that notion in the space of about an hour.

"Peter, let's talk about money for a moment. Now that you are going to be a member of the family, there are a number of things in that regard that you should know about. Before I say anything else, let me make it plain that I heartily support your intention to be your own man in matters of money. That is commendable and I approve of the sentiment, but let me point out the impracticality of certain aspects of this spirit. Money means different things to different people. You are aware that we have considerable wealth, enough to permit me to give rather large sums of it away to deserving causes and people. In time, you will learn something of the philosophy of my philanthropy but for the moment I will only tell you that nothing I give is in the nature of welfare. The gifts our foundation bestows are intended to be what might be called efforts at facilitation. In other words, the funds are awarded where they will permit a task or a goal to be reached in a more timely fashion so as to minimize wasted time, wasted effort, wasted capital. Let's take as an example an inventor who is talented and important, but who is handicapped by lack of money and who is squandering his time raising the needed capital for his true vocation, inventing. A modest leg up for such a man may result in great things. I hate to see talent wasted struggling for adequate funding. You, to take a very specific example, are an inventor of sorts, at least that is what your work can be considered. I don't want you to be preoccupied with nit-picking. I want you to be able to expand and fully utilize your talents without the drudgery and distraction of balancing a checkbook in an effort to prove your manhood, your ability to bring a bison to the cave."

"Susan's grandmother established a trust for her when she was born. Her grandmother had a very substantial estate and much of it went to Susan's trust. She has told me that you know nothing of it, and I think that was proper, but things are changed now. I haven't the least thought that you would abuse the privilege that this wealth gives you. On the contrary, I suspect Susan and I will have to urge you to take advantage of what I am anxious for you to employ in a way that will make life sweet for both of you and allow you to direct your talents without constraint.

"Respecting your intentions, I nevertheless urge you and Susan to pick an apartment, not with an eye to economy nor with an eye to extravagance, but of a size and quality that reflects your alliance with this family and yet is not ostentatious. An apartment that you could afford on your own salary would impress no one, Peter. Unfortunately for your ideals, knowing that you were married to Susan, it would be considered as a pose. You will gradually get used to wealth, Peter. Properly administered and expended, it is nothing to be ashamed of. It has ruined a great many people, but I have no fears for you.

"Now. You're going to need an automobile. That is the type of major expenditure I suggest you make Susan's responsibility. You are not being made a kept man. As for the apartment, as I feel you will want a house before long, you might arrange with the trust officer to make the rental payments so that you will not have to witness Susan writing a check each month. There are all sorts of ways of disguising where the money comes from, and if that is important to you, allow me to advise Susan. I want you to be free to use your mind for your work. And I want you two to have fun. When you can put your work aside, I want you to indulge yourself. Susan has a number of interests that you now share, and I want you both to shake free of professional interests from time to time and expand your horizons. Next, and I hope this doesn't offend you, I would take it as a compliment if you would allow me to send you to my tailor. In no way has your modest wardrobe been unsatisfactory, but you are no longer a student. You will be meeting people and going places regularly now where your appearance will be important. I think I know how you feel about the artificiality of this, but that is the way the world works and you will find that it is easier, at least to begin with, to join them than to fight them. There will be plenty of time to assert your individuality later."

I sat, wide-eyed and chastened. He had shot down the ideals that I had so lovingly and innocently rehearsed and honed. I conceded that he had made a strong case, that I understood, that it would take some time to adjust, but that I trusted his judgment. It is possible that he was not as content with my wardrobe as he had implied since he took me to his tailor the very next day.

My approach to the apartment would have been to look at the classified ads in the Sunday paper. That was not the way it was done. Dr. Grafton called a real estate agent he knew who picked us up and showed us a few places, any one of which so far exceeded my expectations that I was totally indifferent to which one we chose. We settled on one based on it's facing an attractive park, a handsome older building with an impressive foyer, huge, slow, antique elevator, the apartment itself oozing comfort and calm. A spacious living room, a bedroom nearly as large, a small maid's room which had 'study' written all over it. The kitchen appliances bore only a generic resemblance to those at Susan's home, but Susan seemed unconcerned. The bathroom was enormous, an echo chamber of tiled and marble surfaces, the shower the size of the communal shower at school, water closet at the ceiling with a long chain, the pedestal wash basin like something from the Louvre. I had never seen anything remotely resembling this bathroom and was inappropriately amused, I suppose, but I just couldn't help laughing at the thought of living with it. Country boy.

The Graftons predictably came to our rescue in the matter of furniture. They had an attic stuffed with everything imaginable, most of it too antiquated, some downright ugly but a number of pieces of considerable charm and utility. There were some very serviceable carpets, much too fine for an attic, a huge canopied bed and other bedroom furniture, of rather ornate design, but perfect if we could find a mattress of the right size. After we had picked out a number of pieces, Mrs. Grafton volunteered that her intention was to give us furniture for our wedding gift and that she and Susan would go shopping. She ended by having a decorator come in and harmonize the pieces from home with the new purchases, drapes, lamps, just about everything except the things that might be anticipated to come as wedding gifts. Naturally I was appreciative of all the generosity, but it was till awkward for me who has such difficulty in gracefully accepting presents. Almost all of this went on while I was getting acquainted with Phillips, an absorbing and bewildering task.

Susan and I were married in a private ceremony in the Grafton home on the morning of June 26, Susan's twenty-first birthday. Dr. Baxter looked very important in formal clothes, the groom's men the guys in the band and Barney. Susan had only Nancy for her attendant, the first time I had seen Nancy in a gown. She was ravishing, and I had a major rush when we greeted. She gave me a nice smile, noncommittal, a token embrace, all very proper, all very upsetting, especially the electricity I felt momentarily. I was furious with myself that something inside permitted such a thing to happen at my own wedding. The minister was a dorky sort, a Unitarian which seemed to have been an attempt to avoid any show of religiosity. As a result the ceremony was not very traditional, at least as far as the few that I had attended were concerned. But that was just fine with me. All I wanted was to get it over with and get on that plane with Susan. The receiving line was painless, the reception comparatively brief. There were photographs, of course, toasts and hugs and handshakes and on and on, but at last we were allowed to disappear and change and make our farewells.

We took off in a hired car mid afternoon, caught our flight and arrived in Miami for late dinner at the hotel where we were to spend that night. I was starved, Susan could scarcely eat, not so much because of the excitement of the day but for the anticipation of the night to come, I guessed. Poor Susan. She had a little wine, she picked at her meal but had a little dessert. I signed the bill which was arranged by the Graftons and we went up to our room. I cannot believe I have ever felt more compassion for any creature than I did for Susan that evening. I doubt that many girls are as nervous as she, the famous composure, the dignity, the outward confidence nowhere in evidence. She fussed with the clothes that had already been unpacked, rearranging them, taking things from one drawer and putting them in another, checking through her purse, laying out cosmetics in the bathroom. I tried to appear nonchalant and let her putter until it was clear that she needed help. I took her by the hand as she brushed by me once and took her in my arms and held her, feeling her pounding heart again my chest. After a time, I felt the tension in her body subsiding, breathing slower, heart under control.

"Come over here and sit down for a little." She acquiesced and we sat on the sofa and I gathered her to me and stroked her hair and kissed her, softly, gently.

"Susan, I want to ask you to forget everything you have ever heard about wedding nights. I want you to put everything out of your mind except that we two are here together to start a lifetime of knowing and loving each other. We have a lifetime. When and how that lifetime begins is of no importance. What is important is not that it begin today, but that it begin when it seems right. This life is ours to determine and for my part, we will write our own book regardless of whatever other people have written. From this day forward is a blank page, ours to set down what we want and when we want it. I have no thoughts but for your comfort and your happiness. I want you to be you, not what you think I want or expect you to be. I want you to forget every story you have heard at school, every novel that you've read and just be yourself, whatever that is. I'm going to be your husband for our entire lives, so there is no hurry. I want to please you in every way that I can starting this minute and henceforth. Above all, I don't want you apprehensive and upset. You are going to set the pace. You. OK?"

She was quiet now, snuggling for reassurance, and she nodded. We reclined like this for along time, no more intimately than we had on other occasions, until I felt that she had mastered herself. "Tired?" She nodded. "Shall we get a little sleep?" She shrugged instead of the nod I had expected and I inwardly smiled, imagining the thoughts that must have been behind the shrug. Was the image of me as a ravisher not yet dispelled? "Time to shower?" It occurred to me that she might think this an invitation for her to join me but she would just have to take that chance, I guessed. She nodded but didn't move. "You first", I said. Did I detect a single deep breath of relief? I think I did. We got up and kissed and she left the room.

I'm going to pull down the privacy curtain again with no apology for leaving the remainder of this evening untold. I have no patience with people who seem desperate to share what I consider intimacies with others. I still feel that way. I will say that Susan was at first more resigned than hopeful, but kindness, and understanding and sympathy and patience can assuage doubts and fears and sometimes transform resignation to acceptance and acceptance to anticipation and anticipation to desire and pleasure. Something like this took place during the remainder of that long, long night as my bride budded and blossomed and came to full bloom to the inexpressible relief of us both.

15

We spent our honeymoon in the Grafton's cottage in Antigua, a simply decorated modest dwelling on a substantial piece of property fronting on a little sandy
cove, overhung with coconut palms, choked with tropical foliage
and flowering vines, a magical place, quiet other than for the water noises, private, comfortable in a simple style. It was an old
friend to Susan who had visited it all her life, and she was anxious
to show me everything on the island. We had a car, we had bicy-
cles, or we walked, stopping as the mood seized us for a drink,
walking the beach as far as we could and back again. There was
all sorts of skin diving equipment, spears, fishing tackle. We
rented a small sailboat and Susan taught me the rudiments of sailing. We swam and dived and speared fish and had them cooked at
the club, just to say we had done it. We lay in the sun and got
burned and got tanned, we ate like royalty all over the island, we
sat in the shade in front of the house and drank rum drinks and
above all, we used the leisure and solitude to grow closer.

On one memorable occasion, toward the end of our stay,
Susan made a particularly penetrating and uncharacteristic observation that I have remembered ever since, the metaphor so appropriate. We had been snorkeling, admiring the tropical fish, the
coral formations, poking idly at some anemones. One of them had
dozens of slowly waving tentacles sifting through everything that
drifted past, selecting from what drifted by, while an adjacent one
instantly retracted and disappeared into its enclosure when
touched. Susan pointed to them and took out her snorkel to tell
me that the first one was me, the second one, her. We were not in
a situation where anything further could be said, and by the time
we came out of the water, I had decided not to comment, but I

thought about what it implied, how closely she must live with this unwelcome governor that forbade her reaching out, sampling, testing.

It would have been unreasonable of me to expect that after the awakening of her sexuality that Susan would otherwise change perceptibly. This was an acquisition for her but not an epiphany. Our new intimacy did not release any other inhibitions. It was no touchstone to engender a new Susan. Had I thought that it might? Probably. To some extent. I knew better than to really believe that it might, but yes, I had had hopes in spite of knowing how very unlikely it was. She was certainly more relaxed, I will give her that, but this didn't translate into any ability to unbend, to be even a little playful, to laugh. She understood jokes, puns, humorous observations, but they only mildly amused her, and not matter how droll or witty an observation or riposte I might come up with, it was politely received with a pretty smile, but seldom with a laugh, her infrequent laughter soft and almost reluctant. I enjoyed making people laugh. I wanted so to be able to make her laugh. Perhaps I could teach her to laugh.

We returned looking like a young couple who had just come from an idyllic honeymoon, and I believe we both felt it had been just that. There could be no doubt about its success when we greeted Susan's parents before going to our apartment. I don't think I have ever seen Susan more animated and demonstrative. We had a drink and a snack and told them what a wonderful time we had had, both parents beaming. Our happiness was palpable. What a relief this must have been to these two parents, each of whom I felt sure carried a guilt that they were in some way responsible for Susan's emotional barrenness. None of us knew what lay beneath that cool exterior, but now I knew at least partly and they in turn at least suspected that something lay smoldering there that while not a fire, would keep us warm.

Our apartment took on an entirely new aspect now. It was ours and we were alone in it and could be alone as much we chose. I felt a tremendous release when we were in and closed the door. Now I loved the apartment and I pranced around and hugged Susan and pranced around some more, ours, ours, ours. I took off my shoes and jumped up and down on the bed yodeling like Tarzan. Susan laughed so I kept on jumping and acting like a fool. I grabbed her and threw her on the bed and tickled her ribs and she howled with helpless laughter. "What on earth are you doing", she gasped, flushed and panting, holding my hands. "I'm making you laugh. I love to hear you laugh. I'm going to practice making you laugh so I can hear it."

16

The newness of our life as a couple was exciting, perhaps especially for me, new wife, new clothes, new job, new dwelling, new car, new associates. Adaptation to married life was somewhat less bewildering for Susan for whom our style of living was less of a departure from her custom. She was occupied now full time at the Grafton Foundation where she had long since been entrusted with a number of nuts and bolts activities. Now her father was including her in policy matters, grooming her as he had told me to assume increasing responsibility and eventually perhaps heading the organization. Susan had never boiled water, so our kitchen was largely used for toast and coffee and otherwise we dined out. Susan was not exposed to new social contacts, but I had been thrust into a widening pool of associations and our new friends came largely from Phillips. I was a new member along with many others in the lowest echelons of this behemoth, who gravitated for support and comfort to one another. There were cocktail parties to attend in which the men talked of nothing but their work, invitations we declined when it wouldn't give offense as neither of us enjoyed them. Although we felt obligated ourselves to entertain from time to time, we thought of our home as a sanctuary and were reluctant to share it. When it was necessary to return the favor of a dinner, we entertained out. I realized that this insularity that I was gravitating into was unwise in a sense, but other than my commitment to represent Dr. Baxter's thesis, I felt little obligation to conform to the social life expected of the aspirant to higher position and income. Did the security that I had come into with my marriage determine this attitude? I think not. Susan, to be sure had an influence. While capable of being a charming and thoughtful hostess, she was not interested in cultivating new friends, and I found it easy to follow her lead. There were a few, but only a few couples that we found entertaining, and we saw them with some regularity, but we had the reputation of being somewhat distant, aloof. As this was attributed to our known affluence and seemed to be thought a perquisite of the wealthy, it passed not as snobbery but as a privilege of the privileged. We were considered as simply a little different from the rest of our group, not shunned, but not courted. By degrees, we created a style for ourselves that attracted and secured to us those people that we cared for and relieved us of the obligation of enduring those we didn't.

The Unspoken in our lives, at least not spoken of for many months, was parenthood. The subject of children had come up only once in the past, sometime during the time between my proposal and our marriage. Selfishly, perhaps, it had not even occurred to me that Susan would not want children, but I asked her one day if she looked forward to having children. She had assured me that she was anxious to have a family, an unspecified number greater than one, as I recall. As for timing, nothing had been said. Consciously, unconsciously, I'm not sure and it is likely of no matter, I had not even considered contraception. Whether Susan was too modest to inquire or whether she had determined to be guided entirely by me I don't know, but we had taken no precautions to prevent a pregnancy and nearly a year later Susan had not conceived.

Even then, it was not on our own initiative that anything further was said or done. Dr. Grafton one day asked something about our plans for a family and I told him that we were trying but had had no luck. Yes, we had more or less expected that by now Susan would be pregnant but thought we would continue to wait and see. Nothing further was said at the time, but a week or two later, he told me that he thought we ought to consider getting ourselves checked and see if this were genuinely infertility, and if so if something could be done. I told Susan what had been said and asked her how she felt about it. She didn't think anything like that was necessary just now. It had in some ways been fortunate that she had not conceived yet, and she thought waiting a little longer might settle the matter. All this had uncovered the fact that Susan had never been to a gynecologist. Knowing her modesty, I suspected that this might have something to do with her reluctance. We compromised by my volunteering to get checked myself, and I did and it appeared that I was not the problem. From time to time, one of the other young wives would have a baby, there would be showers and christenings and other reminders and I felt I saw some concern developing in Susan, just as I felt some myself. Whether it was a natural increased longing or a result of the frustration I felt at not getting what I wanted, I became increasingly anxious to have a child. Feeling that this was something her father could do with greater authority, I put the matter to Dr. Grafton and he did the selling. An appointment was made with a gynecologist of his choice and Susan went to her first of many such appointments, silent and apprehensive.

She returned home, exhausted and a trifle irritable, reporting that the doctor had found nothing out of the ordinary, and suggested a number of things, all of which we were doing anyway, and more patience. He felt that probably there was nothing to worry about, that it was not at all uncommon to go this long without conceiving, that Susan should get plenty of rest, avoid stress, that we should concentrate our efforts around the time of ovulation, a dozen little tricks that didn't impress either of us as critical, so we went along pretty much as before, waiting, chagrined at every new menstrual period to the point where we found ourselves getting edgy at the approach of each such date. Eventually, it was Dr. Grafton again whom I pressed into service, by which time he had begun to worry along with us on his own. A date was made with another gynecologist who specialized in infertility. Imperceptibly, we were becoming obsessed with having a child. New tests, new advice, more time and nothing changed, and now we were to go to a clinic in Boston, reputed to be the last word in the field.

Dear Susan. She was such a responsible person, and it was difficult for her to accept the notion that such a basic biologic function had so far been denied her. We conferred from time to time with her father, who behind the scenes was checking everything short of witchcraft. In this mood, we packed up all the documents we had accumulated in the several medical offices and went to Boston. This gynecologist was a hot number. I had been around enough scientists to recognize the genuine article when I saw it. He went over all our material, examined Susan, ordered some additional tests that had never been done previously, cutting edge stuff that was not in general use. Tony, an ardent family man, a role I found hard to visualize, had encouraged me to take some time off if we needed it, so we stayed a week. At the end of this time, we sat down for a summing up. We were told that advances were being made every day and that it was most likely that well within the ideal childbearing age, something would turn up and that our hope was not misplaced. This was almost a platitude, though well intended. We had no choice but to accept this and settled in to wait, Susan gracefully, not so gracefully for me.

In contrast to this frustration, my professional life was coming along very nicely. While I still had to report to Tony and justify additional funding, which was annoying to someone like me who hated to ask for favors or even accept them, I had been assigned an immediate superior who was a crackerjack. Perhaps I should have said, "a jim dandy" since that was his name. I wonder at the family that would name a kid something like that, knowing that all his life he would have to smile and go through some no longer humorous acknowledgment of the fitness of the name or whatever. In any event, Jim Dandy was a first rate scientist and we suited each other perfectly. Jim had been very skeptical of the Baxter/Hawkins plan to crack the secrets of productions of certain substances at the molecular level, and my first months of struggling to create some of the most basic techniques necessary to even get started, seemed to confirm his doubts. I felt obliged to share these doubts with Dr. Baxter, but he gave me encouragement, told me we were right and to keep going and keep up a confident front, easier said than done sometimes. At length, we came up with a single but tantalizing success, in itself not significant, but showing that the direction it pointed was promising. Then there were a couple more small successes, and now Jim began to come and talk with me and make suggestions. Gradually, with his increasing help and technical ingenuity, we began to devise advanced explorations that attracted the attention of the head of our division who asked us to make him a secret presentation. Although having no illusions about the economic value of the work if it succeeded, I was slightly intimidated by the secrecy which now came from the top, in anticipation of something economically valuable. Jim brought with him a few of his own guys, and the five of us met with this Dr. Vinson, whom I had never met, all very hush-hush in a small conference room in the lab one Sunday. I made my presentation and Jim then brought him up to date on the mechanics of how to get there, based on the recent encouragement. Dr. Vinson asked Jim's men their opinion regarding time and expenses, then back to me for comments, especially prognostications. I told him that there was still a long way to go but that even though I could not chart the course to a successful conclusion, that we had come on nothing yet to suggest that it was not possible. He had a few more things to ask of Jim's group, then there was a pause for coffee and rolls for the troops while Dr. Vinson left us. We sat around and went over the ground again, checking to see if we should add or emphasize anything.

Dr. Vinson came back and we took our seats again while he asked a couple more questions in a slightly different way that I felt very encouraging. "I'm interested in this project, gentlemen. I don't pretend to be conversant with much of what you have told me, Mr. Hawkins, but it has the ring of plausibility and I think you have presented your case fairly. I don't need to tell you that the implications are staggering if we find a way to realize them. As for your part, Dr. Dandy, it would seem that you have a great deal of work to do and that it will be expensive, is that a fair assumption?" Jim agreed that it was, and Dr. Vinson continued, almost as though discussing it with himself, "I believe I can find the money you will need, probably a good idea to divide it up into pieces and when you finish a piece of work, let me know and if it seems to fill the bill, I'll speak to Tony and you can just keep going through him…but come to me first, you understand and I'll see to it…Dr. Dandy, will you at any point need a separate laboratory, separate personnel? I worry a little about spreading this work out. I wonder if you should have someplace…" Jim interrupted, "Excuse me, Dr. Vinson, I should explain that much of the work will involve techniques that we already have in place and certainly that part we can do just as we do now. For the next phase of the work, I would definitely want a separate lab, and I would like to be able to pick my technicians from our present group and train them."

"Your concerns are related to security?"

"Yes, sir."

"I think we should spend a few minutes going over just how much security is needed here, gentlemen. I feel sure we all realize the value of bringing this to fruition without our work being known of elsewhere. As a new arrival to our company, I feel I should address you personally, Mr. Hawkins, although what I have to say applies equally to each of you gentlemen. I want you to understand that I applaud the selfless motives of the scientist who wants to share what he knows with his colleagues to assist in advancing the frontiers of science, all very understandable and commendable. A necessary stipulation that I must make, however, considering that you are an employee of this company, is that where our commercial interests are concerned, you must be guided by our policies that often require strict secrecy. This project before us is just such a case. Our policy is that important discoveries are handsomely rewarded. You will not labor in obscurity not will you go uncompensated. You must, however, exercise the greatest discretion. It will be next to impossible for something like this not to be anticipated by some other group. If you have any doubts about whether a major scientific advance is being delayed from becoming a boon to humanity, let me put them to rest. There is no faster way in the world for science to advance than in the hands of the economically interested. I make no apology for the money we earn from our patented pharmaceuticals. There are people whose devotion to pure science precludes any economic motivation. We depend upon such people, and you, Mr. Hawkins, are possibly one such, but without capital, hypotheses remain just that. The fastest way to advance the cause you are dedicating yourself to is through enlisting the aid of a company such as us. If this work you propose is doable, it will be done. I want to ensure that it is Phillips that does it. Any questions?" There were none and Dr. Vinson dismissed us.

"May I have a word with you before you leave, Mr. Hawkins?" The rest of the group filed out and at his gesture, I sat.

Mitzi

"I hope you didn't take offense at my suggesting a secrecy that you may find distasteful. I have had dealings with a great many young scientists and I appreciate the idealism I often encounter. At least, I imagine that you are idealistic. Most bright young men your age seem to me to be. Secrecy is probably contrary to your ideas of honesty and decency. In fact, it is quite consistent with such traits. Economic competition is a fact of life, Mr. Hawkins. You have possibly not heard of industrial espionage, a rather grand sounding euphemism for stealing. I won't insult your intelligence by implying that our own company does not send spies, for that is the proper word for them, into competitor's workplaces to steal secrets from them to turn into profit for us. While I deplore such practices, they do exist and all of us have had losses to such activities. This is what creates the need for complete secrecy. I must ask you to be vague but convincing with anyone about your work. This must include even your wife. No doubt she knows already that you are involved in something that might be important. In all likelihood it will come up in her conversations with other wives or friends. You have no idea how exciting it is to some people to pass on such a tidbit. I would suggest that you tell your wife just what I am telling you if you think she is totally trustworthy with sensitive information. Otherwise, I would suggest you tell her that your project has hit a stone wall, will be scrapped or whatever other fib you think will do. Now, this may all be unnecessary. The whole thing may come to nothing, but until it does, we must be very close about it. Dr. Dandy is an old hand at this and you can trust his judgment if you need it. He'll be more strict with you than I am, but I felt it was important that you know that this attitude goes all the way up. Now, just one personal matter. You certainly have made an impression here in such a short time. How is it that you don't have a doctorate? You really should have one, you know."

I replied that I simply had not had the time and what with this project, couldn't see where I could spare the time for independent research and writing.

"You were graduated from Corinthian University, I recollect?"

"Yes, sir."

"If you have no objection, I'd like to talk with those folks. I think we should be able to work something out. It seems to me that you have done quite enough here already to make a dissertation out of, if we can pick out a body of your work that will not tip our hand here. You must face the prospect of being famous, some day, you know, and it just wouldn't do to be Peter Hawkins, B.S.,M.S., would it?"

"I could live with that, I suppose, but I'd hate to embarrass the company." He seemed to like that and he laughed and clapped me on the back, then shook my hand, wished me luck and told me to call on him anytime. I left feeling pretty high and went home to tell Susan about our new cloak and dagger status.

I contacted Dr. Baxter and arranged to meet him the next evening. I felt a little foolish asking him what he thought about the Ph.D., but he took it in stride and said he thought that would not be a problem. He was particularly happy with the idea of having a separate lab and an experienced and loyal staff. "Keep them interested, Peter. If you hit a snag, let's go over the ground immediately. These fellows are ravenous, and we must keep up their interest. Jim is a very capable man; I think you are most fortunate that they have put the two of you together. As for the secrecy, you can't be too careful. Let Jim help you devise a plausible cover that will stand scrutiny and on which you can talk knowledgeably. This sort of thing isn't my natural inclination either, but I take their word for its necessity. How are things with you and Susan?" I told him just fine but that we were a little disappointed in Susan not getting pregnant. He made a face. "Well, there's lots of time yet. Be patient," and we were, I guess.

We got the new lab and the staff and the money, nearly a blank check to start with and came up with some very provocative data. More new equipment, a little more space, a great deal of work and we arrived at a plateau where the basic thesis seemed vindicated and it was largely a matter of a laborious grind to replicate enough volume of material to start the first test to establish the practicality of genuine production. This was largely Jim's field and other than tweaking things, I was at a pause point. With the additional time at my disposal, I completed a thesis that Dr.

Baxter and I had agreed upon, closely related but peripheral enough to our project for Phillips that no inference would likely be drawn that would jeopardize our secrecy. Oddly, the graduation ceremony and the doctorate were anticlimactic. I hardly had the feeling of having earned it, so preoccupied with our project that seemed more like hard work than investigation. A short time later, Dr. Vinson invited Susan and me to a celebratory dinner at his club. He knew Susan's father and was most cordial and attentive to Susan, and had some very flattering things to say about her later.

Work in other words, was fine. And our marriage was fine, the apartment was fine, my in-laws were close friends and we had plenty of money, almost all of it Susan's. As agreed upon, we got around the pain this caused me by signing for just about everything, Susan paying the bills out of her funds. As Susan had no interest in cooking, for which I could hardly blame her, we dined out almost every night, settling on a half dozen restaurants that pleased us, and enjoyed the best food and wine and the quality of service that is extended to regular patrons. I do not deny that it was very pleasant to be warmly greeted by an otherwise haughty maitre d' and promptly shown to the same particularly good table. We attended plays and concerts and went to galleries and occasionally entertained those few friends with whom we cared to socialize. Saturdays in season were usually spent at the lake, swimming, canoeing, Sundays at the Grafton's where I could catch up on the piano, play tennis with Susan, visit with Walter. By any standards, it was an enviable life. We enjoyed the compete freedom that wealth and childlessness conferred on us although the obverse, the feeling of selfishness, of self indulgence made me a little uncomfortable. Susan wanted a child, I believed, not just to satisfy what she knew to be a deep seated desire on my part, but for her own reasons, although I never felt that her disappointment was as keen as mine.

All my life I had sought and thrived on novelty, new interests, new challenges, but now I was at a null of sorts. In spite of a satisfying marriage and a promising career, I was restless, lacking a new challenge, some stimulus to respond to and I saw no prospects of something of this sort in the immediate future. My work was stimulating, fascinating, and I had a good gang of guys around me, bright guys, fun to be with, and the days went very swiftly but the fact was that there was a certain sameness at home, a quiet, stable routine that left me slightly bored, a terrible thing to admit but it was a fact. A child was what I wanted and the diminishing prospects of this ever happening preoccupied me increasingly. Possibly as a result, I also began to reflect on my perception that certain aspects of our personal life were not just what I had hoped they might become in time. I wanted more time at home. Going out nearly every evening was becoming a nuisance. It meant dressing shortly after I got home, getting a cab to take us to dinner. We had wonderful conversations during and after dinner, but by the time we got home, it was time to get to bed. Our best evenings were when Susan arranged a take-out dinner, and we could talk over a drink, have our dinner and have the whole evening to read and talk. I couldn't very well tell Susan to learn to cook, but one can eat only just so many take-out meals. Then I would feel guilty and get down on myself for expecting too much--she brought so many gifts to our marriage and was so generous with them that I was ashamed to think ungrateful thoughts, but the feeling was there that maybe I could change her. I knew better but I was unwilling to admit it. If I could change to the extent of enjoying symphonic and chamber music, why couldn't Susan could learn to enjoy some of the things that I missed? A couple of times I had invited old college pals and their wives over for a drink and was able to some extent to recapture the good times we had shared in school, but this camaraderie and its inbred humor left Susan politely high and dry, and I suspected she didn't especially enjoy such evenings. Basically, I was spoiling for something to break into the pattern of living we had gravitated into, something that later I was to read was known as the 'four year itch', a year early here, but with all the earmarks of the four year variety.

Old habits, old behavior dies hard. Although my work was conducted exclusively with a team of men, there were women on the fringes of our turf and where there were women, there was flirting, innocent in almost all cases, but flirting nevertheless. There was a young lady who always seemed to have an unsolicited smile for me before leaving the room after some routine errand. I was not inattentive to moments like this and when I realized that she had somehow become the exclusive messenger from her department, I found myself anticipating the glance and smiling in return. It got as far as a drink in an out of the way bar after work one day, a shameful performance that left me feeling foolish and guilty and the young lady annoyed and puzzled. The effect was to put me on notice that I was out of step with the cosmos.

Urban living, apartment house living, elevators, doormen, taxis, city noises were not much to my taste now that the novelty had worn off, and I decided that a retreat to the suburbs, a house, a yard, flowers, a garden, a shop to fill my mind and hours with wholesome tasks was what was called for. This represented my attempt to externalize what more sober reflection would have identified as internal. Susan was enthusiastic about the prospect, so we contacted the same realtor, gave her some specifications and inside a month had located an attractive, comparatively modest but beautifully designed and constructed home with over two acres of yard, attractively landscaped, a large garage, woods on three sides, most inviting. We closed the deal and moved in and spent the next month shopping for furniture, a piano, redoing some of the landscaping, buying lawn and garden tools, thoroughly enjoying our new freedom and greater privacy, the near silence, the sweet air. I felt relieved and Susan who was accustomed to even grander isolation pronounced herself contented. And I was busy. Plunging into work around the house and yard, I accomplished all manner of things that satisfied me and enhanced our surroundings. Later that summer we decided to have a tennis court built; we had ample room and in the evenings when we had light, we played singles. On weekends Susan invited friends who enjoyed playing and we had some congenial doubles, topped off with drinks and maybe a barbecue afterward. Susan missed the pool she had grown up with, so the following Spring we put in a pool. There was no question but what we had done the right thing by getting out of town. Susan had an aptitude for gardening and we put in ornamental plants, flower beds, decorative trees. I spaded up a little patch of ground for an herb garden and Susan began to experiment with cooking, nothing grand, but developing a modest repertory of simple but special dishes and a few of the down-home standards that so appealed to me. Now, with the drive involved if we chose to dine out, we often ate at home during the week, a most considerate deference to me. In short, we were becoming typical yuppies, a term unknown at the time. We still attended the theater regularly, went to the ballet all season, attended concerts, took in an occasional movie, went to a few parties, gave them only rarely, and joined a country club. While this provided a certain amount of pleasure, I was unable to persuade myself to invest the time needed to develop a respectable golf game, so that much of being members was lost on me, but Susan enjoyed the pool and the tennis during the week when she was not at the Foundation.

17

It was at the club that Susan for the first time came across Nancy on a regular basis. They had an occasional lunch together and I heard Susan talking on the phone with her from time to time. The friendship, while not having cooled, had been somewhat neglected on both sides, for quite different reasons. Nancy was looking very well, Susan said, and had a new gentleman friend whom she appeared to be fond of. What in heaven's name was my problem? My first emotion at this bit of news, delivered matter of factly by Susan and with obvious pleasure for an old friend's happiness, was jealousy. After my pique subsided, I determined that I should feel relieved to have this loose cannon tethered, but that wasn't what I truly felt. Jealous and ashamed of the jealousy was what I really felt. The two girls saw more of each other now, the boyfriend apparently a fixture, so when Susan reported she had asked them over for drinks one evening, I had stabilized sufficiently to agree that that would be nice.

As the date drew nearer, so did a certain amount of anxiety surface. Given a choice, I would not have had this evening take place. Ever. In spite of the prospect of seeing Nancy again and learning what effect it would have on me, I was abnormally fearful that something would be said that would betray our greater familiarity than could be explained by the only contact that Susan knew of. I fantasized about how to get Nancy aside and pledge her to treat me coolly, not to talk about horses or anything where a slip might be made. I wondered if I dared call her on the phone and arrange all this. I thought as hard as I could about everything we three had talked about at the horse show, resolving to take the initiative on this topic to get any reference to horses out of the way. It was bound to come up. Better to bring it up myself and try to control it than risk it getting out of hand. I was in a funk and feeling very unhappy about this threat to my marital tranquility, but in the end I decided to hell with it, I'd hope for the best.

The day arrived, and I left work early, which was a mistake. I was edgy and worried again, and for some reason felt I would do better at home, but instead I simply I had more time to think about the impending meeting and to dread it. They arrived right on time, which I thought was inconsiderate, and Susan admitted them as I cowardly came to greet them a few seconds later. Susan was exchanging greetings with the man which left Nancy and me to do our own greeting. I had a raging conflict going on as to what it should consist of, considering our presumed only nominal friendship. Nancy solved this by advancing boldly for a hug and a discreet kiss on the cheek, no more than friends would be party to, and actually, not inappropriate for the occasion, although full to bursting with significance for me. As we parted, I glanced quickly at her face and was most relieved to see an expression of cheerful innocence, no 'look', no fire, no nuance, just the pleasant face of my wife's dear friend. The two girls greeted each other affectionately as the guy and I exchanged names and shook hands. I had no idea what name he had given me until it came up in conversation later, after I had settled down and had my wits about me.

We sat out on the screened porch on this balmy evening and after a couple drinks the evening began to take on the aspect of being pleasant, for which chance I would not have given much an hour earlier. The guy's name was Byron Harvey, his calling something to do with insurance and at a level that seemed to permit him ample leisure to be at the club during the day. He was a tall, strapping guy, good looking in a slightly vacuous way, but affable, outgoing, easy to talk with and clearly enamored of Nancy which he made a point of impressing upon us at regular intervals. Developing a modest distaste for the fellow as he droned on made the jealously more tolerable somehow. As for my apprehension about the stables coming up, nothing was ever said. Instead, we talked about mutual friends, coming and past events at the club, news from Willoughby, everything but horses and stables. My work was touched on briefly, and we passed on to the insurance business, about which Byron seemed to have a good bit to say. As a matter of fact, once begun, he went from excess to boring to tedious. The firm was Oswald, Grinnel and Harvey, an outfit I knew of as being pretty heavy hitters. Byron was not shy about announcing that he was a vice president and as the boss's son, both Oswald and Grinnel long dead, had very few responsibilities. I looked at Nancy during this self congratulatory essay. She sat quietly, her face frozen in a benign, tolerant smile that defied analysis. I couldn't believe a person like this would be attractive to her. She had plenty of her own money, that surely couldn't be it, I thought. On and on he went, Nancy making no effort to reel him in and Susan much too polite to take the lead, so we sat and let him gush until finally Nancy announced that they must go. Susan preceded us into the living room which gave me a chance to look at Nancy privately as we followed. She clearly anticipated such a moment and met my openly puzzled look with one of inexplicable blandness but sustained so unreasonably long that I felt it must be an attempt to transmit something, I knew not what. There was no hostility, no resentment, no criticism I could detect, but she held it maddeningly, tauntingly until the group came together and the good-byes and promises and thanks were entered into. Before long they were gone. We tidied up the party things and sat down to some dessert in the kitchen.

"Well, what did you think of God's gift to the uninsured public?" Susan gave me a slightly reprimanding look as she regularly did when I started to trash someone.

"He seems like a nice person. I must say that he does tend to go on a good bit about himself, but perhaps he was just nervous. Nancy seems to feel he is quite special. She tells me a great deal about their relationship, for some reason. I suppose she's more of less sounding me for an opinion. He certainly is no one that I would want to cultivate, but if Nancy is happy with him, that's all that matters."

"Do you think she's serious about him?" I felt it was important to take a neutral tone in all this, quickly running over in my mind just how much I was supposed to know about her, separating one visit from the other frantically, aware that I wanted to know everything Susan had heard without appearing to.

"I wouldn't be surprised from what she says. They've dined with his parents several times and they went to New York with them for a weekend not long ago, so I guess there must be something there. I can't say that she seems very excited about the man, but you know, it's been a long time since she and Roger broke up, and Nancy is such an attractive and such a vivacious creature. I wonder that she hasn't found someone long before now. I enjoy her company so. She will make someone a wonderful wife, but I must say that I would rather see her with someone other than Byron. He is definitely not her type, but there must be something we don't appreciate in him that attracts her."

We let it go at that. I was disappointed in Nancy. I thought her taste for someone like Byron considerably deflating to my own ego. Worse than that, I realized I was jealous that some idiot like that would in all likelihood marry her. What a waste. Before long, it got worse, as Susan and Nancy began to see a good bit of each other at the club, Nancy confiding everything about her romance to Susan, who innocently repeated it to me as a matter of interest. The only consolation I could take from all this was that if Byron married her, I would have plenty of reason to discourage much contact between the two couples and spare myself many further meetings. Whatever the long look meant that one evening, I felt vaguely threatened by it as though there might be something hazardous to my mental health. I concluded that the less I saw of Nancy the happier I would be. Good, let her marry the insurance peddler.

And she did. Within a few months, Susan greeted me one evening with the exciting news that Nancy had told her she and Byron were to be married soon. Susan would be in the bridal party, of course, so she had a lot of contact with the prospective bride and kept me up to date on the details. The wedding was big and expensive and widely reported in the papers. Nancy looked stunning, of course, elegant gown, lovely girl, lots of photographs and ceremony. Byron looked like the cat who had swallowed the canary, the meathead. Once out of the reception line, which I knew might be a rush for me, I could consider the matter closed. Susan preceded me and was busy congratulating Byron while I faced a demurely smiling Nancy, gave her a chaste kiss on the cheek and for my discretion, got a hard pinch on my arm and a little lifting of the eyebrows, the smile broadening into what in private would have been glee. Wicked Nancy! Damn you, you vixen, I thought, but I couldn't suppress a big grin at her boldness, the first sign that the Nancy I had known was alive and well and still full of mischief. I had to revise my thinking. What was going on, I had no idea, but she was still Nancy and while I knew I had to be wary, I realized she was still my pal and that the blah evening at our house was some sort of act. Nancy, what are you up to? What in the world are you doing with this lump you just married? Well, I figured I'd find out some day. We were friends again.

A few months later, another of the Willoughby girls got remarried after the customary first failure and we attended a party in honor of the happy couple after their return from the honeymoon. It was held at the club on one of the last fine evenings that fall and of all people for me to meet, Susan clutched at a man walking by, embraced him enthusiastically and introduced me to Roger Barnes. It didn't take very long to figure out that all the reports were true. What a grin this guy was. I had an idea of what to expect, but I had no notion that I would be so charmed by this cat whom Nancy had dumped, who couldn't leave the booze alone, everybody's friend. We got to talking and in no time I was howling. With total ease and instant familiarity, he said some of the funniest things I had heard in years. We stood and drank and talked and laughed until Susan had to come to drag me away to meet the bride, with a promise that we would have Roger over for an evening soon. In twenty minutes, he seemed like an old friend, he was that sort. So this was the guy that Nancy had found irresistible. Small wonder, the more I thought about it. It gave me a warm feeling about Nancy again, the kinship that people who love to laugh feel for each other. If Roger was her cup of tea, then a lot of things I had suspected about her were right.

I went on with Susan to meet the bride, a breezy, airhead type, wound up awfully tight for the occasion, laughing too much at too little, so after some mindless polite conversation, we moved on. Susan spotted Byron and said we should have a word with him. I suggested that she go ahead and that I would get a couple drinks and join her. I was scanning the room for the nearest bar when I saw Nancy. She was standing alone in the back of the room near a pair of French doors that opened off the room on that side. Our eyes met and she gave a tiny tilt of her head and walked out of sight onto the balcony outside. It was an unmistakable invitation and I felt it would be reasonable to accept. She was standing in the near dark with a light shawl around her shoulders, hugging herself against the cool air. I walked up to her, quickly, aware of how brief this must be, but how desirable.

"Hello, Peter," she said.

"Hello, Nancy", I replied. We stood, looking at each other, neither of us certain of what our role should be, I suppose. At least that was the case with me.

"Susan is talking with Byron, but I can't stay long," I said.

"Relax, Peter. We're friends. What could be more natural than that you should have seen me come out here and came to say hello?" She looked up at me and slowly leaned against me. I very gently but very deliberately straightened her up.

"Hold on a second, Nance. Look…this isn't going to work. Susan and I are getting on just fine, you're settled, we're settled, everything's cool and I'd really very much like to keep it that way, just say hello now and then, have drink or dinner but not get things all stirred up again. OK…I admit I'm still attracted to you. I don't deny it. I wish it weren't true but so far there doesn't seem to me much I can do about it but you're not helping. Susan and I are very happy and I want it to stay that way. Byron is not exactly my dish, but let's just settle for getting together occasionally as friends and not start anything. I just can't handle it."

"Byron is not exactly your dish," she scoffed. "God. You don't have to live with him."

"Well then why did you marry him in the first place? What was that all about? I couldn't figure you two together for shucks."

"I was bored, Peter. Bored to death. I didn't love the man, I don't love the man, I don't intend to love the man at any time in the future. I was bored, I was frustrated, I was angry with myself and I just thought it would be something to do. And nobody knows better what I was angry about and frustrated about. No, don't worry, I'm not going to get into it, but if you want an answer, that's the answer. Byron is a brainless tomcat, and I give him all the rope he wants. He's my companion and I'm his trophy so we go places and do things, but that's it. Does this put me on your conscience? I suppose it does and I apologize for dumping on you. I didn't entice you out here to give you a burden, Peter, but in case you still don't know, you are it for me, and you have been it for me since I first told you that, and I don't see anything that's going to change. So let's just go along and see how things work out. Don't hate me, Peter. I'm doing the best I can under the circumstances. I just haven't been able to change my dream." Oh, man. Why does she tell me this stuff? This was no help at all. This was just what I didn't want to hear. I took her two clenched fists, kissed the knuckles and went back inside.

I got the drinks and went to Susan, said hello to Byron, told them I had just seen Nancy to say hello and the whole incident was over except for the interminable reflections. I had to accept everything Nancy had said, including the apology for the guilt she had created. Poor Nancy. Impulsive Nancy. But regardless of the sympathy I could feel for her rotten situation, it was after all of her own making. As a matter choice on my part, we saw increasingly less of them, occasional club functions, but no dinners, few parties, their crowd quite different than ours.

18

There seemed to be less and less of this type of socializing over the next year or so, our life together reverting to the routine that I still had not come to terms with, just the least bit bored, waiting for an inspiration as I have done so many times in my life. It came from an unexpected quarter, Susan. One Friday evening, she mentioned that there was a dog show over the weekend that might be fun to attend and we took it in. How could I have missed this annual event these several years? I had never even seen anything about it in the papers. We had such a fine afternoon. I had had a couple dogs in my boyhood who were great pals, but between college and the apartment, having a dog again had not crossed my mind. The dogs I had had were mutts, just country dogs that appeared in the yard out of nowhere, skinny and lame, and once fed, took up residence with no further formalities. They were dropped off along the road by folks who couldn't afford to feed them or spay them even if they thought of it. I had never seen more than an occasional purebred dog and here was an arena full of them. We wandered around the periphery of the show, much less interested in the judging than in watching the exhibitors groom and prepare their animals, talking with them about their breed, admiring these handsome creatures. Something inside me simply insisted that I get a dog. I was convinced that this was exactly what I needed and I felt instantly happy and light hearted at the prospect. Later that day at home, I broached the subject to Susan who was surprisingly enthusiastic, even though she had never had a pet of any sort. While a puppy is not a baby, it occurred to me that this would take a little heat off of Susan until we somehow broke the jinx. What had started as a selfish indulgence became a thoughtful gesture. So I told myself, anyway.

There had been a dozen breeds at the show that I thought were just what I wanted. It was like being a kid in a candy shop. I favored the large breeds, Susan had in mind something much smaller. The important thing was to get one before Susan thought better of it. Nothing would do now but what we get a dog at the earliest possible moment. We had the property, we had the safety of a dead end road, a big yard, woods nearby, a dog's paradise. Susan knew someone who bred Yorkshire terriers, and while I had no special feeling for the breed, the important thing was to get started looking. We visited this kennel, nice people, cute dogs, but just not at all right for me, and I felt in this instance I had the right to a veto, anyway, as I was the dog man. There were certain breeds that were right and there were some that were plain wrong, nothing against the dog, but the dog and the owner must match up somehow, and I never fancied myself a Yorkie or a poodle or a Scottie man and so forth. We looked at some German shepherds, gorgeous, intelligent dogs that were too serious for me and simply frightened Susan. We tried cocker spaniels, right for Susan, wrong for me. Hounds were out, we were advised, are you sure a poodle wouldn't suit you? No, sorry. Then came the collies, so beautiful, but Susan balked at the grooming and I was just as content to pass on them. Susan was beginning to realize the nuisance of having a puppy which I had taken pains not to get into and she was beginning to show signs of disinterest. She was helping at the Foundation almost every day, volunteer work really, but enjoyable and important to her. The prospect of taking a substantial amount of time off to get a puppy started was a little sobering. In all fairness, Susan was not the kind of girl that you visualize sitting at home, cooking, gardening or anything else, and I got to thinking that the choice of a puppy was perhaps unfair to Susan, so I decided one afternoon a few weeks later to check the animal shelter.

I had no idea what to expect and was gratified to find that the place was neat and modern with well cared for runs of substantial size, really quite as nice as the kennels we had gone to, and of course, much larger. I went in and spoke to the only girl there, outlining my problem. She gave me the patter about what they cost, what the shelter would pay for, that females must be spayed and so on. All I wanted was to get a look at the dogs and see if mine was there. The expenses were so modest that I wondered how they managed. At length, she told me to go back out and just walk up and down the line of pens and check out what they had. If there any one that took my fancy, she would get it out and I could play with it and see how we got on.

I started out and hadn't gone by more than a half dozen cages when I came on a white dog, a youngster, sitting politely, quietly and staring at me with huge, soulful dark eyes, projecting unimaginable earnestness, beseeching me to accept and reciprocate the love that my appearing there had aroused in her. Her message was simple and poignant. "Somehow I have become the victim of a dreadful mistake. I have been taken from my home and confined in this place and I beg you, I implore you, take me with you, let me be yours only and I will repay you with a lifetime of affection and gratitude. But take me, love me." I stared back, her roommate running around and yapping as though demented while the white dog sat and stared back, tail quietly wagging, ears drawn back affectionately. I knew I had found my dog. I knew it as surely as I would a year from then, knew beyond a doubt that I had uncovered a treasure, that this was the thunderbolt, the unambiguous transference of a heavy dose of love that stamped her indelibly as mine, this true love at first sight.. As I stood there wondering if I owed it to myself to at least look at the other dogs, another automobile pulled in and a couple got out and I panicked. I looked down once more at my beauty and there she sat, staring and pleading as only a dog can do, and now she played her ace, the tip of the tongue slipping in and out, blowing me little kisses. That did it.

I charged into the office and impatiently waited while the girl went through the same litany with the couple. It seemed forever before they started on their own quest, and I told her I thought I wanted the white dog in the fourth or fifth cage. She reflected and asked did I mean the yellow Lab. Yes, I felt that must be the one and would she bring the creature out. She left and shortly reopened the door and asked me if this were my choice. And there she was, smiling and now wagging wildly but shyly, assuring me in her own fashion that I had chosen wisely and that she was immensely grateful.

I paid the fee and asked if she would accept a donation and wrote a much larger check than was expected or usual, to judge from the effusion from the girl. I asked her what she knew of my new prize and was told that she was a runt from a litter of pure-bred dogs from a private home, not professional breeders. The litter mates had all been sold and after failing for the longest time to sell her, not wanting her for breeding or for a pet, her owners had brought her here. Checking her papers, she reported that she was nearly a year old, had no bad habits, had not been spayed which I must do, had been raised outdoors, got on well with cats. She had only arrived the evening before. It was the girl's opinion that I was very lucky to have come by when I did as a dog that pretty would be picked out very quickly. I agreed.

We went out to the car using a throwaway lead of some awful plastic. I had no idea if she had ever been in a car before, but that was quickly settled when she panicked and dragged me back toward the office, absolutely terrified of the car. I knelt and petted and cajoled and talked and petted, but when it was obviously a losing game, cradled her up and after a brief tussle, got her into the front seat. Once again, we sat and I talked and she looked at me and I talked some more and gradually she accepted my explanation and lay down but breathing heavily, unhappily. Remembering that I had nothing for her at home, I headed immediately for a pet store. There was a moment of consternation as I got out and she showed that she had no intention of letting me out of her sight without a protest, but then she settled into staring disconsolately through the window until I came back with the collar, the lead, dishes, a bag of chow and got her properly decked out to meet Susan.

She seemed to warm some to the ride, getting up and looking out at everything, then over at me for approval and possibly to be sure that I was still there, throwing kisses, leaning over to lick my hand and then making the lick-lunge for the face. Somewhat reassured, I could now think of what to call her. How easily this came. It was Good Friday and passing an open market on the way home, I saw massed banks of Easter lilies and although my passenger was technically a yellow Labrador, she was nearly white and so I dubbed her Lily and as such she was introduced to Susan when I got home.

Susan was in the yard when I arrived and at the sight of Lily's head peering at her through the window, stopped and waited for me to open the door and let our new arrival jump out. Lily had by now decided that the car was acceptable, but she was certain that getting out was the wrong thing to do and resolutely declined to. I got back in the car and we sat and talked and after a time I lifted her out and carried her into the house. There was no question about her having been raised outdoors. She was very suspicious of everything and wouldn't leave my side, but when I walked around the room, she followed as though separation from me would mean sudden death, and so I paraded her everywhere, telling her what everything was and how much fun we would have. A bowl of water boosted her morale some although she drank while constantly keeping her eyes on me. I took her out and we walked the yard, Lily all but attached to my leg, but now she began to relax, sniffed here and there and everywhere, wandered short distances away and then quickly returned, and then in the course of only seconds, or so it seemed, she came to a decision that all would be well, and the tail started up, and the face became animated and she began a little prancing in place, and then suddenly in total abandon, began racing around the yard in circles, with an occasional little yip that could only have been joy. The chasm had been bridged. Something had clicked and all would be well and we were pals. Now she wanted to meet Susan and apologize for her timidity. Susan cautiously reached down and stroked her head with the distinctive clumsiness of people who don't know dogs.

I told her the story and how the sight of this youngster had so captivated me that there was no question of leaving her behind. Susan seemed pleased that the whole matter had been settled to my satisfaction, the entire dog business something to which she brought little personal opinion. We returned to the house, Lily like a shadow and when I sat, likewise sat within reach of my hand, and gazed up at me with the devotion only a dog can give so convincingly. Now for the first time I noted what had made her dark eyes so huge and alluring. In spite of the nearly white coat, the skin around her face and muzzle was black and where the hairs were very short or absent, the black skin outlined her eyes as though she had been heavily made up with mascara. With her black lips and nose set off by her pale yellow coat, she had a theatrical glamour. My own harp seal, I thought.

"Would you like to feed her? She's probably starved." We went to the kitchen and Susan put a dish of chow on the floor and we stood there and watched as she wolfed it down and looked up for more. I encouraged Susan to come outside with us again and we walked around some more, Lily now more curious and confident and beginning to associate Susan with home, but intent on staying near me. "What do you think? Isn't she a pretty thing? I like the idea of her being a reject, somehow. Poor thing. How could someone have given up on such a pretty creature? I doubt she's ever been in a house before, and that makes you wonder just how much love she's had. We'll make it up to her." I got down on the grass with her and that seemed to please her and in no time we were wrestling with each other and she was yipping. As evening came on, I realized it would be impossible to turn her out, even if we had never discussed this. Susan took the prospect of Lily being a roommate well and when we went to bed that night, I invited Lily in to the bedroom, knowing full well that if I didn't she'd be miserable and pass it on to us, so she came in and lay down on the floor on my side. As soon as the lights went out, there was a little whimper and shuffling and a couple paws on the bed. I eased her down and dangled my hand over to let her lick and caressed her and gradually she became quiet. There were a few more brief episodes of insecurity, but we both got a pretty good night's sleep. Of course, one night in the master's bedroom is a lifetime habit and Lily slept there ever after.

I spent the next day with her almost constantly, throwing things for her to fetch, grooming her, petting her, talking to her. I had some concerns about what would happen when I left for work on Tuesday so I was most anxious that Susan feel not only comfortable, but affectionate toward our new charge. It amounted to a crash course. She got to the point where she would get in the car, but what it did for her, I don't know, as she spent the whole time looking at me; the world outside the car of no interest whatever. We took trip after meaningless trip until she would leap in when I opened the door, and from that weekend on, if I went in the car I had to do some fast talking to leave her behind, but she took it like a champ once she had been waved off.

By the end of the week, I thought she was totally happy and adjusted, so the next morning when we went for breakfast at the Grafton's, I took her along, not to stay in the car but to be free and learn to be a good guest. Dr. Grafton took to her immediately and made a big fuss over her while Mrs. Grafton looked distressed and I knew she was thinking about her carpets. We were promptly invited into the solarium with its marble floors and had breakfast there, Lily a model, staying as tight to my left leg as it she had been to school, lying quietly beside my chair all through breakfast to the point where Mrs. Grafton actually praised her and asked if I thought she should have some water. I honestly didn't know whether she would disgrace herself given the opportunity, so I took a stroll outdoors a couple times, very casual, and dear Lily immediately relieved herself and we would drift back in. The whole morning went very smoothly and I was of proud of her.

I waited a couple weeks until she seemed to be completely settled down before getting her spayed. A neighbor suggested a vet whose office was located near us in the careworn older house in which the original owner of all this land had lived. The vet turned out to be an unhurried mature gentleman, slender, slow and bemused whom I felt trustworthy for all the absence of bustle in the waiting room. He suggested a day and a fee, painfully modest I thought, and on the appointed morning I took a hungry and thirsty Lily for her surgery. How it is that dogs sense things, I'll never fully appreciate, but even though I was very conscious of being casual--was that my mistake?--she steadfastly refused to get into the car for the first time since she had come home and there ensued an undignified scene at the end of which she was captured and loaded. We were a little late, but Dr. Thomas took it philosophically and I proceeded on to work, unreasonably preoccupied with her welfare. I picked her up on the way home and although a little goofy, she was wagging and so happy to be back with us, sleeping away the rest of the day.

With the joys and rewards of this early experience with Lily, I began to become aware of the things I had anticipated from a child, someone with whom to share the things I felt important, some creature to shape and teach and guide, someone that having grown with me, might be like me. This was to be Lily's role now, at least for a time and to an extent. When she had completely recovered from her surgery I enrolled the two of us in an obedience class in the evenings. Susan came along to observe and we went through the half dozen classes in grand style. In the evenings at home, Lily and I would practice, and by the time of the next class, she had mastered her homework. When our instructor began to use us as a demonstration of what the others should be doing, I knew we were going to ace the course. Lily was as excited as I was, knowing how well she was doing and so pleased to have these new tricks to gratify me. By the time the course was ended, I felt that I had a genius on my hands, and we won the graduation day exercise hands down, the independent judge hired for the competition, telling me what a fine job I had done and what a clever pet I had. We took the certificate home and I had it framed and hung it on the wall in the hallway where we had a few important photographs. We continued to go through our lessons for several more weeks at home, not so much to cement them in Lily's mind but because she enjoyed them so. It was a game at which she was good and she knew it. When I left her for long periods commanded to sit and stay, she never looked bored, but alert with her play face, just waiting for me to call 'Lily, come!" at which she would fly to my side and sit and look up for the praise and petting. What a marvelous thing she was! I was so proud of her. Susan remained a respectful bystander, enjoying seeing me work with her but declining to be part of it.

The days were warm now and we resumed going to the lake on Saturdays, when the Graftons opened the cottage. Lily had never had the opportunity to swim before. I don't know just what I expected, but it was not what Lily gave us. I let her out of the car and the three of us walked down to the edge of the water. Lily waded in up to her belly, drank a little, walked some more and then came out, sort of an anticlimax for her owners. Hoping for something better, I picked up a stick and threw it, much farther than I had intended, thinking of our sport in the yard, and with that, Lily flew toward the water and launched, a powerful, long leap through the air and a great splash. With no practice that I knew of, she was a strong, confident swimmer, retrieving the stick and dropping at my feet, tensely waiting for the next throw, not even bothering to shake. What fun we had! I walked her out on the dock then and now she really showed her stuff. The dock was only a foot off the water, but this little additional elevation gave her just that much more elevation that her leap was longer the splash more dramatic. She came ashore, ran out onto the dock and dropped the stick at my feet. I don't know how long this might have gone on. I never did succeed in tiring her before I was ready to call it quits.

We took her out in the canoe after lunch, a model passenger who simply sat in the center and watched the water going by, fascinate at the train of bubble and the bow wake. We pulled into a favorite gravel beach and played stick for a time before Susan and I just sat and watched her exploring in the shallows, looking intently into the clear water, pawing first, then lunging her head in, biting at minnows, stalking, stalking, tail erect, ears tensely elevated, oblivious, other than for periodic reassurance that we were still there, of anything but her intended prey.

When I took the cover off the pool at home the result was as expected. Fortunately, we had had steps put at the shallow end, so Lily could get out quickly and bring me the tennis ball which she never could retrieve too many times. She had become the focus of much of our spare time together, and as parents take their children to the playground and are entertained by watching them play, so we did with Lily who became our surrogate child. Perhaps because we had been thwarted for so long in conceiving our own child, we made too much of our pet. It can happen. Everyone has seen some pet tricked out in jeweled sweaters, ribbons and bows, dyed coats. We weren't that bad. Our indulgence--perhaps I should say my indulgence--took the form of having Lily accompany us almost wherever we went. Weather permitting, she could be left in the car with the windows open when we dined out or visited where a dog was out of the question. With most of our friends, she was accepted and lay quietly somewhere while we ate or played bridge or visited. Even Emily Grafton seemed to enjoy Lily's visits, rather proud of herself, I thought, at coming around to accepting an animal in the house.

Lily was in a class by herself. She worshipped me, she idolized me. I think it's fair to assume that in her primitive mind, I had saved her life. Whatever was her concept of my adopting her, she behaved as though I had snatched her from the very jaws of doom and therefore had become my loving slave. When I sat and read in the evening, she lay in such a way as to able to look at me, an alert, intelligent stare that on my catching her eye, ever so briefly, turned into a look of love, the ears laid back, eyes slightly narrowed, throwing little kisses, just that finger breath of tongue gliding out rhythmically, tail stirring restlessly, all in proportion to the intensity and duration of my look, melting completely if I smiled ever so slightly. If I stood up, she stood up, waiting. When I sat down again, she lay as before. The mere crook of a finger brought her to my side for contact, eyes nearly closed as I stroked her head, and in moments of uncontrollable ecstasy, her jaw chattering ever so slightly. I loved it. Lily was giving me that unselfconscious, unconditional overt love that I had been so missing.

I was aware that Susan took all this in, watching the two of us with an enigmatic smile. At times I was concerned that Susan might feel Lily was a rival for my affections, but not only was I unable to make a case for this, but came to believe that Susan was relieved that I had a playmate at last. It was rejuvenating to drive in after work and meet a wildly joyful companion who needed release, as I myself did, and we would run around the yard doing whatever came to mind, chase, stick, tug of war until Lily was satisfied that I was going to stay for dinner, and then Susan and I could enjoy our cocktail together and talk, while Lily sat, looking now from one to the other, listening, wagging when her name was dropped in conversation, listening, waiting, loving.

She was very considerate in most regards, but had her own ideas about the days of the week. On Saturdays and Sundays when we tended to sleep in longer, at the time when the alarm would ordinarily go off, there would be the soft tapping of toenails on the wooden floor at my side of the bed, Lily literally tap dancing, creating this tiny staccato of nails on the floor that was just sufficient to awaken me enough to drape an arm over the edge of the bed, her pacifier. Susan customarily got up before I did, and when she had left the room, I allowed Lily to jump up in bed and lie beside me, a great sigh of contentment escaping her as she settled her back against me. She rarely barked, although in her frustration sometimes at not being able to jump up on Susan or me, would prance in place and squeal softly. With strangers, she was friendly, polite, but just the least bit distant, never soliciting affection from strangers, letting everyone know that she was ours exclusively. When Susan and I both went somewhere not suitable for taking her along, she simply lay down in the living room and waited, no barking, no chewing, just waiting for her loved ones to return and her life to resume.

Now, in addition to all these other wonderful attributes, Lily had a sense of humor. She was not just a lover, she was a comedian. When the mood was right, there appeared a look in her eyes of pure devilment, pure tease, pure silliness, and off we would go, she with the wild look, totally disobedient, completely certain that all rules were suspended, and that this was play time, the time to cut up and have fun. There would be fierce charges and leaps at me, snapping at cuffs, grabbing of sleeves, refusal to drop the tennis ball, simple tearing around the yard maniacally, barking, growling. What a sketch! No matter how bushed I was, she could turn my mood in an instant into helpless laughter. She was the antidote to my restless ennui.

There are as many definitions of love as there are lovers, it seems to me, and yet I rarely see or hear of this emotion in humans equaled by what passes between the owner and the exceptional dog. The love of a good dog is selfless, constant, inextinguishable. To know that the happiness of a devoted creature is entirely dependent upon you is an enormous responsibility. We can explain to humans, but no matter how we deceive ourselves by talking earnestly to our dog why we are not taking her someplace, all she knows is that she cannot be with her beloved and it hurts. Witness the unbelievable joy and excitement when you return from the briefest errand from which she has been excluded. Without overdoing it, I am convinced that during our absence, our pet's mind is filled with thoughts of us, us, us until we return. Could anything be more flattering? We might be anathema to our wife, a pariah at work, a failure at golf, but to our dog, we are a hero, a lover, a lord. Much, I believe, is hoped for, but virtually nothing is insisted upon in return. This love is a gift, freely given, totally given. Where else in all of life can one command a loyalty to compare with that of our dog? And this loyalty was not taught, perhaps not even sought, yet it is there for us whether we expect it or not. The dog that rolls over on its back to acknowledge its master's superiority is cute and engaging but this is submission and servility, not the love I refer to. The dog that maintains it's dignity, that continues self possessed, that meets one's level gaze and still radiates it's veneration toward its master is in love. Mature, changeless, deep seated love.

Lily's attitude toward Susan was one of somewhat detached affection, very much what would be expected. When they were at home alone together, Lily would do whatever Susan commanded, and do it willingly, but as Susan reported, she was just putting in time until I returned home. They went on walks, but Lily didn't volunteer to heel, walking near Susan but on her own track. On the occasional night when I was out of town, Lily slept on the floor on my side. Susan fed her, Susan brushed her, Susan stroked her and talked to her as they became better friends, but her heart belonged to Daddy. A friend of mine from home once remarked that in a lifetime, a man has the right to expect one good woman and one good dog. I thought I was doing pretty well.

As our parenting of Lily went on, I was acutely aware and amused by the reflection that Lily's undisguised crush on me was satisfying that need I had for expressed and unabashed love that Susan was incapable of, no matter how deeply she might feel it. There was never a doubt in my mind about her love for me, or whatever she called it in her private thoughts, but I wanted something more overt, something that I could see and feel and take reassurance from. Lily had stepped in and was doing the job. Odd how words, hollow as they can be and no substitute for deeds, are sought after, are welcomed and often taken for the deed. Now, in the absence of the word, I had the constant demonstration that I was loved to distraction by a lovely creature whose love I returned. Not surprisingly, this not only retained its appeal but enhanced my tenderness toward Susan. That Lily was bridging an emotional gap that had always existed between us, there was no question in my mind, and I thought Susan had intimations of this also.

With this new love in my life, with the fun and diversion that Lily brought to me, the disappointment of Susan not conceiving was mitigated and gradually we came to accept the idea that we might remain a childless couple. We didn't talk about it much, especially now that we had a youngster of sorts to raise. I had thought occasionally of the prospect of adoption, but had rejected the idea as being far too hazardous. We knew one delightful couple, the most gentle and sweet people one could imagine, well educated and affectionate who had adopted a baby boy who turned out tragically to have a criminal mind, a dreadful child who eventually ended up in prison for a serious offense. Another well intended couple who had two children of their own, out of consideration for the wife's health, adopted a third child who became so hateful with its new siblings that the harmony of the family was all but destroyed. At that time, the debate between nature and nurture was heavily weighted in favor of the latter, and both these families accepted the guilt of having failed their new charges, where in fact, they had simply been dealt kids with bad genes.

As much as I wanted children, I was so against the prospect of taking such a gamble with some else's random mating that I would have declined if Susan had suggested it. While not a child, Lily was almost filling that void and had made my life so much richer. And so we drifted along. Susan was being given greater responsibility at the Foundation and was enjoying all the interesting contacts there. My work was actually flourishing and I was now familiar enough with all it's aspects that I felt I was carrying my weight. Dr. Baxter was pleased, Tony DeMarco was pleased, Jim was actually happy, Susan was happy, Walter and Emily were happy, I was making decent money now and it looked to me as though it were going to be clear sailing from then on. There is a delicious feeling of knowing that all is right in one's world, no clouds on the horizons, no money worries, stable home, good job, good health. If that isn't the dream of success, it must be pretty close.

I mentioned that our neighborhood was a very private one, only a few homes, all with large lots, acres of fields and woods. In spite of all the temptations this might offer to a dog, Lily was quite particular not to roam. True, there were times when I had to call to fetch her from the woods around the house, but her habit was to stay close to home. One day, a day I'm still reluctant to call to memory, I had come home, expecting her usual effusive greeting, but no Lily, uncharacteristic but in no way troubling. I called and called, without effect and after a time, I decided she would just have to come at her own pleasure and went in and had a drink with Susan. As the light began to fail, the nagging concern I had been trying to ignore became an imperative, and I got in the car and toured the area, stopping now and then to call her name without success. Truly worried now, I returned home and set off into the woods behind our house, calling and listening, calling and looking. As I descended a slope that led to a tiny creek, I saw a patch of white in the brush beside the stream. Suddenly stricken with fear of what I might find, I plunged through the undergrowth and found my darling, lying on her side, with her front paws in the stream, to all appearances dead, blood all over the place, coming out of her rear, out of her mouth. Oh, God, what a grotesque sight! Scarcely able to even comprehend what I was seeing, I knelt and stroked her and called her name and noted she was breathing and trying to stick out her tongue the way she did when she threw me a kiss. I carefully turned her, apparently without pain, looking for a wound, a gunshot, something to explain this unbelievable state, but nothing. Frantic now, desperate to get help before it was too late, I gathered her up and stumbled wildly through the woods back to the house where I found Susan, wide-eyed and frozen with her hand over her mouth at this hideous sight. I gasped out that I was going to the vet's, put her in the front seat and set off for Dr. Thomas's. Susan, exercising the good sense I was incapable of at the time, had called ahead and had found Dr. Thomas still at the clinic so that when I pulled in, he was waiting in the driveway with his big black helper. I choked out the story and without a word the helper carried her into the examining room. Dr. Thomas went over her quickly and told me that she had been poisoned. He said it with such conviction that there was no doubting his diagnosis. He gave her some shots to help stop the bleeding. In very short, blunt sentences, he told me that he kept a donor dog in the kennel and would give her a transfusion to hopefully replace enough blood to sustain life while her body attempted to cope with dealing with all the destroyed tissue and the poison itself, a very chancy thing, not knowing how much poison she had ingested. There was no emotion, just a very honest observation that he felt her chances slim, but certainly worth improving to whatever extent we could. He suggested I return home and that he would call when he had something to report. I have never felt so totally helpless, so baffled by the orderly world I lived in which had just become a nightmare. I simply nodded and went out to the car and sat there, uncertain just what to do, trying to absorb the events of the last half hour, trying not to believe that this precious creature might never greet me again, might never put her head in my lap as we drove along. I felt that it simply could not have happened. How in the world could she have gotten into poison? All but impossible. Who would put out poison? Someone trying to poison rats? There couldn't be a rat problem where we were. Could anyone have deliberately set it out to poison a dog? I simply couldn't believe it of the people we lived among, even though I knew very little of them. The whole idea was so dreadful, such an ugly, ugly, thing to contemplate anyone in a civilized community setting out poison.

At length, defeated and depressed as I had never been in my life, I slowly drove home and got out of the car. Susan was waiting for me outside the house, just standing there looking at my face to see what she might find there to answer her unspoken question. I looked at her and shrugged and told her that Lily was alive, barely, that she was getting a transfusion and that the chances of her surviving were pretty slender. Susan's face contorted as I had never seen it and she began to sob and fell into my arms, her body shaking uncontrollably. We stood like that for some time until Susan became more quiet, and finally walked into the darkened house, Susan having stayed outside all the time I was gone. We sat in the living room in the late twilight, neither wanting to face the reality that light would have revealed.

Eventually, we got up and went to the kitchen and Susan got out some leftovers and made a small meal. We had gotten over the shock and now it was time to go over the whole matter, the way people do when they calm down and try to better understand a shocking event. I told Susan in more detail what I had told her earlier about the poisoning and while each of us held to the weak hope Dr. Thomas had offered, I was preparing myself for life without Lily although I said nothing to Susan of this despair. We sat up for a time, waiting to get a call perhaps, but not willing to bother the doctor and eventually went to bed to a very broken sleep, awakening repeatedly and having to relive and reaccept the gloomy prognosis and the void, the bleak void that her death would leave behind.

We were aroused from our mutual reluctance to arise the next morning by the phone ringing. Susan looked at me in alarm and I got up and went into the kitchen and answered. It was Dr. Thomas, he was sorry to disappoint us, but Lily had died during the night and he had felt it better to wait until morning to call. He asked if we would like him to dispose of her body or would we like to come for her. I thanked him and told him I would be over shortly. I returned to the bedroom and told Susan, who took it in silence. She got up and made coffee while I got dressed and went out back with a spade and dug a deep grave at the edge of the flower bed. Dr. Thomas had put Lily's body in a large cardboard box, and he helped me put it in the trunk of the car, a terrible moment for me, visualizing her leaping into the front seat, sitting bolt upright and smiling, waiting for me to get in. Lily in the trunk. My dear, sweet Lily, in the trunk. I can still feel it.

I shook the doctor's hand and thanked him for all he had done. He accepted my praise and gratitude quietly and modestly with little comment. I was somehow reluctant to go, and he stood quietly, letting me take the lead. After a moment's indecision, I had the nerve to ask him if his final opinion was that it was rat poison. He nodded. Having broached the inconceivable, I asked him if he had any idea how it could possibly have happened. He looked steadily at me and told me that this was the third case of rat poisoning in a dog he had had in the past two months. One had survived. I was aghast! Three? What in heaven's name was going on? He shook his head gravely.

"You have no idea how many people there are that hate dogs, Mr. Hawkins. It's very difficult for someone who loves animals to accept the fact that there are people willing to murder them on the most trivial excuse. They leave a mess in their yard. They chase their cats. They bark at night, they frighten their children, they tip over garbage cans, they might have rabies. These things tend to run in cycles, it seems to me. It could be a neighbor you think you know, it could even be a person who drives through your neighborhood and drops off pieces of poisoned meat, a lunatic that simply hates blindly and kills what he hates, regardless of the innocence of the individual pet. You'll never find out who did it, Mr. Hawkins. If you're thinking of trying to find out, I would recommend you don't. I've never known of anyone to accurately identify a poisoner, and if you should, then what? I would suggest that you wait to get over this and then get another dog and fence in your yard. It would take a lot of nerve for someone to throw poisoned meat over a fence in daylight. Still, you never can be sure. I have a very low opinion of the average man's humanity, Mr. Hawkins. I much prefer the company of animals."

Completely drained and disillusioned, I drove home. Susan helped me carry the box out to the grave but then left. I took my poor darling out and lowered her gently into the hole and ar-ranged her so that she appeared to be sleeping with her head on her crossed paws, as she so frequently did. I lay there for a time looking down at her and grieving until a shadow fell across my field of vision and I found Susan standing there. She had come to comfort me, my dear Susan. We stood for a minute, holding each other and looking down at our pet. Susan went back in and I filled in the hole, mounded it over neatly and went into the house.

Lily's death was the first personal tragedy either of us had experienced. We comforted each other, rationalized as best we could, and with time, put it behind us and went on living, al-though the memories only slowly faded and for the longest time, I looked beside my chair by reflex to catch her eye, looked down carefully beside the bed as I got out to be sure not to step on her. Her presence was everywhere for months and on the wall in the hallway thereafter, a lovely photograph I had taken of her and had enlarged, tugging at my emotions each time I passed it, my sweetheart, gazing out at me with those enormous dark eyes.

19

We finally began to talk about it, but I found it very difficult to consider getting another dog, a fact that surprised me. Only months before I had actually told someone whose dog had died of natural causes that they should get out right away and get another dog. I believed it sincerely. Get a new puppy and the cute little fellow will soon have you smiling again. It's not disloyal to the old dog, it's just the best answer to the grief of losing an old companion, but when the time came for me to take my own advice, it seemed no longer to apply to my case, our case. It was not just a matter of replacing our dog. It was a matter of replacing Lily and I didn't feel that was possible. Susan was all for it but even though I felt that I should be also, it didn't seem right and I trust my instincts when I feel them strongly. The result was that the longer I procrastinated, the more certain I was that I hadn't healed and that there would be no new dog for the time.

I got by with this for a time, but one evening a few months later, Susan took the initiative in such a determined way that I had to attach importance to it. She pulled up a chair and sat close in front of me and I knew we were in for some serious talking. She asked me to put my book aside and listen to something she had to say.

"Peter….Peter, you are not yourself, do you know?" I professed surprise and asked in what way.

"It's not having Lily, Peter. She was so terribly important to your happiness. You may not realize completely what her presence did for you. She was so much more than a pet. I'm not concerned about your grieving. I think we're both pretty well over that, but I don't think you realize what an important role Lily

214

played in this house. You were so cheerful and amusing and cute with her. I used to love watching you two playing and mooning over each other. I really think you need that, Peter. You were a different person when Lily was with us. She gave you something that I doubt anything or anyone else could, something that took you away from everything ordinary and allowed you to be just yourself for a little. I think that is very important for you. Do you understand what I'm trying to say?"

Of course I did. I knew all about it. I had complex reasons for not wanting another dog now, but the importance of a foil for the part of me that needed that foil was often on my mind. It was not a matter of recognizing it but rather how to deal with it. Without having said anything to Susan, I had begun once more to think about adoption, fretting and wrangling with the pros and cons that were already so familiar to me, but now seen in a different light.

"Yeah, I understand. You're right. I've been thinking about it a lot. I guess it's time for us to reconsider the whole adoption business again. Is that what you're thinking about?"

She nodded. "I don't mean that I've given up hope for our having our own child, but realistically, maybe we ought to think some more about it. I know you've never been enthusiastic about it, but it seems to me that it's either a dog or a child. I'm glad that no one but you can hear me saying that, but I think that's where we stand. Shall we start to think about it again? Seriously?" No avoiding it longer, it seemed.

"Yeah. OK. I guess we should. I'll go over all my prejudices again and see how they're doing. The problem with being a biologist is, that I know way too much about genetics to brush them aside and say, OK, give me that one over there in the blue blanket and we'll see what we end up with."

"Oh, Peter. Don't put it like that! We're two intelligent, loving people, and I don't see why we couldn't raise a perfectly nice, intelligent child. If other people can do it, can't we?"

"Of course we can, Suze. But what if we get a lemon? That's not just a little lump of clay in that bassinet, you know. That's a fully programmed kid that may be a genius or may be a dope and no matter how nice and how loving we are, there's nothing we can do about that. He could be an Abe Lincoln or a Charles Manson. I have some grave misgivings about rolling the dice like that for something we're going to live with and be responsible for a lifetime. If you get a really bad dog, you can put him down and that's that, nothing said, just start over, but with a kid, you're stuck forever." Susan was puzzled and thoughtful.

"You're trying to tell me something, but I'm not sure just what it is. What do you mean about fully programmed and Charles Manson? I'm talking about going through a legitimate, experienced agency, not just advertising or something like that. I don't quite understand why you are so negative about taking someone else's child and raising them. People do it all the time and I'm sure they are not only fulfilling their own need, but giving a good home to such a child seems to me to be the responsible thing for people in our circumstances to do. I don't see what makes you so hesitant to even consider it"

"Look Suze, it can work. I'm sure there are plenty of people out there who have adopted kids and are happy with the result. It just happens that I know two of them that are miserable. Like those people, you think you can take in a kid and if you give him love and material advantages and a good example and a good education, you will have the kind of kid you think such attention should produce. It doesn't always work that way. I don't know what it is that makes people think that we are any different than the rest of the animals in the world. I don't want to get too clinical, but very simply, breeders know that if you breed two good animals, you are likely to get a good offspring. Two bad ones, bad offspring. One good, one bad, something in between. Not every time, of course, but the odds are in favor of it. For some reason, ego maybe, people seem to take that 'all men are created equal' phrase to mean that if you do a good job of parenting, you'll have a good product. Not even close! It simply doesn't work that way and that's what has me concerned." Susan didn't have any rebuttal, but she didn't seem convinced, so I took it a little farther.

"Susan. Let me be more specific. Assume that a bright Willoughly girl gets knocked up by a graduate student at Corinthian. If you adopt that baby, chances are good you're going to have a winner. No guarantee, but darn good odds. Now let's say we mate a Bowery bum with an upstate hooker and we take that kid.

216

Chances are good it's going to be a disaster. Not for sure, but most likely. So we go to an adoption agency and what do they tell us about the parents? Almost nothing, is what I've heard. Hush hush, privacy and all that. They're very anxious for the adopting couple not to guess the real identity of the parents. You read about it all the time. I don't know the law behind it, but it seems the secrecy is cast iron, for whatever reason. I guess they couldn't function without it. Now if somehow we personally knew the baby came from the Willoughby/Corinthian match up, we'd take the baby in a heartbeat. But from an agency, how would we even guess that the kid wasn't the Bowery/hooker model? That's what gets to me. I don't think there's any way you can get the truth out of an agency that's trying to place these kids. And would you believe them if they hinted that this kid was the products of just the quality match you're looking for? I know I wouldn't. They can tell you anything they want to and how can you prove they're deceiving you? I think all that stuff is strictly off limits to the adopting parents. OK. That's it in a nutshell. Am I missing something? Am I way off base here?"

"I'm not trying deliberately to misunderstand, Peter. I accept all that you say, but my point is in the emphasis you give it. I'm sure people have occasionally been stuck, but it seems to me that almost all the adopted children I have heard about were pretty normal." I interrupted. "Susan, dear heart, consider. You're not going to hear about the flops. People don't brag about the flops. You're going to hear the heartwarming stories of the Orphan Who Triumphed, finds a cure for cancer, becomes a famous statesman. People hide the flops. It makes them look bad not to have succeeded raising a good kid after all their effort. They keep them under wraps. OK, I know of only two bad flops, but I worry about having number three." Susan was deflated. I hated to shoot down what might be our only hope, but I just couldn't let her get into this business without knowing the downside from my standpoint. We sat there stewing in our indecision for awhile.

Susan was taking this all in quietly, now, and I knew this meant she accepted what I had to say but it didn't buoy her spirits much. "But it could be a good combination and we could have a good child, even a bright child?"

"Sure. We could have a genius, a Miss America, a Mickey Mantle. Or we could get a Juke or a Kallikak. I know, I know... but you can see what I mean about it being a crap shoot. Well, that's all I can say. So what should we do, now that I've hung crape all over the place."

"Oh, Peter. I hate it that it's so complicated. I don't know what to say. What to you think? Should we just give up on it? Don't you think we should at least contact some place and see what they have to say? Should we take a look at what's available?"

"Sure. All right. We've got to do it someday, I guess. Nothing to lose by at least seeing what's involved. Let's just do it. You can tell I'm not excited about it, but what the hell. I suppose we at least ought to get our feet wet. I just want to go on record before we go by saying that I'm not going to believe anything they tell me about any kid. They have no idea what that mother was taking or doing during her pregnancy. Or who the father was, if the mother herself knows. That sort of stuff. And even if it is known it's going to be swept under the rug. Who's going to challenge whatever they tell us, if they're pledged to secrecy? Oh, man. Pig in a poke. But OK, I'm game. Let's give it a go and see what happens."

"Oh, Peter, I think you're being unfair and you're making it harder for me. If you go into it with such a negative attitude, we might never agree on how to proceed. At least please don't say any more until we've had a chance to see what this is all about. If we are going to do it at all, let's try to approach it with a more open mind. Don't prejudice me against even trying, Peter. I think we owe it to ourselves to at least look and maybe we'll be surprised. Let's at least not judge until we've done some checking."

As it turned out, my fears were largely unnecessary. For practical purposes we never got to first base. Susan did her homework and came up with the name of several organizations, variously recommended by friends, and we arranged to meet with them and did so only to find that there was a glut of adopters and a dearth of adoptees, such a dearth that the list of prospective parents was so long as to be daunting. We ended by leaving our names and the necessary information, thanking them and going home to regroup. Susan kept calling around and occasionally came up with a small organization who professed to have some girl just about to deliver, but these almost furtive type arrangements really got to me, and we had to admit defeat for the time being. We put out the word to Susan's' friends who from time to time came up with an idea, but what seemed doable seemed illegal and I had no intention of getting involved in something like that.

I continued to see Dr. Baxter almost every week, less often now that we were mostly occupied at work with the drudgery of doing procedure after procedure of the same nature before we could get on. He had been following our domestic frustration particularly closely because he felt that his advice about taking advantage of the good Grafton genes had tipped the scales for me, and here we were, high and dry, those genes not including fertility in this particular generation, it appeared. I told him of my fears concerning adoption, which he shared but perhaps not as glumly, pointing out that there was a substantial chance that the adopted child might be quite to our taste. He did, however, make a very provocative suggestion that we look into foster homes for a child grown to the point where we could form an opinion of their character. Such a thing had never occurred to me, but the more I thought about it, the more I liked it. It certainly would give us an advantage against the possibility of ending up with a really wrong kid. I had enough confidence in my ability to size people up to think that I could scope out a child and not be too badly fooled. At least it seemed to have some promise, and when I came home I put the matter to Susan. Could she poke around and find out where there were foster homes and what sort of kids they have in residence and so forth? I figured that even beyond our own good judgment, the foster parents, unless they were pretty dull, must have formed some opinions of their own and could help us make a good choice. If they would level with us. Susan agreed that it sounded reasonable and so she started looking.

There were a surprising number of foster parent homes around. I had had no idea it was such a widespread business. It was left to Susan to try and decide who was worth visiting. What we didn't know was that a lot of these homes were just ways of people making money from the state, taking the kids in and getting paid for their care and not necessarily doing it because they loved kids and wanted to help them. Well, I guess that's all right. If the state looked in from time to time, as I hoped they did, the kids were probably better off than in the homes they had come from. Susan was drawing a lot of blanks, however. Once in awhile she'd think she might have something and we would drive out and see what was what. Absolutely a total waste of time. The whole effort was getting to be more of a chore than a quest when one day I came home and Susan reported that she had a lead. She had called a home and spoken to a cultured, articulate woman on the other end who seemed to be doing this from the goodness of her heart and who cordially invited us to come over some time in a way that impressed Susan as being almost a social invitation. We made a date for the following Sunday morning. It turned out to be a most memorable morning.

20

We drove to a section of town that I was unfamiliar with, attractive older homes, quiet streets, huge trees, very dignified. The house numbers were set so far back that we were having trouble finding 2100 when we came on a low stone wall leading to an open, gated entrance with the number 2100 on it. We parked on the broad street and walked to the door. Before I could ring the bell, the door was opened by a bespectacled little woman in unfashionable clothes whom I took to be Mrs. Armbrewster. No, she protested, she was the teacher; Mrs. Armbrewster would be here shortly. She ushered us into a large living room furnished with rather unattractive antiques, comfortable and lived in and probably decorated a lifetime ago just as we found it. We heard noises that sounded as though they came from upstairs, the sound of children, and Susan and I looked nervously at each other, our first foray into the real life world of children cast adrift, neither of us knowing what to expect.

Brisk footsteps across the wooden floored foyer preceded the entry of a vigorous, no nonsense lady of uncertain years with the blue-white hair and careful grooming of ladies of her age in that period, a warm smile and direct manner that put me at my ease. She looked like the sort of person that one could trust, a type I felt comfortable with, not unlike Susan's mother. She marched up to us, introduced herself, shook hands with authority and asked us to be seated. I helped with the chair she seemed determined to draw up to ours and we sat in a tight little circle, smiling politely.

"I'm so glad you could come. I'm always thrilled to meet people who love children. My husband and I raised four fine boys, each of them a credit to us all their lives but sadly, all living so far way and so involved in their own careers and affairs that we get together only a few times a year. They all have children now, so we have, oh heavens, eight... no nine, it is now, nine grandchildren. Darlings every one. We have such fun when they visit. I just love them. My husband passed away four years ago and I was so lonely, I just thought I had to have some children around, so I applied to be a foster mother and that's the whole story. They send a new one to me from time to time when I have a vacancy, and I enjoy them so. Every now and then someone takes one of them from me, sometimes a relative who surfaces and says they would like to have them. I do so hope they are happy. Sometimes a child comes along that is just too much for me, not very often, but you know. Some of the boys are just too spunky for me and I have to ask them to place them somewhere else. Not bad boys, just misunderstood, I think. Well, well. I think that's about the story of this place. Your wife and I had a nice chat the other day. I gather you young people are thinking about adopting a foster child. I think that's wonderful. So sad that you have been unable to have your own children, but not everyone is blessed that way. And then there are some who don't consider it a blessing at all, and these are the children we have here. Such a pity. Poor dears. Well, now, what would you like me to do? Would you like to meet the children? They love to have visitors. We don't have very many, I'm afraid." She looked brightly from Susan to me and back to Susan.

"If that wouldn't be too much trouble, yes, we'd love to meet them," Susan said. She tinkled the little bell I had noticed in her hand and presently a young Mennonite girl came in and our hostess asked her to bring the children down, please. The girl left and we resumed our conversation. I told her very briefly of our concerns about adopting an infant. She nodded sagely, but I don't think she really understood. First there was the noise of children leaping and crashing downstairs, the clatter across the foyer, then the shushing instructions of the Mennonite girl, some suppressed giggling, a hasty recovery of a more controlled deportment and then an amusing, stiff parade into the room of several boys and girls of various ages, fighting hard to contain their urge to laugh at the solemnity of the entrance which clearly was not their usual style. I glanced at Susan and found she was enjoying the act as much as I.

"Boys and girls, I'd like you to meet two friends of mine, Mr. and Mrs. Hawkins." She beckoned to the oldest boy, a real actor I guessed. He came over, still trying to control his mirth, looking back at the others to see how his formality was playing. He gave what he considered to be a theatrical bow and then overcome at the absurdity of the situation, started howling in a croaking laughter that reduced the other kids to fits of their own. Mrs. Armbrewster was smiling and shaking her head in defeat.

"Children, children, do please come to order. This is certainly not the way to behave with visitors. What will they think of you? Now. Let's try to be more like ladies and gentlemen. This is Arnold," taking the clown by the hand and pulling him to one side. "Now, Jeffery, come over here and say hello, that's a good fellow. This is Jeffrey, Mr. and Mrs. Hawkins," and so on down the line, some of the novelty having worn off, the younger children now shy and quiet and uneasy. Our hostess looked around.

"Anna, where is Mitzi? Did she come down with you?" Anna indicated she had not. "Well do go and bring her down, Anna. Tell her we have some very nice people visiting and that I want her to meet them." She turned to us. "Mitzi has been here only a short time and she is still very shy. Sweet little thing, but very quiet. I think it's important for her to meet people, don't you? She'll be down shortly. In the meantime, maybe the children would like to tell you what they are doing in school. We have a perfectly marvelous teacher who comes in and gives the children their lessons right here. I think you must have met her when you arrived. Really a very capable woman and doing such a splendid job with them. Martha, can you tell the Hawkinses the poem you learned? The one you told me this morning?" Martha was dumbstruck at first, but one of the other girls raised her hand as though to volunteer something of her own, and that set Martha off. The poem was delivered in the tiniest voice imaginable, and Mrs. Armbrewster called her over to us to do it again so we could hear. She came as close as she dared, and while looking resolutely at her shoes, once more delivered her little poem. We praised her and told her how much we had enjoyed it and she quickly walked

back to the group. At that moment Mrs. Armbrewster looked behind her and exclaimed, "Ah! Here's our Mitzi. Do come in, dear.
I want you to meet some friends of mine." Mitzi stood rooted just
inside the opened doors, staring resolutely at the floor. "Won't
you come over, dear? The Hawkinses would love to meet you. Do
come over and say hello, Mitzi, won't you?" We waited as Mitzi
very slightly shook her head, standing perfectly motionless. "Oh,
very well, dear, just make yourself at home and you can meet
them later on. That's a good girl." Attention was turned to the
other children who had decided to do some more reciting, now a
contest instead of a duty.

I could hardly understand a word the kids were saying as
they insisted on correcting each other's recitations, bickering,
voicing wounded exclamations. Losing interest, I turned and
looked again at Mitzi, a frail, slender little waif in a worn, plain
garment, perhaps an adult undergarment of some sort, tattered
little ruffles on the straps, clutching a battered Teddy bear. She
had long, straight black hair kept from her face with a simple
black ribbon, still standing frozen in place but now staring not at
the floor but at me with great black eyes, serious, unblinking, un-
wavering. In the space of a heartbeat I felt a profound wave of the
deepest empathy with this strange little spirit, this otherworldly,
unnaturally sober little fairy child. I smiled. Nothing. I enlarged
the smile and gestured to her to come to me. She continued to
stare at me without a trace of expression. I assumed a look of exaggerated disappointment, trying to tempt her to please me, gesturing again for her to come to me. Balked, I glanced at Susan
who I realized now had been watching us. Susan was smiling and
trying to coax the child to come over with no better success. Who
had any idea of what had gone on in that child's life that made her
so what? cautious? fearful? Was she perhaps retarded? I gestured
once more and looking now at the floor, she came slowly over
and stood in front of me, her chin on her chest, slowly wringing
her tiny hands.

"How do you do, Mitzi. I'm very pleased to meet you. My
name is Peter. Will you shake my hand?" There was no sign of a
response as I put out my hand to her, but then after a bit, she
slowly put her hand where I could take it in mine and give it a

tiny squeeze. "That was very nice of you to come over to see me. I was getting lonely. Will you keep me company for awhile?" The head stayed down, but it nodded a little. "That's such a pretty name. Mitzi. I've never known a girl by the name of Mitzi. Would you like to be my friend?" A little shrug, the head still down. "I don't have very many friends. It's so lonely not to have a friend. Won't you be my friend? Please?" This time she nodded. "That's very nice of you. I hope we'll be good friends. Would you like to sit on my lap?" A little shrug. "If I help you?" A tiny nod, so I cautiously lifted this delicate little creature onto my lap and steadied her with an arm around her shoulders. And now the face came up. Face to face, the great black eyes meeting mine, carefully searching my face, thinking who knows what, and then as something about me seemed to satisfy some dream, some standard, some expectation or hope, put her head on my chest and with her little hands, clung to my jacket. I scarcely dared breathe. It was like having a bird fly out of the forest and light on one's finger. Without stirring, I looked over at Susan, my unemotional Susan who sat with tears in her eyes, ramrod straight, cheeks flushed, turning quickly to brush her eyes and back again to gaze at the tableau before her.

With the noise of the remaining children competing for attention with their garbled recitations, the fragile creature on my lap was utterly still and so quiet that I looked at Susan who could see her face, and she nodded, yes, she was asleep. Mrs. Armbrewster, who had been attempting to bring order from chaos saw the three of us and herded the rest out of the room and closed the doors. She came over and sat near us, charmed at the scene nearly in tears herself, I thought.

"This is the first time I have ever seen this little dear anything but unhappy. How sweet she looks! You must have a special charm, Mr. Hawkins. Just look at how she clings to you. I think she's asleep, isn't she?" Susan nodded. "Poor little thing," our hostess continued very softly, "I really have no idea of how things have been for her. The mother recently died in a hospital. Some sort of cancer, I was told, but other than that, I know very little about her. The mother apparently was one of those women who was unable to resist men and I gather life must have been rather unkind to her, don't you know? On her birth certificate the father is listed as unknown, and from what I gather, there were quite a number of men who could have been the father. Dreadful business. So sad that we have people in our midst so unfortunate. And this is what happens. Poor little child. Heaven knows how long it's been since she has had someone hold her like that. Are you getting tired? Shall I have Mary come take her upstairs?" I told her that I would just as soon sit a time longer, if that were all right, and she said of course, she understood and asked if we would like some tea or coffee. The coffee was freshly made, so we had a cup, Mitzi now slumped into a tiny, angular bundle, sound asleep and undisturbed by my squirming to resettle her. We sat thus, quietly for the most part until Mary came in, showing some concern that I was being burdened and came forward to retrieve her charge. My permission was requested and at this point I felt it proper to let her go, and she was carried out to continue her sleep elsewhere.

"Mrs. Armbrewster," I began. "This has been a rather unusual experience for us this morning. I wonder if it would be inconvenient for you if I arranged to call you and come over again sometime and try to get to know this little lady better. She seems to be attracted to us so perhaps I could visit some and get better acquainted and see how we get along. Would that be agreeable with you?"

"Why of course! Please do. We'd be so happy to have you come by any time. I'll arrange it so that the other children won't interfere. That would be better, wouldn't it? That was such a touching scene. Well, well. One never knows, does one?" We rose to leave.

"Thank you so very much, Mrs. Armbrewster. You've been very generous with your time. I'll call you as soon as I know when we can come visit again. Will you please tell Mitzi how sorry we were that we had to leave before she was awake? And that we will come again very soon and that...well, just tell her whatever you think would reassure her that we like her and we want to be friends. Or something. I guess what I am trying to say is that we want her to know that we will come back again soon, but...well, how are we going to tell her anything without getting her hopes up? We're absolutely new to this business of shopping around for a child and even though I'm very anxious not to disappoint Mitzi, there are still things my wife and I have to talk over. The last thing I want is for that little child to be hurt. Can you be vague but hopeful, or something like that? I'm not getting this over very well, but am I making sense?"

"Perfectly, Mr. Hawkins. I understand completely. I'll tell her something that will make her happy but not put you in an awkward position if this just doesn't fit into your plans. I think I know exactly what you're going through. They tug at your heart strings, don't they? I have this happen to me all the time, and I don't think I'll ever get to the point where it doesn't happen to me from time to time. That's what makes this work so rewarding. I'll take care of it. You can trust me."

We left and sat in the car. I looked at Susan and Susan looked back at me. I raised my eyebrows and shrugged. "Is that the hand of fate, or what?" I said. Susan shook her head thoughtfully. "Talk about being smitten! How are we going to be able to walk away from that little angel?" We sat for a time longer, recovering from the emotions we shared from this meeting.

"I think what you said we would do is the right approach," Susan said. "We'll just have to come over and visit until we see if what we just went through is the real thing or just our first experience with an orphan. I must say, I can't remember ever having been so touched. The sight of that little thing coming over to you at last and then that fierce hug when you took her up on your lap. That was a sight I'll never forget. You must have melted."

"Did you ever see eyes like that? Those huge, black eyes? The little sharecropper dress and the long hair hanging down? It was right out of Dickens. Dear, poor little thing. What in the world do you suppose she has been through? The way she hugged me! I wonder if she's ever been held? Poor baby. I feel so badly about not being there when she wakes up. I hope she doesn't think we've abandoned her. Mrs. Armbrewster seemed to understand, though. I think she'll know how to handle it, don't you? We've just got to come over again very soon. Do you think we could try to make it tomorrow? I just can't stand the thought of that little girl wondering when she'll see us again. And of course, we've got to get to know her better. At least she seems to understand what I said. She surely must talk, at least I hope so. We've really got to make sure we're not being nutty about her just out of sympathy for her. I know it sounds hard hearted, but I'm going to promise myself that she's got to show me somehow that she is at least normal. I mean, she doesn't have to be Phi Bet' material, but I've got to be satisfied that she's at least average. What do you think?" It was only form, but I felt that if nothing but for the sake of form, I had to make a stab at objectivity. There had to be some common sense along with the sentiment, I thought, and common sense said I should take it slowly and try to keep my instincts reined in.

"Absolutely," Susan answered, "but she'd better pass the test because I don't see how you're going to be able to walk away from that child. That was pretty convincing, the way she just so much as told you that you were hers. But yes, of course, let's find out as quickly as we can if this is going to work. The longer we think back on today, the more certain it is that we'll take her home." The phrase 'take her home' seemed so natural that I realized I had already made my decision and would be just going through the motions of evaluating her suitability. The very thought of 'evaluating' her was such a joke. The decision had been made by Mitzi when she got up onto my lap and I couldn't conceive of not taking her home. But I would go through the motions. I would go through the motions, and then take her home.

I arranged to leave the lab early the next afternoon, called Mrs. Armbrewster, then called Susan but was unable to get her at home or at the Foundation, so having made the appointment, I went to the home. The first order of business, now that we were prospective parents, was to reduce the level of formality it seemed. Mrs. Armbrewster told me her name was Helen, as she would prefer to be addressed, so we became Peter and Helen.

"I told Mitzi that you were an old friend and that you were coming to visit me again, and asked if she would like to say hello, so you are under no suspicion of being here to see her, if that will make it more comfortable for you. I think it very considerate of you not to get her hopes up and then perhaps dash them. There must have been so much of that in her life already. Mary will bring her down. The other children are at their lessons." We sat and talked a few minutes before Mary arrived with Mitzi. She was wearing the same dress, which I learned had some particular significance for her and which she insisted on wearing every day. Our eyes met as she came into the room, Mary discretely withdrawing.

"Well, hello little Sleepy-head. You were so tired yesterday and so sound asleep that I decided not to wake you to say goodbye. How nice it is to see you again! Come give me a hug," and she came over close to me and looked up shyly, but not showing any signs of giving the hug. "No hug today? Well, that's all right. Sometimes I don't feel like hugging, either. Would you like to shake my hand?" She nodded and smiled a tiny smile and held out her hand. I took it and solemnly shook it…and shook it…and shook it some more, a little harder up and down, a little harder and soon I was shaking it wildly up and down and she began to giggle and then laughed a gap toothed laugh, high and musical. I looked at her in mock dismay. "What's so funny?" I asked still shaking her helpless little arm up and down. "This is," she giggled. "Well now, just a minute," I said, continuing to shake her hand, swinging it, making circles, up and down, "shaking hands is a serious business! What makes you think it's so funny?" She was really laughing now, and I suddenly stopped and let go of her hand. "Well, if you think shaking hands is so funny, maybe we'd better hug. What do you think?" A big grin now and she held out her arms and I scooped her up and stood, hugging her and bending forward and backward and side to side, delighting Mitzi who laughed and squealed. I stopped. "More!' she cried, and I gyrated some more and stopped. More!" she cried again but now I pretended to be exhausted. "Oh, my. I can't go on. You've worn me out, completely worn me out," and I panted and heaved. She was thrilled. "You'll have to let me rest a little while I talk to Mrs. Armbrewster. Here, come sit on my lap and be nice while we talk."

She sat still and I talked of the weather and whatnot with Helen, who took up the game and seemed amused and grateful for the little bit of fun I had created. Mitzi spent the time staring at my face, touching my hand, and when occasionally I looked down at her, she smiled a little smile. A few times she put her head against my chest, then she would seem to think of something and sit up and look at my face as I talked to Helen. Whatever was she thinking?

Helen gave me a look and asked if I would excuse her for a couple minutes, there was something she had forgotten to do, so she left us sitting there and now it was time to talk to Mitzi. "So your name is Mitzi, is it?" She nodded. "And how old is Miss Mitzi?" She looked down at my hand, more solemn now, the spell of some sort that we had woven, gone for the moment and she whispered "Six."

"What a wonderful age to be! That used to be my favorite age to be. Or was it seven? Or eight, ornineortenorelevenor...I forget." A little smile. Does Mitzi have a middle name?" She shook her head. "Does Mitzi have a last name?" Negative again. "So it's just Mitzi? Well that's all the name you need, as far as I'm concerned. That is a beautiful, beautiful name. Can you spell it for me?" She shook her head. "Can you write your name yet?" She signaled no. I guessed that she had had no teaching of any sort, even from her Mom. I was getting concerned now about having asked so many things that she was unable to respond to. "Do you like stories?" I asked. She shrugged. "Would you like me to tell you a story?" No response. "Would you like me to tell you the story about the three bears?" She shrugged, that habitual little gesture, probably not one of indifference as much as uncertainty. How very much uncertainly she must have dealt with in her short life. I decided to take the lead and I told her the story. As I imitated the various voices, especially the bears, her head came up and she started watching my mouth, interested now, and when I came to the voice of the Papa Bear, she giggled, looking at me, and I capitalized on the breakthrough and gave Papa Bear a lot of lines he was not entitled to.

By the time I was done, she was giggling and presented me with the demand that only a child can make: tell it again. Now I had a rapt audience who occasionally volunteered a line of dialogue she had remembered, and when I came to the Papa Bear, she got nearly hysterical. "Say it again!" she would plead of a favorite remark Papa Bear might make and I would say it again.

Mitzi

This went on until I was getting to that point that parents can get to, and mercifully Helen returned. Now what animation! "Oh Helen, he told me the story of the Three Bears and Goldilocks sleeped in their beds and sat in their chairs and she got caught and Papa Bear said who's been eating my porridge and ..." Well, you get the picture, formerly nearly mute, she was babbling to Helen who was expressing amazement and disbelief and all the things we express to children to reward them for such efforts. "What a wonderful story, Mitzi. You must be sure and tell the other children, I'm sure they would enjoy it. Do you want to go upstairs now?" She put her head down and shook it vigorously. "Well, then, you can stay down here and talk some more to Mr. Hawkins. Would you like that?" She looked up at me and I gave her the encouraging look she seemed to seek and she treated us to a little smile and a nod. "Did you say thank you to Mr. Hawkins for being so nice? When someone does something nice for you, you should say 'thank you'. Can you say thank you, Mr. Hawkins?" Now the head is down and again and she shrugged. I signaled Helen not to pursue it and knelt down in front of Mitzi so that we were eye to eye.

"Would you like me to come again tomorrow and tell you another story?" She nodded but the head stayed down and I guessed there might have been other promises made and broken and that she had little faith in this one coming true. "I've enjoyed talking with you today, Mitzi. You're a very nice little girl and I like you. I'll see you tomorrow and maybe my wife can come with me. Would you like that?" She shrugged and I began to feel that I should go slowly with anything that merited only a shrug. I held out my hand and her downcast eyes saw it and now the face came up with a smile and she grabbed my hand with both of hers and shook it as hard a she was able, giggling and grinning and we parted on this high note, although she declined to return my parting wave as I went out of the house.

I told Susan about the visit and my tentative impression, that the child seems to have been badly neglected and was certainly behind in accomplishments for her age, but had remembered some of the dialogue in my story and had shown that little burst of joy when she told Helen about it. She was not retarded, it

231

seemed certain, but woefully mistrustful and somber. I told Susan that I thought it might be better for me to go alone the first few times and not overwhelm the child. I had made a contact that I felt could be improved upon and that would give me a better idea of what was inside that mysterious little head and Susan agreed that it should be my show for the present.

On the way to our next meeting, I bought an illustrated book of fairy tales, making sure that the Three Bears was included. Mitzi was in the living room with Helen when I arrived and she smiled shyly. I stood where I was at the entrance to the room and stuck out my hand and she uttered a shy little sound of some sort and ran over and grabbed my hand and shook it vigorously and we seemed to have reconnected. As I talked with Helen for a few minutes, I noted that she was looking very pointedly at the book and the illustration on the cover. Helen excused herself and I settled on a couch with my audience who seemed mesmerized by the book and seemed very impatient for me to open it. "Isn't this a pretty book, Mitzi? Look at all the pictures," I said as I turned through the pages with no purpose in mind other than to make the book fascinating and something she wanted to explore. Suddenly she put a finger in the book and said, "There he is! There he is! That's Papa Bear!" It wasn't, but she had seen it and I had to leaf back a little to come to the proper page and sure enough, there were the three bears and a penitent Goldilocks confessing her guilt to an authoritative looking Papa Bear. A fine figure of a bear indeed. Mitzi was in raptures. She put her finger on the bear and told me over and over that that was Papa Bear. We went over the entire picture and she identified everything correctly and wondered over things, no concept of porridge but accepting my explanation that it was just another name for hot cereal. Did she know what hot cereal was? No. "What did you have for breakfast, sweetheart, what did you like for breakfast when you were with your Mommy?" Looking down, she shrugged, that defensive little gesture. "Do you like milk, Mitzi?" No answer. I decided I needed some help, so I excused myself and left Mitzi with the book and sought out Helen.

"Do you have any idea what this little girl was raised on? She doesn't even seem to know what milk is. What does she eat for breakfast here?" She excused her ignorance and said she would check with Mary who was responsible for breakfast. Mary came quickly to tell me personally that Mitzi just ate dry cereal, liked plain bread and any pastries that were served. Was she offered milk? Yes, but declined it and seemed most content with just dry cereal. She liked orange juice but was suspicious at first. Having been there only days, not much more had surfaced for me to go on, but I guessed she had been left to feed herself with the cheapest and most expedient nourishment Mommy was able to provide. Helen tut-tutted and seemed a little embarrassed that this had been going on without her knowing it. "You can be sure that I'll have something to say about this, Peter. Dear me. That's shocking in this day and age." I was beginning to feel that there were a great many worse things in Mitzi's background that would shock both of us if we knew of them.

I returned to Mitzi to find her totally absorbed with the book looking carefully, turning the pages with exaggerated delicacy. I sat down quietly beside her and let her keep the book on her lap.

"Would you like for me to read you a story? You pick out the one you want and I'll read it to you." She took the longest time, selecting just the picture that seemed to promise the best story and having made up her mind, put her finger squarely in the middle of the picture and said "This one." I read her the story, tracing the words with my finger to establish the idea that they were associated with what I was saying, not knowing whether even this fundamental relationship was known to her. Satisfied that it wasn't when I finished the story, I told her how she could 'tell the story to herself' when she learned what the words said, as I was doing. She seemed interested, so I went to the Three Bear story and found 'Papa Bear' and pointed to the first word and told her that it said Papa and the next word was 'bear' and then I started to scan the page and pick out each 'Papa' and each 'Bear' and very shortly she picked out her first 'Papa' on her own and I praised her and told her how proud I was and how she would learn to read in no time. I picked another common word and we played the same game, and now she was getting excited. She made mistakes, of course, but they were understandable. The important thing was that I thought she was catching on quicker than I had expected.

"What a smart little girl you are, Mitzi! You are learning how to read already. I'm very proud of you. I want to shake your hand but not so hard. You might hurt me.

That tickled her, the notion that she could hurt a big man, so she gave my hand only one hard shake and looked at me for approval. "Very good. Much, much more ladylike. Now, would you like me to read another one?" and of course she did.

I must have read for an hour, slowly, tracing the letters, Mitzi every now and then seizing on a recognized word in advance of my reading, and giddy with excitement when I praised her. That was a lovely afternoon, seeing this darling child responding to love, witnessing her mind responding to attention and instruction. I'm not sure how long this might have gone on if Helen hadn't come in and politely announced that the children were having dinner and that Mitzi had to wash her hands and face and take her place, which she seemed to do cheerfully, looking back at me as she left the room and then, remembering something, returned quickly and gave me a quick hug and a smile and then flew off again.

I drove home slowly, thinking very hard about this experience, convinced that she was at least normal, possibly bright, badly, badly in need of schooling and love. I found that knowing more about her past was less and less important to me. That was over. There was nothing, I felt, to be gained from hearing sordid details from people who might have known the mother, even if I could find them. The important thing was to put the past behind us without attempting to bury it and get started with a normal life for this little girl.

Susan was impressed at the things I told her about our growing closeness, but in spite of my urging, declined for the moment to join me on my visits, my wise Susan. "I think this should be your affair for now, Peter. There is plenty of time for her to get to know me, but I think it will be much better for her to be getting only one message until she can absorb more. As shy and insecure as she is, I think it might be a mistake to overwhelm her," and of course, she was right. I had told Jim about what was going on and he encouraged me to take as much time as I needed, so I went to visit Mitzi every afternoon that week. Each day I told her what time I would be there and made it a point to be on time, as I learned that she had learned how to tell time and was to be found hovering near the door as the hour of my arrival came due. By now it was obvious to everyone that we were going to take this little creature home, but I hung on grimly to the letter of my quest and asked to see her medical records from the Health Department. Such as they were, they told me almost nothing. I wasn't a doctor, but I could smell boredom in a report when I saw it and I had little faith in what I read, so I arranged to have her taken to a pediatrician that Dr. Grafton told me was a bright guy. Helen took her, as I felt it better not to be associated with anything she might consider frightening. This report was much better. Lots of observations about behavior and background that I'm sure were close to being on target and pretty much matched mine, but as for physical health, undernourished, a trifle under developed physically for her age, otherwise OK. Specifically, no evidence of physical or sexual abuse. Teeth needed some attention, lab work about normal although somewhat anemic, nothing we couldn't fix.

I don't know why it was such an emotional occasion when I told Helen, not in the least surprised, of course, that we would like to adopt Mitzi. She was thrilled and set about telling me what to do with the State and so on, but I had determined and Susan agreed that we would prefer to have an attorney handle the whole thing so that there would be no slip up. I was so anxious that we do it right, so much seemed to be at stake. The mother was definitely dead, there were no surviving relatives of the mother, the father was unknown, so it must have been pretty open and shut for the attorney, and the papers were prepared in very short order, cleared with the State and we were nominally Mitzi's parents, a fact of which she was unaware.

At this point I thought I ought to consult the principal in the case and the following afternoon when we had finished reading, I said, as though the thought had just come to me, "Say! Would you like to come and live with me? For ever and ever and ever? Would you?" The notion seemed to baffle her. Where would she sleep? I told her she would have her own room with a nice bed and a soft pillow and a soft rug and her own bureau for her clothes and her own closet. And we would read stories every night until bedtime. She thought about this quite seriously. Would Helen be there? No, but she could come and visit anytime at all. Would Mary be there? No, but she could come and see her, too, when she had time. She thought a long time, and I felt it might be just as well to let the idea simmer. "You can tell me some other time. You don't have to decide right now. Ask Helen and Mary what they think. Maybe tomorrow you will decide what to do." I left a puzzled, thoughtful little girl, asked to appeal to her own resources for such a momentous decision. I had no doubt about the eventual outcome, but I wanted her to arrive at the decision on her own, with plenty of help from Helen and Mary, if necessary, of course. Susan was profoundly disappointed that I had not come home with her, everything in readiness and no Mitzi but my explanation was duly approved and it was agreed that I would call and announce success when it occurred.

The next day when I arrived, there was no doubt about the answer. She ran to me and asked when she could come to live in my house. "Oh, my! So sudden. You certainly make up your mind in a hurry. Well, now let me see. I'll tell my wife. Then we'll have to fix up your room just the way you want it. Then, lets' see…" She was dancing up and down, in a fever of excitement. "Well, I guess we had just better go right now. Will that be all right?"

She squealed with delight and grabbed my hand to start out of the door at a run. I gathered her up and told her to hold her horses while we got her clothes, all packed of course as Mitzi had come to her decision shortly after I left and had been unable to talk of anything else since. Mary came with a little shopping bag of clothes and the dreadful looking little teddy bear, hairless and soiled, a treasure, no doubt. I thanked Helen warmly and told her I would come by and keep her posted and started to carry Mitzi out. "No, no. I want to go out myself!" and when I put her down, she grabbed my hand again and started to run. She was so excited that she had to be urged to kiss Helen and Mary goodbye and thank them. That done in haste, nothing would do but she drag me to the car she had seen me get out of and pile into the front seat. She seemed awed by the interior, and ran her hands over every-thing, watching intently as I shifted gears, the big black eyes alert and excited. She was surprisingly quiet when we arrived and she saw the house that was to be her home for ever and ever and ever.

Susan came out to meet us and Mitzi was painfully shy and held my hand with grim determination. Susan knelt and kissed her and talked to her in the tone that women have, and by degrees, Mitzi seemed to accept the notion that Susan was to be her new mother and we went in to her very own room, which had the ef-fect of rendering her mute and I suppose unbelieving. We went over every item of furniture, 'your' bed, 'your' closet, 'your' chair, 'your' own bathroom. I wonder what was going one in her little mind. It would take some time. We went out to show her the living room and our bedroom and the dining room and the kitchen and then went out and walked around the yard to see the flowers and pick a couple which she clutched for the longest time after-ward. We had talked about the first meal and decided on ham-burger and French fries, some fresh fruit, ice cream, sound choices, it turned out, except for the fruit. Cocoa seemed to go down well and she had two mugs with the result that when I sat to read to her after dinner, she was asleep in no time and Susan took her up and got her bathed and in a new little nightie. She brought her out to say goodnight.

"Goodnight, sweetheart," and she tottered over to me and gave me a big hug and seemed unlikely to let go the grip she had on my shirt, so I took her up and we both went in and put her in bed. There was still some concern in her face, and I asked if she would like to hear a story. She nodded so I launched into a low voiced Goldilocks and in no time, she was fast asleep. We sat and grinned at each other. "Well, Ma?," I said. "Well, Pa?," she re-plied.

The next morning we realized we had not established our new identities with her, just never having gotten around to it in the excitement of the arrival. Susan got her up and dressed and when she came out to breakfast, she was a little bewildered again. All this must have seemed a dream, I suppose.

"Did you have a good sleep, sweetheart?" I asked. She gave the little non-committal shrug that I had become used to. "Are you still sleepy, darling?" She gave a little nod. "Did you say good morning to Mommy?" She looked down in the way I had seen when she was distressed. I reached out and brought her to me, turned her to face Susan and put my arms around her. "Can you say good morning to Mommy?" She shook her lowered head. "Why not, baby?" I asked gently and at last she answered so softly I could scarcely hear. "That's not my Mommy. That's Susan."

I looked up at Susan with the obvious question in my face, and she nodded. "Can you say good morning to Susan?" I whispered softly into her ear and now the head slowly lifted and she nodded and in a tiny voice said, "Good morning, Susan". Before Susan could answer, I whispered again," I don't think Susan could hear you. Try again!" and she repeated her greeting a little louder. I shook my head at Susan and whispered "Louder!" and now she looked around at me with the beginning of a tiny grin and then facing Susan said in a normal voice, "Good morning, Susan." And once again I whispered "Louder!" and now she giggled and yelled "Good morning, Susan!" as loud as her little voice would permit and broke into a fit of giggling. Susan had a broad smile and knelt down and took her in her arms and said "Good morning, Mitzi. My, what a loud voice you have," and thus Susan came to be called.

I was sure I was going to be Peter to her, but when Susan asked her to say good morning to Daddy, she replied, "That's Papa Bear!" in a loud voice and more giggles and that became my title, soon thereafter for most purposes shortened to "Papa" although still the full, more formal "Papa Bear" on occasion.

There was so much for both sides to learn. Mitzi was painfully shy with Susan for many days, but girls do have that affinity for each other, and the personal attention of a devoted mother must have grown to be terribly important to Mitzi. The two of them were together all day, and I had no thought of telling Susan how to handle this new situation. Almost day by day when I arrived home, there was visibly a closer bond, but in spite of this, Mitzi was my constant companion when I was home, sitting with me to talk about her day, walking around the yard to inspect, holding my hand. When I was quiet, she sat where she could look at me, the closer the better, not staring now, but smiling her little crooked smile with the dimple in her right cheek. Sometimes I was concerned that Susan might feel she was being slighted, but she insisted that she loved to see the two of us together, and I knew she meant it.

We had talked about education and both agreed that she must stay at home with us at least until she showed enough confidence in her new existence to be put in school and not feel she was being abandoned again. For the time, then, we decided that Susan would teach her at home and we would think about school later. As it turned out the occasion never arose for us to consider schooling anywhere but at home, as Mitzi thrived so on Susan's tutelage that going to school would have been a demotion. Beyond the pleasure Susan got from seeing this keen little mind learn, she enjoyed Mitzi's company, which became more and more charming. After a time I realized that Susan was staying away from the Foundation more by choice than by obligation. We got a book on phonics and Susan began the type of reading program that we had grown up with, going through a pile of children's books that had been favorites with us both. She learned by leaps and bounds. She was thrilled to sound out letters and recognize that they made familiar words. 'Goldilocks' came out and she loved to sit and painstakingly sounding out every word she could, finally memorizing the story, or so it seemed to me. Now in the evening, after I had read to her, she insisted on reading to me, so pleased with herself, almost hugging herself at her new ability and the feeling of accomplishment. She could do something that her grown up Papa Bear and Susan could do.

We had a television set, but neither Susan nor I were very much attracted to the programming in those days, so aside from an occasional program, Mitzi was raised on books and music and conversation. The little progress examinations that were required for home taught children were embarrassingly easy for our little prodigy. She was so far ahead of the standards that it almost seemed insulting to ask her to take them, but she laughed about it and endured it with good grace even though she was well aware of how advanced she was.

Susan would take her shopping and she was outfitted in the things that every little girl needed, but when it came to what might be called optional clothes where Susan allowed her to choose, she had very definite and interesting tastes, picked up from who knows where, firm about her choices which though not always to Susan's taste, were tasteful in a different way. While she was willing to be dressed in 'Susan's' clothes, when she picked her own things to wear, we could hardly get her out of them, even at her pleading allowing her on occasion to sleep in a particular dress that was too precious to remove.

Emily's quiet but undisguised objection to our even considering adoption, especially of a child from such a sordid background, had been difficult for Susan for a time, but Mitzi's charm was undeniable and Emily slowly relented and was won over, the victory entirely one of Mitzi's doing. Despite Emily's also disapproving the plan to teach Mitzi ourselves, she was eventually brought to acknowledge the progress Mitzi made between our meetings, which we continued as a tradition to observe each Sunday.

Mitzi had entered a new world which must have seemed to have been inhabited by unimaginably nice and thoughtful and generous people, and she responded in kind, showing so much uncritical affection for Emily that it was irresistible and Emily simply had to yield and accept this little waif as the adorable child she was becoming. Our little sprite was beginning to flourish as she came out of the darkness in which she had lived so long, all this potential poised within her like a nearly bursting bud, waiting for the opportunity to blossom, and blossom she did. She had an insatiable curiosity and a challenging thirst to learn, gobbling up ideas and words, studying Susan and me, thinking, remembering, rehearsing and playing back select material out of which she was fashioning herself. Her native talent for mimicry made her so easy to teach. As though all this were not enough, she was in the bargain, cheerful, anxious to please, considerate of the adults in her world and such a joy simply to be with. Her mouth was shaped in such a way that she seemed always on the verge of a smile with the result that people instinctively smiled at her when they saw her. It was just not possible to feel down when Mitzi was around. Her delicious spirit infused the atmosphere around her with an innocent curiosity and delight that was infectious.

It was the three of us now, outside of my working hours. An only child has such advantages, as Susan knew so well. We unconsciously, or perhaps consciously, determined to make her more of a companion than a dependent. With little effort, her table manners became quite acceptable and we regularly took her with us to dine in the homes of friends and to restaurants where she deciphered the menu (with occasional help) and ordered for herself, invariably charming the waiters. She learned to greet our guests with confidence and seemed to love to meet new people, unspoiled by the excessive attention her precocious charm attracted to her, natural in a way that reflected an unaffected simplicity and genuineness that was beguiling. As a result, she became everyone's pet. Susan and I could scarcely believe what we had stumbled into. Mitzi exceeded even the highest expectations I had imagined for any child born to us.

We came to believe that she could do most anything and we arranged for her to start piano lessons. Susan spent hours working with her on all sorts of art projects. These were very special to her and when I came home, I could usually anticipate Mitzi running out to the car with papers in hand to show me her latest crayon or watercolor or handwriting lesson. Susan spent a lot of time with her in the pool and Mitzi took to swimming like an otter. With her long black hair, which she insisted on not having fastened when she swam, her olive skin which tanned almost in the course of a day, she looked like something out of a Gaugin painting. Susan's approach to swimming was one of discipline and style. She was a strong and graceful swimmer and enjoyed the pool almost exclusively as an opportunity to exercise, to swim laps. She encouraged Mitzi to learn the backstroke and the butterfly, but all Mitzi wanted to do was swim a very effective and speedy if not classic free style and cavort and swim underwater and do acrobatics and play. She could fly through the water, but had no interest in racing or competition of any sort, something of a disappointment to Susan. It was the same with diving. Susan was not a competitive diver, but she was quite good at several dives and taught them to an utterly fearless Mitzi in the course of a summer but could elicit no further interest in diving, once she could do those few dives she had been taught reasonably well. Susan taught her to play tennis and over time she became a good player, better than I, but having reached a certain level of competence, she was content to settle for that. There was no suggestion that she took pride in simply winning at something. We arranged as often as it was practical to have kids come over to our house to play. Having a pool and a tennis court didn't hurt. Mitzi was better than her peers at most of the things that kids do but she had a knack for not permitting a playmate to feel inferior. She made light of her successes and had genuine praise for the efforts of others. There was never a cross word that I heard of. In a group of kids her age, she was the peacemaker. She was the impartial judge. It was Mitzi who saw to fair play and sharing. This decency and honesty and sensitivity didn't make her the leader in her group, that was not her style. But she was the one they looked to for responsibility.

When we started her in dance, we struck a rich vein. Here she found her métier, not in ballet which was our first thought, but in modern dance. She loved it to distraction and with a little effort was able to give a convincing imitation of much of the dancing she saw in movies. But she tired of formal training, and was satisfied to dance just for her own amusement and ours. Her teacher had told us that she had the kind of talent that very possibly would take her to a professional level, but Mitzi wasn't interested. She loved to dance but on her terms, it appeared. In the evening, she might take a sudden notion that she wanted to dance. Sometimes she just wanted to dance for her own pleasure and Susan and I would sit and watch and applaud. Other times, she wanted to dance with me, and I would take off my shoes and we would glide around clumsily or even better try to jitterbug. She was so weightless that I could fling her around as though we were at the Roseland Ballroom, and she would squeal, hair flying, game for any acrobatic foolishness I would attempt. Often as not we would collapse in a heap at some point, Mitzi's eyes wide and bright, grinning from ear to ear, "Let's do it again!" and off we would go until I had to call it quits.

"Oh, Papa! Your hair is all mussed up! Do you want me to comb it for you?" and I would sit on a footstool and she would get a dish towel and put it around my neck. It was my job to hold a glass of water with a comb in it until the brushing was done and the styling began. This involved a wide variety of locations for the part, most of them fore and aft, but sometimes from one side to the other, this last accompanied by derisive peals of laughter. She would run and get a hand mirror and ask me to check it, waiting for the outrage which was the desired response.

"Mitzi, you fiend! You've ruined my hair! I won't be able to go to work tomorrow!"

"Then you can stay home and we'll play," the impish grin now. "What's a fiend?"

"A fiend is somebody who parts hair the wrong way. I knew I should never have sat down here. I think I'll just get up and do what I can to repair the damage. I may lose my job! You unnatural changeling!"

"What's a chainling?"

"Changeling."

"But what is it," hoping for something horrible.

"I don't think you're old enough for this."

"Yes I am! Yes I am! Tell me, Papa, tell me!" jumping up and down.

"Some times when the fairies have a really rotten child, a real stinker, they slip into someone's house and change it for a nice little girl and the parents wake up and their nice little girl has turned into someone who tries to ruin their hairdo."

"Is that me?"

"Who else? It's the only explanation. Can you talk like a fairy? They have a very strange language."

The face becomes pensive, then lights up and looking me right in the eye, utters some gibberish with an air of great expectancy.

"That's it! That's fairy talk! I knew it, you're bewitched!" Squeals of utter delight.

"What does bewitch mean, Papa?"

And so it would go, I would get a pigtail, or perhaps three pigtails, I would get bobby pins, ribbons, more water, comb,

comb, comb, step back for an appraisal, puzzled dissatisfaction. Redo, reappraise, still not right, redo, ah, perhaps, what did I think? with the mirror held in front of me reflecting a section of the ceiling. Perfect. Just perfect. I knew you could do it and I would sit the remainder of the evening with the new tonsure, Mitzi regarding it critically and occasionally coming over to revise it slightly. Now it was read-to-me time, and Mitzi would select a book and squeeze into the space beside me and I would read to her. What a great number of books we read, Mitzi absorbed, squirming in anticipation, commenting. Occasionally at some injustice in a story, her eyes would grow wide and her body tense and she would interrupt and tell me in detail her opinion of the matter. The story about Hansel and Gretel was particularly difficult for her. She was so incensed at the witch! She told me all the horrid things she would have done to that witch had she been Gretel, and we sat and devised elaborate punishments for that miserable creature which Mitzi usually chose to act out in front of me, simple recitation inadequate to the magnitude of her indignation. How she lived the stories! When I would tuck her in bed, she would go over the plot again, praise here, damnation there, highly moralistic.

Mitzi knew nothing about cards. It didn't appear that she had ever seen a deck of cards, but as soon as she knew her numbers I taught her to play slap jack and go fish and crazy eights, simple games but what a shark this little lady became! She learned to shuffle and deal with amazing dexterity, she plotted and schemed and gloated behind her cards, anticipating her next coup, not in the least concerned about my seeing her hand, perfectly willing to tip my cards down to see what I was concealing, not above cheating but stoutly denying it when challenged. She loved to win and whooped and ran to report if to Susan, repeating the sequence of play in rapture, reliving the triumph. When we got to double solitaire, it was a free for all. Mitzi always played standing up, jumping up and down, eyes darting around, nimble little fingers snatching up cards and slamming them down where I had missed an opportunity with a cry of delight, moaning if she thought she was getting behind, accusing me of all sorts of irregularities. She had a way of making up new rules that seemed to favor her situation at the moment. I would roar in anguish, threaten to quit if she were winning, all this bringing Mitzi to fit of laughter that occasionally put her right onto the floor, unable to control her helpless mirth at my discomfort.

We passed on to rummy of several sorts, cribbage, back gammon, game boards all over the living room during the winter. We got jig saw puzzles, and wouldn't you know, in my absence during the day they would be put together completely, disassembled to please me and then done again, those sharp eyes regularly beating me to the desired fit. When at last I taught her how to play poker, I finally had the upper hand. Bluff just wasn't in her. She emoted, she wrung her hands, she agonized and when she got the cards she wanted, she yipped before putting on her best poker face. As she got a little older and had read more, I brought home a game of Scrabble, Susan sitting in now, and didn't we learn some new words! Mitzi was a most imaginative wordsmith. When a few high counting markers were involved, she could come up with some absolutely dazzling neologisms. Not only come up with them, but stoutly defend them before dissolving in giggles.

I got a volume of Uncle Remus stories and read them in the enchanting and lovingly written dialect that Harris transcribed so well. Mitzi was captivated and nothing then would do but she practice speaking it. In her high pitched, childish voice, a great deal was lost, but what remained was hysterical. She put on Tar Baby for us, using a pillow and playing the Fox for all she was worth, a performance that had even Susan holding her sides. We had such good times, just the three of us, Mitzi enjoying her own acting as much as we, laughing along with us, never able to keep a straight face. I had found someone who loved to be silly.

In the fall and winter, we took Mitzi with us to all the theater we attended, to the concerts, to galleries and museums, to football games, occasionally a hockey game, baseball in the Spring. Mitzi adored parties. She liked to dress up in something of Susan's that could be somehow fitted onto her and pretend she was co-hostess. She loved passing hors d'oeuvres, fetching napkins, setting the dining table properly, taking coats and what not. She freshened drinks with more ice, she helped Susan serve at dinner, and as a reward was seated with us and sat through the meal, speaking if spoken to and not otherwise. Can you believe it? She shook hands with everyone as Susan had taught her, although the women insisted on a kiss in addition. It seemed unavoidable that all this attention and the extravagant compliments would spoil her, but it never happened. She simply took all the compliments in stride and thanked her admirers graciously and that was that. Easy to see why I called her Perfect Child.

But Mitzi had a serious side, too. It seemed to center around me. I had rescued her. I had brought her hope when she was at her lowest ebb and that had created a dependency of enormous strength, the depth of it appearing only gradually. When she had first come to us, there was a minor crisis each morning when I left for the lab, Mitzi troubled that I would not return and requiring lots of reassurance. This improved, of course, but even after a year or more, our leave takings in the morning were not occasions for cheerful good wishes, but for earnest hugs and sober emotions.

Our work at Phillips had to some extent taken a new turn. Despite our best efforts, a number of other institutions both here and abroad had begun work on the same project. Science is like that. These other people were just as smart as we were and Dr. Baxter's theory inevitably occurred to other bright minds who were just as anxious as we to be the first to exploit it. We had known for some time that a half dozen or more well funded groups both here and abroad were hard at work trying to overtake us. We naturally thought we had an edge, but every now and then we would get wind of some bunch coming up with a new approach to some phase of the work that we had not considered. Now we must hastily check out this idea and either incorporate it into our work or abandon it. What had been secret for a time was now the subject of seminars and conferences. In some cases there was limited but genuine sharing of data. In others such as at Phillips, there was still a shroud of jealous secrecy. The high moral ground that Dr. Vinson had staked out for the company was under assault and a more Machiavellian approach evident. Jim was absolutely petrified at being on a podium and it had been decided that I was to be the mouthpiece for our lab at the symposia.

Mitzi

The first such opportunity was to address a group of my colleagues in San Francisco. I came home full of this exciting news
only to find that when it sank in that I would be gone for nearly a
week, Mitzi slid into a funk. I did what parents from the beginning of time have done. I told her how short a time that was, that I
would bring some exciting presents for both of them, that I would
be home before she knew it and absolutely hit a stone wall. This
poor little child became uncommunicative, head down, feet scuff-
ing and nothing I could say or promise had any effect. She went
to her room, not in tears but close to it, and I sat with her for the
longest time and told her how much I loved her and how important it was for her to cheer up and be a help to Susan while I was
gone, but nothing made an impression.

"What is it, sweetheart? Is it because you'll be lonely?
There's so much to do here, and Susan will keep you busy. It
won't be very long and I'll be home again."

She said something too softly for me to hear and I leaned
close and asked her to repeat it. She did, and I still couldn't make
out the words. She tried again and this time I realized she was
asking what if I didn't come home. I gathered her up in my arms
and rocked her. "Oh, Mitzi, precious baby! I would never leave
you! I will always come home! You must never, never think that I
would leave you. You're the only Mitzi I've got and I wouldn't
lose you for the world, the whole world. Don't be sad, Mitz. It
makes me so unhappy when you're sad. Is that really what you're
so unhappy about?" and her little head nodded slowly. We sat for
a long time this way, much the way we had sat the first time I
lifted her up into my lap, her arms around me in a determined
embrace, he face averted and quiet. At last I gave her a kiss, got a
tiny smile for my effort and we went out together, the worst of the
blow behind us.

That night after Mitzi had gone to bed, Susan asked what had
gone on and I told her.

"Let's all go, Peter. Let's pack up Mitzi and all three of us
go. There's nothing to stop us. I can take her around the city and
we'll have a great time. I was only a little girl when I was there
and I'd love to see the city again." So simple. And that is just
what we did. Mitzi was spellbound at the prospect of riding in an

airplane, going all the way across the country and staying in a hotel in a strange city. And not being separated from me. It made the trip. Seeing much of what is commonplace through the eyes of an enthusiastic and appreciative child is a rare treat and we savored each moment of it. When we met in the room at the end of the afternoon, Mitzi was all but incoherent, frantic to tell me all the marvels they had seen, the places they had been. She pounced on me and sat me down in a chair, standing in front of me and lecturing to me about her day, replete with sound effects and broad gestures, eyes wide, hair thrashing around her shoulders. The whole thing was an outstanding success and when we got home, it was decided that from then on, the Hawkinses would go as a team.

The travel opportunities multiplied as our project crept nearer to successful completion and we not only went to most of the big east coast cities but to Toronto and Mexico City before we hit the European circuit, London, Paris, Amsterdam, Rome. For a country boy born and bred, regardless of the cosmopolitan arena at home, this was heady stuff. For Susan, it was not unfamiliar, but for Mitzi and me, it was our own Disneyland. Mitzi was transfixed most of the time. Eyes wide, jaw slack, lips dry, her brain saturated with newness, overloaded with the landscapes, the languages, the dress, the buildings, the very automobiles, all so different, the sounds and aromas, the food, the manners, all but overwhelming. Gone was the wild recitation of the day's events while we dressed for dinner. Now it was question after question, the serious face reviewing, daydreaming, overawed. Mitzi became a globe trotter.

21

We approached Mitzi's teen years with some trepidation, Susan especially, a result I thought of her own mother's fears and prohibitions that had so complicated our early relationship. Perhaps it was because we had such a unique child, such a treasure that we were more than ordinarily concerned about her safety, her contacts as she entered that vulnerable period of her life. The home schooling, of course, had paid handsome dividends in terms of the trust and confidence that had developed between us three. Mitzi loved her home and her parents and chose to have her friends come to her. On weekends for half the year, between the tennis court and the pool, it was open house at our house to a dozen kids. Mitzi had friends from her piano lessons and dancing as well as the children of our own acquaintances. The sleep-overs were at our house, the weenie roasts were in our backyard. We held dances in our living room. Canoeing parties were on the lake and the kids used the cottage to change and snack and hang out. The boys liked Mitzi and they liked us and we got to know them, and what a difference that made. Mitzi had such good sense, and on the few occasions when we had reservations about some boy or girl and mentioned it to her, she was ahead of us and making the necessary rearrangements.

As she emerged from her childhood, she became such a pretty young lady, not a beauty in the sense that Susan was, but to my taste, equally attractive, more the type of girl I had been drawn to before I met Susan. Her face was lively and mobile, she had cute little expressions that suddenly appeared as though to illustrate what she was saying.

She still mimicked and clowned unaffectedly, but she had serious moods that were convincing and spoke to her basic nature, which I knew had deeper overtones than her ingratiating cheerfulness might suggest. As much as we kidded back and forth, there were many long and thoughtful conversations between us, Mitzi given to uncommonly deep reflections about people which occupied a large part of her thinking. I supposed that the adult associations we had encouraged had taught her to see things denied most youngsters her age. We discussed and analyzed her friends and ours, fearlessly and frankly even when what I had to offer was not flattering to some adult friend. My thinking, contrary to Susan's, being that Mitzi could not know too much nor too soon about the adult world and what made them behave the way they did. As clever as Susan was in judging people and motivation, she was reluctant to share much of her intuition with Mitzi, worried that it might distort her approach to people, that she might adopt our opinions uncritically and not form her own.

Boys at this age can be very unattractive. How humbling it was to see myself in some of these gawky, clumsy, croakers, so loud, so self conscious, so clueless. There were a few pretty neat kids, though. I made it a point to get to know them and talk to them. Most of them were children of co-workers either at Phillips or friends of Susan's from the Foundation, so for the most part we knew something of their backgrounds. As popular as Mitzi was, she never seemed to have a favorite, although there were a number of boys importuning her to 'go steady', whatever that meant at that age. Mitzi resolutely declined that honor and as a result, was more sought after than ever. I don't think she was a coquette. She liked these boys and she was sincere with them, but she was not inclined to favor any one to a point where he felt he had an inside track. I kidded her about her stable of beaux and how she kept them dangling.

"Oh, Papa, they're nice boys, but they act like they are never going to grow up. I mean, they are lots of fun and all but they do such dumb things and say such dumb things just to try to impress us girls. It's all right, I guess and most of the girls like it even if they say they don't, but it seems so silly. I wish they'd just be themselves and not be so stupid all the time. They must not think we know anything. We have a lot of fun together, but mostly it seems they just want to show off and do dumb things. I tell them to just be normal and they can't. They're always trying to outdo each other, you know? It's boring, really boring."

One of the things that so set Mitzi apart was this precocious maturity. She was so far ahead of the boys emotionally that they just weren't cutting it. She had her share of dates but turned down a lot, it seemed to me, just not attracted to her age mates until a particularly nice kid came along, Karl Meissen, the youngest of two sons of a German biologist whom we had recruited at Phillips a couple years before. The father, Oskar, was an urbane fellow, considerably more at ease in this country than some of his countrymen I had met, reserved, serious but easy to talk to. He spoke excellent English and was married to a French woman, Nicole, whom I had met on a couple occasions but had never become acquainted with until we gave a family picnic at the lake for a small group and decided to include Oskar and Nicole. Everyone brought their kids, and Karl shortly after arriving surveyed the group and seemed to take a particular fancy to Mitzi. He was a tall, fair, athletic looking kid with a very engaging personality, very polite and proper, asking me to my secret astonishment and pleasure if I would introduce him to Mitzi whom I had pointed out as our daughter. I took him to where she was talking with friends and performed the ceremony, catching Mitzi's glance of curiosity at this unexpected formality, wondering whatever was going on.

The Meissens were an interesting pair. They were cultured in the European style, well informed, widely traveled, enthusiastic people whom we found to be good company, Susan and Nicole shared a number of interests that seemed to create a certain bond between them. Susan had spent considerable time in France and spoke French much better than I, and although Nicole was articulate in heavily accented English, she clearly enjoyed having someone to talk to in her own tongue, and they conversed at great length, Susan more animated than usual, which was a good sign. This pleasant day ended with the Meissens the last guests, the four of us sitting around on the porch with a last drink, content not to have the day end so quickly. Karl, his brother and Mitzi joined us and we sat and swapped tales until dark, making a date for them to come to dinner the following week with the boys.

After our guests had left, I asked Mitzi what she thought of Karl and was a little surprised to hear her say that he was very nice and very interesting and that she had enjoyed his company, the most praise I had heard her extend to any boy yet, so Susan and I exchanged glances and I asked more about him. "Well, he's so much more grown up, you know? He's traveled a lot and been to some places even we haven't been to, and we just talked about places we both knew and how he liked America and where he was going to school and what he wanted to do and so forth. He's a very nice boy who seems to know a lot and is really interesting. He's going to Corinthian just like you did, only he wants to be an engineer. He says he wants to stay in this country and become a citizen. I think he's really neat. Oh!...and Papa!...Get this! He's going to ask you if it's OK to ask me to go out with him! Can you imagine? He's so proper and kind of shy about it! Are you going to tell him yes?"

"Hmmmm. I don't know about this, Precious. These foreigners coming over here, seeking out our maidens with who knows what in mind. The mere thought of my darling consorting with that T-T-T-Teuton is like a dagger, cold and sharp, plunged here in my bosom."

"I take it that means yes?" and with that came over and plopped herself in my lap.

"Of course. Not only that, but I want it noted that I think the idea of his asking my permission antique and delightful. Nevertheless, I propose to quiz him closely about his intentions." She gave me her little lopsided grin and patted me on the head.

"You are kidding, Papa?"

"I are."

"You won't embarrass him, will you? He really is shy."

"Not to worry, Perfect Child, he will be treated with tact."

And of course, he was. At the end of dinner when I had left the room to fetch a book I wanted Oskar to see, Karl approached me respectfully and asked if it would be acceptable to me for him to take Mitzi to the movies. He explained that she had said she would like to go, that he had his car and that she would be home before midnight. I told him that I appreciated his asking and that he had my permission and that I hoped they would have a good

Mitzi

time. They excused themselves in some excitement and were gone. I told Susan and the Meissens what had just gone on and how I thought they could be proud of their son's thoughtfulness and manners which I found very refreshing. They were pleased, of course, and told us a good bit about the boy, who seemed on all counts to be a credit to them. In turn, they had the nicest things to say about Mitzi, and each couple felt that their child had found an estimable friend.

This began a rather long relationship between these two, one that I found very hard to decipher. Mitzi certainly enjoyed Karl's company, and he in turn seemed to adore her, but Mitzi simply wasn't interested in any steady relationship. She had a wide circle of admirers and dated a few other boys, favoring Karl above the others but unwilling to forego dates with others. Oskar and Nicole were puzzled and perhaps a little disappointed as they had made it clear that they thought the two very well suited to each other, and likely were thinking in terms of marriage somewhere down the line. Susan and I had discussed the possibility, more or less by way of being prepared, and we both agreed that Karl seemed a good match on all counts except for Mitzi's unwillingness to accept him as a bona fide suitor. At nineteen, Mitzi was young for marriage, but her maturity was such that the calendar didn't tell the whole story.

There was the question of further formal education and college had been discussed a number of times, but Mitzi was firm in her opinion that she didn't want to leave home. That brought up the prospect of her attending Willoughly as a day student, but here again, she had no interest. Susan had gone into this at some length in their talks and it turned out that Mitzi simply felt that college didn't have that much to offer her academically or socially and we had to admit that this was not far from the truth and we decided that she should be permitted the liberty to decide her own destiny. She had absolutely no career ambitions, and from the financial standpoint, had no need of one. Still, I had the feeling that she should have some sort of dedication, some goal or other.

Here we had this attractive, talented and personable young lady who seemed to waiting to be touched by something, but by what, we had no idea. We were so enchanted with her, simply having her with us, that we had given very little thought to where she was headed. Now with this ambivalence about such an eligible suitor, I felt I should ask Mitzi if she had anything particular in mind for her future. One evening when Walter was at a hospital meeting, Susan announced that she was going over to have a visit with her mother, and this seemed like the time to have my own visit with Mitzi. I sat on the couch.

"Hey, babe. Come over here and talk to your old man for awhile." She sat beside me and I put my arm around her and she snuggled up as she had done for years.

"What do you want to do with your worthless life? Any ideas? I haven't thought much about it until just recently, but I get the impression that you're not excited about marriage. I don't mean just Karl--that's your affair, of course. It may be he's just not your ideal, but what do you want to do with yourself, Mitz? There's no hurry, God knows, I'm just curious. Any thoughts?" The question didn't faze her.

"Nope," she said, matter of factly.

"Nope?"

"Nope." She looked up at me with her best little smile and I kissed her.

"Just going to stay here with the old man, huh? Hang out with the old dude?"

"Yep."

"Come on, Mitz. What's going on? What do you want to do? I don't care if you don't want to get married. I'd be happy if you waited a good long time. You'll just make that much better a choice. Karl is a nice kid, but the woods are full of nice kids. You'll find one some day. Or are you going to be an old maid? Hell of a waste, babe. Some great guy is out there somewhere yearning for you."

"Not interested."

The way she said it, some sort of intonation, made me pause. She was serious. It was not just a careless dismissal of my casual remark.

"OK...why not?"

"Because I want to stay here. I just want to keep on the way things are right now. I don't want to go anywhere. I just want to stay here with you."

I gave her an automatic squeeze of appreciation for the compliment. Compliment it was, all right. At least that was the way I took it even though there was a hint of an indefinable gravity to the remark that percolated in my consciousness briefly and then retreated but didn't entirely disappear.

"You can stay forever, sweetheart. We love you to pieces, and what you want is what we want. Nothing is more important to us than your happiness, sugar. I asked just out of curiosity. There's no one I'd rather please than you, so you just do what seems best to you and you know we're behind you." She gave me a hug and we continued to sit like that in silence. I was involved in sort vague reverie when she spoke again, softly.

"This is all I want," and then she was still again.

We sat that way in silence until we heard Susan drive in. The spell broken, we got up and resumed our lives.

It was not long after this that I had come home rather late one evening, Mitzi on a date with Karl, Susan with a preoccupied air about her, enough that I asked if she were all right. "I'm fine, Peter, but I'm concerned, I suppose. Mitzi mentioned to me that she had recently noticed a little lump in her left breast that she was sure had not been there very long. I imagine that sort of thing happens perfectly innocently, but even so, I can't help but think about it. Do you think we ought to have someone look at it?" I tossed this around a little, slightly worried myself at anything unexpected of this nature, telling myself it could not possibly be significant.

"I doubt it's necessary, Suze. I don't think anything serious in that department could occur to someone her age. Why not just ask her to keep an eye on it, and if it gets any bigger, sure, take her to Wilkins and see what he thinks. I wouldn't worry Mitzi with any show of concern on our part, but she should learn to be observant anyway. Why don't you just handle it and I won't even mention that you told me anything. I don't think we should upset her by appearing to take it seriously, do you?"

"Well. No. But still, I'd feel better if someone who knows would reassure me. Would it be all right with you if I just made an appointment for a routine physical for her and tell Dr. Wilkins that we would appreciate his opinion specifically about this lump? Mitzi might not mention it. Besides, she hasn't seen anyone for years, and she should probably have an internist to call her own, don't you think? I'd just feel better if she were examined." I agreed that that sounded fine and so Mitzi saw Dr. Wilkins, a first rate man, I thought. Mitzi came home perfectly nonchalant, reporting that she was in great shape and from her standpoint, that was that. I called the doctor the next day and asked him about the lump. Yes, there was a tiny lump that he had no concern about although he suggested that if in a couple months it was changed any, that we let him know and he would send her to a general surgeon for his opinion, just to be sure. Susan marked it on her calendar, although I could tell that she didn't need this to remind her, and after the suggested time had lapsed, she casually asked Mitzi about the lump. Mitzi didn't know, but checked and said she wasn't sure, that possibly it was a little larger, but maybe not. She certainly hadn't seemed to be very interested in the thing. Susan came to me with this report, and there was no doubt that Mitzi was headed for the surgical consultation, mostly to satisfy Susan, I thought, but if that was what it was going to take, fine.

So Mitzi was referred to a Dr. Ed Claiborne who Dr. Wilkins assured us was as good as they came. Susan took her over there, mostly to be able to talk to the doctor personally after the examination, Mitzi awfully casual about everything and possibly not to be depended upon for detail. He examined her, confirmed the presence of a lump, but considering her age and the fact that this was the first time he had seen it, felt that she need do nothing for a couple months, but to return then for review whether it was larger or not. A mammogram was ordered and reported to us later as simply confirming the presence of a "mass", such an ugly exaggeration for so small a lump, but that seemed to be the way they talked. At least we could shelve that problem for a couple months and we did, or at least I more or less did, Susan scarcely ever mentioning it, although it was clearly on her mind.

Mitzi

Two months passed and now it was considered an admissible topic, so Susan asked Mitzi if she thought it was larger, and Mitzi said she was pretty sure it was, although not much. Why this struck such fear into both our hearts I can't say. Once again, her youth rendering anything serious out of the question, but in spite of this, we seemed to catch each other's apprehension and without admitting it to each other, were worried. Susan told me that evening that Dr. Claiborne had said that since it had slightly enlarged even though it was still small, that he felt that it best to remove it, a very simple and brief operation. It almost certainly was a benign condition of some sort, but that in spite of its location and lack of any other suggestions of abnormalities in the remaining breast tissue, that it was better to remove it. The whole thing could be done without distorting the breast and we'd be finished with it, whatever it turned out to be. I think we were both relieved to know that something definitive was going to be done, Mitzi taking it very well, but just a tiny bit off her usual buoyancy. Susan called the next morning and made a date for the following week, such a small case that it could be slipped into an otherwise full schedule.

It is perfectly ridiculous how something like this can infect a home. I was certain it was nothing, Mitzi was generally unconcerned as to the nature of the lump, only slightly apprehensive about going to the hospital at all. But Susan, for all she tried to be her usual self, was not, and both Mitzi and I caught her anxiety and lived uneasily with it until the following Tuesday. It was to be an outpatient procedure, or at least she was not to stay overnight although she had a light general anesthesia. Dr. Claiborne stepped outside the operating suite to reassure us that all had gone well and that the tissue was on its way to the lab for diagnosis and that he would have his office call us in a few days, Mitzi to return in a week to get the stitches removed. I couldn't forebear asking if he had any opinion from the appearance of the lump, and he shrugged and said he preferred not to speculate about such things but would give us a complete rundown when the report came through. Mitzi was a little goofy from the anesthesia and her pain medication and after eating scarcely anything, went to bed early.

"I think I'll call your father, Suze. He can undoubtedly expedite that examination. I don't think under the circumstances that Dr. Claiborne would object, do you? I never told him about Walter being your father. The sooner we have this behind us, the happier we'll all be." Susan agreed and I called Walter and told him about Mitzi's surgery. We had not mentioned it to either of them before and Walter was a little surprised. By all means, he would expedite the preparation and get it read tomorrow and give us a call. That was the beginning of the nightmare that was to follow.

Late the next day Walter called and said he would come over if that was agreeable. I said by all means, and we settled down to wait, all three of us unnaturally quiet. Mitzi sat with us, and while I wished in a way she were not there until we heard whatever we were going to hear, I felt she must be part of the truth, whatever that was, and so she sat with us, waiting also. Walter came in, outwardly his usual self, but had no more than gotten seated than it was apparent that he was troubled.

"Most unusual bit of tissue. Not at all what one would expect. I had Horace read it and he came in to me and showed it to me. I took it to a couple more of the boys and they all agree that it looks like a bad actor. Lots of abnormal cell division and jumbled architecture, characteristic beyond much doubt that it is, ah...", and here he balked, looking to us for help, a word, a sign of how to proceed. I took the leap without daring to frame the thought more artfully and suggested a conclusion to his sentence, "...malignant?"

He looked pained and uncomfortable. "I'm afraid so. I really can't make it to be anything else, but I'm going to assume that all of us could be wrong, and considering the rarity of the diagnosis, I've already sent another section of it to a fellow in Chicago who is collecting these rare birds and who will give us the best answer we could get anywhere on the planet. I really don't have any serious thought that he will contradict us, though, so I propose to call Ed first thing in the morning and tell him our opinion and what we've done to confirm it and let him talk to you people tomorrow sometime and make what ever plan he thinks best. It will be tomorrow evening before my pal in Chicago can talk with him, but he will know, if anybody does, what the preferred treatment will be. I have no way of even giving you an idea and wouldn't if I could. I think Ed will have to hear the statistics and go from there. You can absolutely depend on him doing the right thing. Don't have any worries on that score. I can't imagine you being better off anywhere than right here with that man."

He looked at Mitzi who was clearly stunned. "Don't worry, sweetheart. We'll take the best care of you and things are going to turn out all right. There is no doubt in my mind that you will be completely cured and have a long and happy life. It's just going to take a little effort on our part and patience from you, but you've got a great team and we can solve this. Poor baby. I'm awfully sorry, honey. I wish I had better news, but the good part is that we have caught it absolutely at the beginning and it will soon be a thing of the past." He declined a drink and after a very little more socializing, no one interested in anything but this bombshell, he excused himself and we were left with the agony of suspense over the safety and well being of our precious Mitzi. She didn't cry, she didn't ask questions, she just seemed to want to be by herself and went to bed, dejected and disbelieving.

The next day Dr. Claiborne called me at the lab and told me that Walter had called and what he had said. He asked us to wait until he had a chance to discuss the matter with the Chicago pathologist. He would call as soon as they had spoken and arrange to see us in his office, with Mitzi in attendance, to discuss the treatment. I reported this to my ladies that evening and we did what we could to pass the time which hung so heavy with us. I played double solitaire with Mitzi and after a time, she began to recover her normal animation and by bedtime, seemed almost herself. Well, the worst was over, we all seemed to think. It had been a nasty shock, cancer, of all things in the world, but the thought had settled now and the prospects of eradicating it promptly and getting back to normal made us feel some better. We were getting the best medical help possible and before long it would all be behind us.

We met late the following afternoon at Dr. Claiborne's office. He was still in greens, but tired as he was from a long day, had some emergency waiting for him after he finished with us. He had talked with the man in Chicago, a man he knew well by reputation and in whom he had complete confidence. "Unfortunately, there is no doubt about the accuracy of the diagnosis. It is rare, but this particular malignancy does occur in young women and when neglected has an abysmal record. It's unusual to catch it this early according to his studies, but when this does occur, the results are quite good with comparatively limited surgery. Walter had a great many additional slides of the tissue made and there is not a single sign of its being even close to the margins of what we took out, so the possibility of spread is remote. Nevertheless, he feels we dare not presume on our good fortune thus far and in his opinion a simple mastectomy is mandatory." He looked at Mitzi. "That means removing all the breast tissue on that side, Mitzi. I know that sounds awful, but it's not really so bad. The scar will be under the breast where it will never show, and after you're all healed up, we can have a plastic surgeon insert a prosthetic breast of the same size as the other breast and you'll be in great shape again. I know it's a terrible shock, young lady, but think of how lucky you are to have picked up this thing so early that we can put everything right again. We're going to do a couple additional x-rays, but the surgery is all that is required. There is no advantage in taking chemotherapy or having x-ray therapy on your chest after the surgery. No one likes the idea of being operated upon, but it's got to be done and the sooner we get to it, the sooner it will be over."

He turned now to us. "Is there any family history of breast cancer? Mitzi told me she knows so little of her family background. Anything you might know of in this line?" I told him that all we knew was that her mother had died rather young, in a hospital, but of what, we knew nothing. "It wouldn't have any bearing on our treatment. Just curiosity. There's a pretty strong correlation with other family members having the same type of tumor, although this is certainly a good bit earlier that most. Well, I've got to get back. I'll leave instructions with my office nurse and you can call tomorrow and set something up after you've had a sleep on it. I'd rather get going and get it done pretty shortly. I suspect you would, too. Call me anytime if you have questions. Mitzi should be in and out in a couple days at the most. Just the same procedure she had before, only a little more so. And don't you worry, Mitzi. I'll take good care of you." We shook hands all around and thanked him for his time and trouble and went home.

What does a pretty young girl think when she is told she will have to have a breast removed? What does she imagine about how she will look, what people will say, how will she tell her friends? What will she tell her friends, for that matter? What will it be like to stand in front of a mirror and look at that trim athletic body, the white swathe of skin her bikini tops have sheltered from the sun now ugly, flat, misshapen and empty on one side, an empty sack of shriveled skin perhaps, waiting for a blob of jello to be inserted and what then? What will that look like? I have no idea that Mitzi thought anything like this, but very likely she did. She had never shown the least sign of vanity that I could detect. Her attractiveness was so natural, so inherent that I wonder if she even realized the extent of it. She never used makeup and seldom wore jewelry, she chose to leave her long straight hair very simply pulled back from her face with a simple band, her clothes by choice were simple, tasteful. She made no effort to call attention to herself and yet she was the center of attention with her friends simply by virtue of her effortless charm, her spirit, her enthusiasm, her wit, her charity…how was this dear sweet child going to handle it?

We drove home in silence, sat down to a pickup dinner, none of us feeling like a restaurant or cooking. As the leader of the pack I suppose I was expected to set the tone, and although I wanted more time to think about it and talk about it elsewhere, I felt we had best begin to get through it.

"That's a really crappy break, honey," I said to Mitzi. "Damn, damn. Rotten luck. But what can you do? We'll just have to get through it and get on with things, I guess. What a hell of a note. Did you pretty much understand everything Dr. Claiborne said, baby?" Mitzi nodded without eye contact and I knew she was suffering. We got up and I went over to Mitzi and took her hand. "Let's go sit down for a little and brood together. I'm really mad at fate and I need someone to sit with me." We sat on the sofa, Mitzi with her head on my chest, my arm around her, slouched and sprawled.

"Look, sugar, it's going to be a mess for a little while and if you like, we can go someplace and hide out for awhile until we get our wits together and get used to the idea. That may not be what you want to do when the time comes, but the point is, if you're feeling blue and don't want to have to deal with it with your friends and all, we'll do whatever suits you. Probably thousands of women are going through this same thing right now. Breast cancer is a really big deal and people talk about it all the time and women grow up checking themselves and being checked and getting x-rays and so on. We expect it will happen to a certain number of people we know and we all accept it and those women accept it, I suppose. What gets me is that you're so doggone young. That's what gets me down. It's so bloody unfair to have to deal with something like this before you might expect it." We sat some more, Mitzi not moving or saying anything.

"Can you deal with it, baby?"

"I guess. I don't have much choice."

"No. Guess not." Susan came over and sat on Mitzi's other side and we all snuggled together and sat quietly until Mitzi said she'd like to go to bed. Susan and I sat up for a couple hours, talking quietly. It didn't appear we had missed anything. There was no question about the accuracy of the diagnosis, the necessity of the surgery. As far as timing was concerned, the sooner the better and we agreed Susan would call in the morning and make a date. She was also going to inquire about a temporary prosthesis and when Mitzi could start wearing one. We felt it would be very important to Mitzi to look as normal as possible as soon as possible until she could have the cosmetic surgery to give her a permanent solution.

"I talked to Walter about this particular tumor. He had a long talk with his friend in Chicago. There is a high likelihood of the same thing occurring on the other side. Is this thing ever going to give up? Can you imagine at this age losing both breasts? What a kick in the butt. I'm just sick about the whole miserable thing. Poor baby. If there is anyone who doesn't deserve another whack, it's our little sweetheart. You know, I suppose there's no particular point in trying to track it down, at least from our standpoint, but I'll bet Mitzi's mom died of the same thing. Walter thinks it very likely too. Nothing to be done about that, of course. I suppose the docs would really like to know, though. I think I'll ask if they'd like me to contact Helen again and see if she knows anything more. Do you suppose she's still around? I haven't thought of her for the longest time. She might be interested in hearing from us. Then again, maybe not. I think I'll call, though and see what she might have to say. I don't know how much of her denial was just protecting...what? A dead woman? There'd be no reason for her not to tell us which hospital and what last name if she knows. I might as well call." Susan didn't seem very interested but sat thinking her own thoughts.

"Mitzi is down even more than I would have thought, Peter. It's a terrible blow to someone so young, but still I'm a little surprised at how she's taking it. We think of her as being so tough, the way she survived whatever her childhood involved, some pretty bad scenes, I imagine. Even after years of what might have been near hopelessness, she bounced back so quickly when she came to us. I'll keep her busy and be with her. I think I'll ask if the office knows someone who talks to people who are going to have this sort of surgery. I think the more she knows the better, don't you?" I agreed, of course and after a time, we sort of shrugged and decided to turn in. What a day.

Mitzi rallied. She certainly wasn't herself, but she took on a semblance of herself over the next couple days. Susan did a wonderful job of doing things for her and with her. They talked to a nurse in the office of the plastic surgeon that Dr. Claiborne recommended, a slick girl not that much older than Mitzi who went through the whole drill with her, telling her that her doctor was capable of turning out a figure indistinguishable from normal, assuring her that she would be in a bikini again before she knew it, possible a slight exaggeration, but comforting nevertheless. She showed her a sample prosthesis they kept around and the whole thing began to seem doable to her, I thought. At least she talked about it, and she ate, and we resumed our cribbage games in the evening and sometimes she laughed. With all the worry and distraction, I had forgotten how important that tinkley little laugh was to me and how I had missed it recently. Susan seemed adjusted to the idea of the surgery and Mitzi put on a pretty good show, but I was having a difficult time of it. I had truly come to think of her as perfect. I realize that sounds silly, but I simply could not think of a flaw or a fault. She was the essence of the ideal girl I thought and it grieved me so to see anyone this precious, this wonderful having to suffer at all, at all. Well, that was my own problem. I couldn't share it with anyone, but it truly hurt.

By the time the day came to go to the hospital, Mitzi seemed just fine, actually professing to be anxious to get in and get it over with and get home to her Papa and Susan. We went in with her and after she had gotten settled, sat and talked and made plans for where we would go to celebrate when she came home and so on. At the end of visiting hours, we kissed her goodnight and went on home to sit and worry. Why, I can't really say. The surgery was really quite simple, according to all our information, a couple days in the hospital on account of the drains and antibiotics and maybe also because we were Walter's family. In any event, Mitzi came out of the operation with a good attitude, not all that much pain, a routine course of recovery after surgery and in no time was home again, bandaged and a little sore but so happy to be home again. We fussed and pampered until she began to assert her independence and before long we found we were able to behave normally. At least that is what we imagined we were doing. Not long after the sutures had been removed, Susan had approached Mitzi to see the result, feeling that it was not to be a mystery and that it would be good for her to share her deformity. I was unaware of this sharing until that night when after Mitzi had gone to bed, Susan told me she had been shown the operative area.

"Oh, Peter! I thought I would faint. It is just so ugly and abnormal, a pathetic little squashed mess with a nipple at the bottom of it, just awful, awful, awful. I could hardly stand it! It was all I could do to keep a straight face and say something without showing what I really felt. I'm just sick about it, Peter! My God, that poor child! The picture of health in every other way, and to have such an ugly, ugly thing to deal with. I can't wait for her to get a bra with a prosthesis for that side. She says it is not very sore, and so as soon as she feels she wants it and the area is not tender, I'm going to take her to the place they told me about and get her at least looking better until she can have the plastic surgery." Nothing was normal. The joy was out of Mitzi and that meant that the joy was out of me. The wound healed and while Mitzi was not ready for reconstructive surgery, she was ready for the temporary prosthetic bra and Susan undertook to take her to the prosthetist. There was nothing to criticize about the prosthesis. Susan and Mitzi had both agreed that it was a good disguise, but somehow, it never had the desired effect on Mitzi. In fact, I think it made her feel worse by making her increasingly conscious of the fact that it was deception, that she was hiding her deformity, that it was a cop-out. When I came home that night, there was an artificial tension in the air and I was aware that Susan was putting on a front and that Mitzi was depressed.

"Well, we got it done! Show Papa your new figure!" Mitzi stood slowly, wearing a cotton blouse that draped over the protrusion of the left breast which was formed accurately to the size of the opposite breast and made her look her usual self.

"Hey, sugar! All right! You're back in business! Looks great, honey, what a relief that must be. Give me hug, precious," and I took her in my arms and hugged her very gently, not knowing yet what was permitted. She sensed my restraint and assured me that she wasn't tender, but there was no feeling the remark, it wasn't an invitation to hug and smooch the way we were accustomed to. We had a bottle of champagne with dinner, which wasn't a very good idea after all. We not infrequently had a bottle without an occasion because we all liked it with certain meals, but as this had a celebratory air about it, it didn't go over well and it quickly became apparent that the less that was said or noticed about the new figure the better. Mitzi was having a great deal of trouble sleeping and after she had gone to bed early, Susan I resumed our talking about her, which subject occupied every waking moment together, so anxious we were to find a solution to the gloom that had settle in our house. We concluded time and again that we would be supportive, create a happy environment, let Mitzi call the shots and be patient. We simply had nothing to go on. Mitzi had always been so resilient, so immune to the blues, such a rock for her friends when they were down.

Susan took up the problem with Dr. Wilkins who agreed we were doing the right thing. He gave her some sleeping pills, feeling that with better rest she might perk up, and for a time, this seemed to help although the sleeplessness persisted. My situation at Phillips was such that I could write my own ticket, the company so thrilled at the riches that had started pouring in as a result of Jim's and my efforts, their stock soaring as rumors of our nearing success was getting around. Susan and I both felt that we should get away completely, away from the phone away from the sympathy. We packed up and went to the Antigua house where Mitzi had always had such fun. We talked about the swimming suit business, knowing that she would be in one a good bit, but in complete privacy, and we thought this might be a way of getting her less self conscious if that was the problem. The prosthesis made bikinis out of the question but Susan and she shopped around and bought several less skimpy suits that were still cute and stylish.

Mitzi would put on her suit and then a big cover-up wrap of one sort or another. She took off the wrap to swim and then put it right back on. When she and I skin dived, she chose to wear a wetsuit top which she had never done before. Sure we had fun. We sailed, and walked the beach and went out in the evening occasionally to dance, Mitzi and I anyway, and she was as graceful as ever, but the life, the feeling was gone from it. We fished and ate more than we should have, did a lot of underwater photography with the new underwater cameras. While Mitzi was much less modest about her attire with Susan, when I appeared she was quick to put on some wrap. I mentioned it to Susan who had been aware of it all along and confirmed my suspicions. "You must realize that you are her ideal man. Of all people, she is most concerned about your good opinion of her. Perhaps she has taken the Perfect Child term too literally. Whatever the reason is, she is still ashamed of the way she feels she looks in your eyes. I think she has an idea that she has somehow let you down, disappointed you. I simply can't put my finger on it, Peter. It's so frustrating. She should surely know better than to have any such ideas. I suppose we'll just have to wait it out. She's so level-headed ordinarily. Do sit down with her again, Peter, and see if you can do anything." I tried every approach I could think of, but nothing seemed to make much difference. She was just withdrawn in a way I had never seen. The sleeplessness continued and she took naps during the day, so uncharacteristic. We came home, no better for the vacation.

The time came have the implant. And Mitzi balked. To our dismay, at first she declared herself not ready just yet, then gradually adopted a position of not caring about further surgery and finally decided that she just didn't want it done. The two of us were seated on the couch one evening while Susan was showering, and I brought up the delicate subject again. Didn't she think she would be better in the long run to have the surgery, no more stuffed bra, no longer the artificial padding but something that looked like a real breast? She sat up and turned to me with a look of utmost seriousness and after collecting her thoughts, said, "Papa...will you always love me, no matter what?" I hugged her too me and rocked her as we had when she was young.

"Dear, dear, precious creature, you know the answer to that without having to ask. You will always be the most beloved creature in my world. You must never have any doubts about that. How many times I must have told you that from the time you came to us. Have you any reason to doubt, little one?"

"No, Papa.....but...I feel like I've let you down."

"Oh, Mitzi! Let me down? Whatever in the world would possess you to think such a thing? Dear little lamb, you could not possibly let me down! Whatever gave you such an idea? Never, never, in this world, love! Please do put any such thoughts out of your mind. Is this what had been troubling you these weeks? Oh, Mitzi, Mitzi, if that's the reason for your unhappiness, please put it out of your mind, sweetheart. I had no idea you were brooding about something that silly. Oh, Mitzi, you numbskull! Susan and I would never have dreamed of such a thing, baby. Come on now, sugar. Let's get back on track. I don't care when you have the surgery but let's at least clear the air here and get back to being ourselves again. What do you say? Hey, you. Say something."

But she didn't. Something was not happening with Mitzi. There was no release, no embarrassed apology, no snuggle of contentment. She just lay in my arms, not returning my hug with conviction. Suspicious, I sat back and looked at her and she was as baleful as before, not a tear, not a shy grin, nothing that suggested I had helped the situation.

"What is it, baby? Wrong track?" She lowered her eyes and shrugged, that enigmatic little shrug scarcely seen for many years. We sat like that for an eternity, I despairing again after that transient relief.

"It's just not the same, Papa. It's not like it used to be. It's never going to be the same." Now I noted that she was silently crying, the tears tracing around the corners of her mouth and falling silently. I was helpless, frightened, a wretched little burst of adrenaline setting my heart pounding at her grief, her unfathomable grief. Knowing of nothing constructive to do or say and fearful of making things worse, I sat and watched the tears fall. Then they stopped. And her breathing became easier and at last she relaxed and became quiet. I still said nothing, but just held her until she announced that she was tired and thought she would go to bed. I kissed her and she gave me a tiny smile, one of the nicest in weeks, and went into her room.

When Susan came out to say goodnight, I suggested we walk outside for a look at the moon. I had not the slightest interest in the moon, of course, but I had to tell Susan about this strange and upsetting scene. I told her in complete detail what had been said and how Mitzi looked. Susan was upset and we sat quietly on a bench for some time, thinking.

"I'm not entirely surprised at this, Peter. I had no idea that it ran so deeply, but I've had hints that she was feeling guilty about not being just what you have always assured her she was. No, don't take that wrong, Peter. I think your 'Perfect Child' and all the other pet names were cute and very much appreciated. I think the way you did it was very loving and not at all something that would challenge a child, if that's what you're thinking. No, she took all that with the humor that was intended, I feel certain. Please don't feel guilt about something you have no reason to. It was never overdone, I enjoyed it and I know Mitzi did. But you know, the surgery, the second surgery seemed to change something fundamental. In spite of her sunny disposition and all, I expected that there would be tears, or shock or something. And there wasn't. It was just as though something fundamental to her happiness had just suddenly shut down and I had this sinister feeling of....something...nothing I could put into words. Something ominous. I'm not trying to be dramatic, Peter, but I think we need help."

"Shrink?" I asked.

"Peter! I know your not being flippant, but I really dislike that term. But yes, I do think we're in over our heads and if it's agreeable to you, I'd like to call my father and ask him who we should take her to. It need not be a psychiatrist, I suppose. Maybe I should call our old pediatrician first. I imagine youngsters might do better with less threatening counseling. Anyway, is that all right with you?" I agreed that there seemed to be no question but that we needed help. This was really getting me down, and for all of Susan's calm, I knew she was worried, too. We sat up quite awhile, had a drink, thought, worried and finally decided to call it quits and went to bed.

22

The next day was the sixteenth of June. It was a Saturday. Susan awakened first and woke me and we lay there a time, thinking about last night. Susan was concerned that the pediatrician's office would not be open and we were both anxious to have the reassurance that we were getting closer to a solution for our worries. We arose, got cleaned up and dressed and went out to the kitchen and made coffee. The house was silent. We sipped, made some toast and sat out on the screened porch to eat, neither of us very hungry.

"At least Mitzi seems to be getting some sleep for a change. She must be totally worn out. Do you think I should wake her? It's after nine."

"Let her sleep, I'd say. At least she's not struggling with whatever it is while she's sleeping," so we were quiet. I got the paper and we shared it over more coffee until another hour or more had passed.

"Perhaps I should get her up, don't you think?" Susan asked.

"Yeah, I guess so. Such a pretty day. Maybe we could go over to the lake for lunch. Lovely day for it. Might be good for all of us."

Susan agreed and left the room. I remember I had just reached for the first section of the paper to review an article on a proposed new municipal bond issue when I was frozen in horror by the sound of a hideous, hoarse, alien cry, too grotesque to be Susan yet unmistakably Susan, then loud, strangled wordless reiterated cries, muffled and unreal. Momentarily paralyzed with apprehension, I rushed to Mitzi's room, the door open, Susan wildly sobbing, on her knees at the bedside, clutching onto the motionless, hair-tossed figure of a young girl, pale, still, lifeless. I choked, nearly vomited, fell to the floor beside Susan and clutched at the cold hand, fumbling for a pulse, utterly disbelieving, powerless to think, destroyed as nearly as a human can be and survive. All I could say was No! and I said it over and over and over, nothing else occurring to me other than by this incantation to try to turn time back. We knelt there like this until we were utterly drained of all emotion except disbelief, denial, defeat. We were finally able to look at one another, poor Susan's face so contorted with agony and despair as to be scarcely recognizable. We threw our arms around each other and tried to comfort each other, but what comfort can there be at a monstrous scene like this? Exhausted at last, we got to our feet and stood, looking down at this pathetic figure, the nightgown with its delicate lace and openwork only slightly disarranged, the long black hair spread widely over the pillow, her eyes closed peacefully, lips slightly parted, and all so still, so very still.

Eventually, both of us thinking in the same terms, we glanced around the room. At her desk were four prescription bottles, empty of course, the caps off and lying beside a drinking glass. So she had been planning this for a long time, saving the pills until she had plenty. I thought my heart would break. All this time, unknown to us, Mitzi was planning her own destruction. All this time that we were supporting and being patient, she had made up her mind and needed only the time to collect the means. How perfectly, perfectly hideous! How unutterably sad! Perhaps we were within days of uncovering this appalling plot but now it was too late, just a little too late. What in this whole world can possibly be worse than losing a child, a sweet, treasured child that one has loved and cherished and watched grow and fulfill all one's dreams? Staggered, silent, we slumped onto the bench in front of her vanity where I had seen her so often brushing her long hair, smiling her crooked little smile at me in the mirror, the reversal of the usual little crookedness so comical that I would laugh and she would scold me for laughing at the asymmetry. On the vanity top lay a single sheet of paper with Mitzi's unlikely large scrawl easily identified. I picked it up and we read it together. There was no salutation. It simply said "It will just never, never be the same.

I'm so very sorry. Please forgive me. I love you, love you, love you."

There was nothing left to say. We finally got up and left the room, closing the door behind us but leaving it ajar.

"Who do we call? The police? I think I'll call your father. He'll know, and we must tell them shortly anyway." Susan had nothing to offer, so I called Walter. Poor fellow. He was terribly upset and had a time composing himself and telling me whom to call, yes the police, our internist who had prescribed the pills and would have to certify the cause of death, a funeral home. Walter said if the toxicology report confirmed the barbiturate level expected that an autopsy would not be necessary. I had never even thought of the possibility and wondered how I would have taken the idea of someone dissecting my Mitzi.

The house was a mess the rest of the day, strangers, big bustling strangers who were all wrong inside our house, doing the things they had to do, Dr. Wilkins doing a perfunctory examination, commiserating very kindly and feelingly, and finally Mitzi's lifeless form disappearing into a vehicle and the house quiet at last. I put the note away, discarded the pill containers, stripped the bed and had a stiff drink of whiskey which didn't help a bit.

Susan had absolutely collapsed. Literally collapsed. I had put her in bed shortly after the tragic scene had played itself out, Susan with a blinding headache, nauseated, staggering. Clarence had looked at her and prescribed a sedative which Susan declined, Clarence, poor fellow, sensing the possible inappropriateness from our standpoint of prescribing yet another sedative, gave me a prescription anyway to be administered later. It almost seemed merciful that Susan was so stricken. She was not a bit better the next day, but it was Sunday, and she had the medication which did help. There would be nothing in the papers until Monday, so we turned off the phone and hid which was all I wanted to do. Walter and Emily came over, Walter in a terrible state, Emily not much better. Walter and I found a quiet corner to brood in while Emily stayed with Susan to comfort her as best she could and we passed a couple hours this way, no one knowing what else to do but sit and occasionally offer some random personal reflection.

They went home and Susan and I were alone again. I was more concerned about Susan now than anything else. On Monday, she was still absolutely prostrate with her headache, light-headedness, nausea. Walter and Emily came over and spent the greater part of the day, good for both of us, but after they had left I called Clarence's office and asked if he would be good enough to come out after hours and see what he thought. Good old Clarence, never an excuse, came by and talked to Susan, felt as I did that it was a migraine type headache brought on by the colossal shock of being the one to find Mitzi. He gave me a prescription for some pretty strong analgesic, advised a darkened room, ice bag, privacy, diet as she felt up to it. We left Susan and went into the living room and had a drink together. Clarence seemed relieved to be able to sit and relax a moment before going home. We knew his wife casually and her reputation as a termagant and I thought I owed it to him to allow him to sit and chat and unwind before going home to who knows what, day after day. He had not had time to express his profoundest sympathy for Mitzi's death. I told him in even greater detail what had been going on for the months since the second surgery. He was inclined to take some blame on himself for making the sleeping pills renewable to that extent, but I assured him we thought they were necessary and that with her personality we never imagined that she was that blue. I told him that we were to have made an appointment with some one to talk to her about her depression this very day. Everything in retrospect seemed so lame and ineffective, but he quite rightly pointed out that we almost surely could not have prevented it if she had been planning it that long. The decision, for whatever tragic reason once made seems to have been irrevocable to her. Clarence left after he had finished his drink, declining another, and asked that I keep him posted..

The next day Walter and Emily came over again and we behaved a little more rationally, got something to eat and sat around and discussed what to do next. There would have to be a death notice and we prepared a short one. There were only a few calls to be made, both families so small that it was almost only my parents and my sisters who needed to be told. Time after time, I told the short story, went through the grief again with each of them and was emotionally drained by the time I had finished. I urged them not to come down just yet, that Susan was down and out with the shock and that it would be better to wait until I called them again. Emily sent over Martha each day and that kind and capable lady fussed over Susan with tempting dishes and gradually we got onto some sort of schedule. I felt strongly that we should pack away all Mitzi's clothes and things. I didn't think I could bear being reminded by all the personal touches of hers that the room contained but the prospect of packing up that roomful of memories and dreams involved much too much pain. Susan understood and Emily and Martha packed up everything in cartons and I took them into the attic.

It was slow, but Susan improved a little each day and aside from lassitude and fatigue, reported that the headache was better and began to get up and around. I passed all this on to Clarence and we began to take things a day at a time. The mortuary delivered Mitzi's ashes and I found I couldn't even bear to handle the urn and asked the man to put it on a shelf in the kitchen. I told Susan nothing about it, but after she was up and about and feeling better I told her that they had been delivered and that I had not decided what to do with them. Susan didn't want to consider the subject and nothing further was said until it occurred to me that the fittest place I could think of would be in the garden where Lily's grave lay, marked by a single flagstone. I broached the subject after I had thought it through and Susan agreed that that seemed proper. I dug a deep hole on the other side of the flagstone with a posthole digger, lay down on the ground and placed the urn in the bottom, much as I had done in arranging poor Lily's position. Nothing was said by either of us, and Susan in tears went back in to lie down while I replaced the dirt and the sod.

Both of us were so wiped out emotionally in the following days that it was some time before I realized that Susan's incapacity seemed to be taking an awfully long to clear. Although she was better, she was lethargic and uncharacteristically dull and although she reassured me that she was getting on, I was so sensitized by now that I was seeing problems where likely none existed. I urged her to see Clarence at his office instead of my calling in progress reports. Susan agreed that she was tired of being tired and we made the appointment.

Clarence had me called into his office to discuss his observations and I was relieved to have him suggest that Susan see a neurologist, the headache gone but still a couple things about the whole matter that had Clarence uneasy about missing something. It would be exhausting, but Susan was anxious to getting the air cleared and putting her grief and infirmity behind her, so it was in that spirit that she told me she that after the neurologist had seen her, that he had ordered a CT scan.

"Did he say what he thought might be the trouble?"

"No. Awfully impersonal and uncommunicative. He just did his examination and told me to get the X-ray and come back tomorrow." The test was performed and the following day we were to see Dr. Vanderwort again and go from there.

We got to our appointment a little early and were ushered into his office, scanning his credentials on the wall, impressive even to me, jaded by all the certificates one sees that seem sometimes to have so little behind them. Well, he certainly seemed to be well qualified but then he arrived, and what an odd duck. I formed an instant dislike for the man the minute he walked into his office, tall, skinny to the point of it being his dominant feature, a long cadaverous face and a personality to match. There was no greeting other than a nod, no handshake, no preliminaries before he settled into his seat and pulled over to him a thin folder with Susan's name on it, opening it and extracting a single sheet of paper. He sat down and with no preamble, looked from one to the other of us and announced, "The CT scan shows that you have a mass in the mesial temporal lobe on the left in the basi-frontal region. This is most likely a tumor, the nature of which is undetermined. I recommend that you be seen by a neurosurgeon of your choice. Any further investigation should be under his direction. I'm not in a position to recommend any particular surgeon, but I'm sure Dr. Wilkins can guide you."

A mass? Mesial temporal lobe on the left? What in heaven's name is this ghoul telling us! Again that riveting, sickening squirt of adrenaline as the translation into 'brain tumor' leaped into my consciousness. I felt this simply could not be happening! There has to be limit of what one is expected to bear. It was asking too much to have us faced with another possible disaster. I looked at Susan who sat, immobile, staring at the doctor, her faced suddenly drained of color.

"This mass. I'm not sure I understand what you're saying. Can you give us a better idea of what it might represent? I mean, could it be a blood clot, or are you implying that it might be a tumor... or what?"

"My expectation would be that it is a tumor. Beyond that, I prefer not to speculate." And then he sat there, staring at us. Neither of us moved, I suppose hoping that he might come up with something even slightly consoling, some hint that all might come right, but not a word. He had done his duty and that seemed to be the end of his responsibility. After another motionless silence in each of us, he added, "I suggest you arrange your appointment without delay," and he rose and held the door open for us. Neither of us spoke as we left. Miserable creep! God, how unreasonably I hated that man! How could a guy like that make a living?

"Look, Susan. Let's go right on over to Clarence and tell him what's going on. I know it's not proper, but I'm sure he'll understand, and damn it, I just can't sit and wait. This is just too damn much! Clarence can get a copy of that report and talk to the man who read the x-rays and maybe get some sort of slant on this thing. I wouldn't believe that guy Vanderwort if he told me the sun rises in the east. I really don't want to go home until we have done something after that pounding we got in there. What do you say?" Susan nodded dully and we drove to Clarence's and talked to his girl who passed on the message. Clarence was on the phone and we sat while he finished his call.

"I had them send me a copy, Peter. Let me see if Sharon has it. He called his girl and she brought it in and he sat and read through it. "Did he read it to you?' he asked.

"He read off the part about a mass on the left side in the temporal lobe but he didn't elaborate and we left there with a serious dislike for the man. All he said was to get your help in getting to a neurosurgeon and to do it right now, so here we are, although I don't think he expected us to just barge in like this. God, Clarence, this sounds pretty grim so far. Can you give us any better idea of what's going on? We're just up to our ears in bad news recently and I'd like to hear something better, if you can come up with something." He sat soberly and rereads the report and put it down and took off his glasses.

"These scans are pretty accurate things, Peter. There is no doubt about a pretty big shadow where there shouldn't be one. The man who read the x-ray, who is very good, incidentally, just calls it a mass. That's all he can do, I suspect, but the chances of it being a tumor it seems to me are pretty high. Vanderwort is a zombie in many regards, but he's very good and that's why I sent you to him. He may not have a friend in the world and I almost wonder what he's doing in medicine, but he is very capable and we must take his advice. Any one of the three neurosurgeons here would be perfectly fine, but I'm inclined to suggest you go with Don Evers. He's old enough to have experience and young enough to still be hot. Plus, you'll like him. If you like, I'll call him right now and get you in to see him without any wait." I looked at Susan and she nodded. Clarence called and after a little polite chat, he told our story, read the report, answered few questions about Susan's general health and then with appropriate thanks, hung up and told us that he would see us today about six, and that we should go to the hospital and get the CT scan films and take them with us. Gloom, gloom.

Dr. Evers turned out to be the sort of person you'd like to have as a friend. He was a solid, tough looking guy with a big smile, a relaxed manner, serious as the occasion called for, but putting us at our ease and most of all, inspiring confidence. He went over the whole history of Mitzi's death, Susan's collapse and severe headache, her gradual improvement, the weariness and somnolence which because of its persistence had finally concerned us. He did a few perfunctory neurological checks on her, looked at the film for a long time and then got down to business.

"I can't tell you what kind of a tumor this, is, but it is a tumor. It just happens to be located in an area that when disturbed, doesn't cause all that many symptoms, and for that reason this type of thing is often missed or neglected. The length of time since Susan first got the severe headache until now is not all that long, which of course is good. I don't think there is much doubt but that the initial onset of the severe headache represented a bleeding episode in the tumor. Tumor cells can and frequently do erode blood vessels in their midst and the sudden increase in volume from the bleeding causes the headache. As the blood is absorbed and the volume of the tumor goes down, the symptoms improve, but they don't necessary stop, depending on the size of the tumor. Now, as to the exact nature of the tumor, I can't say and I'm not going to guess. We have one obligation and that is to expose it, and remove it if possible, and the sooner we get at it, the better. That will establish our definitive diagnosis and therefore the prognosis. I don't mean to sound mysterious and I'm not leading you on or sparing your feelings. It is just that there is no point in speculating until after we have done the one imperative thing, the surgery. Luckily, this is an area where a substantial amount of tissue can be removed without serious losses. That cuts two ways, of course. That very plus is also the reason it got to this point without declaring itself.

"Now, for specifics. I'll want you in one day before surgery so that Clarence can check you over again and I can get some lab work and some additional x-rays. You'll have to get a haircut, not a very flattering haircut, I'm afraid, but it will grow back. I don't expect you to have much pain after the surgery, and whatever you do have we can take care of very easily. Now, I may do a frozen section, that is a quick and dirty exam that I might want to guide me, but unless it very clearly tells me all I need to know, we won't have a final accurate diagnosis until the day after, if you can get Dr. Grafton to expedite the tissue examination, and I'm sure he will. I would judge you would be out of the hospital in a week, maybe less." He paused and looked around on his desk top for something and didn't find it.

"Now, there is one final thing I want you two to think over. If the tumor in my judgment can be completely removed, I will of course do just that. If it is benign, case closed, recovery with some trivial losses of function. If is malignant, there is still a chance that I can get it all and once again, a happy ending. Now let's look at a worst case scenario, the possibility that this is a malignant tumor that cannot be completely removed without serious functional loss. I'm speaking now of losses that would not be acceptable to many people, a vegetative state, for instance. If you are willing to accept any potential loss for the sake of preserving life, I will pursue the tumor until I either feel I have removed it entirely or to where it is apparent that this is impossible. It is not always possible to know even with the tissue right in front of one, whether it is wise to proceed and make the attempt at total removal. Finally, if the frozen section shows the tumor to be malignant and the exploration shows that total removal with survival is next to impossible, simply backing out and leaving the patient as little changed as possible and allowing events to take their course is an option." He stopped here, and walked away to look at a document on a side table, an errand I thought might be to give us a moment to absorb this ominous prospect without having to look him in the face. He came back with a paper in his hand and sat down again.

"It is never pleasant to talk about such morbid things. It is certainly the worst part of this business and I hate it, but there are things you must know, and there is nothing that I won't tell you truthfully and accurately if it is within my power to tell you without speculating. I would not accept whatever decision you gave me right now about this last question. I want you to go home and consider first, whether you want surgery at all. I don't think I have to ask that, but there is no law against doing nothing about this matter. Assuming that you do want to have surgery, I am going to put you down for admission on the twentieth, surgery on the twenty-first. If you decide to do nothing, please call and I'll scratch the admission and the surgery. I'm going to give you this paper to look at and think about. You'll see that there are several different options of permission that you are going to grant me before surgery. If any one of them fits, that is the one we will have you sign in the hospital. If there is any little tailoring you feel you have to do on the one you select, take it up with me before admission and if it is reasonable and doable, we can work out the language. I think, though, that you'll find that one of the permissions on the sheet will satisfy you. And once again, please call and leave a message about anything you question and I'll call you back sometime in the late afternoon or evening. I want you to both feel that you know everything you need to know before we get started. These things demand a high level of confidence on both sides to get the best result. OK. Anything I can clear up right now?"

We were both so emotionally exhausted and as we later agreed, so relieved, if that is the word, to find at last someone who was authoritative, understanding and who exuded professionalism, that we both declined, gave him our thanks and were shown out by him personally, a touch that somehow seemed special. As paradoxical as it seems, we actually felt some better when we got home. The natural optimist, I gave Susan a long hug and a kiss and told her that I thought we had found the guy who could pull it off. Hadn't he been encouraged at the relatively short period of time Susan had had symptoms? Couldn't a lot of the present shadow on the x-rays just be blood that hadn't yet been absorbed? Or maybe some new bleeding? Why shouldn't the tumor itself be small? And removable? And while we're at it, why could it not be benign? I don't know that all this did a great deal to lift Susan's spirits, but I was talking myself into feeling a good deal better about the thing. At least we had a good man and we were going to get right on it, and ...Right. We're going to get right on it. Now I had to think about the alternative and I not only had to think about it, but the two of us had to sit down and make a decision that would be binding, a decision that would be Susan's, and right now Susan was in no condition to do anything more than get a little something to eat and get to bed.

I sat up until quite late, reading the paper Dr. Evers had given us and turning over the language, the significance, the options. Poor guy. What if he finds that the thing is malignant but has to pursue it all over the place before he decides he can't get it all? He then has to back out and perhaps have nothing to show for his attempt but a bedfast remnant of a patient who is going to die anyway. Or even worse, after taking out all this brain actually does get all the tumor and now has left behind the bedfast remnant who instead of at least dying, goes on and on and on, never becoming a functional, thinking human again. And how does he live with the thought that maybe he was wrong, that he could have cured the patient and didn't go far enough, thinking to spare the family the bedfast remnant?

I had a long talk with Walter who had dogged our steps and talked with both Vanderwort and Evers. I didn't have the nerve to ask if they had shared anything with him beyond what we had been told. He had nothing optimistic to offer, and certainly knew from long experience what the tumor was likely to be from the wording of the CT report. We really got no further than telling each other in as many ways as we could invent, how unfair it was, what incredible misfortune we had had lately. He and Emily would be over in the morning if that was all right and we ended our talk and I sat there over a drink and thought what were surprisingly gloomy thoughts for me.

Susan went into the hospital with her usual courage and dignity, although I could tell the little differences in her demeanor that meant tension. I sat with her that evening until bedtime. She had had her haircut, accepting the option of having only half of it shaved with the idea that she could do something or other with it after surgery, sort of a comb-over. As far as the permission was concerned, we had left it that if there was no prospect in the surgeon's judgment of getting it all, that he would back off and leave her as nearly as possible as she was presently. I had been pretty sure this is what Susan would choose. When I was called much sooner than I had expected, my heart sank as I concluded that it must not have been operable or surely it would have taken much longer. I was ushered into a little private cubicle and was joined by Dr. Evers in his scrubs. I was right. "Not very good news, I'm afraid, Mr. Hawkins. I exposed the tumor without any difficulty, a pretty large affair, and took a sample and had the lab go over it. It had all the gross characteristics to my eye of a glioblastoma, and that is what pathology assures me it is. The technical name is glioblastoma multiforme, a bad actor unfortunately, very malignant, and associated with a very low survival rate even when it is small and all of it that can be seen with the naked eye has been removed. I'm afraid we didn't have that option here. I explored the edges and everywhere I went I was cutting across tumor. In my judgment, it would not be possible to remove it all without removing very large and important areas of normal tissue, and even then I have grave doubts that it would have been possible to eradicate it. I didn't want to dishearten you when we first met, but that scan looked very ominous to me. I doubt, though, that anyone would have had the nerve to suggest to you that on the basis of the x-rays alone that removal was impossible. Even though we not infrequently think so before surgery, we feel obliged to prove our suspicion, and occasionally we're rewarded by a successful salvage when things looked unlikely on the films. I'm awfully sorry not to be able to bring you better a better report. Susan will be in the recovery room for a few hours, and then you can visit in her room. Don't expect too much today, she'll be groggy and medicated, but tomorrow you should find her better, I think. She can go home anytime after about three or four days, when she feels able to navigate. I'll be seeing her in the office next a week to take the sutures out and we can talk then about management at home or whatever your choice is." There was a pause and I knew he had more to say and I was pretty sure I knew what it would be.

"As for the long haul, I really can't tell you much. I don't expect much in the way of pain, mostly just the drowsiness you have seen. We can arrange easily to take care of any symptoms that arise. Susan has indicated she wants to remain at home under any circumstances, and I see no problem with that. As far as activities are concerned, or diet or anything at all, just let her do what she pleases. As for the unspoken question, which I thank you for not asking just yet, I don't know. A major bleed could bring an end to this matter at any time. Under the best of circumstances, I'm thinking in terms of weeks, not months, although such a thing is possible. I hope you can understand my reluctance to give you something more specific. I have fallen on my face so many times trying to do that that I have given up. Take each day for what it is and hope for as many of them as possible. That's about the best I can tell you. If there are legal affairs that require her competency, I would suggest that they be taken care of shortly. There is just that much uncertainly in a case like this that has already had one bleeding episode of really major proportions. Call me anytime. We'll help in any way we can. Keep up her spirits. And yours, too." We shook hands and he left and I left the hospital and drove out to the Graftons.

Emily had specifically asked that she not be expected to be in the hospital that morning and Walter had felt he should stay with her. The look on my face when I went in must have told the story, and we three sat glumly at the dining table, Martha's apron showing behind the edge of the kitchen doorway. I told them of what Dr. Evers had said, Walter staring at the table top, Emily watching my face. Walter had been in touch with his staff and confirmed that the tumor had shown a markedly aggressive growth pattern, just a hopeless situation, although he had told Emily nothing until I came. Oddly, we were all dry-eyed as we shuffled our feet under the table. Emily asked Martha, now in helpless tears, to bring in some coffee, no need to repeat what she had heard.

"Susan wants to stay at home, no matter what. I'm going to extend my leave of absence indefinitely and stay home with her. It's understood that it's open house to you folks. Come anytime you can and stay as long as you wish. I've got a ton of writing to do and I can break away or not, anytime. You won't be in the way and I want us all to share as much of Susan as we can. The doctor mentioned that anything of a legal nature that required her competency had best be taken care of pretty quickly. I can't believe he meant as an emergency, but on the other hand, he did mention the possibility of a sudden event, another episode of bleeding, you know. We two made out wills long ago and I suppose I should get that attorney to check Susan's and make sure it's OK. I hate to do anything right now, though. It seems so final. I don't want Susan to think we're already planning our lives for after she's not around, but like it or not, I guess we are. What a rotten business! Well, anyway. There it is for whatever it is." We sat and talked and drank coffee for a while, but the atmosphere was terribly oppressive and I declined lunch and went home to a beer and a sandwich and the telephone. My parents were very upset, of course, but there was nothing they could do and I suggested they just wait until Susan was home and feeling up to it and then if they wanted to visit, fine.

23

S usan did quite well, I thought. She was a little unsteady and
used a walker for a day but then that seemed to pass and on
the fourth day, we went home. I had put in a hospital bed on
their advice so she could change her position as she chose. She
spent much of the day there, only occasionally getting up into a
chair. Her hair was a mess, but once the stitches were out, she
devised a little arrangement with a band that held the remaining
hair over her head and made her look more like herself. All the
legal work was soon over, the Graftons settling in, as I had, to a
vigil of unknown duration, trying to make everything as natural
and rewarding as possible. Through this period, it was we who
were the ones under stress, Susan calm and at peace, seeming to
have come to terms with the inevitable. She had an occasional
tolerable headache, increasingly frequent, I realized, and had begun to spend more time in bed, the periods of near normal alert-
ness gradually shortened between naps. Surely she knew that time
was getting short, and one Sunday morning, with what must have
cost her an enormous effort, she began a most poignant confession that must have had a long and difficult gestation.

"Peter, dear Peter. I'm afraid there's not an awfully lot of
time left, is there? I lie here and I think of so many things. Without planning it, I seem to going through some sort of summing up.
I think of so many things I have put off, promising myself that
some time I'll do them. And still when I think of them, I tell myself that there's still time and my first instinct is to put them off a
little longer. I'm not really a procrastinator, but some things are
so difficult...but I'm coming to the point where I don't think I can
put it off. I do so want to explain, Peter. Please help me. For some
stupid, stupid reason it's still so hard for me to say some things.

Mitzi

There are so many things...things I have never been able to say that so desperately need saying..." She paused and thought for along time, a struggle of some sort taking place in some remote area of her mind beyond my reach and as it transpired, beyond my imagination. Looking resolutely at the bedclothes or alternately at some undefined spot on the wall opposite, so different from Susan's direct manner of looking at the person she addressed, she began in a small voice to which I had to pay close attention to hear.

"I don't know why it is. It has been the source of so very much anguish to me that I have always, since I can remember, found it impossible to talk about emotions. You would have no way of knowing how deeply I have felt about so many things, and how impossible it has been to put them in words and how frustrating it is to look out from inside at people to whom I have never found the words to communicate the most sensitive thoughts I have had. I am painfully aware of how cool I must seem to so many people. It's not that I'm indifferent to deeper emotions, not because I don't feel them but because I don't know how to express them. Or I'm afraid to show them. Sometimes I don't know which. God knows I have fought and fought to be able to say what I really feel, but the words just won't come no matter what, and there are so many people I'll never be able to make all this up to now. But I want to try to make it up to you, Peter. I want to try to tell you what I have felt all these wonderful years with such a wonderful man." How impossible it would have been for me to have articulated a signal syllable at that moment, so choked with emotion at this tiny glimpse into the emotional center of this fragile creature. For all the hints, I had never been sure of Susan being capable of feeling more than what she had with such difficulty expressed on rare occasions. There was a certain amount of apprehension in considering what might be coming, the tears which started now confirming that we were on the verge of opening into recesses in Susan's secret world that I had never been permitted to enter.

"I have decided that I cannot leave you, Peter, without trying to tell you so many things that I have so longed to tell you over all these years. I simply must. Please be patient with me. It is such an

285

effort to even bring these words to consciousness, much let to utter them. How can I have been so cursed with such a burden, not being able to say the simplest things I feel if they are tinged with the least emotion? You will never understand how dreadful it has been, like living among people whose language you simply couldn't learn and with whom you cannot share your...feelings. You see! I meant to say..." and here her voiced became all but inaudible as this forbidden word, in this context, was whispered, "...love." She looked up at me and met my eyes in the most piteous stare and held them for an eternity, it seemed.

"There. I've said it. I've used the word to you that I have never spoken before to you. To anyone. Anyone! Not to my father, not to my mother. No one. What in the world is so badly wrong in me! It's so infuriating! What must you have thought of a girl, a wife, who has never spoken that word to you? Oh, Peter! I want you to know that I have felt it so strongly that at times I thought I would burst, and yet I have never been able to use the very word, the simple, simple word that everybody else in the whole world uses to express their affection for one another! Never! I can't tell you what a nightmare it has been, hoping that you would sense, would know even though I never said as much....that I...loved you. That I loved you with every fiber of my being, that I loved you to distraction, possibly even more because I couldn't be sure you understood how I felt about you. Peter, Peter, please forgive me. Please forgive my poor, pathetic inability to tell you how deeply I have felt about you since the first day we met. You have no idea what went through my mind as we talked that first day. I could scarcely believe what I was feeling and yet I have no doubt that you didn't have a clue. Even then I was determined not to show my feelings. When we talked about Romeo and Juliet after class, I might as well have been Juliet herself. I was swept off my feet with emotions I had never had before, and yet I'm sure you never realized it. I was so anxious not to betray this to you, and you must have felt, what a heartless girl, how serious, how unemotional and I was in agony that you might feel this way, because if you had and had never approached me again, there would have been no way for me to explain and try to salvage what I desperately wanted to become a romance. Can you believe my using that word, 'romance'? Even now? But I wanted a romance with, you, Peter. I wanted you so badly to like me without my having to tell you the things that everyone else would have had no difficulty in expressing to their beloved. It seems so very odd to speak words like this that I have never used other than abstractly. Abstractly. I couldn't even say I 'loved' a movie, or 'loved' a gown or a party or a painting. It was a word so charged with emotion, so extreme that it threatened me. I simply could not articulate it in any context, as though uttering it would somehow make me vulnerable...to what? To utter it was to violate a taboo that I couldn't transgress even when it became imperative that I do so. How you ever managed to take me as your wife without ever having heard me express in the simplest terms the depth of my feelings for you, is simply miraculous. You can have no conception of the enormity of your actually asking me to be your wife, when I despaired of it ever happening."

She closed her eyes. She seemed nearly exhausted by the effort these admissions had demanded. "Would you bring me a cold drink, Peter? Please." I returned to find her outwardly more composed. She drank a little from the glass and put it down on the nightstand.

"Our courtship had me a nervous wreck. I agonized over every contact with you, hoping to see something more than just the attraction we had for each other based on simply our common interests. All that time I was hoping for some sign that you intuitively guessed that...that I was in love with you, miserable with the uncertainty of whether you could ever return my feeling, furious with myself at not being able to give you a hint. You will never know how defeating it is not to be able to communicate your most precious thoughts with even one, just one other person. Not one. Can you believe it? I couldn't even tell a girl friend, my mother, anyone. I had to live, night and day, with the unbearable thought that you might not see through my helplessness and just drift away. I felt with the utmost conviction that I must spend my life with you, somehow, in some capacity. At whatever cost, I must not lose you, but you, you poor creature, you must guess what I felt, how earnestly I was soliciting your affection without giving you a hint. I can only imagine what you must have thought, week after week, dating the Snow Queen, as my class-mates called me. I'm not in any way asking for your sympathy, Peter. That was just the way Susan was and Susan had grown up accepting it."

I sat and held her hand, giving it a squeeze when I thought it might signify my sharing her distress as she unveiled all this tor-tured uncertainty that had been her side of our courtship. She paused now, and took a few sips of her drink. "I'll have to rest a bit, Peter. I feel so tired. I have a great deal more I want to tell you, but I can't do it now. Just let me rest some and then I want to go on. It will be easier, I think, now that I've started. Odd, how now that I've broken the ice, it doesn't seem quite so formidable. But it had to come to...to this," she said, gesturing to her head. Just let me rest a little, Peter, and then do let me go on." I kissed her and closed the door behind me.

It was late afternoon before she awakened again. I had fixed her some poached eggs which was what she wanted now for some reason. She ate this little meal and seemed revived by the coffee and was anxious to continue. I sat beside the bed and took her hand and let her set the pace.

"I can't tell you how many times I have gone over those months when we were dating, the torments I went through, trying to make you like me better than anyone else. I simply was not up to the job. I felt so helpless about not being able to laugh and joke and be amusing to you. When I met your friends that day and was in their company, or when you tried to interest me in jazz and dancing and things like that that I simply couldn't take part in, I was miserable, so crushed. I felt so inadequate and I knew I was disappointing you, that you needed things like that in your life and that I'd never be able to provide them or even be a part of them and I absolutely despaired of winning you, so often that I don't care to remember. Do you remember the time I was telling you about the scene I had had with Brad and then you're telling me that you didn't think you could possibly fit into what you de-scribed as my crowd, as though I were a part of an affluent bunch of brainless, idle rich. I thought I would perish, just stop breathing that very moment, and that was the closest I ever came to throw-ing myself at you, but all I could say was that I really liked you and that I hoped you wouldn't give up on me. For me, that was the equivalent of telling you that I adored you. I can't express how relieved I was when you relented and kissed me. For the first time, I began to think there was hope.

"I was so happy that you and my father got on so well, and as ridiculous as it may seem, I realized he was in a sense, courting you for me. I had that feeling that anything at all that would make me seem more desirable, might be the deciding factor, and I told my father again and again how much I liked and admired you, and actually hoped that he would help me win you. And the same with dear Dr. Baxter. When he realized that my shyness, as he called it, was a handicap, he as much as told me that he would see to it that you appreciated what a prize I was…that sweet man, so loyal and so devoted to my father. He never said anything further about it, but he was so pleased when we got engaged. I even asked Nancy to help and when I took you out there that day, I had asked her if she wouldn't say something nice to you about me. I was desperate, Peter. I wanted you so badly."

Oh Susan! Don't make me think about this, not now. How painful it was to have this infidelity cast up to me so innocently! Bad enough to have betrayed my precious, unsuspecting Susan that day, but to learn that Nancy had also violated her trust so flagrantly. Dear Susan, thank God you never found out, my dearest. I am so ashamed.

"I don't think I ever told you that Brad came home a year or so later with his boyfriend on his arm. Yes, boy friend. The Montgomerys were simply horrified and he went back to Italy and has been there ever since. So that was my first beau. My only other beau." She made a rueful little face before going on.

"I truly am an awful prude Peter. There is simply no getting around it. I don't know why, any more than I don't understand other things about myself. I know mother was very protective and very stern about the whole topic of sex. I don't know what my parent's love life has been like, but it would appear that it was not much. I don't want to blame my mother and I won't, but it is true that I was raised with the idea that boys did evil things and I had an unwholesome and fearful attitude for so long. And I know I

projected that. With Brad, it was just what I had been led to believe, disgusting when he started his groping and I reacted as I felt
I should. But then when you and I started dating, I would have
allowed you so much more liberty if I had had the nerve, but I just
didn't, and I know I must have intimidated you. You were so understanding and considerate, but what must you have thought?
What must you have wondered our honeymoon would be like? I
can scarcely imagine your trust, Peter, your wonderful trust that
you were not getting into a nightmare of frigidity. But don't you
see, there was no way in the world I could tell you that I wanted
you and would be good to you and everything would be all right. I
didn't know with complete certainty, but I felt sure that with a
little time I could please you." I could only nod and smile reassur-
ingly at such a tender and vulnerable admission.

"I was frantic, Peter. I wanted you to want me and I simply
didn't have any way of telling you how much I longed for physical love with you, and so, in my clumsy, fumbling way, I bought
that latex swim suit, as embarrassed at simply buying it as though
it were something kept under the counter. I felt that somehow I
had to at least momentarily excite you with my... my....oh, Peter.
Charms? I don't want to try to give it a name. You know what I
mean. When I stepped out of that changing room, I might as well
have been naked. I could hardly function, not knowing what
would be your response, and when you looked up at me with that
air of total shock and what I thought of as plain lust, I panicked
and dived in the pool and wished I were anywhere else where no
one could see my humiliation. What a fool I was! How ridiculous
I must have seemed to you, but how sweet you were about trying
to make me feel better. I was deeply touched, but all I could think
of was to get out of the water and get a huge towel and recover
my dignity. And then in the depths of this degradation I had arranged for myself, you proposed to me, and from those depths, I
was resurrected into the greatest joy I have ever felt in my life.
How I kept any composure at all, I don't know. I remember very
distinctly that I wanted to weep and weep and weep. I was so
happy! All my anxieties, all my insecurities behind me. It was
over. We were going to go through life together. It was an indescribable moment for me. Out of the blue. So completely unex-

pected! I owe you so very much, my dear Peter. You have made my boring, orderly life such a pleasure, so exciting, such a joy, even though you may not have seen it. I want very much to have you know it now."

She was tired and her voice was failing some and I proposed that she rest and she agreed and before I had even left the room, seemed to be asleep. I stood and watched her breathing for a time, in this climate of uncertainty, I was conscious of having to reassure myself at moments like this that she had not gone beyond sleep. Grotesque, to be thinking in such terms.

The next morning, I got a call from Nancy, of all people. She knew about Susan's situation, had sent flowers to the hospital and a couple notes, but had not asked to come visit until now. There was no awkwardness between us, rather the contrary, now that all the dust had settled, and I encouraged her to come over about ten when Susan usually was at her best. She looked wonderful, as usual, dressed modestly for such a serious occasion. We kissed chastely and I asked her if she would like coffee, Susan not yet awake. We sat and talked, and I brought her up to date about her condition. Nancy was genuinely grieved at our tragedies. She had met Mitzi only a few times, had been very taken with her and had been very touching in her expressions of sympathy when she learned of her death. She asked me how I was getting on with all this misery, and I assured her that the worst was finally over, that I had recovered as nearly as I was ever going to recover from Mitzi's loss and had accepted the fact that Susan's death was not very far off. She asked what was I going to do and I told her that I would keep the house, I thought, and go back to work but was thinking of hanging it up and traveling some, simply getting away. She had been divorced from her goon for some time, it came out, and was breeding and training horses, living at her family home. She still saw Roger from time to time, the two of them amicable again, Roger still drinking himself to death. I couldn't help but feel sorry for this girl who in spite of all her advantages and her attractiveness had somehow never gotten things together. I checked again and after Susan had gotten up and gotten refreshed, I took Nancy in and after a bit, excused myself so that they could talk.

I was a little surprised at how long Nancy stayed there, concerned that she not tire Susan. When she came out, she was looking surprisingly relaxed. I thanked her for coming and she said that Susan was most anxious for her to come again soon, and that she would call and be sure it was convenient. She apologized for having taken that much time away from Susan and me. Susan looked ever so much more at ease when I returned to her, actually beaming a little at the fun she had had talking with Nancy about school and mutual friends, most of whom she had made no effort to follow.

"Nancy is such a tonic for me, Peter. I miss her very much and I just haven't thought of insisting that she come over. She was concerned that we would want to be alone, and I assured her that we did value our time, but that she must come and talk some more. She made me feel so good even though it was tiring. I want so to go on with our talk, but I must have a little sleep first. Maybe I'll feel like it this evening. Could you just bring me one of those pills for the headache? Not the big one, just the other one. I'm just a little achy and I think it will help me rest."

She awakened for some dinner and then went back to sleep and I didn't have the heart of awaken her again. In the morning, she was awake and seemed rested and had a good breakfast, considering. The coffee helped and she asked me to please sit and talk.

"I was just thinking about when we first got home and got started, how apprehensive I was. I was worried about so many things. I had such a wonderful time on our honeymoon, just the two of us, getting used to being with each other every minute. It was such a thrill for me that I forgot what it would be like to come home again to your responsibilities, you gone all day, a new apartment of our own. And I wondered if you would be happy. All the old feelings of inadequacy resurfaced, the awareness of how very different we were from each other in spite of the things that we both enjoyed. I have never been able to be part of what people call fun, as you know so well. My father was playful and witty and I enjoyed it, but I was never able to be part of it. I think that is part of why you two get on so well. I seem to take after my mother. She smiles a lot but you almost never hear her laugh. I wasn't much aware of it until you became a regular visitor and then I realized that only my father and you laugh when we are together. I like the sound of laughter and I like people around me to be happy, but it isn't that important to me to be amused or have fun or play. That and my maddening inability to be even the least bit demonstrative, to initiate a hug, to welcome you home with open arms, to take your hand when we walk...I was so afraid that you would tire of my detachment, my aloofness from some of the things that meant to much you. Please forgive me, Peter, but jazz for some reason repels me and I can't seem to change my feelings about it, no matter how hard I have tried, and I did try, Peter, to please you. Everyone except me seems to enjoy dancing, and when I see couples dancing together who enjoy it, I am so envious. They look so attractive, holding each other. Maybe it has something to do my shyness about displaying affection in public.

"After we had lived in the city for awhile, I noticed that you were becoming restless and as it increased, I grew so apprehensive because I felt certain that you were wondering whether you had made such a good bargain after all, marrying Miss Sobersides..." I started to protest but Susan continued, "...and were having second thoughts, and I was so miserable. At first I blamed it on my being unable to conceive. Surely a child in the house would make a big difference give us both a new thing to share. Maybe a child would bring some much needed warmth into the house, someone to play with and laugh with who might compensate for some for my failings, but it was just not to be and I was left with the certainty that it would be my sole responsibility to save myself, and I wasn't at all sure I could." Susan sat quietly for the longest time before she resumed.

"When you proposed to move out of downtown, I was thrilled, feeling that perhaps it was the city after all, and not me. In any event, if it would please you, it was what I wanted also. I so enjoyed watching the pleasure you took in the garden and the plantings and your shop, but I saw that underneath all this newness, there was the same restlessness that had upset me before. You were bored, you would find someone else, you would ask for a divorce...dreadful thoughts and I couldn't get them out of my head. When we went to that dog show and I saw how much you enjoyed being around those dogs, I felt I had stumbled onto a possible solution. And I was right, Peter! Oh, I was so right and I was so proud of myself! Dear Lily was the answer to my prayers! You have no idea how you changed, overnight it seemed. That sweet, sweet animal gave you what was missing. I was so happy! For the first time since we had come home from our honeymoon I was certain that you were happy again. How devastated I was when she died. What a terrible day for us both, of course, but for my part, with the grief came the old apprehension. While I could understand your reluctance to get another dog, at least for a time, I knew I had to have the kind of help that Lily had become.

"And it fell in our laps. Sitting there in that room with Helen and looking up and seeing you and Mitzi staring at each other, seeing that little urchin finally go to you and sit in your lap and hug you as though she would never let go, brought me to tears of joy. I knew as surely as I have ever known anything that all would be well, and I had no question at all in my mind about taking her home. I would have done so that morning, I was that sure of the rightness of having her with us. You were so touching, going back time after time as though to convince yourself, and doing all that investigating, being so proper about it, and all the time I knew you were madly in love with her and she with you. Thirteen years of near bliss. Thirteen years of the loveliest, most angelic being in the world, filling our lives with happiness and pride and delight. She saved me, Peter. She literally saved me and by saving me, she saved us. In a sense, she made me whole, she relieved me of the whole burden of agonizing over my incompleteness, I'll call it. It was a though I had been reborn whole, complete and had become the person that I so wanted to be for you. Mitzi took up all the slack and then went on to provide her own special magic. You always insisted that it was genes, that she was destined to be the way she was and that we were just lucky to have had the pleasure of seeing the inevitable unfold. I have never accepted that, Peter. In spite of your science and what it ways, I say that you created that child in your image. She was your creature, Peter, say what you will."

I chose to say nothing. What did it matter where the credit lay? Susan's face was slightly flushed the way it became with emotion, and I knew she was having the same difficulty with her feelings as I. "I want to go on with that, Peter...but not now. There are some things I want you to know about Mitzi that are more than I can manage right now. Things I feel you should know. But not now. I'd like to get a little sleep, I think. And the little pain pill and some water, please. Just leave them on the stand. Maybe I won't need them."

I was getting the idea that things were moving to a conclusion with my dear wife. She either slept of was restless the remainder of the day, and I didn't feel I should encourage her to do anything other than what she chose. As had happened before, after a rather bad patch, she seemed better, not really alert but happy to have my company. "You said you had something to tell me about Mitzi. Do you feel like going into it? We can wait if you want." No, she wanted to do it.

"For all of your having been such a favorite with Mitzi, she and I were perhaps closer than you knew. We spent so much time together, and although I always had the feeling she was just waiting for her Papa to come home, she discussed a lot of things with me that I don't believe she ever mentioned to you. Most of it was about you and as with anyone, she needed a confidant. It would serve no purpose to tell you how unbelievably attached to you she was. I think you must know that the sun rose and set on you in her world. She would repeat to me what you had said, how you had looked, what you were planning on doing together, where you would go, how much she hoped you would take her, and how very, very happy she was with us. Meaning mostly you, Peter. Please don't feel that I have ever felt slighted. I owe so very much to that dear child who literally saved my married life, I'll forever be grateful. Well," she added ruefully, "that won't be such an awfully long time, though, will it? She filled in all the blanks and without her..." She trailed off with her eyes closed and I thought she would pass into sleep, she was quiet for such a time, but it was only thinking that she was involved in.

"Well...enough of that. It is about her taking her own life that I thought you ought to know my feelings." I wasn't at all sure I wanted to hear what might come next. I don't remember exactly what I anticipated, but my instincts were to leave that part of the past alone.

"First of all, I can assure you that it was not you who created the passion in Mitzi to be perfect for your sake. It was her notion entirely, and I don't believe you even suspected it, nor did I until Karl came into the picture and we had reason at one point to believe that they might get together and marry. I was curious about why it was that getting along as well and they did and having as much fun as they seemed to have, that she could be so casual about such a nice young man. In bits and pieces it came out that she wasn't disinterested, that she was very fond of Karl, but she gradually made it plain to me that Karl was out of the question because she was already committed. And that of course, was to you, Peter. When I sensed that she was perfectly serious, I asked her about what her long term goals and plans were, and she insisted that all she ever wanted was to be with us forever, and make you happy. To imagine that she understood her importance to me in this regard is almost too much. Without ever saying it in so many words, she felt that she owed her entire life to you, Peter, and that she was going to stay with us--you--forever. I chose not to mention it, partly because I thought it might simply be an exaggerated compliment that was not to be taken literally. But that wasn't the case.

"When she had the second operation, and went into such a funk, I spent a great deal of time talking with her. She was very difficult to reach. I tried every approach I could think of. She mentioned repeatedly things to the effect that you would no longer regard her the same as you had before, as though her not being physically as perfect as she had been would be a deterrent to your love or your pride in her or your esteem ...I don't know what, but it was very clear to me that she had some obsession that depended on her being as she had been before the surgery. I urged her to realize that cosmetic surgery would almost surely restore her to a cute and natural figure, but she would have none of it. She kept saying that it would never be the same...never be the same, and nothing I could say seemed to shake that belief. I think it entirely possible that a commitment of sorts was made, in some elemental but powerful way when you and she first met. When we imagine, as we have, what we--you--rescued her from, such an intelligent and sensitive and precocious a child, it wouldn't surprise me in the least if at that moment in her childish way, she determined that you were hers for eternity. I believe that is what she felt she owed you. How fortunate you are to have inspired such devotion in such an exceptional being. And how terrible sad that her obsession with pleasing you, with being perfect for you was taken to such an extreme. Arriving at this thought and passing it along to you can't begin to lessen the pain of her death, but I simply couldn't rest until I had something that made sense to explain it. I think it is very important for neither of us to feel that we failed her. We didn't, Peter. We didn't fail her. I hope you believe that. I do."

Susan died quietly three days later in the afternoon while I was on the phone talking to Walter. I called him back when I had satisfied myself that she was gone, and they came over and we sat and looked at each other. Emily looked terrible but was dry-eyed. Walter asked had Susan expressed any wishes about burial? I told him she had chosen to be cremated and her urn placed beside Mitzi's.

"Please, Peter. Would you please allow us to have her buried? I know you made a promise, but I hope very, very much that you will permit us to bury her where all my family is buried. It would mean a great deal to me." I agreed, of course, and a few days later stood at a graveside on a day that was far too beautiful for such solemnity and watched my dear Susan put in the ground among her forebears.

What an emotional flogging I had had and I felt every blow of it. I decided to end my services at Phillips. I just didn't have any desire to strive any more, the fun had gone out of things and I felt that immersing myself in work again, which was the conventional advice, was not the solution in my particular case. They urged that I not go completely and asked only that I come in when I chose and talk. I told them that I'd think about it but I doubted I wanted any more of the same. I had achieved more fame than I deserved, I had discharged my obligations to Charlie Baxter, I had exceeded my own aspirations and I wanted to rest and think and heal at my own pace.

I closed the house and went down to a little village in a remote area of Mexico we had become fond of and took a small apartment. The couple who were the curators of the local folk art museum had become good friends over the years. I wanted company. I didn't want to go somewhere and be alone but the company had to be right. Anxious to avoid spoiling our meeting after a few years, I wrote them about Mitzi and Susan and explained that I just wanted a quiet retreat and some friendship. It was the beginning of the healing I so badly needed. I sat with these two understanding people and we talked art and literature and the ancient colonial churches Enrique was restoring. We gorged on the local whitefish from the lake and drank bootleg mescal. I ended up spending nearly a month in their restorative company and felt almost whole by the time I returned and opened the house again. It was still oppressive with memories and I momentarily felt I had done the wrong thing to come back. There was a huge stack of mail that needed attending to, there was dining with the Graftons and explaining what I proposed to do, still uncertain, but not returning to work. Even their house had changed for me and seemed unbearably lonely. Did I want to take any of Susan's paintings? I thought I might and ended taking a couple and went on home to play the piano some and make plans.

It was about three weeks after I had returned that I heard a car drive up. It was Nancy. Nancy in jeans and a sweater and loafers. Nancy looking great, as usual, rested and natural looking, no sign of the solicitude I was still getting from the few people I had seen since my return, just her normal, knowing face, her breezy confidence.

"Stranger! How in the world are you? May I come in?" We embraced quickly as I welcomed her and got her a drink. She was anxious to hear about my trip and we talked the way old friends do who like each other and feel comfortable in each other's presence. It was so easy to talk to Nancy. It had been a long while since we had felt at ease talking with each other, and I found it such a pleasure to laugh again, and kid and joke and exaggerate, you know, the way people do. She declined a second drink and I thought this was preparatory to her leaving, but she instead she came over and sat next to me on the sofa and looked at me very seriously.

"Peter, I want you to do something for me." I smiled benignly and said that I would be happy to.

"I want you to pack what you think you will need, lock the doors and come home with me." I stared at her in utter disbelief, realizing only slowly that she was completely serious. I sat stunned for long enough for her to take it up again. "I mean it, Peter. Don't sit and think up excuses. Get rid of this house and what it means to you and come live with me. I'm serious, Peter. I want you to come and live with me. It's the natural thing to do. It doesn't make any sense for me to sit alone in that house of mine and you sitting here in this house of yours when we could be together. No objections, Peter. Just go put some things in a suitcase and come with me and we can get the rest later."

We stared at each other for a time and finally I had to grin at the boldness and determination of this woman. I got up and packed a bag, locked the doors and we drove over to Nancy's house.

24

That was eight years ago. After twenty-five years of sparring with each other, here we are, eight years of happiness for us both, together at last as we seemed to have been destined. Strange. All the permutations we had been through, both of us, waiting for this pairing. Nancy had been right and had known it for years. I had known it very briefly before I chose to deny it out of a feeling of chivalry, obligation, what you will. There was a great deal of newness at first, shifting gears, rearranging attitudes, but it was all there, simply a matter of my accepting it and the acceptance was painless. Suspecting perhaps that I might have some regrets, considering how suited for each other we are, Nancy has pointed out that if it had not been for Susan, there would have been no Mitzi.

I did go back to Phillips for a time, but it wasn't long before I realized that I had shot my bolt the first time. We had missed the Nobel, not by much. Several years later Jim and his gang got it for a still more advanced application of our original work and I think Jim will go down in the annals of science as a pretty fancy operator. Jim offered to put my name on the paper because some of the background had my fingerprints on it, but I declined. There was a time when that sort of glory would have attracted me, but that has passed and I'm very well satisfied to live in professional obscurity with Nancy.

Emily died not long after Susan, not of grief but a stroke. Walter had made me his sole heir, but I felt badly about this. I didn't need the money and we finally agreed that when the time came, the whole pile should go to his Foundation with the understanding that I would act in an advisory capacity as far as evaluating grant requests in my field. I felt this little effort was due the memory of Susan which is still very dear to me. Not to be morbid about it, but I can still hear her heart-breaking confession, I suppose it might be called. I owe her so very much.

Not infrequently I reflect on the first conversation Susan and I had about whether there was such as thing as instant recognition of your beloved, an instinctive affinity for another as though there were a receptor mechanism in our psyches that was prepared to recognize the match that perfectly suited it. Sounds a little like romantic clap-trap, I know, but I've decided that it is possible to put it in such a way that perhaps it makes at least a little sense. The biologist, specially the molecular biologist, is well aware of the near flawless identification and attraction that takes place between innumerable molecules in our body every instant of our lives, this molecule seizing and uniting to the only other molecule that will allow them to fulfill their proper function. Traveling backward in the history of evolution, we must inevitably get down to some very simple living creatures whose survival depended on just such bondings. Now granting that, which is not much to ask, is it not conceivable that these innumerable 'biases' that have ensured survival might not also function to guide the whole organism into desirable decisions and avoid bad ones? If this instant key-in-lock identification between essential molecules is critical to our very survival, could it not over billions of years through the natural selection among biases endow the organism itself with an instinct for identifying a suitable mate? Further, this knack having developed over such a great span of time, can we not imagine that at least in some individuals it became refined to the point of being able to identify not only a suitable mate, but an ideal mate? We don't balk at using the term 'instinct' and 'intuition'. What is instinct but just this, a 'hunch', a 'gut feeling'? We see a certain face, certain body language, a particular gait, a gesture and we feel there is some sort of destiny there.

Consider staid, conservative Susan confessing after all those years that she had fallen hopelessly in love the first time we spoke together, yet feeling at the time she should deny the possibility. There was Nancy's sudden recognition of me as her proper mate, a seemingly inexcusable betrayal of her dear friend at the time. Yet what if a deeply rooted mechanism, something developed over the millions of years of human life on earth, a mechanism designed to enhance human survival, overrode her normal self control and simply insisted that she and I were meant for each other? Is it unreasonable to assume that a mating instinct might not trump a friendship instinct?

I think now that my profound responses at first hearing a good jazz pianist, first seeing a Van Gogh painting, the moment of instantaneous emotional bonding with Lily, were the honing of my emotional responses, sensitizing and preparing me for the transforming moment of my first meeting with Mitzi, that epiphany that confirmed for me the validity of a sudden, irresistible, consuming affection for another.

I can see my fellow biologists smiling as this relentlessly objective researcher betrays a romantic inclination that could make a fool of him. Well, I'm not embarrassed. I see no harm in doing a little tongue in cheek speculating about such a pleasant notion. Perhaps there is something about each of us that has had such experiences that indicates that we are adepts of a sort, a fortunate minority just slightly differently constituted to be particularly receptive to such lightning insights. Very likely even Dr. Baxter and his Ellie felt the same thunderbolt. Given the testimony of my mother that she had fallen in love at her first meeting with my father, perhaps my own inclinations or preconditioning in this direction have some subtle inheritance to explain them. Well, so much for idle speculation. I certainly have not shed new light on this mystery, but nevertheless all these reflections have come to be regular visitors to my daydreams, tantalizing me as to their origin and significance. Imagine then how delighted I was recently at having a most provocative experience. Nancy had gone out to the barn to check on one of our mares. We were expecting a new foal very shortly. I was reading a volume of Christopher Marlowe's poetry that I had bought years ago and scarcely opened. Totally unprepared for such a discovery, I stumbled upon the following poem:

It lies not in our power to love or hate,
For will in us is overruled by fate.
When two are stripped, long ere the course begin,
We wish that one should love, the other win;
And one especially do we affect
Of two gold ingots, like in each respect:
The reason no man knows; let it suffice
What we behold is censured by our eyes.
Where both deliberate, the love is slight:
Who ever loved, that loved not at first sight?

I rest my case.

THE END

Printed in the United States
69472LVS00001B

9 781598 243918